OUT OF THE FRYING PAN . . .

Hamid-Jones said a brief prayer that the Assassins' bomb had not killed them all.

"We'd better sit it out here for a while," Aziz said as Hamid-Jones started to get up.

But they didn't have that luxury. A trembling began around them, and Hamid-Jones felt weight pressing him to the floor. "The controllers must have seen the antimatter flash and turned on the creation engines ahead of schedule."

Very soon, the acceleration was going to crush them to the floor, not that it mattered much. They were trapped on a runaway spaceship that was on its way to turning into a black hole . . .

By Donald Moffitt
Published by Ballantine Books:

A GATHERING OF STARS

Book Two of
The Mechanical Sky

Donald Moffitt

A Del Rey Book

BALLANTINE BOOKS • NEW YORK

"Try to imagine how the War of Independence would have gone if news of Bunker Hill had not arrived in England until Disraeli was Victoria's prime minister and his urgent instructions on how to deal with the situation had reached America during President Eisenhower's second term. Stated in this way, the whole concept of interstellar administration or culture is seen to be an absurdity."

ARTHUR C. CLARKE

CHAPTER 1

The mullah's knife flashed, and a spurt of arterial blood drenched his white robes. He continued sawing away at the sheep's throat until he was satisfied, then untangled his fingers from the woolly head and let it drop limply to the plastic sheet that the spaceport janitorial crew had spread to protect the inlaid floor of the departure lounge.

"Well, you're guaranteed a safe voyage, at any rate," said Hamid-Jones's baby-sitter, an impressively self-possessed young attaché from the Centauran embassy. "Are you going to go over there to dip your fingertips for luck?"

"I don't think so," Hamid-Jones said.

Droplets of blood were hanging in the air, settling imperceptibly in the almost nonexistent gravity of Deimos. A couple of members of the maintenance crew were sweeping the air with large sponges to catch stray drops escaping the tarpaulined area, but one jet of blood had traveled twenty feet, and another coveralled worker was hurrying to intercept it with a catch basin.

"Wise decision," said the watchdog. "Your ident's as good as we could make it, but it's best to stay in the background as much as possible till you're safely aboard Centauran territory."

The mullah was winding up the sacrificial rites with a prayer. A number of passengers were self-consciously lining up for individual blessings.

"What about the person whose place I took?" Hamid-Jones asked.

"He'll be sent back down to Mars in the same diplomatic

1

pouch that brought you up, and we'll do a lot of computer shuffles over the next few months to pass along the hiatus till it's diluted enough to be wiped out. How was the ride? Uncomfortable?''

"It wasn't too bad."

The "pouch" had, in fact, been a sealed cylinder large enough to stretch out in. An outer shell was filled with an inert gas and lined with a lot of sophisticated baffles, some of which projected false images of the cylinder's interior. An inner suspension contained a cocoon that protected the passenger against jolts. There was a miniaturized life-support facility that provided enough oxygen for thirty-six hours, and a rather embarrassing sanitary facility that relied heavily on stickybags that would have to be disposed of later by someone or other. Hamid-Jones had had a few bad moments when the pouch had been dropped or turned upside-down, but once out of Mars's gravity field it ceased to matter. On Deimos, the Centaurans had extracted him without being detected.

Hamid-Jones reflectively fingered the curls of his false beard, which was done up in ribbons and squared off Centauran style. False was not exactly the word, since the whiskers had been force-grown from his own DNA and grafted, hair by hair, to a three-day growth of his own stubble by molecular machines. A coppery dye job disguised the disjunction at the roots, which could be presumed simply to be growing out again and gave him the properly foppish look of a young foreign service officer. He had also sacrificed the fleshy pad of a forefinger in the unlikely event that a DNA sample might be required at exit; he would have a sore finger for a few weeks aboard ship as the graft was rejected and his own fingertip, already seeded for cloned regeneration, grew out again.

He had balked at losing an eye, even temporarily, and the ambassador had upheld him against the insistence of the intelligence *wallahs*. "A retinal check is extremely unlikely," the ambassador had said. "Mars has adhered to civilized standards for over two centuries. The last time they interfered with diplomatic personnel was in the first unsettled years of the usurper, and even then they only checked the identities of new arrivals, not returnees."

"Don't worry," the attaché laughed. "You look like a proper Centauran. Your build is a plus; it's fortunate you were born on

Earth. The gravity on our capital planet is two and a half times that of Mars—about ninety-five percent of Earth gravity. You won't have any problems adjusting—our ships boost and deboost at close to a standard G, so you'll have two years of subjective time to toughen up."

Both of them turned to look at the view outside the huge curving windows of the departure lounge. Lit from one side, Mars was an enormous breast in the sky, with Olympus Mons for a nipple. The view from Phobos, of course, was more spectacular; there, Mars filled the sky—almost *was* the sky. But on Deimos, at least, one had the sensation that one was looking *up* at it, not in danger of plunging down into it at any moment.

"Here it comes," the attaché said. "If you look close, you can just about make it out."

Hamid-Jones strained his eyes and was rewarded by the sight of a glimmering mote at the exact center of the planet. Of course that was the only place it *could* be—at Mars's equator and directly below, or rather "above," the tiny moon. Even the east-west and west-east mail satellites, which dropped their own skyhooks from orbits a little above, or below, synchronous orbit, were constrained to an equatorial run.

As he watched, the mote grew more bright. It made the 12,000 mile trip up its spider's thread in a couple of hours, and at about a hundred miles the braking rockets had to cut in to keep it from smashing into Deimos. Its flattened nacelle shape was visible now. The last time Hamid-Jones had seen it, it had been unreeling itself from the Martian sky with a belly full of soldiers.

"It's the last one," the attaché said. "Do you want to board ship before the crush?"

"No, I'll wait," said Hamid-Jones. "I want to see if anyone I know gets off."

"Hmm, yes, there's that," the attaché agreed. "A starship's big, but it's best to see what inconvenient persons you might have to avoid for the next two years."

"Five years," Hamid-Jones corrected.

"Yes, five to us stay-at-homes. But time will fly for you. The time dilation effect won't be very noticeable for most of that initial year of boost, but by the time you get up to within about one millionth of one percent of the speed of light, it'll reach a factor of approximately seven hundred. So you'll do the entire middle part of the journey—covering some three and a quarter light-years of distance—in what will seem to you to be about a day and a half. Turnover will take place halfway through that day and a half, and I guarantee that the captain and crew will be very busy. There's no gravity for several hours—while the ship is coasting through that appalling void at ninety-nine point nine thousand nine hundred ninety-nine percent of the speed of light—and I believe the passengers are confined to their cabins for safety reasons. Actually it's to keep them out of the crew's hair. Then comes deboosting and another year of shipboard boredom.''

''You seem to have it all down pat,'' Hamid-Jones said. He was getting tired of being on a leash, even when the other end of the leash was held by a succession of scrupulously agreeable people like the attaché.

''Oh, I've given the tour many times,'' the attaché said. There might have been a tiny shade of resentment in his tone, too. ''There'll be a lecture aboard, I believe, for those passengers who are new to star travel.''

Outside in the blackness, a last firing of retro rockets had slowed the hangar-size nacelle to a stop. It strained at the end of its tether several hundred feet up, like an enormous flattened balloon. The passengers inside would be technically upside-down—but that hardly mattered in Deimos's negligible gravity. A misty puff from the attitude nozzles flipped the traveling terminal over on its belly, and it started slowly to settle into its docking cradle. Hamid-Jones's eye was just quick enough to see the ²ick of the detached tether as it snaked into its slot beside the cradle.

The stars above were suddenly occulted as the nacelle mated with the departure lounge. Craning his neck around the curve of the observation window, Hamid-Jones saw the great lid come down and connect the two structures. He felt a faint vibration under his feet as the lounge rang in vacuum.

''Quite a circus,'' the attaché murmured as the first embarkees came through.

Passengers in the lounge stared at the newcomers making their way across the vast floor. At the head of the throng was a wave front of four-armed dwarfs in gaudy puffed costumes and turbans like fat pretzels. The little men were laden with suitcases, gladstone bags, small sea chests, brass-bound coffers—one to each arm. Many of them were outmassed by their burdens, and though weight was no problem in Deimos gravity, the dwarfs must have been enormously muscled under their flaring finery to have managed all that tonnage on the surface of Mars.

"Product of Palace bioengineering?" the attaché asked.

"I'm afraid so," said Hamid-Jones. "The Emir always went in for that sort of novelty."

"Handy for carrying a gentleman's luggage," the attaché said dryly.

"They're not a particularly elegant example of gene redesign, like sandipedes or hexapodal camels," Hamid-Jones said with professional distaste. "They were created by a rather crude form of somatic replication—the Palace cloning department uses a lot of shortcuts. They wouldn't breed true if, in fact, they weren't already sterile."

"That's a relief," the attaché said as the little men marched past, the weight of their multiple loads keeping their buskined feet more or less in contact with the floor. "I'm sure they're much esteemed here on Mars, but they wouldn't be a very suitable gift from one sovereign to another if there was any danger of their spreading."

Hamid-Jones suspected the attaché was making fun of him, but he could detect nothing but seriousness in his expression.

"My word, look at that!" the attaché exclaimed. "Your Emir certainly does have a taste for these prodigies!"

Following the dwarfs was a gaggle of four-legged dancing girls in scanty, sequined costumes that left no doubt of their profession. Their faces were concealed for travel, but the leg-veils billowing below were gauzily transparent. They moved across the floor like skittish racehorses, their dancers' skills doing for them what anchoring weight had done for the dwarfs. The effect of the double-hipped platforms bearing all those slender, upright torsos was rather like a procession of candles on trivets.

"If one may ask," the attaché said, "does two sets of legs, ahem, also imply two functional sets of other apparatus?"

"They're capable of bearing children at either fork, if that's what you mean," Hamid-Jones said, annoyed.

"Two in one!" the attaché exclaimed. "That truly would be a princely gift from royalty to royalty—if the recipient had a taste for the bizarre. Our Sultan, however, is a man of uncomplicated though hearty appetites. He'll probably pension these dancing quadrupeds off. I have no doubt they'll all find husbands. But did I understand you to say that they're not sterile?"

"That's right," growled Hamid-Jones. "But they carry a sex-linked lethal recessive that goes with the quadrupedia. So any surviving male children would be back in the genetic mainstream."

After the dancers came a matched set of two-headed singers capable of performing duets with themselves—the pair of them constituting a quartet.

"What, one wonders, is their repertoire?" the attaché drawled. A lowering look from Hamid-Jones cut off his further comment.

The amazed stares of the spaceport bystanders changed to admiration as the next offerings of the Emir filed past—a succession of handlers and grooms with some of the finest animals in the Solar system. There were prancing salukis, their silky ears flying in the low gravity, held down to the floor only by the pressure of the leash; fierce, caged Marsfalcons with magnificent plumage.

"The poor creatures will never fly on Alif Prime," the attaché said, serious now. "Those great fragile wings would snap like matchsticks at first flutter. They'll have to be sent to one of the moons and kept in a zoo."

Hamid-Jones's heart stopped as he recognized al-Janah leading the string of Mars stallions being escorted by Royal Stables grooms. Had someone else—Rashid or Ja'far—completed the cloning project he'd started? After he recovered from the first surprise, he realized that there wouldn't have been time to carry a clone to maturity. The horse was unmistakably al-Janah, but he would have to be the product of an earlier cloning.

"Wonderful animal," the attaché said. "Is something the matter?"

Hamid-Jones turned away. "I hope that none of those grooms can recognize me through this disguise."

"You won't have to worry about them once you're aboard. They'll turn the horses over to our own stablemaster and return on the next tethershuttle."

Porters with padlocked cases, in lockstep with armed guards, followed the animals, and then came crews of navvies floating pallets with huge crates, big enough for elephants, a few inches off the floor. Jewels, perhaps, in the smaller cases. The contents of the crates could only be guessed at. In a previous exchange of gifts between rulers, the Emir had sent a custom-built state yacht, tested on one of the enclosed palace lagoons and then dismantled in sections; the Mars-made craft could not have stayed afloat for five minutes in Alpha Centauri's seas, but as a gesture it was hard to top.

Last of all came the new Martian ambassador and his considerable retinue, who were to present the collection of state gifts. The current ambassador, four light-years away, could have no inkling that he would be replaced upon the arrival of the starship. Even the news of the bogus Emir's "recovery" from the ambushed operation would not arrive by radio until a year before the ship. The distant ambassador was a Rubinstein man. He was definitely on Ismail's list. Hamid-Jones wondered whether there was a killer in the replacement ambassador's retinue, or whether the execution would wait until the old ambassador returned to Mars.

"Is there anyone in that bunch who might know you by sight?"

Hamid-Jones studied the ambassadorial staff. There were too many eunuchs among them—about fifty out of a total of a hundred or so. The uncastrated men tended toward civil service fops, some of them as gaudy and overadorned as the eunuchs.

The ambassador himself, a cadaverous fellow with shifty eyes, was not a eunuch—that would have been an insult to the Sultan—but he was Ismail's man nevertheless. It was more than four light-years to Alpha Centauri, but fear made a long string.

"I don't recognize anyone offhand, but you never know."

"If worse comes to worst, you can put yourself under the captain's protection. He won't be able to acknowledge you openly—there's already too much diplomatic strain between Mars and Alpha Centauri—but perhaps he might tuck you away somewhere. I don't know how many coverts are traveling with that dressmaker's circus, but it's unlikely that even the loosest cannon would compromise his ambassador's position with a shipboard attempt on your life." His teeth gleamed in a perfect smile. "Governments generally hire the Assassins for that sort of skulduggery."

"That's very comforting," Hamid-Jones said.

"There go the last of them," the attaché said, turning. He was a bit of a fop himself, but when his short Centauran-style chlamys parted, Hamid-Jones clearly saw the outline of a shoulder holster. "You'd better get a move on. Do you have your boarding pass?"

"Yes."

"Good. I'll leave you here, then. I'm not cleared past the gate. Good trip and all that."

"Thanks."

Hamid-Jones picked up his carry-on luggage and joined the last-minute flow to the departure gate. There were fewer than a thousand people left. They parted in two streams around the mullah, who was cleaning up the remains of the sacrifice while an impatient custodial worker rolled up the edges of the plastic tarpaulin. A number of passengers were pausing to dip their fingertips or pick up a fragment of the laser-charred mutton. At the last moment, Hamid-Jones did the same, popping a blackened morsel into his mouth with a mumbled prayer.

As he moved in a low-gravity shuffle through the long transparent passage that curved over Deimos's small horizon, never more than a hundred yards away, he lifted his eyes with almost everybody else to watch the rising of the starship above the pocked skyline.

It was a vast onion shape, over a mile in diameter, that would flatten out still further under acceleration. He could see the gossamer shroud clinging to the ship and all the complicated rigging and stays that would unfold it in flight to protect the craft from the howling storm of charged particles that would impinge on it at relativistic velocities; the superconducting fabric was gaily painted with colorful Kufic calligraphy, though the decorations would char away long before the ship reached even a fraction of its final speed.

The ship itself, of course, was mostly wood, varnished to a glossy sheen. Wood was the most practical material for large structures built in space. It didn't have to be lifted at great expense out of the gravity wells of planets—it was sent spiraling inward from the cometary belt, where the forests of mankind had been growing for five centuries. The great shipyards beyond the orbit of Uranus fashioned the comet-grown lumber into starships, space stations, habitats, intrasystem liners—everything except the small craft designed for atmospheric reentry. The giant trees, bioengineered to live in a vacuum, subsisted on the water, carbon, and nitrogen of cometary ice and in the absence of significant gravity grew to immense size. Timbers a hundred miles long, used in the construction of habitats, were not uncommon.

For a starship like the *Saladin*, timbers and planking a mere mile or so in length sufficed. Hardly a bolt or fastener had been used in the *Saladin*'s construction. Like the Arab ships of yore, it was sewn together—not by coir, as in the ancient seagoing vessels, but by thousands upon thousands of miles of rope made from monofilament fiber. The stitched construction gave the starship the advantage of flexibility. Like a living thing, it could change shape and adapt itself to the enormous stresses of continuous one-G boosts over periods measured in years. Wood and cord were far more sensible materials than metal, which would have had to have been worked into movable joints, or plastic, which was inclined to deteriorate under exposure to the shorter wavelengths or, still worse, to snap.

Wood had been an underrated material in the early days of space exploration, but once mankind had outgrown its tin cans, the engineers had begun once again to appreciate its virtues of high tensile strength, elasticity, and superior insulating qualities. The cedars of Lebanon were reborn—this time in the cometary wilderness. Someday, when the spreading ecology had transformed the Oort Cloud, the greater portion of humanity would live on comets.

"It looks almost like a giant mosque, doesn't it?" remarked an elderly gentleman who was shuffling along beside Hamid-Jones, holding a bird cage. He peered nearsightedly at the wooden onion with its slipcover.

"Er, yes, I guess you could say that," Hamid-Jones agreed politely.

"And the covering with the sacred inscriptions—it reminds me of the embroidered covering of the Kaaba. Have you been to Mecca?"

"Er, no, not yet."

"The inscriptions—will they protect us from harm, do you think?"

"Well, uh, when the magnetic umbrella opens up it will certainly protect us from all the hydrogen atoms that will rain on us at relativistic speeds."

The old man squinted rheumily at Hamid-Jones. "Don't I know you from somewhere? Have we met?"

"I don't think so."

"Just a minute and I'll have it," the old man said.

"It's been nice talking to you," Hamid-Jones said, and hurried to leave the old man behind.

A smiling steward was waiting to greet him at the head of the gangplank. He compared Hamid-Jones's boarding pass to a list summoned up on a palmscreen and said, "Welcome aboard, *sidi*. A porter will show you to your cabin. There's plenty of time to get settled—we don't cast off for another hour and a half. I suggest you go to the observation deck to watch our departure. It's a grand sight. We borrow Deimos's orbital motion to assist us, and as we pull round on the sunward side, you'll see Mars go through all its phases in a half hour. A full Mars at only twelve thousand miles is worth seeing! There won't be much to see after that—Earth will be visible to the naked eye for only about a week, and two weeks after *that*, the Sun will be only another star. By the time we reach a third of the speed of light, the stars themselves will start to disappear—blind spots will appear both ahead and behind as the stars Doppler through the spectrum and become invisible, below infrared behind, beyond ultraviolet forward. The blank disks will enlarge, squeezing the rest of the stars between them into rainbow hoops, until there's just a thin band around us. We ride through a void after that. So see the sights while you can."

"Thanks, I will," Hamid-Jones said.

"Don't worry about acceleration, though. You'll have plenty of time to acquire your space legs. We'll give you about six hours to get up to a Martian standard G—takeoff's practically unnoticeable—and then we give the passengers a month to work up to a standard Centauran G. There are exercise programs available to help. We suggest strongly to all Marsborn passengers that they sign up, but if you're Centauranborn or Earthborn to start with, and you've only lost tone on Mars, the gradual increments of acceleration are generally sufficient to get you back in shape—though mind you, an hour or so daily in a penguin suit can't hurt."

He was looking curiously at Hamid-Jones. Hamid-Jones remembered that while he was dressed and coiffed as an Alpha Centauran and traveling under a Centauran name, his accent was distinctly Solar—Martian with an underlay of Anglo-Arab. His sturdy frame though, forged in Earth's gravitational field, had more in common with Centauran physiques than those of most of the inhabitants of the Solar system.

"I'll keep that in mind," Hamid-Jones mumbled.

The steward snapped his fingers. A porter appeared at Hamid-Jones's side, dressed in blue pantaloons and a white jacket. He touched his tarboosh respectfully and gently pried the bag from Hamid-Jones's hand. "Would you like me to carry you, too, *sidi*?" he said, producing a wraparound girdle with two handles.

Hamid-Jones had no intention of being toted like a log of wood. "No, thank you, I can manage very well in low gravity," he said snappishly.

"Very good, *sidi*," the porter said, and launched himself in a flat trajectory, leaving Hamid-Jones to follow as best he could.

The cabin turned out to be more like a stateroom, with its own tiled bath and a curtained sleeping alcove. There was plenty of room aboard a starship, the economics of interstellar travel being what they were. The prayer nook contained a circular rug that perfectly illustrated the nature of star travel with its continuous boost. Instead of a pointed *mihrab* to align the worshipper properly, the prayer niche was round, with a circular target for the forehead. Mecca would always be directly below during the first half of the journey, directly above for the second half.

He washed his face, fiddled with the holovid to see what the ship's library contained, sampled a piece of fruit from the bowl on the table. A pamphlet told him that the *Saladin* possessed its own orchards that were supplied with light in the growth spectra diverted from the awesome glare of the total annihilation drive, its own flocks of sheep and chickens for fresh mutton and poultry, grew its own garden vegetables and heterochronic grains—though there were bulk suppliers aboard for a two-year subjective voyage should blights or poor harvests afflict the hydroponics cages. There were also several paradises aboard, with purely decorative trees, flowers, and songbirds. Passengers were cautioned to be careful about letting songbirds escape when entering or leaving through the double doors.

A chime sounded, and a pleasant disembodied voice reminded passengers that the ship would cast off in one hour, for those who wished to secure a good place on the observation deck. Hamid-Jones struggled for the better part of a nanosecond against the desire not to appear overeager and unsophisticated, then jammed the unfamiliar tarboosh back on his head and joined the trickle of passengers moving through the corridors. It wasn't every day that one set sail for the stars.

With a groan of protesting timbers that was audible within the ship but went unheard on Deimos's airless surface, the *Saladin* cast off its mooring cables and started to rise. Slowly, ponderously, like a vast squashed balloon, it drifted upward on the momentum imparted by the loaded springs of the landing cradle. Once, the gentle nudge had come from compressed CO_2, but worried Sufi environmentalists had pointed out that the molecules tended to linger, even on a body with an insignificant gravitational field like Deimos.

Deimos fell behind, a smallish potato crisscrossed with the glittering threads of enclosed tubeways and studded with the thumbtack shapes of the hotels and spaceport facilities that had grown there over the centuries. Two of the potato's eyes were glazed over—Swift and Voltaire craters wore bubbles containing, respectively, a park and a low gravity recreational lake over a mile in diameter. Somewhere in Swift Park was a monument displaying a replica of the first Deimos lander, a Russian craft of the early twenty-first Christian century.

The intrasystem fusion drive kicked in when the *Saladin* was far enough away from Deimos not to endanger it. The initial boost was at a gentle one hundredth of a gravity. Within the ship, loose objects, including people, began to settle to the floor. Water stayed in basins. Flower arrangements in cabins showed the slightest droop. People weighed a pound or two—more than they had when the ship was berthed at Deimos.

Steadily, weight increased. In ten minutes it had doubled. At the end of the first hour it was up to about six percent of a Terrestrial G and still increasing. The ship's modest hydrogen reserves would be used up long before it crossed the orbit of Jupiter, but by then it would be safe to turn on the Harun drive— at that point the *Saladin* would be traveling several million miles below the plane of the ecliptic, no inhabited body of the Solar system would be anywhere near its path, and the memories of the Solar system's traffic computers would have been searched to insure that no spacecraft had strayed from the ecliptic on a course that would risk intersecting the trajectory of the *Saladin* at close range.

The Harun effect was well understood after six centuries, and there had been no major accidents since the unfortunate release of the antihydrogen cloud that had wiped the surface of Hygeia clean and turned it into a ball of fused glass. But one doesn't take chances when one rends the curtain of Creation.

The great wooden bubble, a world in itself, steadied and trimmed until it was aligned with the Centaur. Once, that constellation's brightest star had guided Arab mariners venturing south of the equator by pointing the way to the Southern Cross. Now it shone as a yellow beacon beckoning toward another of Allah's kingdoms in the sky.

"I beg your pardon, but could you help me to a seat? I can't seem to stay on the floor."

Hamid-Jones turned his head and saw the old gent who had been carrying the bird cage. He was clinging for dear life to the backrest of Hamid-Jones's seat; evidently he had lost his nerve while trying to negotiate his way toward one of the few empty chairs.

"Here, take mine," Hamid-Jones said, springing to his feet and managing to stay anchored himself only by grabbing a knob on the armrest.

"Oh, I couldn't . . ."

"That's all right. Sitting or standing, it doesn't matter much at a sixteenth of a G. Here, let me help you. Maybe you'll be more comfortable with the safety belt fastened."

The old man settled gratefully into the cushions. "Oh, you're the young man I spoke to at the spaceport."

"Er, yes." Hamid-Jones started to edge away.

"I was afraid I'd bounce up too far and fall into *that*! It makes me quite dizzy just looking at it."

He gestured toward the central well that rose through the mile-wide acreage of the observation deck. It was a thousand feet across and surrounded by a chest-high railing. It was there to allow for expansion as the *Saladin* changed shape, and it was the core of the ship. From the lounge chairs drawn up to face it, one could look down into a chasm that at present was a half-mile deep, or up to see the destination stars of Centaurus. Most of the ship's passengers were seated a halfmile away to watch the retreat of Mars through the ports that girdled the ship, but the more romantically inclined had taken their positions here, to dream and to speculate.

"Oh, there's no danger of that," Hamid-Jones assured the old man. "If you look close you can see the safety threads rising from the railing. They're very fine, but you'd have to be really determined to squeeze through them. The well can't be glassed in, of course, without a lot of expansion joints that would spoil the effect."

"I suppose one couldn't really get hurt, even if one *did* fall through," the old man said, pulling at his snow-white beard. "You'd just float to the bottom."

"Oh, don't make *that* mistake," Hamid-Jones warned. "You might only weigh nine or ten pounds at the moment, but that's quite enough to break your neck at the end of a half-mile fall."

"I've been thinking about where I could have met you. Have you ever gone hunting in Tharsis?"

A finger of ice ran down Hamid-Jones's spine. "No."

"Perhaps I'm mistaken. I've catered hunting parties there. My name's Izzah Zarrab." He peered expectantly at Hamid-Jones.

For an awful moment, Hamid-Jones couldn't remember his Centauran name. "Murjan Khalil Khulafa," he said with a gulp.

"May your hands be blessed, *ya* Murjan," the old man intoned.

"And yours, too, *sidi*," Hamid-Jones said.

"I could have sworn—"

"Have you traveled to the stars before?" Hamid-Jones interjected hastily.

"*Ya satir,* no! They say that star travel makes you young, or at least you come back not as old as you're supposed to be, but I don't understand such things. But I haven't the years left to try to find out. I'm going to live with my daughter. She was taken to Alpha Centauri by her husband, an artisan, many years ago. He's very kindly offered to take me into his household. That's what the message said, though it took them almost nine years to answer me." His watery eyes were trying to puzzle out Hamid-Jones's tarboosh and facial curls. "And what brings you to this journey?"

"Family," said Hamid-Jones, and left it at that.

"When the sky shall split and become doors," the old man said indistinctly.

"What?"

"It's a verse from the Koran. The seventy-eighth surah." The old fellow fumbled with a chain around his neck and brought forth a charm with a scrap of paper in it. "The mullah gave it to me to protect me through the splitting. Will that happen soon?"

"Oh, when they turn on the Harun drive? I suppose the sky does split in a way, but not the way you think. I gather it's more like opening a faucet. I shouldn't think that would be for another day or two. They have to get up to a certain speed. There'll be an announcement beforehand."

"I would have thought such a thing impious. But the mullah assured me that what Allah allows must be Allah's way. Do you agree?"

"Yes," Hamid-Jones said, seeing a note upon which to make his escape. "It must be Allah's way."

"More caviar?" the steward said, bending over the table.

"Thank you," Hamid-Jones said. He pushed aside some of the eggplant appetizer to make more room on his plate.

"There'll be another seating for the lecture after lunch in the small theater on jim deck," the steward said, spooning out a generous portion and arranging several wedges of flatbread. "There are still a few seats left. Would you care to go?"

Hamid-Jones wiped his mouth with a napkin. "Yes, I would. I tried to get into the breakfast seating, but it was jammed."

"The response caught us by surprise. More than four thousand passengers signed up—about a fifth of the passenger list. That's almost twice the usual number. The poor cosmologist and his assistant are giving five lectures a day, and they've roped in the first officer as well."

"I'll look forward to it."

The steward leaned closer. "I've got you into the assistant cosmologist's talk—frankly, the chief is a bit of a stick. It should be a little livelier than the ones you missed—if my spies have informed me correctly, and if the captain doesn't change his mind, we should switch to the mutual annihilation drive sometime during the lecture itself. So be sure to wear your seat belt."

"Thanks, I appreciate it," Hamid-Jones said.

"Here, let me give you a little more caviar."

"Oh, I couldn't. It's very good, though."

"It ought to be. It was collected this morning. That's as fresh as you can get."

"Don't tell me you have sturgeon aboard?"

The steward laughed. "Our pools aren't *quite* that oceanic. No, this is heterochronic caviar. It reproduces itself without an intervening generation of sturgeon. Don't ask me how. You'd have to be a cloning technician to understand it."

"Uh, I suppose so." Hamid-Jones popped a wedge into his mouth and became too busy to talk further. The steward smiled at him and left.

The cosmology officer was a stocky young man with smooth rosy cheeks and an air of intrinsic self-confidence. He was natty in a blue uniform decorated with the triplet of gold, orange, and red stars of the Centauran service and a specialist's patch showing a representation of the universe surmounted by a Feynman diagram in gold braid.

"You've all heard the announcement, so I won't waste time by repeating it, except to say that nothing much happens when the annihilation drive goes on. Your weight goes off for a minute or two after the fusion engines shut down and before the Harun drive cuts in, that's all. Then we'll take about fifteen minutes to bring the ship up to full thrust again—the drive techs will be fine-tuning the proportions of matter and antimatter. So sit tight for the first few minutes. You can move around freely for the present, but when the buzzer and warning light go on, please fasten your safety belts."

"Excuse me—I thought we were supposed to be weightless for several hours," said a nervous passenger in the front row.

"You're thinking about turnover. That won't happen until a year from now. A year of ship's time, that is. About two and a half years will have passed for the rest of the universe. We'll have spent the first year of that getting up to within about one ten-thousandth of one percent of the speed of light. In the process, we'll travel about half a light-year. Time will hardly have seemed to slow down at all for us during most of that time. But when we get to about ninety-nine percent of the speed of light, the relativistic effects will begin to increase very rapidly, so that at our top velocity, time will slow down by a factor of about seven hundred. In other words, the *remainder* of the first leg of our trip after that year of boost—about twenty months at very nearly the speed of light—will go by for us in less than a day."

"Oh . . . I see . . . it's not today, then?"

The cosmologist took a deep breath. "No. We won't experience prolonged weightlessness till midpoint in our journey. Then we'll have about six hours of it while the captain turns the ship around and realigns it precisely. We'll be coasting at our top speed then, and our six hours will be more like six months for the folks back home—we'll travel half a light-year in that time.''

"I see," said the passenger, more confused than ever.

"But we don't have to worry about all that right now," the officer said with heavy professional patience. "I'm going to start with a little history."

He moved to one side of the large holo frame that had been set up on the stage and looked around the small theater to assess the comprehension level of his audience. There were about two hundred of them, mostly Martians and other Solarians. The Alpha Centaurans who were returning home, of course, would have been exposed to orientation lectures on their way out and would consider themselves seasoned star travelers.

Hamid-Jones took the opportunity to study his fellow voyagers, too. He saw rows of earnest expressions, the faces of people determined to squeeze the last drop of significance out of this—for most—once-in-a-lifetime journey.

The cosmologist, on the other hand, might have made the crossing six or eight times, despite his apparent youth. Each round-trip would assess him only four years of his lifespan, while stay-at-homes aged a dozen years.

It was an arresting thought to Hamid-Jones: that fresh-faced youngster had probably been born before most of the graybeards in the audience. It brought home the magnitude of the journey. The people around him would be his neighbors for the next two years. And when he finally disembarked at Alpha Centauri, he would be separated from everything and everyone he had ever known by a gulf of time. Lalla would be a woman of mature years, older than he, before he could return to her; Aziz, if he were still alive, would be declining toward middle age.

"The key to feasible travel between the stars was discovered in the eighteenth century of Islam—the twenty-fourth century for those of you in the audience who are Christians."

The cosmology officer made sure he had their attention before going on. "Until that time, launching an interstellar vessel of any sort was a ruinous and impractical enterprise that even a rich society could afford only once or twice in a generation. Here's what some of those primitive starships looked like."

The holo frame flickered into life and began to show a procession of improbable shapes. There were great scepterlike objects with bulbous ends, their scale impossible to guess. Collections of checkered spheres in frameworks. Flatirons at the ends of poles. Double-ended umbrellas turned inside out. A thing like a dandelion gone to seed. Even something that looked like a child's kite.

"These early efforts divide basically into three groups. Ships that carry their own fuel. Ships that collect their fuel on the way. And light sails and other schemes for getting a free kick from something that remains in the Solar system, like mass drivers."

The audience gaped at the collection of antiques. Hamid-Jones heard a few oohs and ahhs. There was something impressive about those brave, ungainly shapes. They showed the indomitable spirit of man.

"Let's take the fueled ships first. They came in many styles. Ion drives. Various fusion reactions—deuterium-deuterium, deuterium-tritium, deuterium–helium three. There was an interesting *fission* engine using a boron 11 to helium reaction that needed a hydrogen fusion reaction to *trigger* it, but that provided a better push than any of the merely fusion drives. And would you believe that there were actually plans for one early star drive that depended on the explosions of nuclear bombs—one every few seconds—to kick the ship along?"

He gave the audience a look at the ship—a bundle of cylinders with something that looked like a snowball at one end and a goblet of steel at the other.

A hand popped up in the third row, and the lecturer said, "Yes?"

"Excuse me," came a hesitant voice, "but you didn't mention any kind of antimatter drives."

"You're getting ahead of the story, but yes, there *were* crude beginnings in that direction, too. They knew how to make antimatter as a laboratory trick—not too practical for producing antimatter in industrial quantities. An antimatter factory was actually built out past the orbit of Neptune. A Triton-Swiss enterprise, I believe. The accelerator rings were about fifty miles in diameter, stacked in a cylinder a couple of hundred miles long. It was able to produce about a gram of antimatter per day."

After a pause to let that sink in, the cosmology officer allowed the ghost of a smug smile to steal over his face. "Pity. Because gram for gram, an annihilation reaction produces about one hundred forty times the energy of, say, hydrogen-helium fusion. Even so, they'd have been lugging along moonlet-size tanks of hydrogen and antihydrogen—the antihydrogen being stored in some kind of gigantic magnetic flask with its own ticklish engineering problems. And then, a ship the size of the *Saladin* would have to carry seven times its weight in fuel to reach sixty percent of the speed of light. The time-dilation effect would be negligible—about one point two four. A trip to Alpha Centauri would take five years of our lives instead of two. Perhaps civilization could manage. But a trip to, say, Delta Pavonis would cost us about thirty-three years of lifetime instead of, essentially, the same two years. Impossible! And to get up to ninety-nine percent of the speed of light with a time-dilation effect of seven to one—still not as well as we do in modern times—a ship like the *Saladin* would have to carry forty thousand times its mass in matter and antimatter. So we see that the annihilation drive by itself is not the answer."

He began to pace a little. "The problem with all star drives that carry their own fuel is the same: the great satan called mass ratio. The faster you want to go, the more reaction mass you must carry—and all that additional reaction mass itself must be accelerated, at ever-increasing energy cost. For example, that ship whose picture I showed you would have to carry one hundred fifty times its weight in nuclear bombs in order to travel ten light-years in one hundred fifty years. To shorten the trip to eighty years, it would have to carry twenty-two thousand times its own weight. And then it would have traveled only as far as Epsilon Eridani."

He fiddled with his holo wand and produced tables of figures to which no one paid attention.

"So the ships that settled the nearer stars were slow boats, traveling at five or at most ten percent of the speed of light. The first load of colonies to Alpha Centauri took ninety years to reach there, and when they landed, they found the children of the second colony ship waiting there to greet them. Some of the generation ships are still undoubtedly out there in the void. We can only wish their inhabitants well and hope for a safe planetfall for their descendants."

Hamid-Jones's attention strayed to one of the rows in the next

aisle. Out of the corner of his eye he thought he had seen someone there twist a head to look in his direction, then look quickly
away again. But when he turned to see, there was no one to meet
his gaze—just a row of earnest profiles engrossed in the lecture.
One of the profiles was obscured by a fringed headcloth as the
man slouched forward in his seat to get a better view of the
stage. There was nothing to distinguish him; by his headdress
and natty robes, he looked like any Martian prosperous enough
to afford passage on the *Saladin*.

Hamid-Jones remembered the attaché's warning about Assassins and covert government hit men and decided he was being
morbid. So what if someone had glanced at him? Other passengers, their attention wandering, were also sneaking looks at their
fellow voyagers; he was doing it himself.

He returned his attention to the lecture.

"So much for ships that carry their own fuel. But what about
ships that scoop up their fuel on the way? Fuel that then has
only to accelerate the payload and not itself?"

The holo frame showed a tremendous web floating in space.
It was insubstantial enough for stars to shine through it. The
holographic window rushed toward it at dizzying speed until it
finally zoomed in on a tiny mite at the center of the web. There
was another adjustment of scale, and the mite became an enormous vehicle, a double-ended cone assembly bristling with many
spokes. One could see that the machine was spinning its own
web with a thimblelike hub that was rotating like a whirligig.

"This is something called a Bussard ramjet. The theory was
that it would scoop up hydrogen atoms in interstellar space,
squeeze them in a magnetic field, and initiate a fusion reaction
whose efficiency would increase as the ship went faster. The
hydrogen not used in the fusion reaction would be shot out the
rear as reaction mass. There was no theoretical limit to the speed
such a ship could attain, and velocities in excess of ninety-nine
percent of the speed of light were thought possible, giving the
Bussard ramjet a relativistic advantage over ships that had to
carry their own fuel, and making possible the same sort of interstellar commerce we enjoy today."

He shook his head sadly. "But this promising vehicle finally
foundered on engineering difficulties. Hydrogen is thin in ordinary interstellar space—on the order of one atom per cubic
centimeter. Magnetic scoops thousands of miles in diameter

would be required. To keep such a scoop extended, it would have to spin round its hub, and if the spin failed it would collapse and destroy itself. Then there was the problem of the mass of the scoop itself. A very modest thousand-ton vehicle would need a scoop the diameter of Earth's moon, with a collecting area of about four million square miles. Translated into something even as insubstantial as a one-mil superconducting fabric, that would add up to over two hundred million tons—twenty thousand times the mass of the spacecraft itself. You're back to the same kind of mass ratios as when you tote tanks of hydrogen.''

The child's kite appeared again in the holo window and resolved itself into an immense hexagonal figure braced by struts and stays. A flealike reentry vehicle gave it scale. The kite disappeared, was replaced by a radiating burr with a tiny pod at the center. The burr, in turn, gave way to something like a shiny parachute trailing a small pendant orb from its shrouds.

''Now,'' the cosmology officer said, glancing at his watch, ''let's dispose of our third method of propulsion—light sails and other forms of energy transfer. Two of the designs I've just shown you were actually built, and they both worked! The heliogyro, the one with all the vanes, never came to anything. But the disk sail, the best of the designs, actually got up to about twenty percent of the speed of light. We know that from the Dopplered radio signals it continued to send back for some decades. A colony ship—fifteen men with four wives each—with enough life support for a century. It was sent on its way by a battery of laser cannon set up on Phaeton, an asteroid whose orbit takes it closer to the sun than Mercury. Since light pressure as a force varies with the inverse square of distance, this spacecraft worked up most of its velocity before even clearing the Solar system. The problem was stopping. There were no laser cannon, of course, at the destination star, Epsilon Indi. The engineers devised a brilliant scheme, known for some obscure reason as the 'Forward Maneuver.' Forward is an English word meaning *ud-dehm*, 'up front.' At an appropriate braking distance from the target star, a much larger light sail was to be deployed and separated from the ship. The original sail was to be reversed—a tricky proposition requiring jets of gas to keep it from folding up. It would then receive reflected laser light beamed from Phaeton eleven point six light-years earlier, in time for the maneuver. The light would be upshifted to make up the deficit caused by

Dopplering toward the less energetic red part of the spectrum because of the ship's high terminal velocity. Aim and timing, as you can imagine, were critical!''

He had them leaning forward in their seats. Someone breathed, ''What happened?''

''Back in the Solar system, a kingdom had fallen a generation earlier. The new regime had different priorities—and budget problems. It wasn't terribly interested in funding visionary schemes that had been set in motion by its predecessors. A belated rescue effort was cobbled together by the United Islamic Nations with a special *zakat* levied on its members. But by that time, much vital engineering data had been lost. And the laser installation on Phaeton was in disrepair. The eight-year slug of laser light that was finally sent off may have been too little and too late, and the precision of its aim over a distance of eleven light-years may have left something to be desired. At any rate, when later colonists arrived in succeeding centuries, there was no trace of a sailing ship ever having landed anywhere in the system. We can presume that they're still sailing outward into the void.''

There was a general sigh of sympathy. Someone murmured piously, *''Ya khabar abyad!''*

''Similar uncertainties hold for other propulsion schemes involving forms of energy transfer. For example, there was a very creditable plan for using a mass driver of the kind we're all familiar with in lunar and asteroid mining—still an inexpensive way to accrete mass for new habitats. A stream of pellets, accelerated to about twenty percent of the speed of light, would be aimed at a bucket at the rear of the ship. The bucket would have to be large enough to form an umbrella for the ship, of course, and be cushioned by appropriately gargantuan shock absorbers. But aiming matter is even trickier than aiming laser light, particularly at interstellar distances. And then there's the problem of stopping. You can plan your trip well in advance, and first shoot off a stream of slower pellets that will be waiting to collide with the ship when it gets there. This removes any worries about palace revolutions back home. At least you have the consolation of knowing before you leave that your braking mass is presumably waiting for you, having left before you did. But will you hit it exactly on target? There's not much leeway for course corrections. And you still must depend for several decades on the mass driver back in the Solar system for getting you to your preplanned terminal velocity—no more, no less. And that's subject to error, equipment or people failure, unanticipated revisions that you can't tell them about, and political cancellations. Basically it boils down to the fact that it's risky to leave your motor and brakes back home."

He cocked his head and seemed to be listening for something. Then he shrugged and said, "So, to sum up, of our three methods of star travel, one proved to be inefficient, one was impractical, and one was undependable. What was needed was a *fourth* method—some way to *create* your fuel at the moment of its use. But that was fundamentally impossible, wasn't it?

"So though the Solar system and its bodies had been claimed for Allah by the faithful during the first few centuries of *Nadha*, the stars essentially remained beyond our grasp. Travel time to the stars must be measured in generations or, if speeded up, payload had to be reduced to very small automated probes. Still, our forefathers were persistent. A handful of tiny colonies planted with great difficulty on the very nearest of the habitable star systems painfully took root in isolation. And there matters stood for the next few centuries.

"And that brings us to Harun al-Mudarris—Harun the Teacher—and his marvelous insight into the ways of Allah. For Creation did not stop at the first picosecond of the Big Bang. It is about to recommence in—" He glanced at his watch again. "—about one minute, if the engine room is on schedule."

A buzzer sounded. Above the small stage a green sign began flashing. A pleasant baritone voice from nowhere said, "Attention, please. Find the nearest seat at once and fasten the safety belt. If you are not in your cabin or a public area with seating, grasp the nearest wall stanchion and hold it firmly. Our intrasystem drive will be shut down in exactly sixty seconds, and the ship will be in a condition of weightlessness for approximately two minutes until the Harun drive opens to full aperture. Acceleration will resume steadily after that, but it is recommended that you remain seated and in restraint for approximately another ten minutes, until conditions of full weight are restored."

Passengers fumbled with their seat belts. The cosmology officer hooked a toe under the base of the lectern and waited in a posture of elaborate unconcern.

The buzzer repeated. "Attention, please. We will be in a

condition of weightlessness in exactly fifteen seconds. Please make sure you are seated and strapped in.''

Weight went off. A few loose objects began to float. Passengers grabbed at possessions, and one, whose belt had not been fastened, levitated a full six inches before pulling himself back to his seat in embarrassment.

The cosmology officer swayed like a sea anemone, anchored by his toe. His voice took on fire. "At this moment, the portals of the universe are opening for us in the combustion chamber. Matter and antimatter are beginning to collide and annihilate each other, as they did at the beginning of time. Soon a stream of photons and virtual particles with pseudomass will be ejected at the speed of light behind us. The effect will increase rapidly. In a moment you will feel the hand of Allah.''

Hamid-Jones thought he could sense a faint vibration beneath him. In the next minute the walls began to contract with a creak of wood. A neighbor's hovering book of poems settled again into its owner's lap. Though the feathery pressure on his thighs and buttocks told Hamid-Jones that thus far he would tip the scales at only a few ounces, there was no doubt that weight was returning to the ship.

Appropriate exclamations of awe came from all sides.

"Curiously enough,'' the cosmology officer told his tethered audience, "a theory of continuous creation had been discredited in the second half of the twentieth Christian century. Its proponents were a group of British astronomers at Cambridge—still a hallowed center of learning under the Protectorate—named Bondi, Gold, and Hoyle. They asserted that the expansion of the universe and the redshift could be explained if it were assumed that single atoms of hydrogen were somehow coming into being constantly in the depths of space—perhaps about one hydrogen atom per year in a volume of space equal to that of the Great Mosque. The universe would always have the same average density no matter how much it grew. It would have no beginning and no end. Theirs was known as the Steady State theory, in contrast to the Big Bang theory of creation.

"But the Steady State universe was demolished very quickly by newer cosmological discoveries. If the Steady State model were true, then the observable universe should be the same in all directions, at whatever distances. But there was a very much larger number of quasars, for example, in the distant past. If most quasars, as indicated by their extreme redshifts, were more than nine or ten billion light-years away in distance, then they also must be nine or ten billion years away in time, and therefore must belong to a past era of the universe. And, more devastating, background radiation from the Big Bang was detected soon thereafter. The expansion of the universe had to be explained by a mechanism other than the continuous origin of matter. Fred Hoyle, Steady State's chief proponent, had to publicly eat crow.

"The Big Bang model strengthened, growing ever more sophisticated to accommodate such refinements as bubble universes, inflationary universes compartmented by domain walls, a so-called 'chaotic inflationary' model, eleven-dimensional space-time with the extra dimensions tucked away at every point, a four-dimensional space-time wrapped around a more complicated shape to form a boundless universe with both homogeneity and inhomogeneity, and so forth. Cosmologists probing the Big Bang eventually found a method for getting beyond Planck time at 10^{-44} second—the wall beyond which physics doesn't work—and even today there are reputations to be made in this area."

He lowered his eyes in a way that suggested that he himself was one of those hoping to make a name for himself by staking out a small area behind the Planck wall.

"But somehow, the idea of continuous creation refused to go away." He gave a wry little shake of the head. "Little fascinating intimations kept cropping up that in some sense or another matter *could* be created out of nothing. Not in the sense of the early Cambridge model, of course, but in some way that was not incompatible with a modified Big Bang theory. And, after all, it had happened before, hadn't it?

"One such intimation was the demonstration that matter and antimatter in the form of matched pairs of virtual particles can and do arise spontaneously as a result of quantum fluctuations of the vacuum. And why not? The universe itself originated because of a quantum fluctuation known as the Big Bang."

He regarded his audience owlishly, as if trying to decide how far to go. "The key to creation, we now know, was expansion. In an inflationary period, though the sum total which is the energy of the cosmos remains balanced at zero, the sums from which the zero is produced are many times larger. So the number of particles created also is many times larger—a whole universe in a fraction of a second, in fact. But the universe is *still* expanding as we sit here, albeit the *rate* of expansion keeps decreasing as the size gets larger and larger. So out of the net gain of a larger and larger 'zero,' virtual particles still form out of the decay of the vacuum.''

He had acquired enough weight by that time for the soles of his feet to settle to the floor once more. Cautiously he left the security of the lectern and continued his exposition, trying not to gesture too violently.

''Now it is the fate of virtual particles to vanish as quickly as they appear. But they decay briefly into other particles before they do—sometimes whole chains of them. And out of these jigsaw pieces of Creation, mayn't more stable units of matter sometimes be assembled? After all, that's what happened in the thicker quantum soup of the early universe. Isn't it possible that at least some of this peek-a-boo matter might linger?

''Some theorists thought so. They pointed to the unexplained matter in the universe—matter that had no right to be there. For example, there's more hydrogen loitering around the galactic core than there ought to be—and it seems to be constantly re-newed. It's in the form of a sort of orbiting 'smoke ring' with a mass of about two hundred million suns, twice the mass that theory says could be accounted for by core explosions back in galactic history. The only problem was that *if* hydrogen was being created, it was being created in the wrong place—not in empty space but in the vicinity of a hypermass, the hundred-million-sol super black hole that sits in the center of our galaxy! Legions of theorists bit the dust trying to explain this untidy evidence in terms of the decay of the vacuum or by some tor-tured version of the old Bondi-Gold hypothesis. The clue re-mained inconveniently unexplained, however. It was waiting for another Einstein or Hawking to come along and fit it into an-other grand synthesis.

''That mighty theorist, as we all know now, was Harun al-Mudarris, possibly the greatest scientific mind of all time.''

He paused reverentially while the holo frame showed the con-ventional portrait of Harun—the gaunt, saintly face with the sickle beard, the flashing eyes, the elegant turban wrapped round with a string of pearls—as he copied data with pencil and paper from the screen of an old-fashioned desktop computer.

''Like other giant figures of science, Harun made his mark early, at the age of nineteen, with his earthshaking paper on electron decay—the paper that revolutionized physics by challenging the law of electric-charge conservation. His thesis supervisor lost a right hand for stealing it from him when, a year later, Harun followed up with his famous paper on tauon decay and it was realized by the proctors that both brilliant concepts could only have come from the same luminous mind.

"Harun was only twenty-two when he set that mind to the centuries-old problem of the unexplained hydrogen orbiting around the galactic center. He realized at once that Hawking radiation was the key. That, in fact, Hawking radiation served as a metaphor for Creation. When pairs of virtual particles pop into existence in the vicinity of the event horizon of a black hole, instead of mutually annihilating each other, one may be sucked into the black hole while the other is free to spiral outward. The black hole doesn't care what it eats—matter or antimatter. If it is the antimatter particle of the pair—say, a positron—that escapes, it will probably meet its doom by encountering ordinary matter and disappear in a burst of radiation that, in fact, can be detected. If it is the matter particle—the electron—that escapes, then it is free to join the inventory of the universe. Now Harun turned that powerful mind of his to De Sitter space. De Sitter space is the stuff out of which all those bubble universes are made. Event horizons are everywhere. A Hawking contemporary named Gott had reasoned that, like the event horizons of black holes, the event horizons in De Sitter space must also generate Hawking radiation. Such a result was, in fact, implicit in the special case postulated by Hawking. Gott filled his bubbles with Hawking radiation, adding a mathematical constant that turned it into what, even today, is called 'Gott fluid.' The Gott fluid itself drives the expansion of the bubble universes and gives us a sort of universal foam in which Creation continues apace.

"Harun returned, as a mathematical exercise only, to the old Steady State universe and made a quantum leap of the imagination. We need not postulate a homogenized universe, he said. The hydrogen which so infuriated the Big Bangists is part of the fabric of space-time, and leaks into the observed plenum at different gradients. It tends especially to leak where space is stretched by the presence of a hypermass. Thus it overflows and spills out at points where galactic superclusters then form. This, for example, would explain quasars as part of the evolution of newly formed galaxies when the geometry of a smaller universe facilitated an exchange of matter between the various domains of eleven-dimensional space-time. Expansion in our domain, by the way, is reserved for only four of the dimensions, while the rest remain curled up.

"Harun remained locked in his study for five days and four nights, not sleeping, refusing the trays of food which his servants brought to the door. When he emerged, weak and faint but ecstatic, he brought with him his Modified Steady State theory—the keystone of the Grand Unified theory that he completed forty years later. He showed that the bubbles in the foam are not casually disconnected as orthodox Big Bangists would have it. Out of the quark-lepton stew that fills the interstices of the multiuniverse comes causality and creation. Hydrogen is the stuff that ends up on the plate. Hawking radiation is the gravy around the edges. The account books of the universe are balanced. And Harun balanced them in one beautiful equation, the second most famous equation in history, as simple and elegant as Einstein's $E = mc^2$.

"There was only one problem about the hydrogen. It would require that protons and electrons be somehow squeezed through the cosmic strainer in matched pairs. Harun got around this difficulty in a final burst of abstract mathematics, showing that it was actually neutrons or antineutrons that were spilling through the domain walls, depending on whether the adjoining reality was mirrored or not—the universes themselves coming in nested pairs that are curled up as mere points in the infinitely small Kaluza-Klein dimensions.

"The neutron quickly decayed to a proton and an electron—plus a discarded antineutrino, which goes on to perform a different chore in Harun's universe—while the antineutron decayed to a positron and an antiproton, plus, of course, the required neutrino."

The cosmology officer faced them, beaming.

"And *voilà*! Hydrogen and antihydrogen!"

Murmurs of appreciation came from the audience, some of them cognizant and some merely polite. There was a small upwelling of whispers as some of the more scientifically inclined explained to their less-informed neighbors that a hydrogen atom may be assembled from a single proton and electron, and an antihydrogen atom from their mirror particles.

"The antihydrogen quickly disappears in our predominantly non-anti universe, through collisions with other floating particles, the released energy leading to the isotropic radiation predicted by theory. A good deal of hydrogen disappears in the process as well, but of course there is a net gain. Enough hydrogen sticks around through the ages to give rise to such observed phenomena as that stubbornly self-replenishing 'smoke ring' hovering around the Milky Way's central hypermass.

"I'm oversimplifying, of course. The intermediate steps of Creation are a bit more complicated than that. An electron-positron collision first produces a photon—pure energy, you see—that then decays into a quark and antiquark, and so on. And when a proton annihilates an antiproton, it produces a pizero meson one-third of the time, and a charged pion, a muon, and a neutrino two-thirds of the time, after which the pions and neutrons promptly break down to electrons and positrons, photons and neutrinos. And I won't even attempt to trouble you with such refinements as vector bosons and Higgs fields and the like.

"What *is* important is that Harun's theories had a practical effect—just as Einstein's theories ushered in the nuclear age. His central point—that the plenum leaks where it is stretched by a hypermass—was experimentally confirmed by simple apparatus carried aboard one of the early automated probes to the stars. The Harun effect was detectable at velocities approaching twenty percent of the speed of light, when the relativistic mass of the vehicle reaches a value of approximately one point oh three. The experiment was repeated on the interstellar probes that followed, and it was found that they were followed by clouds of virtual particles in the exact ratios predicted by Harun's equation.

"After that, it was only a matter for the engineers. The first practical starship was launched within fifty years. Harun, a vigorous nonagenarian tending his garden on the Moon, lived to see it."

The cosmology officer gave a deep sigh. "And so today starship travel is a free lunch. We don't need fuel tanks or ramscoops anymore. We simply tap the plenum for unlimited quantities of hydrogen and antihydrogen and pour it on as we need. No physical laws are violated, as the conservation of mass-energy is balanced at a higher level. Adjusting the proportions of matter and antimatter is a simple matter of polarization as the stuff comes through—one becomes the other when rotated through a Kaluza-Klein dimension. The plasma engineers don't even have to worry about containing the antimatter because it appears in the firing chamber where it instantly interacts with its opposite—starships of the *Saladin* class are actually a good deal simpler than the primitive fusion-powered vehicles that started it all.

"In fact, matter and antimatter can be created in such enormous profusion—depending upon the size of the rent in the plenum—that the really hard part of the engineers' job is to valve *down* the flood, in order to limit the boost to the constant one gravity that passengers will find comfortable. Theoretically—with mountains of matter and antimatter being turned to pure energy every second—starships could be accelerated at hundreds or thousands of G's, and arrive within a whisker of the speed of light within hours! But the passengers would be smeared to monomolecular paste over the aft bulkheads."

A nervous ripple went through the audience as people contemplated the thick wooden walls around them. The man next to Hamid-Jones played with his worry beads and moved his lips in prayer.

The cosmology officer gave a reassuring smile. "But we don't need to accelerate instantaneously like that. After that first year of boost, starships travel so close to the speed of light that for all practical purposes subjective time is the same for *any* length journey, whether ten light-years or fifty. The relativistic curve goes up very steeply once you get to within about one ten-thousandth of one percent of the speed of light. After that, even with the Harun drive continuing at full blast, we can only shave smaller and smaller fractions from the remaining sum. Even if the *Saladin* were going to Arcturus instead of Alpha Centauri, the trip, as far as we're concerned, would seem to take only an extra few days."

That was too much for the man next to Hamid-Jones. He was a white-knuckle traveler. "Allah have mercy on those who venture into the Deep!" he burst out.

The cosmology officer heard him. "It's true that we seem to abruptly lose radio contact with starships that travel much beyond a fifty light-year radius," he said with a frown. "That's about as far as man has gotten—unless we can credit the new rumor that Gamma Virginis has planted a colony on Mizar, another ten light-years away. But star travel is only a few centuries old. I'm sure a scientific explanation will be found."

"They vanish!" the worrier said. "Allah did not mean man to leave his allotted sphere!"

"We don't know that they vanish," the cosmology officer said with patient condescension. "One opinion is that they keep going, with time aboard relativistically continuing to wind down to some point of critical sluggishness that makes radio communication impossible. After all, at a gamma factor of, say, seventy thousand, a one-minute message would stretch out to seven weeks of ordinary time, to say nothing of the redshifting of the radio waves themselves to beyond the level of detectability."

He was not satisfied with his own explanation, Hamid-Jones could tell from his defensive tone. He himself had described the loss of radio contact as "abrupt," not gradual.

And surely there was more to it than the loss of radio contact. The awesome hadronic light of a Harun drive could be seen over a distance of light-years. Hadn't there been old reports from some of the far colonies of that light suddenly winking out? When growing up, Hamid-Jones had been as avid a reader of Friday supplement stories as any other boy, and he could still remember some of the overheated purple prose about ships being "swallowed up" in the void.

The young cosmology officer, suddenly all official charm, turned a smarmy smile on his audience and said, "But none of that need concern us here aboard the *Saladin*. The road to Alpha Centauri has been well traveled for centuries. Our speed will remain relatively sedate. With only five years to build up our delta-vee and then lose it again, our gamma factor—which determines time dilation and our relativistic mass—will never increase more than seventy-fold. We'll be perfectly safe and snug in our wooden bubble, with all the comforts. Your only problem is to keep from getting bored by your fellow passengers in the next two years of subjective time."

Tension broke. Laughter was heard. Hamid-Jones smiled with the rest, but the harmless joke had made him suddenly edgy. It reminded him that two years was a long time to conceal himself among the twenty thousand passengers. Mars was a small place. And there were an awful lot of Martians aboard.

"I see that our weight is almost back," the Centauran officer said. "You can unstrap now and move about, if you wish. Have a little stretch. The *farash* will be here in a few minutes to serve coffee, and then, for those who wish to remain, we will go on to the second part of the lecture. Mr. Yahya, our second assistant engineer, should be able to leave his duties momentarily, and he will be here to tell us all about hadronic gamma ray exhausts and other fascinating technical details . . ."

Hamid-Jones stood up and stretched with the rest. A movement in the rows opposite caught his eye. It was the passenger in the fringed headcloth who had sneaked a look at him earlier. He was trying to slip out, his face averted, but he had tripped himself up over a pair of knees.

This time there was no mistake. The man glanced over his shoulder to see if Hamid-Jones had noticed him and he was holding up the corner of the headcloth to veil his lower face. When his eyes met Hamid-Jones's, he turned hastily away and pushed his way past his seatmates toward the exit.

It was too late for Hamid-Jones to hide. If he had been identified, he had to know who it was that had recognized him. He ploughed through the people in his row, scattering apologies, and plunged through the exit door his quarry had used.

He spotted the man as he tried to disappear down a side corridor. He caught up with him easily; the fellow moved with the clumsy waddling gait of someone who was not adapted to the near-Terran strength of Centauran gravity, though he was not as handicapped as a Loonie or a native of one of the giant outer satellites would have been. That made him a Martian for sure.

"Just a minute, *sidi*," Hamid-Jones said.

The man kept going, and Hamid-Jones, risking an embarrassing mistake, put a hand on the man's shoulder. The other shriveled at his touch and hunched over, not turning around.

"Who are you?" Hamid-Jones demanded, "and why are you so interested in me?"

"I don't know what you're talking about," the man said in a voice muffled by the shawl. "Let go of me."

The voice was all too familiar. Hamid-Jones swung the skinny form around to face him.

"Aziz, you scoundrel! What are you doing on this ship?"

Aziz's eyes widened in spurious surprise. "Master, you don't know how good it is to see you! For a while, I thought you were dead.''

"Don't lie to me. Why were you trying to avoid me?''

"I was planning to come to your cabin later. I didn't want to draw attention to either of us in public—not when the ship is crawling with Martians. I was afraid of catching you by surprise—you know, master, you're not the most discreet man in the world, or the best actor.''

Some passengers were emerging from an elevator down the corridor. Hamid-Jones let go of Aziz's robes. "You've come up in the world,'' he said, eyeing the other's prosperous middle-class garb. "Where did you get the money to buy passage to Alpha Centauri?''

"Forgive me, master. When I thought you were dead, I happened to remember the slip of paper with the number of the secret Ceres bank account. I can account for every dinar—''

Hamid-Jones almost choked. "The bribe money?''

"It was just sitting there, doing nobody any good. The Centaurans already had paid it in, after all. The harm was done. There was no sense in letting it go to waste.''

"Are you working for the Centaurans now, is that it? Did they hire you to keep track of me?''

"Master, I don't know any Centaurans. I work only for you.''

Hamid-Jones clenched his fists. "How did it happen that you were able to escape the skyhook ambush in Mesogaea?''

"Master, it smelled to high heaven, that's all. Remember that I warned you to be on your guard.''

Aziz had an answer for everything. Hamid-Jones ground his teeth. "And why are you on this ship? Don't tell me it's coincidence!''

"It was the first starship I could book passage on. Master, remember that my skin is forfeit, too. If that patchwork Emir is going to become Caliph, I wanted to be out of the Solar system entirely.''

"By Allah, I want some straight answers for a change! You're too slippery by half! I want to know exactly how you got away at Mesogaea, what you've been doing since, and where you got exit papers good enough to fool the spaceport authorities!''

"Please, master, not here!'' Aziz rolled his eyes in the direction of the passengers who had come out of the elevator and who were heading down the corridor in their direction. "I'll come to your cabin later and explain everything."

The two of them smiled with glassy cordiality at each other while the party from, the elevator passed. There were four of them in an assortment of ages from youth to oldster, and they all wore white *dish-dashas*, brown mantles, and neatly tucked turbans.

"Ismailis," Aziz said when they were out of earshot.

"What's that got to do with anything?"

"Assassins are an Ismaili sect. The Nizaris."

"That doesn't mean that all Ismailis are Assassins. They're perfectly respectable people, and entitled to worship Allah in their own way."

"It doesn't hurt to be cautious. You're still listed in the Assassin data banks as a wanted man. It's the duty of any pious Assassin to kill you."

"Don't try to change the subject with tales meant to frighten children," Hamid-Jones scoffed. "The Solar system and all its planets will be far behind us a month from now. And—" He fingered his curtain of coppery chin whiskers. "—I'll stay in disguise till we reach Alpha Centauri."

"The arm of the Old Man of the Mountain is long," Aziz said balefully. "As for your disguise, it might fool a half-witted child."

Hamid-Jones turned red. "See that you're in my cabin before teatime!" he said stiffly. "And you'd better have your story straight by then!"

Aziz came to him during the hour of the third prayer, when no one was moving about the ship. He slipped through the door with exaggerated caution, holding a finger to his lips while he closed it behind him.

"All right," Hamid-Jones said. "We'll start with the raid on the caravan."

Aziz launched into a long, complicated story about how his camel had shied at that first thunderclap from the sky, throwing him to the sand and then bolting riderless while he was dragged along by a foot caught in the rope boarding ladder. The camel had been cut down by automatic fire as it emerged from behind the last vehicle in line, and he had immediately burrowed into the sand beneath one of the immense mesh tires. Fortunately he had been able to retrieve the spare air bottles of a couple of nearby corpses and so had remained curled up in his pressure suit, like a buried chrysalis, for the next twelve hours, while the soldiers mopped up, departed with their prisoners, and the caravan moved on with its escort. Then, Aziz said, he had rounded up a stray animal that had bolted and wandered back, loaded it with salvaged supplies, and ridden four hundred miles to the oasis settlement at Nodus Gordii. Once among civilized people—if you could call the inhabitants of a hick town like Nodus Gordii civilized—it had been child's play to spin out the succession of tales and identities that got him back to *real* civilization, where he could make the contacts that gave him really *good* forged documents; documents impeccable enough for him to risk an approach to the branch office of the Bank of Ceres and to arrange for exit visas and all the rest. "I thought you were dead, master," he said mournfully, "but I spent good money getting you a visa and papers anyway, just in case you should turn up later. I didn't resell the spare papers until the last minute, when I was ready to board the Deimos skyhook, and believe me, I had to take a big loss as a result."

He immediately began to spill out a profusion of long, boring details that made Hamid-Jones's head spin.

"All right, all *right*!" Hamid-Jones said after another ten or fifteen minutes of it. "I can't sort it out anymore, and I don't suppose it matters anyway. You can tell me anything you want."

"Thank you, master," Aziz said, smiling broadly. "I appreciate your trust. You won't be sorry."

CHAPTER 2

At two and a tenth light-years from Sol, the *Saladin* fled through a lonelier darkness. Even the comets of the Oort Cloud were far behind it, except for a thin scattering of strays that mingled here at midpoint with the maverick iceballs on the fringes of Alpha Centauri's own cometary cloud.

Sol itself was invisible to the naked eye, blotted out by the Doppler shift that had nudged its spectrum past the infrared when the ship had reached a velocity of thirty percent of the speed of light. At that speed, the stars behind began noticeably to redden and crowd forward, leaving a blind circle, while the stars ahead, Dopplering in the opposite direction through the ultraviolet, disappeared into a second blind spot. At three-quarters the speed of light, the squeezed stars merged into rainbow hoops around the ship, with bands of violet, blue, and green at the front edge, yellow in the middle, and orange to duller and duller reds at the rear. The hoops kept growing narrower. Individual stars could no longer be seen, and there was only darkness ahead and behind.

There would have been nothing in either direction for a passenger to see in any event. The magnetic umbrella that warded off a rain of lethal radiation had opened up early in the voyage, blocking the view up the *Saladin*'s central shaft, and there was no view downward—only an eternal sunrise of hadronic light leaking round the edges of the drive baffle in a halo bright enough to blind the unprotected eye in seconds. Those passengers who still retained a taste for scenery gravitated to the lounge around the waist of the ship, from whose three-mile circumference the starbow could be seen like a rainbow sash.

Several thousand idle passengers were wandering through the lounge this morning. There wasn't much else to do. The crew was preoccupied with the approaching turnover, and social activities had been suspended for the day. The dining room service was still superb, and such sports as tennis, golf, and squash remained available for the time being—though the swimming pools had been drained in anticipation of the coming weightlessness—but the staff had little time to spare for individual attention to passengers.

"I don't see why we'll have to stay in our cabins," the old man grumbled. "I'm a light sleeper. Sometimes I get up in the middle of the night for a walk. One of the night porters on my deck—a very nice man named Haffiz—will make me a cup of tea if I come to his service cubicle, and we have a nice talk."

"It's for our own safety, Mr. Zarrab," Hamid-Jones said. "They don't want a lot of people wandering around the ship during all those hours of weightlessness. And besides, the crew will be awfully busy. We don't want to get in their way."

"And does Sindbad have to stay in his cage, too? I like to let him out for exercise. He likes to fly around my cabin. He's very good company late at night, you know."

Sindbad was Mr. Zarrab's pet parakeet, an ill-tempered bird whose presence he occasionally inflicted on other passengers in the breakfast room. He liked to feed Sindbad bits of biscuit or toast.

"I don't think that's necessary, as long as you keep your cabin door closed so he doesn't get out in the corridors." He added hastily, "It's for his own protection, you know."

"You're a very thoughtful young man, *ya* Murjan," the old man quavered. "I never had a son, only daughters, but if I had a son I'd want him to be just like you."

"Thank you," Hamid-Jones said uncomfortably. He had spent a year trying to avoid Mr. Zarrab as much as possible, with varying degrees of success. It was best, he'd found, not to be caught outside his cabin door immediately after dawn prayers or to take early afternoon tea in the small salon on the garden deck.

"You'll have to give me your address on Alpha Centauri," the old man said. "But there's plenty of time. We have another year to get acquainted. I don't know why we hardly ever seem to bump into one another."

"Yes, of course, *sidi*. Excuse me. I think someone wants to see me."

Aziz was standing by a cluster of potted palms near an elevator bank, gesturing urgently. Hamid-Jones let him know with a nod that he had been noticed and gratefully rose from his deck chair.

"Go ahead," the old man said indulgently. "You young people have things to do. You're a good boy to spare time for an old man. Your friend is a fine young man, too—never too busy for a smile or a hello."

He squinted rheumily at Aziz and gave him a mottled smile with a set of teeth that were badly in need of recloning.

Aziz pulled Hamid-Jones round one of the potted palms and looked in both directions before speaking.

"I was right, master. Do you remember what I told you when we saw the Ismailis? There's an Assassin aboard!"

"Oh, for Allah's sake!" Hamid-Jones said in exasperation. "It's been a whole year. Nothing's happened in all that time. If there's an Assassin on this ship, he probably has business on Alpha Centauri like everybody else. There's no reason to go into a tizzy about it."

Aziz pulled a long face. "It's not strictly true that nothing's happened. A passenger was murdered last night."

"What? Are you sure? Nothing was said on the morning newscast."

"It's being hushed up till they can put a good face on it. They're going to say it was some kind of heart attack or asphyxia. There wasn't a mark on him. The autopsy showed only that the blood supply to the brain was cut off."

"Well, then . . ."

"The autopsy also mentioned a slight reddening of tissue around the neck. Probably a padded garrote. Assassins use something like that when they don't want to call attention to a death—like on a ship where they'll be cooped up with the authorities for a year."

"Nonsense. Are you telling me that you have only a few vague suspicions to go on? Dying people often grab at their own throats when they feel themselves choking."

"The autopsy also showed undigested fragments of cake, with cardamom, anise, and nuts, in the stomach. Probably he found it at his bedside and thought it was a bedtime snack provided by the kitchen. The captain's no fool. He's suspicious, but he doesn't want to start a panic when he can't prove anything.''

"Where are you getting all this information?''

"I cultivated a morgue attendant. I play backgammon with him once a week.''

"Who was the victim—not that I'm admitting that he *was* a victim, mind you.''

"One Iyadh ibn Jareer. A Jovian from a habitat in the Patroclus cluster of Trojans. A small merchant. No enemies that I could find out about, except possibly the relatives of a wife he divorced before selling out and buying passage. Not the sort of person who's important enough for someone to send an Assassin after him on a starship. You're right, master. The Assassin probably has other business on Alpha Centauri. But he got tired of twiddling his thumbs after a year on the *Saladin*. They like to keep in practice. Probably he got bored and started scrolling through the wanted list in his personal data bank. He must have had a lot of time on his hands to have sifted through all the Jovian local notices. Jovians settle everything by assassination. The Assassins' Guild there gives a discount for volume.''

Hamid-Jones scowled. "Say you're right. Then we still can forget about it. Your supposed Assassin's done his job. He'll want to pack up his kit and lie low for the rest of the trip.''

"I don't like having bored Assassins around, master. Idle hands are the satan's workshop.''

"That's right—and you're the prime example. Let it go. Nothing's going to happen on this ship until after turnover anyway.''

Aziz studied the fingernails of his recloned right hand. "I think I'll do a little scouting. There's still about twelve hours until they button up the ship. Did I tell you that I made it a point to do a little fieldwork among the Ismaili passengers after that little discussion of ours? I cultivated the stupidest of them, a young ox-brain named Wasil. Oh, the hours I endured while he read Ismaili scripture to me, trying to convert me! I encouraged him to believe my faith was shaky. He'd got as far as hinting that the Ismailis have a secret recognition signal in case aid or support is required by other fellow travelers of their sect. Then Wasil's father found that he'd been talking too much to an outsider, and I haven't been able to get near him since. But if that *was* an Assassin's hit last night, you can bet that the Ismailis will be buzzing today, and Wasil will be bursting to spill a few beans. I think I'll just saunter down to his deck, and see if I can strike up a conversation.''

He departed, leaving Hamid-Jones shaking his head. More people got off the elevators to look at the starbow's lovely wash of colors, like a luminous striated fence circling the ship at the distance of infinity. Hamid-Jones peered through palm fronds to check for the old man. He was gone, his deck chair vacated. Hamid-Jones had been about to opt for an early lunch but thought it prudent to wait awhile. He went back to his cabin to read for an hour.

"As I thought, master, the Ismailis ordered a cake from the catering department yesterday. With cardamom, anise, and nuts. They said it was for a birthday party, but nobody in their group had a birthday yesterday. My young friend doesn't know what happened to the cake. None of the Ismailis got even a crumb, that's for sure. It vanished somewhere along the way by prearrangement.''

Aziz looked tired after his long day. Hamid-Jones had not seen him at lunch or dinner. The kitchens had been closed down for a couple of hours now. Everything aboard the *Saladin* was being battened down in preparation for turnover. Even the evening prayer had been hurried through by the ship's muezzin.

"Have you eaten?''

"Don't worry about me, master. I stopped at a snack bar earlier. I had some kebab and tea. You can rest easy for the time being. I made the acquaintance of an assistant pastry chef in the catering department. No more cakes have been ordered.'' He couldn't help preening a little. "If one is, I'll be the first to know.''

Hamid-Jones laughed. "Aziz, you're remarkable.''

"Thank you, master.''

A chime sounded. The little ceiling loudspeaker that customarily transmitted the muezzin's call cleared its throat. "Thrust will cease in approximately thirty minutes. All passengers are requested to return to their cabins and remain there until the completion of turnover. Please see that all loose objects are secured. Knives and other sharp objects should be put in drawers. Use of sanitary facilities if necessary is suggested now. In approximately twenty minutes from now all plumbing will be automatically drained. Do *not*, repeat *not*, leave water in sinks or tubs. Wet towels are provided in the hamper next to the sink, and you will find drinking water in the carboy over it. If use of sanitary facilities becomes necessary during weightlessness, please turn on the vacuum switch beneath the handle, and be sure that the commode lid is closed and the switch off after use.

"The captain regrets any inconvenience. Thank you.

"Repeat, thrust will cease in approximately thirty minutes . . ."

Aziz gathered his robes about him and stood up. He looked quite presentable in his prosperous middle-class costume. Even the scruffy beard had been improved by weekly visits to a ship's barber.

"I'd better get to my own cabin," he said. "I'm sorry I can't stay here with you. I promise I'll be a proper servant again after we get to Alpha Centauri."

Hamid-Jones became irritated. "I don't need a nursemaid," he snapped.

"In the meantime," Aziz continued imperturbably, "you'd better take this."

He lifted the hem of his robe, exposing a hairy ankle, and removed a small flat object that had been tucked under his garter. Hamid-Jones was so unprepared for the sight that it took him a moment to identify it as a plastic gun, the kind carried by ladies when traveling in unfamiliar parts, with a clip of pastel-colored bullets showing through the transparent handle.

"What's this for?" Hamid-Jones said with distaste.

"It doesn't hurt to take precautions, master," Aziz said.

"Where did you get it? And how did you smuggle it past inspection?"

"Don't be naive, master. It's easy as pie to get a weapon past inspection, unless it's some heavy duty automatic firearm or a bomb. There must be hundreds of these things aboard the *Saladin*. Anyway, I don't take chances myself. I, er, found it in somebody's cabin. The lady it belonged to will never dare complain that it's missing."

"I don't want it. Get rid of it."

"Please, master, indulge me. Look, I'm putting it in the drawer of your night table. Please keep it close by you."

The chime sounded again, and the loudspeaker went through its litany once more. Aziz shrugged helplessly and went to the door. His hand on the doorknob, he paused for a final wheedling admonition.

"And be sure to lock the door after I leave."

The ship floated free in its hoop of mashed stars, like a great turnip of varnished wood. But though the awful fire at its tip was extinguished, it was still traveling at its terminal velocity of ninety-nine point nine nine nine percent of the speed of light. The blackened parasol that it held over its crown was awash with a seething flame of energetic particles slamming into it at relativistic speeds. Had that canopy ever failed for even a second, the *Saladin* and all within her would have fried to a crisp.

Brave men in spacesuits crawled like mites over the planked skin of the ship, inspecting the rigging and the enormous trolley that ran on the ravine-size tracks that stretched like a zipper along a meridian of the *Saladin*. The tracks had to be clear of obstacles; the rigging free of potential tangles. On the delicate maneuver about to be performed rested the safety of the ship and its twenty thousand souls.

Slowly, with a silent screech of metal that could not be heard in vacuum, the gigantic trolley moved down its tracks, bearing with it the titan's mast that it held aloft, while computers played out the ropes that kept the umbrella spread in position. The ship counterrotated with it, making sure that the protective canopy was always pointed precisely in the direction of the line of flight. An error of a few degrees would be fatal. Men walked the tracks, eyeballing every inch of the way. Computers are marvelously clever, but they are not inspired by a healthy fear of death.

When the mast bearing the parasol reached the *Saladin*'s opposite pole, there was a further delay while computers and human navigators refined the axis to be sure that the ship was aligned exactly along its previous line of flight. Alpha Centauri was still a long way off, and any errors would be multiplied at the destination. The minutes ticked by, each of them consuming an hour and eleven minutes of ordinary time. In each of those oddly stretched minutes, the *Saladin* hurtled another billion miles onward. But the time had been allowed for. Unless there were some totally unexpected and disastrous hitch, the men in the spacesuits would have ample opportunity to get indoors before the engines fired again.

When that happened, the fragile-looking canopy, long shorn

of its brightly painted inscriptions of faith, would be instantly shredded and incinerated by the hadronic gamma ray photons of the Harun drive.

But it wouldn't matter anymore. The umbrella's work would be done. The ship would be protected against interstellar hydrogen by the terrible exhaust of the Harun drive itself.

It was a pleasant dream, induced by weightlessness. Hamid-Jones was floating in an emerald sea, surrounded by little darting golden fish. A sun burned above, shaped like an onion. It shed a comforting warmth. Hamid-Jones made swimming motions but found himself restrained.

One of the fish brushed against his face and woke him up. The ocean receded. The restraints had been the straps that kept him from rising too high above his bed. There was a dark bulk behind him, sensed rather than seen. Instantly alert, Hamid-Jones remembered the little plastic gun in the night table drawer and made a lunge, but before he could get at it, a padded yoke whipped around his neck and snapped shut.

Hamid-Jones wasted three seconds grabbing at the collar and trying to pull it apart, and another three seconds in ineffectual thrashing. Then, awkwardly, he got his hands on the person behind him. He was stronger than his assailant, but busy fingers had all the while been turning a sort of wing nut in the yoke. The pads pressed inexorably against his windpipe, his carotid arteries. A red curtain dropped over his vision. He flopped weakly. He could still hear and feel, after a fashion, but he could not speak or move. A dreadful lassitude had taken possession of him, turning his body into an object perceived from afar. The only exception was a remote consciousness of a burning pain traveling up the sides of his neck to below his ears. It felt as if his head was going to explode.

The man behind him leaned closer and spoke almost fondly in his ear. "There was no time to write down the poem. I always got low marks in calligraphy anyway. I'm sorry. I don't want to cheat you. But I'll have to recite it instead."

Hamid-Jones tried to move and actually got his numb fingertips to graze the padded contraption around his neck. The Assassin batted his hand away, like someone admonishing a child, and whispered to him in a singsong rhythm:

Death is an obligation
That must be paid.
You were in arrears,
But now the bill is settled.
Your body is the receipt.

The Arabic rhymes were pedestrian, mere doggerel. It flashed through Hamid-Jones's expiring thoughts that the verse must have come from some kind of Assassin handbook with quick recipes and ready-made poems in it for emergencies. There was a fragmented resentment that he was not being treated to a first-class execution.

Then the Assassin was flinging his limp body over one shoulder and swimming with the weightless burden toward the door. A turbaned head poked through to check the corridor. Through the red veil over his vision, Hamid-Jones saw the corridor floor streaming by as if in a dream, and then he was at the major junction where the central well ran through the ship like a stack of curved porticos.

The Assassin lifted him effortlessly to the rail and balanced him there with his legs dangling like a rag doll's. Hamid-Jones could see the Assassin's face now through a flickering red that was turning dark. It was the old man, Mr. Zarrab, who had been going to join his married daughter on Alpha Centauri and who had a pet bird named Sindbad. He didn't look old and frail now, and his eyes were no longer watery. He might have been about seventy, but he was a tough and stringy old gent whose bushy white brows worked with concentration as he unscrewed the wing nut that held the hinged yoke in place.

There was an incredible rush of pain as the blood surged back to Hamid-Jones's head. He went totally blind for a moment and thought that he was going to throw up. Before his vision cleared, he felt the old man's spread hand against his chest, giving him a push. The safety cords brushed by him as his body squeezed through, and then he saw the railing and the old man's face behind it receding into the distance.

It had been a carefully calculated push, not hard enough to make him float all the way across the thousand-foot well to the opposite side. Air resistance began to slow him, and he found himself floating helplessly, at least a hundred feet away from the brink of the shaft.

A half mile above him—at least in the direction he was used to thinking of as "above"—the familiar canopy was no longer in place. Through the thick glass dome he could see only the velvet blackness of eternal night. It was the rearward blind spot, the blank disk that concealed a redshifted Sol. The absence of the protective umbrella could only mean that the outside crew was well through the preliminary chores of the turnover maneuver. At any moment, the engines might fire and weight return to the ship.

He twisted his neck for a downward view—the direction that would be "down" when the drive resumed. He saw an endless stack of rings—the circular railings at each level—diminishing down a half mile of shaft to the metal grates that barred the way to the thick baffles beyond which were the chambers of hell, where matter and antimatter rushed together in an inferno of mutual annihilation.

It wasn't going to matter how slowly he fell at the start. By the time he reached bottom, he would be going fast enough, and would have fallen far enough, to smash himself into pulp.

He looked back in despair toward the Assassin, a cricket-size creature in black robes, now turning jerkily away from the rail.

It took him a moment to realize that the spasmodic twitch was not a natural motion. It had been caused by another tiny figure behind the Assassin, a half-eclipsed form in sober brown robes. The newcomer was swinging a toothpick-size object that must have carried a lot of inertia, from the way its solid thwack lifted the Assassin off his feet and slammed him against the railing. The black cricket remained pinned there for the moment, with no gravity to make it slide to the floor. The Assassin was not moving; he was either dead or unconscious.

"Halloo, master, are you all right?"

At that moment there was a faint tremor through the ship— Creation clearing its throat. Hamid-Jones made frantic swimming motions, but he could make no headway.

"Don't panic, master!" Aziz called.

"Can you get a rope or something?"

There was another shivering of timbers, and they both knew that Aziz could never find a rope or improvise a hundred feet of torn bedsheets or drapery cords and get back in time. Nor could he possibly get through to the captain and explain the urgency of the situation in the next thirty seconds or so.

Hamid-Jones pulled off his pajama bottoms, wadded them up, and threw them away from him as hard as he could. Newton's third law moved him a few inches at best before air resistance brought him to a stop. He hung in midair, staring at the half-mile drop below.

"Courage, master!"

Aziz picked up the Assassin's body by the scruff of the neck and the seat of the robes, and, planting the soles of his feet against the floor in a vector, he flung the limp figure horizontally toward Hamid-Jones.

"Here's reaction mass for you, master," Aziz cried hoarsely. "For God's sake, don't miss!"

He had calculated the force of his pitch nicely, as the Assassin had with Hamid-Jones. The Assassin's body had come almost to a dead halt when it reached Hamid-Jones, and when he snatched frantically at the robes, it carried him only a few more feet outward.

"Hurry, master!"

Hamid-Jones grabbed the body by a wrist and an ankle and swung it back and forth a few times to build up momentum. He bobbed in the opposite direction at the height of each swing, hovering more or less in the same spot. At the optimum moment he let go and saw the Assassin's body soar toward the center of the shaft like a great black crow. He was moving, too, drifting toward the safety of the railing.

But just then there was a distant roar below, and he felt weight returning. There wasn't much of it yet, just a bare suggestion of the presence of his body's mass. But his trajectory took on a downward curve. Weight ate up a fraction of his momentum. Spread out like a flying squirrel, his pajama top flapping, he watched fatalistically as the level of the railing rose beyond his reach.

Aziz had already sprinted for the emergency staircase. He was waiting at the railing of the deck below as Hamid-Jones glided into view, making encouraging gestures.

Hamid-Jones was just out of reach when his lateral momentum petered out. He began to settle downward like a water-logged sponge. Aziz held out the crowbar with which he had brained the Assassin. Hamid-Jones made a grab at it, and Aziz hauled him in. Hamid-Jones clung weakly to the rail, and when he had caught his breath, Aziz helped him to climb over it.

Both of them turned to look at the Assassin's body. It was

another hundred feet farther out than Hamid-Jones had been, and it was sinking slowly, picking up speed at a rate just fast enough for the eye to detect. Hamid-Jones saw the old man stir to consciousness; Aziz's blow had not killed him after all. Their eyes met. The old man did not say anything. His face was set in a stoic expression as he dropped, more quickly now, out of the line of sight.

"They'll find him later, after the ship gets back to normal," Aziz said. "They'll think any bruises on the head were caused by the fall. The porter will tell them he was in the habit of going for night walks. He was an old man. He didn't understand the dangers of weightlessness. They'll decide he was leaning over the rail and got caught by the return of gravity."

Aziz looked at the object in his hand. It was the padded garrote. It was an ingenious thing, with a spring clamp at the hinge in the rear to make it snap securely into place, and a catch in front. Aziz tossed it over the rail after the falling black figure.

"It'll give them something to think about," he said. "They'll remember the marks on the Jovian's neck and put two and two together. They won't want a scandal. There'll be no further investigation."

"How . . . how did you happen to come out into the corridor just at the right time?"

Aziz grinned. "I put a thread across your door, fixed to set off a little radio beacon if it broke." He held up a little adhesive patch no bigger than a flake of dandruff. "Maybe a younger Assassin would have caught it."

Hamid-Jones stumbled over a sincere thank-you. Perhaps he had done Aziz an injustice to suspect him of treachery on Mars.

"Think nothing of it," Aziz said. He looked at Hamid-Jones's bare legs. "We'd better get you back to your cabin. The corridors will be filled with people shortly."

Later, Hamid-Jones regretted his encouragement to Aziz as the two of them sat over a snack provided by a restored room service, and Aziz rambled on obnoxiously about their prospects on Alpha Centauri. "Just think," he babbled, "you have an introduction to the Sultan himself. Even if it comes to nothing, it will impress a lot of people, and we can parlay it to our advantage."

"We have to get there first," Hamid-Jones said with a frown.

Aziz waved the reprimand away. "There's nothing to worry about," he said airily. "It's clear sailing the rest of the way."

CHAPTER 3

Alpha Centauri was entirely different. Most men wore trousers or pantaloons instead of robes—though sometimes with a colorful open overgarment—and a turban or tarboosh instead of a headcloth bound in place with an *agal*. There were more women in public, many of them with bare faces or only light veils, and they seemed very self-assured. And everything—in the streets around the spaceport, at any rate—seemed livelier and more bustling.

The sky was certainly different. Hamid-Jones looked up at a bowl of deepest blue where a golden sun was climbing toward zenith. Puffy white clouds made it seem Earthlike. Then you noticed the tiny orange jewel—Alpha Centauri A's somewhat cooler companion about three billion miles away—overhead, adding its own increment to the glorious daylight. If you looked hard enough, the *Saladin* could be seen as an amber dot, hovering in its parking orbit eighty miles up. As Hamid-Jones watched, the bright spark of a shuttle blinked on beside it.

Perhaps it was the effect of that open sky, but people here seemed freer, happier, more exuberant. Aziz, trailing Hamid-Jones and his escorts, was looking around with bright, speculative interest, frequently pausing to ogle the ampler of the women.

"This way, Mr. Hamid-Jones," said the young palace official who had been waiting at the customs counter for Hamid-Jones to come through, and who had eased the way for him and Aziz. "There's a limousine waiting just at the curb."

"Where are we going?" Hamid-Jones asked.

"To the Triangular City," the palace aide replied. "You're scheduled for an audience with the Sultan—though you may have to cool your heels for a while. His Majesty's appointments are running way behind today—it's been a madhouse." He consulted a list. "You're down for ten minutes. You must have made quite an impression on the ambassador."

"The master is a very important man on Mars," Aziz put in, nudging Hamid-Jones in the ribs to speak for himself.

"Be that as it may," the aide said, "you should understand that you're being singled out for especially favorable treatment. I had to put the Proxima deputy pasha off till tomorrow, and there'll be the satan to pay about that! I'm going to have to squeeze him into the governors' luncheon to make up for it."

He hurried ahead to speak to the limousine driver, and Aziz took the opportunity to make a sotto voce comment to Hamid-Jones.

"What did I tell you, master? We're in clover. If I'd known we were going to be whisked through customs like that without an inspection, I would have stocked up on Martian sapphires. I hear they go for ten times their Solar system value on the Alpha Centauri black market."

"You've already lost your right hand once," Hamid-Jones said roughly. "Are you trying to lose it again?"

"Master, how can you be so unkind?" Aziz complained. He almost collided with the aide's security flunky, who had stopped short to let a footman open the rear door of the limousine.

"This is the life, eh, master?" Aziz gloated.

It was odd to ride in a limousine whose interior was open to the outside atmosphere at the opening of a door or the rolling down of a window. There was no lock—not even an airsleeve. Hamid-Jones settled back in the rear seat beside the palace aide. Aziz rode with the security officer on the middle bench behind the driver and footman. The aide looked thoughtfully at him and pressed a button that rolled up a screen of glass.

"A word to the wise," the aide said. "The Sultan is very direct, very forthright. He has a quick and impatient mind. He appreciates frankness and brevity. So whatever you have to say, be succinct and don't wander." He glanced at Aziz. "And unlike some monarchs, he doesn't like flattery or clever dealing."

"Thanks, I'll keep that in mind," Hamid-Jones said.

The limousine gave a very smooth ride. Hamid-Jones had noticed when he climbed in that it had no wheels, just a four-sided surround of resilient three-foot balls in sockets that evened out the bumps in caterpillar fashion. At the moment, they were riding down a broad tree-lined boulevard faced with shops and outdoor restaurants. Traffic was thick but moved at a brisk pace. There were some astonishing buildings on the skyline—fairytale spires wrapped in the lace of white balconies, a great pearshaped dome of sparkling blue tile, a teetering cuboid fantasy of tinted glass and dressed stone, something like a shimmering sphere divided like the segments of an orange into freestanding slices. Hamid-Jones stared unabashedly at the architectural exuberance. It was a far cry from the drab Martian tunnels with windows carved out of the rock faces.

"Your first visit to the Alpha Centauri system, Mr. Hamid-Jones?" the aide asked politely.

"Yes."

"Our capital, New Medina, is the oldest city on the planet. It was settled six hundred years ago—before the era of relativistic star travel. Even so, there were people who had been born on Earth among the first settlers: octogenarians and nonagenarians who'd hung on till they could set foot on the promised land. The first shantytown was nothing but plastic prefabs and shacks cannibalized from the materials of the starship, the *Gabriel*. It housed all of two hundred inhabitants. By the time the second colony ship arrived, seventy years later, the population was still under five thousand. But it grew rapidly after that, with the new blood, and then of course the Harun drive came along. The original Old City's on the other side of the river—you'll be able to catch a glimpse of it when we turn onto the River Drive."

"How . . . how large is New Medina now?"

"We've got a population of two million if you count the suburbs, the associated urban areas, and the Triangular City—not much by Earthian standards, but we've still got plenty of room to spread out, both here and on the planets of our other two stars. Even so, we've probably got the most concentrated population in human space outside the Solar system."

"Er, we're going to the Triangular City now?"

"Yes—oh, excuse me, I sometimes forget that some of our visitors may not be familiar with the details of our capital. It's our, um, city within a city—our Vatican or Forbidden City or

Kremlin, as it were. Or, more to the point, it's the equivalent of the Round City within old Baghdad built by the Abbasid caliph Mansur.''

The arrogant comparison with the classical caliphs was not lost on Hamid-Jones. Truly the Sultan of Alpha Centauri must be a monarch of overweening ambition, he thought.

"The Sultan built it, then?'' Hamid-Jones asked, thinking of the urban destruction it must have caused. Even the Emir of Mars had built his New Palace out in the desert.

"Heavens no,'' the aide laughed. "It's three hundred years old—quite a monument for a young society like ours. It was built by the founder of the present sultan's line, the great Malik the First. It's still the seat of government, though. It contains the palaces of the Sultan and his top officials, as well as the residences of those officeholders and public employees who are permitted to live there. You need a pass to get inside the walls. There, you can see the Golden Dome now.''

Hamid-Jones followed the aide's pointing finger. He saw a tremendous gleaming hemisphere that must have been supported on a pedestal of equally tremendous scale to be visible at this distance. It was at the corner of what he now perceived to be an immense bottle-green wall stretching across the horizon and forming a glassy backdrop to the urban sprawl.

"Is it the capitol building?''

"No, it's a mosque. It's been called one of the architectural wonders of all time, by the way.''

"Oh.'' The Centaurans certainly thought a lot of themselves, Hamid-Jones thought.

"It's one of three domes, one at each corner of the triangle, to symbolize the three stars of the Sultan's realm—golden, orange, and red. The golden dome, of course, represents our main sun, Alpha Centauri Alif. The orange one stands for Alpha Centauri Baa'—Beta, as the Christian astronomers used to call it. And the dull red dome at the vertex of the triangle represents Proxima, the red dwarf. You can't see it from here; it's twenty miles away. The scale couldn't be preserved, of course. The base of the triangle is only two miles wide; the vertex would have to be seven hundred miles away to suggest Proxima's true distance of a tenth of a light-year. But it still makes for a long narrow triangle. It encloses about twenty square miles of grounds, and it's quite a little metropolis in its own right.''

Taking the aide's hint, Hamid-Jones squinted down the wall's foreshortened angle and could just make out a distant orange dewdrop, luminous in the bright sunlight. The other angle of the wall dwindled to infinity, and nothing could be seen at the end of it.

The limousine crossed a belt of parkland, and then the gates of the Triangular City were looming ahead of them. Monumental pilasters rose on either side with colossal statuary atop them; the Centaurans didn't seem to be inhibited by any religious taboos about representing the human figure. Craning his neck upward, Hamid-Jones made out an angel with a sword and an angel with a lamp.

A smartly dressed guard opened an elaborate wrought-iron gate for them and the limo pulled to a stop beside a gatehouse. A gatekeeper took a cursory look at the aide's holo badge and waved the limo through. There was none of the fuss Hamid-Jones had endured getting into the New Palace on Mars, but he had the distinct impression that the Sultan's security was confident rather than lax.

Inside the walls were the narrow streets of an earlier era. They ran in sensible grids enclosing little parks, walled palace grounds, neat arcades fronting rows of public buildings. Gracious squares with fountains and greenery marked the intersections. The people in the streets seemed busy, prosperous.

The ball-wheeled vehicle moved at a crawl through the colorful pedestrian traffic. Hamid-Jones saw the splendid costumes of what must have been important officials among the casual strollers, conversing and walking unattended like anyone else. One, in a towering cylindrical turban hung with festoons of jewels, skipped backward to let the limousine pass. On Mars, the driver would have been hauled out and beaten.

The limo finally broke through the maze of approach streets and turned onto a broad central boulevard that ran straight and true toward the base of the long triangle. The enclosing glassy green walls on either side, visible at each intersection, opened out to their full width, and after another fifteen minutes of travel, Hamid-Jones could see the shape of their destination.

Equidistant, poised at either end of the two-mile stretch of wall that formed the base of the triangle, were the two mighty domes he had seen from afar. The orange dome, Hamid-Jones could see now, was larger than the golden one, but it was not as magnificent. Both immense cupolas were raised on tremendous cylindrical shafts that lofted them above the outer walls to loom over the streets outside the walls. The tiled forecourts must have been hundreds of acres in extent and were enclosed by a geometric layout of colonnades that led the eye to the tall minarets that flanked the mosque grounds.

Midway between the cornering domes was an apron of parkland that fronted what could only have been the Sultan's palace. Its walls sparkled with bright tile and the roofs of its creamy white buildings rose in a multitude of spires, steeples, and clusters of bell-shaped finials.

The limousine passed through another gate at the park, where the checking of passes was as painless as before, and followed the roadway to the main gate of the palace. The lawns were green and well tended, and banked with lavish floral displays. Hamid-Jones asked about the queer red ornamental plants that crowded enclosed gardens of their own.

"Oh yes, that's Centauran vegetation—a remnant of the original ecology," the aide told him. "It exists very well side by side with Terrestrial species, though it's all dextrarotary forms, so that their saprophytes and decay bacteria can't handle our sort of life and vice versa. We can't use it for foodstuffs, obviously, though some of the species give us some exotic chemicals and industrial alcohol. Terrestrial life's been gradually taking over— it's a little better at competition for some reason—but we're making an effort to preserve the dextrarotary forms in parklands, reservations, and zoos."

Hamid-Jones admired the Centauran equivalent of a tree as they passed by it. It was a cottony pink ball held aloft by a double arch of four slender fronds. The curved legs were not solid; he could see that they were actually complex latticeworks made of triangular braces. Evidently Centauran plant life had never developed anything like a trunk stiffened by lignin. Instead, the large forms gained height by a vegetable geometry of interwoven struts.

"Here we are, the executive office wing," the aide said. "I'll drop you at the audience hall."

The limousine halted at a guardhouse and was passed through after Hamid-Jones's name was found on a computer's checklist. No one questioned the presence of Aziz, perhaps because he was sitting up front with staff. Hamid-Jones marveled at the Sultan's self-confidence.

They pulled up under a porte cochere at the end of a circular drive. Hamid-Jones got out with the aide, and Aziz came round the side to join them. The aide showed them up a flight of broad steps where people stood around in groups having confidential conversations. They entered a room big enough to hold horse races in, where some thousands of people waited on benches and in seating islands. A *farash* discreetly wheeled his cart from group to group, serving coffee. The aide showed Hamid-Jones to a long counter where a score of receptionists handled lines of supplicants. Hamid-Jones got the VIP treatment at an express line where a sign said: BLUE STAR APPOINTMENTS ONLY.

"I'll leave you now," the aide said. "Sit tight. It may be a while."

"Are all these people waiting to see the Sultan?" Hamid-Jones asked.

The aide laughed. "Heavens, no. Most of them will count themselves fortunate to get to see one of the Sultan's one hundred and twenty secretaries."

Hamid-Jones sat down. After a half hour of fidgeting, Aziz said: "I think I'll circulate a while, master. I'll see what I can find out." When next Hamid-Jones looked for him, he was in earnest conversation with a ratty little man in rumpled pantaloons and a battered tarboosh. Hamid-Jones picked up a well-worn flatscreen from a pile on the coffee table and thumbed through a number of droning documentaries about various public works projects on the planets and moons of the Alif system until he found a museum tour of Centauran art treasures.

Some three or four hours later, an usher in palace livery came for him.

"*Sidi* Hamid-Jones. His Highness will see you now."

Hamid-Jones looked around for Aziz, but he was gone.

"So my old adversary is no more, so to speak," the Sultan said. "Except that he's a hydra. One new head after another."

Malik the Eighth was a down-to-earth monarch, a bluff, hearty man with an imposing leonine head and a brick-red beard cut in the square ringleted Centauran style. He wore a simple turban wrapped mushroom-fashion around a conical tarboosh, and a plain shirt with puff sleeves under a leather jerkin that was laced across a bull-like chest.

His office looked worked in, with untidy stacks of documents piled on library tables. There was no throne or dais. He had invited Hamid-Jones to sit beside him on a divan, while a secretary broke off work at a computer terminal to perch nearby on a hassock, fingers poised over a datapad.

Now, as the Sultan spoke, he was stroking the sleek head of a sinuous, graceful creature that he had identified, for Hamid-Jones's benefit, as a Centauran double-ender. It was about the size of a whippet and was shaped like a lyre. Four supple legs, clustered together and splayed outward, made a base for it. It was covered with a fine golden down, and the eyes on either head were like nothing ever seen on Earth—they were silky oval patches that responded to light and shade with constantly shifting patterns that resembled photographic negatives. The mouths were recognizable mouths, though, with velvety pink linings and rows of thornlike teeth. "They're essentially plants, you know," the Sultan had explained. "Motile plants with something corresponding to a nervous system and a brain halfway between the two ends. But they're marvelously affectionate."

"Oh . . . er, do they grow in soil?" Hamid-Jones had asked.

"No, they're hunting plants. They hunt small Centauran animals. But there are bigger animals that hunt *them*—which is the reason for the two ends. So that they can defend themselves while running away. But they're very good at running their prey to ground, as well. There's absolutely nothing in life to compare with the excitement of the chase, with a good horse under you and a fine pack of double-enders to flush out the quarry. I maintain several hunting preserves stocked with Centauran life at various locations on the planet—royal prerogative, I'm afraid."

He had laughed heartily and thumped his knee. The double-ender had responded by throwing back one head and making a sound like a violin; the other head had joined in sweet harmony.

The amenities, though they seemed casual and totally unrushed, were somehow over in about a minute. Then the Sultan had gotten down to business. His manner remained informal, but the questions were penetrating, and it was clear that he expected thought and precision in the replies.

Hamid-Jones reflected carefully before responding. "The corps of eunuchs under Ismail thought they'd installed a figurehead, so to speak, but the clone had all of the Emir's character-istics buried in him, of course, and his will is very strong."

"Hmm, yes, he's been rather rambunctious, I understand. I received a report from our Martian ambassador radioed a year after your departure. It arrived here a few days ago. It thoroughly confirmed your evaluation, you may like to know."

No reply was expected, so Hamid-Jones kept silent. The Sultan went on.

"As you predicted, *ya* Abdul, your refurbished Emir re-frained from making a bid at the Caliphate Congress. The King of Greater Arabia pushed his own claim, as usual, and the Mo-gul of Tau Ceti floated an absentee candidacy—a posthumous candidacy, as it turned out, since he'd died eleven years before the congress began. Even his campaign chairman on Earth hadn't known it. The time lag was providential in a way, since it pre-vented Tau Ceti from releasing its bloc of votes to Arabia. Ara-bia would have knuckled under to Mars, as it always does, and it would have been enough to put the Emir over if he'd been actively campaigning. As it was, the vote was divided, and nei-ther your Bobo or myself was able to get a clear majority. So the congress broke up without electing a caliph, and it's all been put off till next time."

Hamid-Jones answered the implied question. "He'll run. And Ismail will spend the next ten years coaching him."

"Six years, *ya* Abdul," the Sultan said gently. "It all hap-pened more than four years ago. You forget you're just off the boat. Never mind, it happens to everybody. It'll take a little while to adjust."

Hamid-Jones blushed. "Six years. There'll be intensive lob-bying all that time, to get the votes lined up."

"And I can't compete from four light-years away, is that it? Don't be afraid to say it. It's quite true. Still, from my point of view, there's still two years to think of something, isn't there? Two if by radio, one if by ship. Empires have been won and lost on a shorter toss of the dice."

For a moment the Sultan unlidded the extraordinary force and power of his personality. Hamid-Jones knew he was in the pres-ence of greatness, a strength of will that could not be gainsaid. Ordinary men were never this focused. Hamid-Jones was almost ready to believe that the Sultan was the Mahdi, the Expected One, as some of his more superstitious followers maintained.

Then the moment passed, and the Sultan was once again the hearty monarch, the astute politician, the hard-working administrator who ruled a loose collection of three stars with Allah only knew how many planets and inhabited moons and somehow made it all hang together.

"You've been an invaluable aid to me, *ya* Abdul, and you won't find me ungrateful," the Sultan said, and Hamid-Jones knew the interview was over.

"Thank you, your Highness," Hamid-Jones said, getting up off the divan. "Er, do you want me to report to somebody in the proper department for a debriefing?"

"No, no, that won't be necessary. It's all in here." The Sultan tapped a computer terminal built into the cushions. "The ambassador and his spooks did a thorough job. I just wanted to see you for myself. There's no substitute for face-to-face contact, is there?"

"Uh, no, your Majesty."

"Still, I'll want to keep you close by in case something comes up. You fought with al-Sharq's freedom fighters, didn't you? You might be of some assistance to the people here at the palace who run him. It's politically delicate, of course; we still maintain full diplomatic relations with Mars. You wouldn't mind making yourself available from time to time, would you?"

"No, your Majesty."

The Sultan whirled on his nearest secretary. "See that you fix up something for Hamid-Jones, will you? Some kind of place on the organizational chart and the right passes for the Triangular City and all that. And an appropriate stipend, of course."

The secretary nodded and began tapping entries into his datapad. Somebody else came over and courteously but firmly took Hamid-Jones's arm and led him to the door, where the usher who had brought him waited.

There seemed to be some sort of yellow dust on Hamid-Jones's sleeve. He brushed it off. "I don't know where this came from," he said to the staffperson who was showing him out.

The Sultan heard him. He lifted his lion's head from the flatscreen he was scanning and said, "From the double-ender. It pollinated you. You should be flattered. It doesn't like everybody. I'm glad to see my good opinion of you confirmed."

* * *

When he returned to the waiting room, he could not at first locate Aziz. He finally found him half concealed behind an archway, trading whispers with a seedy-looking man who melted away as soon as Aziz caught sight of Hamid-Jones and made a little sign of dismissal.

"What have you been up to?" Hamid-Jones said wearily.

"I've just been making inquiries, master," Aziz said in tones of injured virtue. "I've accomplished a lot already. I've got the lay of the land, found us lodgings, and promoted a small loan to tide us over—an advance against your stipend."

He jingled coins in a purse that he quickly returned to its hiding place under his robes.

"Stipend? How did you know about my stipend? And how did you get a loan on the strength of it?"

"You were in the Blue Star appointment line. Everybody knows what that means. Is-Sawabi saw the Sultan's aide take you there. Of course I may have elaborated a little bit—"

"Is-Sawabi? Fingers?"

Aziz actually blushed slightly. "That's what they call him. He . . . he arranges things. He's the man you saw me talking to after we arrived."

"That rat-faced felon? He had jailbird written all over him. What kind of people are you getting us mixed up with?"

"He's never been convicted of anything. He just likes to help people. He knows everybody. Important people, too."

Hamid-Jones sighed. "And what about our lodgings? Did you fix that up with Is-Sawabi, too?"

"Oh no, master. I got a good lead from Mr. Sarook just now." He nodded toward the archway where he had been doing business. "He's sorry he couldn't stay to meet you, but he had an appointment."

"And what is this wonderful lead you got from Mr. Sarook?"

The sarcasm was wasted on Aziz. "He suggested we stay in the Unbelievers' Quarter. It's cheap, and they're used to foreigners. We won't stand out so much there. But there are some very chic rentals, even if it *is* an ethnic quarter. And the food's very good—lots of little restaurants."

"When you babble on that fast, I know you're up to something."

"Oh no, master. But we've got to save money. Your stipend won't amount to much at first. Mr. Sarook knows all about these things. But we can improve our fortunes once we know our way around. For example, the special pass that gets you into the Triangular City. Do you know what the going rate is from vendors and petitioners who want to get inside?"

"Forget it. I'm not going to get into that kind of trouble."

Aziz led him outside. A taxicab was already waiting, pulled off to one side of the circular drive, its driver waving off other would-be fares. It was an open square platform with a striped awning, floating on a cloud of pink bubbles that concealed some sort of serpentine propulsive tread. A medallion on the post by the driver said it was authorized for access to the Triangular City.

They climbed aboard and seated themselves on the passenger bench. The driver glided off without being told where to go—another of Aziz's arrangements.

"Where is this wonderful place?" Hamid-Jones said.

"The Unbelievers' Quarter? It's just across the river, by the Bab al-Harami," Aziz replied.

"The Thieves' Gate?" Hamid-Jones sputtered, almost falling off the bench.

"Relax, master. It's only an old name. It's a very nice place. You'll see."

CHAPTER 4

"Are ladies on Mars pretty?" Meryem asked, standing next to the table and obtrusively tracing a design on the well-worn carpet with her toe.

Hamid-Jones paused to squeeze a few drops of lemon juice on his breakfast melon before replying. "Yes, I guess so," he said noncommittally.

He tasted a mouthful. It was a Centauran tetraploidal variety, and it was delicious. Produce was always good in the Unbelievers' Quarter, and the landlord, Meryem's father, made a point of getting up early to go to the market.

"Prettier than here?"

"Uh, I don't think so. I don't know many ladies here."

"That's not what Mamma says. She says you go out too much. She thinks you should settle down and get married."

Meryem was about eleven, a skinny overactive tomboy with inquisitive dark eyes, a smudge that traveled from her nose to her cheek to her forehead, and perpetually scraped and grimy knees. She would have been almost old enough for the veil if she had been a Moslem.

Hamid-Jones had not known he had been the subject of discussion. "You shouldn't repeat what your mother says, especially if it's personal," he said sternly.

Meryem showed what she thought of the reprimand by making a rude sound. "Did you have any special lady friends on Mars?"

A bittersweet image of Lalla floated unbidden in Hamid-

Jones's mind. "Well, yes, I was fond of a very fine lady of good family."

"Is that the lady whose picture you have in your room?"

Hamid-Jones had had a holographic blowup made of the little hologram of Lalla that he had carried with him to Alpha Centauri. The blowup was a little blurred in its details, but from a slight distance, or viewed out of the corner of the eye, it gave the illusion of a half-size Lalla on the mantelpiece. Of course he switched it off when he was washing or dressing.

"Have you been in my room again, young lady? You know that's not proper. It's . . . it's *mish-haram*. You're getting too old for that."

She changed tack. "Is it true there's only one sun on Mars?"

"Yes. Meryem—"

"Earth, too?"

"It's the same sun, only closer. Now listen to me—"

"Aziz has a lady friend, too. I saw her. She's fat."

"If Aziz has a lady friend, that's his own business." He looked at her suspiciously. "How do you know what she looks like?"

She giggled. "I followed him. He never knew I was there."

"Now see here, young lady, you can't go wandering around the streets like that. You'll get into trouble." Another suspicion struck him. "Have you been following me, too?"

She giggled again. "You went to that coffee shop yesterday, the one in Pickpocket's Lane where the poets recite and have contests, and then you went to the street with all the book-stalls and looked through about a *million* books but you didn't buy any, and then you got in one of the taxicabs that go to the Triangular City." She stuck out her tongue at him. "You never do anything *interesting*!"

"That's the last straw. When your mother finds out what a nuisance you've been making of yourself . . ."

She was suddenly all wide-eyed innocence. "Father says it's very cold on Mars. Is that because there's only one sun?"

"No, it's because—" He broke off as he saw the reason for her changed demeanor. Her mother, *is-sayida* Roxane, was coming through the archway from the kitchen with a steaming tray.

"Meryem, are you bothering Abdul again? Maybe he'd like to eat his breakfast in peace."

She was a very pretty woman, with chestnut hair and small,

smooth features, but Hamid-Jones could not get used to seeing her unveiled face. Hamid-Jones prided himself on being broadminded and told himself that the landlord, Yaqub, and his wife were decent, hardworking people, even if they had rejected the Prophet's message. It was just a matter of different customs.

He had never known there were so many different kinds of Unbelievers. The Sultan encouraged diversity in his realm. In the crowded, twisting streets behind the Thieves' Gate were little enclaves of Druses, Zoroastrians, Buddhists, Confucianists, Taoists, Shintoists, Hindus, Pantheists, Gnostics, Orphics, Metempsychosans, Dualists, Unitarians. The Sultan even tolerated heretical Islamic offshoots like the Bahai, the Extreme Sufis, and the Yezidi or devil worshippers.

But it was the Christians who were the most abundant and bewildering in the diversity of their sects. There were Copts, Maronites, Nestorians, Catholics—including an American Catholic offshoot known as Eclectics or "Lesterites," Apostolic Preresurrectionists, Third Millenniumists or "Threesers," New Eastern Rite adherents, and Jumpers. Hamid-Jones could see no differences between them, though the Christians themselves seemed to take their differences very seriously. Meryem's family belonged to something called the "Church of the Revision"— an offshoot of the Nestorians, but Hamid-Jones hadn't the foggiest idea of what that signified, except that on Sunday, the Christian holy day, they went to a large stone church in the Quarter that was shared by several other Christian denominations that staggered their services at different hours.

Hamid-Jones gathered that the various religious and national groups had their own homelands among the planets and moons of the Sultan's triple realm; like all minorities, many of them had gravitated to the capital planet in search of a better life. The landlord's people originally came from a planet revolving around the orange star and before that hailed from the old Byzantine empire on Earth.

"Thank you, *ya sitt-hanim*," Hamid-Jones said as his landlady set down the steaming tray. "Meryem's not bothering me. I enjoy talking to her."

"I don't want her to be a nuisance." She smiled. "I think she's developed a crush on you."

"Oh, Mother!" Meryem said disgustedly.

"A little jelly omelet, with sausage," *is-sayida* Roxane went on. "You don't have to worry about the sausage. It's not made with pork."

"You shouldn't have gone to so much trouble. The melon and coffee's fine. I know it's way past breakfast time. I, uh, overslept a little."

The landlord chose that moment to come through the dining room, carrying a mop and pail. Yaqub Yordan was a great big bearlike man with a mop of curly black hair and a cleanshaven face. "It's no wonder you can't get up in the morning, staying up late like that," he said cheerfully. He gave Hamid-Jones a broad wink, man to man.

"I, uh, got invited to an opening night. The *nisrani* dance troupe from Earth that arrived last month. They performed some of their old folk art, something called Lake of Swans. There was a cast party afterward, and one of the dancers invited me—"

He broke off as he realized that the Yordans were *nisrani*s, too. It wasn't really a rude term for Christians—certainly not a pejorative like *ferengi* or *kaffir*—but it wasn't, strictly speaking, correct usage.

"I didn't mean . . . that is . . ." he said in some confusion.

His landlord laughed. "That's all right, Abdul. We call ourselves *nisrani*, too. And *jahil*—nonturbans—as our Druse neighbors put it. Don't worry about it. The Sultan's empire is a tolerant place—we all get along with one another."

"Yes, the Sultan's an enlightened ruler," his wife agreed. "That's why the Triple Suns are so prosperous. Earth doesn't realize what a center of commerce and culture we've become. We have a larger volume of traffic with Sirius, Barnard's Star, Procyon, and Epsilon Eridani than the Solar system does. The nearer stars would rather do business with us than have Earth look down its nose at them. Alpha Centauri's becoming the hub."

Hamid-Jones never ceased being surprised at the way Unbeliever women of all kinds inserted themselves into male conversations. But her husband didn't seem at all put out. He smiled at her fondly before going on to amplify.

"Cross-fertilization—that's the Sultan's favorite expression," Yaqub said. "He believes in cultural exchange as a way of bringing new vitality to his kingdom. That's why your Earthian dance troupe decided to transplant themselves here. There were too many restrictions in the Solar system—not enough respect for them as artists. To those Solar mossbacks, a dancing girl is a dancing girl. They can't believe that dancers in skimpy costumes are respectable."

His wife glanced meaningfully at their daughter, and Yaqub closed his mouth.

"Have you seen Aziz?" Hamid-Jones asked.

"He was up early," the landlord said. "He went out on some errand."

"Meryem, are you still here?" Roxane said. "Run along. Find something else to do. Abdul doesn't want you hanging around him all the time. Don't be a pest."

Meryem made a face and ran away. Hamid-Jones heard the outer door slam shut.

"That child!" *is-sayida* Roxane sighed.

"Talking about Aziz, *there's* a fellow who can't get enough of dancing girls!" Yaqub said. "I think he knows every backroom paradise in the district. I don't know what you pay him, Abdul, but I can tell you that there are plenty of willing hands to help separate him from his money."

"Yaqub, you'll get Aziz in trouble with his employer!" Roxane scolded him. To Hamid-Jones, she said: "Aziz is a good servant. Believe me, I see plenty of them here, skimping on their duties, not attending to their masters' interests. And anyway, if Aziz has been out a lot lately, it's not because he's off carousing all the time. I admit that when he first came here, I thought he was a little bit of a scamp. But he's changed his ways in the last month or so. He's really a different person. I think he's serious about someone. He puts on his best clothes and plenty of perfume when he goes out to see her, and when he's in the kitchen having a cup of coffee and letting his hair down, he talks about making something of himself. Not," she added hastily, "that he isn't happy with his situation."

"Come to think of it, he had his beard all primped and ribboned when he went out," Yaqub said. "Looked quite the dandy."

"Oh, you men!" Roxane said. She turned to Hamid-Jones. "You could do worse than to take a leaf from Aziz," she said with womanly certitude. "He's sown his wild oats; now he's thinking about settling down."

"Now who's being a pest?" her husband said. "Come on, let's let Abdul eat his breakfast before it gets cold."

Hamid-Jones was left alone to breakfast in solitary splendor. The other tenants had long since left the house for jobs or other interests. Hamid-Jones sometimes found his ill-defined hours at the Triangular City an embarrassment—it didn't seem to matter much if he showed up or not—and he filled in his hours by exploring the bazaars, going to horse races and the wildly free-wheeling Centauran polo matches played on double-ended mounts. He had dipped into the capital's cultural life as well. He knew all the major art galleries—where Centauran artists seemed never to have heard of a prohibition against portraying the human form or the face of Mohammed. He had also become addicted to the concert halls, where large ensembles not only played traditional Arab art music and singers performed the classical songs, but where music of a vanished Western culture was being revived. Once, on a luminous afternoon, he had heard the grand ancient composition, the "concerto" by Beethoven, that Rubinstein had played for him so long ago on Mars.

And there were women. The exotic mores of the Unbelievers' Quarter were still a puzzlement and a trap, but Hamid-Jones was beginning to find his way around a little. He had learned the hard way that the fact that a woman was unveiled and free of the harem did not necessarily mean that she was available. But in the six months that he had lived here, he had stumbled into no fewer than three brief liaisons—two with married women whose husbands were away on other planets, and one with a waitress at a café where he sometimes stopped for lunch. He had avoided the dancing girls and the low dives, though Aziz had often importuned him to come along. At the moment he had a convenient arrangement with one of the dancers from the Earth-ian troupe—a pretty but rather bony girl named Ludmilla—though this was destined to end shortly when the troupe went on tour on one of the planet's other continents.

He could not complain about the digs that Aziz had found for them. The Yordans had given him his own sitting room and the use of their living room, a bedroom and a servant's room for Aziz, and a private bath complete with an ablution font for his prayers; though the Yordans were not Moslems themselves, they were used to Moslem tenants. The price was moderate, as Aziz had told him it would be, and was well within the limits of the modest stipend he received from the Sultan.

It wasn't a bad way of life. But somehow it wasn't satisfying.

His undemanding job left him feeling restless. He felt that he wanted real work to do. He determined to have it out today with Colonel Ish-Shamaal, the shadowy figure in the Palace sub-basement to whom he reported. If he failed to get a satisfactory response, he decided, he would ask to see the Sultan again, or failing that, look on his own for a job as a cloning technician somewhere in private industry.

He put down his coffee mug, filled with the unsedimented *ferengi*-style coffee, to which cream was added by some of the house's other lodgers, and wiped his lips with a napkin. Yes, he decided, today was definitely the day he would confront Colonel Ish-Shamaal.

Before he could rise from the table, he heard the front door swing open with the little tinkle of a camel bell, and Aziz slouched into the dining room, red-eyed from lack of sleep, dressed in Centauran finery with ribbons on his scraggly beard, and fragrant with cheap perfume.

"Is there any coffee, master?"

The *is-sayida* heard him and came fussing in with a pot and an extra mug. "You didn't eat breakfast this morning," she accused him. "Just sit there, and I'll make an omelet for you. It will only take a few minutes."

Aziz turned a shade paler, and Hamid-Jones could see that the thought of food did not appeal to him this morning. "No thank you, madame," he said with strained courtliness. "Coffee is all I want."

"Are you sure?"

"Yes, madame, thank you. You are too accommodating."

She left, clucking to herself. Hamid-Jones turned to Aziz and lit into him.

"So, you're not satisfied with your nighttime debaucheries! You have to go out early in the morning to wallow with your paradise girls! And before breakfast—the morning prayer, too! It's disgusting!"

"It's not paradise girls, master," Aziz protested. "That's all over. I'm in love."

"Love, hah!"

"It's true, master. With a very respectable widow. We've done nothing more than hold hands. She's my rose, my treasure, my garden of delights. The reason I went over so early was to deliver her little boy to his first day at the mosque school. It takes a man for such things. He's seven and has no father, poor little tyke. My poor Zubeideh cried and cried to see him go.''

"A widow, eh? She's rich, I suppose.''

"It's true that her husband left her comfortably off. She runs the export-import business herself—women are very independent on Alpha Centauri. But I don't care about her money, master. It's her I love. She's my pearl, my plum, my candle in the dark, my—''

"That's enough.'' He looked at Aziz. "I've heard about your pearl; I didn't know whether to believe it. Why do I have to find out such things from infidels?''

"I was going to tell you, master. I just wanted to be sure.''

"Mosque school, eh? Then she's a Moslem, at least.''

"Oh yes, master, very devout. You mustn't be misled by the freer customs here on Alpha Centauri. A woman may be virtuous and still enjoy the company of men. And she need not wear the veil among friends. But her sister is almost always present, a most worthy woman.''

"A widow, too, I suppose.''

"No, master, never married.''

"Well, true love or not, you have a new job, starting today. I want you to keep an eye on little Meryem. She's been trailing around after me in the streets—you, too.''

"I know, master.''

"You *know*? And you did nothing about it?''

"She's like a fish in water in these streets of the Quarter. She knows them in and out. She can stay out of trouble on her own hook. Do you know, even I almost didn't spot her shadowing me the other day? She's very talented—reminds me of myself at that age. Too bad she's not a boy. With those cat feet and light fingers, she could go far—with the right person to instruct her.''

"I can't believe I'm hearing such things. I thought you were reformed. And you with that object lesson growing out of your right wrist!''

"They don't do that on Alpha Centauri. The Sultan's a liberal—he doesn't believe in legal amputations for criminals. Jail sentences and rehabilitation, that's his style. Anyway, master, you can't seriously believe I'd ever introduce a child to a life of crime. I just admire talent when I see it. Little Meryem's just going through a brat stage at the moment. Soon enough she'll turn into a young woman, give up her puppy infatuation with you, fall in love, get married—''

"She doesn't have a crush on me, she just likes to vex me. And her mother and her father and everyone else around. Now, I'm depending on you to keep her out of trouble. The Unbelievers' Quarter may be picturesque, but it's a rough place. Meryem's not like the little pickpockets and street Christians you see around here. I don't want her falling in with the wrong sort."

"You can stop worrying, master. I'll keep an eye on her." Aziz took a sip of coffee, wincing as from pain.

The landlady came in with a small dish of melon cut up into bite-size cubes for Aziz. He smiled wanly and thanked her.

"Will you be here for supper, Abdul?" she asked Hamid-Jones.

"No . . . I'll be back later." Ludmilla had told him she wouldn't see him tonight—she had a late performance and then a matinee the next day—but he had hopes of changing her mind if he showed up at the theater.

But first he had to put in an appearance at the Triangular City.

Out of the corner of his eye he saw a small twitch of movement, like a flea, but when he turned his head there was nothing there. Hamid-Jones plodded doggedly on, past the rows of bazaar stalls displaying the merchandise of two dozen worlds, toward the end of the narrow twisting alley where a main thoroughfare led to the Thieves' Gate and the cruising bubblecabs that could be picked up there.

Feeling clever, he stopped at an outdoor booth that displayed brightly polished copper bowls and trays. He chose a large flat tray and tried to make sense of the rippling images of street movement that warped across its surface. He thought he saw something dart from a doorway, but when he whirled around for a confrontation there was nothing there again.

"You like the tray? I can give you a very good price on it."

The proprietor of the stall gave him an open zipper of a smile and sidled strategically to place himself between Hamid-Jones and the direction in which he had been heading.

"Uh, no thanks," Hamid-Jones said, putting the tray back.

"It's from the moons of Baa'," he said. "All handwork."

"Some other time," Hamid-Jones said, edging past him.

He made a third try at the corner. A shop selling thumbnail holo sets and basketwork had blocked part of the curb with a towering pillar of baskets. Hamid-Jones made a tight turn at a fast walking pace, put on the brakes, then ducked behind the basket tower. A skinny form in bright calico came to a skidding stop. Hamid-Jones grabbed a bony wrist.

"And what do you think you're up to, young lady?" he said.

Meryem made a face at him. "I was going to let you catch me anyway. That's why I came round the corner right after you."

"You're going home. Right now. And Aziz is going to sit on you."

Her small freckled face clouded. "I only came after you to tell you that a man is following you. He's the same man who followed you once before. I wasn't sure, so I followed *him*. He's sort of sneaky, but he isn't very good at following people. If you weren't so unconscious all the time, you'd have noticed him for sure."

"Never mind making up stories. You're going home anyway."

"I mean it. He's over there right now, where you were looking at that tray. That was a dumb trick, you know. I knew right away what you were trying to do."

Hamid-Jones twisted his neck around and saw a flash of white robe as someone stepped quickly between stalls into the narrow passage leading to the next alley. He could get no impression of the man, except that he was bearded and wore what might have been a Martian-style robe and headdress.

"Why'd you do that?" Meryem said impatiently. "You should have made believe you were still talking to me, then sort of just turned around a little, as though you weren't really looking."

"Very clever, young lady. Who's the next one who's supposed to be following me? The man stopping for a sherbet over there? The little old lady with the market basket? The dog hanging around the kebab stand?"

"Honest, that's the one."

"No more nonsense. You're going home. Right now."

He took her by the wrist and dragged her after him. Damn that Aziz, he thought. He had too little to do here on the opulent capital of Alif Prime. From now on he was going to have to buckle down and play nursemaid.

* * *

"Colonel Ish-Shamaal is occupied right now," said the secretary, a slender mournful man named Halabee. "It's not really a good day."

"I'll wait," Hamid-Jones said, seating himself on the plush satin couch in the outer office. His own little cubicle was down the hall and didn't connect with the colonel's suite. Space, the colonel had told him.

Ten minutes later, the inner door opened a crack, and Hamid-Jones heard a flurry of conspiratorial whispers. Colonel Ish-Shamaal's visitors tended to be like that—furtive, secretive men who looked at you from under the lids of their eyes and who saw hidden meanings in a simple "good morning." All of these urgent whispers were probably about nothing more confidential than the price of eggs on Proxima.

The visitors came out, giving Hamid-Jones and the secretary a sidelong glance as they headed for the door. They were three beetle-browed men in dun-colored tunics and the red-checkered turbans of Sabians. The *Subbi*, as Sabians were called by proper Moslems, had some sort of semiautonomous enclave on an airless moon of one of the gas giants of the orange star, and there had been recent nationalist stirrings among a disaffected few that the Sultan was attempting to quell by funneling more financial aid through the ruling elders. The three men began whispering among themselves again before the outer door had closed behind them.

The colonel himself came out a moment later, bearing an armload of tied and bundled documents that he dumped on Halabee's desk. "Burn these," he said. "And stir the ashes."

He turned to go back inside. "Colonel Ish-Shamaal," Hamid-Jones said. "Could I have a word with you?"

The colonel stopped unwillingly and pretended to notice Hamid-Jones for the first time. "*Ya* Abdul!" he said with a toothy smile. "Of course! Any time! Come into my office."

Hamid-Jones followed him inside and seated himself in the straight-backed wooden visitor's chair opposite the colonel. "Colonel, I—"

"Call me Zeytoon," the colonel invited him. "We're all friends here, *ya* Abdul." He sat back, crisp in his military uniform, and made a tent of his fingers. Colonel Zeytoon Ish-Shamaal was young for his responsibilities and approached his duties with an earnestness and ardor that infected those who worked for him. Hamid-Jones was no exception, though he tried to retain an objective view. The colonel, after all, had been giving him the runaround for months.

"It's the report I submitted six weeks ago," Hamid-Jones said. "I put a lot of thought into it, and I haven't heard anything about it so far, not even if it's been read. But that's just one example. I—"

"Ah, the report," Ish-Shamaal said, rearranging his fingers to close off one end of the tent. His bushy eyebrows lifted to add frankness to his smile. "Very useful. Rest assured, *ya* Abdul, that we're doing everything possible to maximize al-Sharq's potential." He leaned forward and lowered his voice. "This is under the rose, of course, but we're arranging an arms shipment to the Beni Akhdar tribe through our agents on Vesta. It should help to free up some of al-Sharq's forces if there's a general uprising."

"But the Beni Akhdar are the deadly enemies of the Beni al-Rub, who are al-Sharq's allies!" Hamid-Jones cried in alarm. "They work for the Emir as caravan guards, and they only use their position to raid the weaker tribes! I wrote all that in my report!"

Colonel Ish-Shamaal laced his fingers together more tightly. "For all we know, the situation may be completely different four years from now, when the arms get there. The Beni Akhdar may have allied themselves with al-Sharq, or the Beni al-Rub may have gone over to the Emir. We won't know for eight years. This is the game the big boys play, *ya* Abdul. It isn't easy pulling the strings at long range. We can only stir things up and wait for all the elements to fall into place."

"But I was *there*! I fought with the Beni al-Rub! They'd *never* switch loyalties! They're al-Sharq's kinsmen!"

"Being there may have clouded your judgment. We can't trust anybody. That's the name of the game. How do we know where al-Sharq's allegiances might lie once he took over the throne? His propaganda keeps talking about the 'Martian people.' The sheik of the Beni Akhdar's already given certain assurances to our agents. He's sworn fealty to the Sultan."

"Oh, they'd say anything to get money and arms. But they'll only do mischief with them."

"Mischief—isn't that what we want, *ya* Abdul?" The colonel's eyes glittered under his bushy brows. "Stir things up, spill a little blood. Doesn't matter whose blood it is, in the long run. It makes people disaffected, destabilizes the government." His eyes misted over as he contemplated truth and beauty. "When things fall apart, we come along and pick up the pieces. It doesn't really matter who we put in. It so happens that in this particular horse race we've put some of our important money on al-Sharq because he looks like the front runner, but it's a wise player who spreads around his bets."

"It makes sense to support groups like the Christian Jihad, the Popular Liberationists, the Legitimists—even the Committee for an Assassins' Homeland. They know al-Sharq's the front-runner, too. They'll throw their support to him when the time comes. But it's counterproductive to throw sand in al-Sharq's gears."

The colonel mustered a tolerant expression. "You're emotionally involved. All right, I'll tell you what we'll do. We'll send al-Sharq some tactical nukes."

"But there are no troop concentrations he could use them against. He could only use them for dome busting. Al-Sharq wants to liberate the people, not massacre them. He needs small arms, food and clothing, outdoor gear, transportation . . ."

The colonel flashed him a winning smile, the kind that charmed his superiors. "Tell you what. You put all that in another report. And then we'll see."

"But that's not what I came to talk about . . ." Hamid-Jones's resolve faded away. "All right, I'll start work on it. I'll have it for you in about a week . . ."

The rest of Hamid-Jones's day was disjointed. He used his pass to have a swim in one of the grottoed pools the Triangular City maintained for midlevel bureaucrats and followed up with a workout in the gym. Then he had a game of centrifugal squash with a cultural deputy from the Department of Extrasystem Concerns. At loose ends after that, he visited the Golden Dome like any tourist and admired its amazing interior courts with their intricately worked archways and friezes, and the Grand Hall of *Mihrab*s, where astronomical clockwork substituted for computers to swivel the serried ranks of prayer niches toward Mecca.

He left the Triangular City to have a solitary lunch downtown, then killed more time by dropping in on a gallery opening showing the latest avant-garde works from the Proximan art scene.

The exhibition was depressing—it was doused in a dull red light to match the dwarf star's spectrum—but it carried him up to post time for the double-ender races at the uptown track. He placed a few small bets, lost a little more than he won, then looked at his watch and thought it might be a good time to call Ludmilla. He couldn't get through to her—an assistant stage manager said she was in the middle of a run-through—so he took a cab to the theater to try in person. When he got there, he cooled his heels in the back row for a while, watching Ludmilla and the other swan maidens tiptoe around the stage; then she came back to tell him that she really couldn't see him that night—the performance didn't end till midnight, and she simply *had* to get a few hours' sleep in order to be fresh for her six o'clock wake-up call—but that she could spend the night with him on Thursday, the day before the troupe left for its tour of the southern continent.

It was still early enough for him to go home for dinner if he wanted to, but he had already told *is-sayida* Roxane that he would eat out, and he was embarrassed to inconvenience her at both ends of the day. So he had another solitary meal at a poetry club and afterward lingered to hear a long ode by an electrifying young poet from Beta Hydri.

It was past midnight when his bubblecab deposited him at the Thieves' Gate. The night was brilliant—there was no such thing as dark during the six months when Alpha Centauri B remained in the heavens after prime sunset—with the orange dab outshining a hundred full moons and casting sharp-edged shadows. One of its gas giants was visible as a pinprick in the sky beside it.

Despite the bright twinshine, the driver refused to take Hamid-Jones to his door. Night was night, and the Unbelievers' Quarter was the Unbelievers' Quarter. Hamid-Jones was tolerant of the man's prejudices—he congratulated himself on having risen above such narrow-mindedness—and tipped him liberally anyway.

The cab rotated and whispered away, and Hamid-Jones set out to walk the remaining distance. The stalls were shuttered; the after-hours places turned blind faces to the street, though you could hear the sounds of all-night merriment within. Hardly anyone was in the streets: a group of cloaked and hooded young bravos looking for one more place to have an illegal nightcap, a householder hurrying home, a burst of light and music as a door opened for someone calling it quits. Hamid-Jones was amused at the jitters of people like the cabdriver. He allowed himself to bask in a glow of moral superiority. These were his streets and his people; in the last six months he had become one of them. One had nothing to fear from one's neighbors.

A sound of footsteps behind him gradually penetrated his consciousness; he hadn't been paying attention to them. They were keeping pace with his own steps, staying a fixed distance behind him.

He looked around, but not quickly enough, and saw an empty lane. The stall archways were all in deep shadow; there was a flicker of motion and a small scurrying that might have been a cat or a Centauran scavenger plant.

He resumed walking and heard the footsteps again. They were definitely matching his own stride, step for step, trying to mask the sound they made.

His first thought was that Meryem had added nighttime escapades to her usual pranks—that she had sneaked out after her parents' bedtime to prowl the Quarter for adventure—and he became furious with Aziz for not keeping tabs on her.

He tried the trick that had worked before—turning a corner quickly then popping back for a look.

This time he was rewarded by the glimpse of a white robe hastily dodging into the shadow of a stall. There was a suggestion of beard, and a headcloth rather than a turban or tarboosh; it could have been the man Meryem had pointed out to him that morning.

Hamid-Jones became alarmed. With Mars four light-years behind him, he had allowed himself to feel secure. Who, here on Alpha Centauri's capital planet, could be interested in him?

Perhaps, he told himself, it was only a simple mugger. It didn't have to be the same man he'd seen that morning. There were plenty of off-worlders on Alpha Centauri, and the polyglot Unbelievers' Quarter had more than its share of them.

He took the turn ahead with abrupt footwork and immediately broke into a sprint. There was a fork at the end of the alley, and a heaped collection of garbage cans in front of the shuttered shop at the corner. Hamid-Jones dived nimbly to the side and crouched behind the cans—just in time. He heard footsteps pounding past, a moment of hesitation, and then the sound of his pursuer taking the left fork.

He was too smart to emerge then. He waited until he heard the footsteps coming back. They continued down the right fork without stopping. When he judged they were a safe distance away, he jumped out and ran back the way he'd come. He threaded his way through several side alleys, taking a round-about way home. Feeling smug, he entered the cul-de-sac that contained his lodging house and stepped up to the front door, feeling for the key in his pocket.

He was just putting the key in the lock when something hard jabbed into the small of his back. "No tricks or I'll blow you in half," a voice behind him said. The accent was Martian.

Hamid-Jones froze, the key in his hand.

"That's right," the gunman said behind him. "Nice and easy. We're going inside now. Open the door and be quiet about it. We don't want to wake anybody up."

CHAPTER 5

Hamid-Jones stumbled through the Yordans' darkened living room, the gun poking at his back. He brushed by a beaded lamp and set it tinkling.

A door opened down the shabby hallway leading to the back of the house. A yellow night-light within splashed a dim glow across the hallway ceiling. "Is that you, Abdul?" the landlord called.

The gun prodded him in warning. "Answer him," came a whisper. "Make it sound good."

"Yes, *ya* Yaqub," Hamid-Jones replied.

"Is everything all right?"

"Everything's fine. Had a late night tonight." He added a yawn.

"Good night, then." The door closed.

The gunman herded him upstairs, past the doors of other sleeping tenants. He seemed to know where he was going. Hamid-Jones's flat was above what had been a stable in better days, across a bridge from the upper floor, apart from the main house. Sounds did not carry. The privacy had been an important consideration to Aziz when he had rented the place.

Aziz was cowering in a corner of the front bedroom, under guard by a pair of bulky characters brandishing conspicuously large hand weapons. He looked frightened and had the shivers, but he did not appear to have been harmed.

"Picked him up at the *bab*," the gunman behind Hamid-

Jones said. "He's clean—no tails from the Triangle." He threw back his headcloth and stood bareheaded.

The other two appraised Hamid-Jones with hard stares. One was long-jawed, snub-nosed, with a Nordic shelf of forehead fringed by bleached eyebrows. The other was pockmarked, swarthy, with a shovel chin. They, too, had thrown back their head coverings indoors and were bareheaded, but otherwise their robes, like those of Hamid-Jones's captor, were draped Martian-style.

"It's time for you to talk to us, *ya* Abdul," the swarthy one said.

"Who . . . who are you?" Hamid-Jones said with a dry mouth.

His mind was racing: did this have something to do with the clandestine department in the palace basement where he drew his stipend; hadn't Colonel Ish-Shamaal just been going on about military aid to guerrilla organizations on Mars? There was no other reason for Martian *fedayeen* to be interested in him. And these men had the look of *fedayeen*—you could always tell the type.

"Tell him, Musa," the snub-nosed man said.

"Did you sweep the place for bugs?" said the bearded *mujahid* who had delivered Hamid-Jones.

"Yes, there's nothing here."

"Better sweep him, too."

The snub-nosed man produced a palm-size detector that he ran over Hamid-Jones's body. Then he drew a length of collapsible tubing into a hoop and made Hamid-Jones step through it.

"Not a thing on him. The colonel must be losing his touch. Either that or he thinks that webs are spun in only one direction."

"Careful, Tawfiq."

"He won't spill anything," Tawfiq said, showing Hamid-Jones his teeth. "It's going to be *his* neck."

A choked sound came from Aziz in the corner. "He won't say a word. I swear it. Neither will I."

The swarthy one, Musa, looked Hamid-Jones over as if he were deciding the best place to begin carving up a roast. "We're freedom fighters. Of *al-Jihad-al-misih*."

Christian terrorists! He might have guessed it from the uncovered heads. Hamid-Jones kept his counsel. These were dangerous and unpredictable men.

Seeing his reaction, Tawfiq gave a feral laugh. "It's all right, *ya* Abdul. You won't get in trouble for harboring us. We have an office-in-exile here in the Sultan's capital. The Sultan looks the other way. We're even on Colonel Ish-Shamaal's payroll."

"Not for enough," the bearded man growled. "The assistance he sends to our brethren is a joke."

"Is . . . is that what you want from me?" Hamid-Jones said. "I don't have any influence with the colonel."

"No, you can't do us any good there—we know your position." Musa spat on the floor; Christians had filthy habits. "The colonel keeps us on a short leash. He plays off one group of *mujahidin* against the other."

"Even the Committee for an Assassins' Homeland gets more funds than we do!" the bearded man burst out.

"That's enough, Dris," Musa said. "They're our brothers in arms. All *mujahidin* are brothers in arms till the struggle is over."

"You . . . you work with the Assassins?" Hamid-Jones said.

Musa gave him a sardonic smile. "We go back a long way together. Even in the twelfth century, the Assassins made common cause with the Christian Knights Templars against the reigning sultans. We were only infidels. The sultans were their enemies in the faith. It's a question of who you hate the most."

"The overthrow of the Emir and his carbon copies is the overriding issue," Tawfiq said. "We can fight amongst ourselves afterward."

"You . . . you know about the new head-clone, then?"

"*Know* about it? The *al-Jihad-al-misih* were *responsible* for it! We were the ones who sabotaged the head transplant operation!"

"I . . . I thought it was the Legitimists who were responsible for the attack."

The three *fedayeen* looked at one another. "The Legitimists always take credit for everything," Dris said. "We can't blow up a pipeline without them making an anonymous phone call to the press."

"We complain," Tawfiq said, "but they always do it again."

Hamid-Jones saw no reason to doubt their assertions. It was Rashid, back on Mars, who had pointed out that the terrorists in the *majlis* attack had willingly sacrificed their right hands to smuggle weapons into the operating theater. It took a Christian to do that—even though the loss would be temporary. A Moslem would more readily have sacrificed his *zib*.

"We received news of the attack almost a year ago from our colleagues in the Solar system," Musa said. He frowned. "The radio signal was somewhat garbled. Our sources said that the Legitimists had picked you up for questioning. They wanted to know how successful the attack had been. But you brick-walled them. You waited till you could deliver the information to al-Sharq."

"Good show, that, *ya* Abdul," Dris said. "Our leadership was very pleased with you."

The atmosphere was noticeably less threatening. Two of the terrorists had put away their guns, and Dris held his like a forgotten object.

"That's nice to know," Hamid-Jones gulped.

Aziz, over in the corner, had stopped trembling. His face had taken on the familiar bland expression that concealed conniving. "The master's always been partial to Christians," he whined. "Didn't he take up his abode with Christians here in the Quarter?"

The gunmen ignored him. "Yes, your fame has preceded you, *ya* Abdul," Musa said. "The Clonemaster's faith in you was not misplaced. You didn't give in to the temptation to fink on him to save your own skin. The leadership had high hopes for you after the Clonemaster was betrayed. Particularly after you cleverly gained the confidence of the Grand Vizier. For a time it was hoped that you could bore from within at the Palace as even the Clonemaster had not been able to do."

"He wasn't so clever after all if he had to flee, was he?" Dris said maliciously. "He should have allied himself with the eunuch's faction, not the Vizier's."

"How could he know?" Musa countered. "Our money was on the Vizier, too. The important thing was that the Clonemaster trusted him. Why, he even planned to make Hamid-Jones his heir—marry off his daughter to him."

The shock made Hamid-Jones's knees go weak. How stupid he had been! There had been no need for him to have sneaked around behind the Clonemaster's back to woo Lalla. He need only have waited!

"That's why we're going to trust you now, *ya* Abdul," Dris said, fingering his gun again. "I hope we're not mistaken in you."

"We're collecting our dues," Tawfiq added.

"I don't see how I can help," Hamid-Jones protested, his head swimming with the new knowledge. "Mars is over four light-years away. For all we know, the substitute Emir may already have been overthrown—may have been overthrown all of four years ago. Al-Sharq may already be on the throne."

"All that's true," Musa admitted. "It's not important now. You've already done your part for the cause by exposing the Emir clone and giving al-Sharq the propaganda ammunition he needs. And by fighting with the desert Arabs—yes, we know about that, too. In any case, no one here on Alpha Centauri can influence political events unfolding four and three-tenths light-years away."

"Then . . . I don't understand what it is you want of me."

The three exchanged glances. It was Musa who spoke. "We want you to spy on the Sultan for us. Seeing that you have favored status and access to the Triangular City."

"We haven't been able to place one of our own," Tawfiq amplified. "It's hard for non-Centaurans to move freely inside."

Hamid-Jones was appalled. "The Sultan is my host and benefactor—yours, too! That would be a poor return for his hospitality!"

"Host!" Tawfiq spat. "What consideration do you owe someone who invites you to dinner so he can burn down your house while you're away?"

"What are you talking about?"

"The Sultan is a ruthless man. You don't rule three suns without being ruthless. He'll do anything to win the Caliphate. Even destroy an entire planet to put his chief competitor out of the running."

"But that's insane!"

"Is it? Genocide's been around a long time in human affairs. Sargon, Genghis Khan, Attila, Hitler, Pol Pot—"

"But an entire planet!"

"Where the means exist, there's always the possibility they'll be used. Attila had to make do with sword and fire. In our enlightened age, there's a choice of methods. The means to destroy an entire world has existed since the twentieth century— a few thousand nuclear bombs to wipe out Mars's fragile ecology would do the job. Or the planet could be seeded with radioactive dust or biological weapons. Or a starship tethered at

Phobos could accidentally on purpose act as a retrorocket, slow Phobos down in its orbit, and send it crashing down to the Martian surface. It would make the comet that extinguished the dinosaurs look like a pebble!"

"There's no need to be so fancy," Dris said. "A Centauran starship could do a flyby with its Harun drive on."

"Allah preserve us!" Aziz cried from his corner. "I don't want to hear such things!"

"The Sultan would never do such things!" Hamid-Jones protested. "He's not a madman. And even if he were, the perpetrator of such a crime would be a pariah in Islam forever. He'd never get the Caliphate!"

"No," Musa agreed. "That's why he's going about it more cleverly."

"What do you mean?"

Musa looked very grim. "Informers in our network here on Alpha Centauri keep picking up rumors of some stupendous technical project that's supposed to wrap up the Caliphate for the Sultan. There's supposed to be some kind of huge secret installation beyond Pluto, in the Oort Cloud."

"But that's just a communications facility!" Hamid-Jones burst out. "That's what the ambassador told me—"

He stopped. The others were looking at him intently.

"The ambassador?" Musa prompted.

"The Centauran ambassador on Mars," Hamid-Jones said miserably.

"What else did the ambassador say?" Dris said, toying with his gun.

"I . . . I said that only a miracle could make the Sultan the Caliph of Islam, seeing that he can't spare ten years to make the pilgrimage to Mecca and that the laws of nature can't be changed. And he said, what if you didn't *have* to change the laws of nature?"

"Aha!" Dris said. "What did I tell you. It's going to be a flyby with the Harun drive. Only they're going to fix it up so it can't be traced back to the Sultan. It'll be made to look like a runaway starship from one of the farther stars, with no one left alive on board, and the evidence destroyed afterward by diving it into the sun or letting it continue accelerating into the outer darkness!"

Musa gazed steadily at Hamid-Jones. "Some of our information came from a drunken engineer," he said. "He talked about a vast engineering project beyond Pluto—having something to do with the Harun drive."

Hamid-Jones's face went white. "I won't believe it!" he said. "It's too monstrous!"

"Can you afford to take that chance, *ya* Abdul?" Musa said gently. "Isn't there someone you love on Mars?"

"Lalla!" Hamid-Jones choked. "And everybody else!"

"Exactly."

Hamid-Jones snatched at straws. "But the Sultan's been supporting your group—all the other *mujahidin* groups—in the hope of unseating the Emir and putting al-Sharq on the throne. Setting him up to become a Centauran satrap. Why would he go to all that trouble?"

"Perhaps," Musa suggested, "he's lost patience."

"Or maybe," Tawfiq put in, "the flyby is his ace in the hole in case all his political machinations don't work out. His alternate plan."

"In any case," Musa said, "we've got to find out about the secret project in the Oort Cloud. Don't you agree?"

"I suppose so," Hamid-Jones said miserably.

"You needn't feel bad about it," Musa said gently. "If we're wrong, there's no harm done. You can go right on serving the Sultan in your present capacity, and we can go on lobbying him for additional funds."

"You owe the Sultan nothing," Dris glowered. "He's just using you and everyone else for his own ends. Your loyalties lie with the suffering people of Mars—not with this foreign Sultan who's keeping you as a pet!"

It was Tawfiq's turn. It was his job to scowl at Hamid-Jones and turn the screws further. "And if you have any idea about not playing along with us, we can always get you put back on the Assassins' hit list. We checked with them. They've got an office on Alpha Centauri, too, you know. We got them to give you a reprieve for the common good."

"You don't have to threaten me," Hamid-Jones said angrily. "I'll do it—because if there's the slightest chance this wicked rumor is true, I'd work with the satan himself to save Mars."

CHAPTER 6

Hamid-Jones clung like a fly to the ledge, his slippers feeling for footholds. It was two hundred feet down to a concrete parking lot if he lost his balance. The cursed orange star was in the sky, illuminating the night, but fortunately he was in the shadow of a water tower at the moment, in case anyone happened to look up.

He inched his way toward what he hoped was the right balcony. Aziz had triangulated it for him, telling him to look for a stainless steel minaret in the middle distance, then to sight with one eye toward the far-off gleam of the Golden Dome. When the two were aligned, he would be above the right balcony.

He hoped he could trust Aziz's trigonometry. He tried not to think about the consequences if he were to be caught breaking into the wrong apartment, blundering into some angry official's bedroom or harem.

His foot slipped, and before he could do anything about it, he lost a slipper. Helplessly he watched it tumble through space to the parking lot below, coming to rest next to an egg-shaped monowheel.

He should not have looked down. The sheer ceramic cliff he was hugging seemed to dip and swoop. He hung on. After a moment the swaying surface became a solid wall again. The random squares of light resolved themselves into glass terrace doors. The one he wanted was dark, as he had been told it would be.

He looked out across the Triangular City. From up here, it

was a thin slice of greenery and jumbled rooftops carved out of the Sultan's sprawling metropolis. He was closer to the narrow end, where favored officials like Izzat Awad lived in these luxury ant-heaps, so that perspective was skewed—the triangle as it widened with distance became almost a narrow oblong, until the eye took in the scale of the gold and orange domes at the far corners and the Sultan's private park centered between them like a postage stamp. Those engraved geometric lines were roadways, the scattered granular shapes the outbuildings of his royal reservation.

The perfume of jasmine and hibiscus filled the night air; the music of songbirds kept awake by the orange star rose from a thousand walled paradises. The pale arch of the Milky Way could still be seen despite the competition of the twinshine, and the familiar constellations looked the same as they did on Mars, with the exception of Cassiopeia, which had added an extra star to its W-shape—Earth's Sun as seen from Alpha Centauri.

He emerged from the shadow of the rooftop water tank and wormed his way across the last few yards with sweaty palms and nerve that was close to cracking. Then, carefully, he allowed his feet to dangle. His remaining slipper plopped to the balcony below. He let go of the cornice and dropped after it with a thump.

He remained in a crouching position for several moments, catching his breath and listening. No challenges came from the surrounding terraces, no insomniac shouted for the security guards. And he heard nothing from within—no voices or stirrings that would mean that his information had been wrong and that he was trapped on the balcony.

There was no point in having a timidity attack at this juncture. The longer he waited in the open, the greater the chance that he would be discovered. He tried the sliding glass door and discovered to his vast relief that it was unlocked, as it was supposed to be. He pushed it open just far enough and slipped inside, to find himself smothered in heavy drapery. He untangled himself and stepped into the dark room.

A small gasp came from the darkness. "Who's there?" a strained voice whispered.

He couldn't be certain whose voice it was, but there was nothing to do except answer.

"It's me, my love . . . your Abdul."

There was a silken rustling, and a warm body flung itself into his arms. The body was substantial enough to knock him off balance. "Oh, I was so frightened waiting for you, *ya* Abdul!" Mrs. Awad panted, all revved up and ready to go.

"There was no need to be frightened, little one," he said glibly, pouring it on and hating himself. "There's no danger— everything's been taken care of."

He hoped it was true. At this moment, Mr. Awad had better be well into his cups, embarked irredeemably on an all-night drinking bout. Aziz had called less than an hour ago to say that the coast was clear—that Awad had reached the garrulous, sentimental stage, and that if he followed his previous behavior patterns he would progress to drinking himself into weepy oblivion and roll on home about dawn, helped by one of his drinking companions. This time the good samaritan would be Aziz.

"He's the type who drinks to escape, master," Aziz had said when he had called from one of the cellar speakeasies that seemed to thrive illegally in the Sultan's capital. "Something about his work has him frightened out of his wits, but he keeps dancing around the subject. Oh-oh, I better go. He's trying to stand up. He's ready to move on to another joint."

Now the bounteous Mrs. Awad confirmed Aziz's diagnosis of her husband. "I know, *ya* Abdul," she said, pressing against him. "He stays out all night when he gets in these moods. Poor Izzat's been drinking more and more, lately. Something's bothering him, but he won't tell me what it is."

No wonder, Hamid-Jones thought. Being involved in the murder of an entire planet was not the kind of subject one cared to discuss, even with one's wife.

"He brings briefcases full of work home all the time, even though it's against security regulations, and then he locks himself away with it all night," she complained. "He never visits my bedroom anymore—he's either out drinking or shut up with his computer. I'm a passionate woman! I can't stand it anymore!"

Aziz—with a little help from the intelligence files of the Christian Jihad—had filled him in on that, too. Mrs. Awad needed a lot of consoling. Hamid-Jones would not be the first, or even the twentieth.

"All you have to do is keep bumping into her when she goes shopping," Aziz had coached him. "Follow her around like a starved dog. It won't hurt to roll your eyes a lot, either. Try to look as if you're in pain. Mrs. Awad has a high opinion of her own charms."

"But what about her chaperon?" Hamid-Jones had asked.

"She doesn't have one of her own. Her husband subscribes to a eunuch service. They take their clients on outings at a group rate. As you can imagine, they're not very strict. They have to please the customers. And that's the women. The men don't know anything. Except that they're saving money. Women like Mrs. Awad pout a lot for the benefit of their husbands and complain about being prisoners. But they're the ones who tip the eunuch at the end of the week."

Aziz's evaluation had been right on the mark. Mrs. Awad had noticed Hamid-Jones right away and started flirting with him on the second day. They had managed to exchange a few words at a time as they passed each other on opposite sides of the *raba'a-mahram* barriers of the Triangular City's shops and public accommodations, and Mrs. Awad had even contrived to break away from her excursion group for long minutes—while the other women covered up for her with the bored agency eunuch in attendance. They had progressed to passionate kisses and mutual fondlings behind potted palms and around blind corners, and once Mrs. Awad had shown her readiness to consummate matters in a linen closet in the two or three minutes available while she was supposedly on her way back from a visit to the ladies' room of a kebab restaurant. Only the inopportune arrival of a busboy had cooled her down.

"That was fortunate, master," Aziz had said later when Hamid-Jones had reported the incident. "You don't want to take the edge off her with these easy encounters. Tell her your ardor is too intense to be satisfied by a few hurried moments. Hold out for an all-night visit to her bedchamber."

"How did her husband allow her to reach such a state?" Hamid-Jones had said in disapproval.

"She's too much for him, that's all, master," Aziz had replied. "He's just a silly little man who can't handle a woman of his wife's capacity." He snickered. "I hope you escape alive, master."

"That's enough!" Hamid-Jones had said severely.

Now, with Mrs. Awad panting in his ear and rubbing against him like a cat, Hamid-Jones remembered Aziz's words and gave a shiver. He had his night's work cut out for him; he could only hope that the night would be long enough for him to complete what he had come to do.

"You are shivering with passion, my poor Abdul!" Mrs. Awad breathed. "Don't worry, no one will interrupt us. We don't go in for large household staffs here in Paradise Towers, despite Izzat's position. All services are supplied by building maintenance, even the bath maid. Izzat has only one thief of a personal servant, who disappears every time Izzat does. I don't know how Izzat lets him get away with it. He sees the signs of Izzat's binges days in advance and takes off on his own—he won't be back till the yellow sun rises."

Hamid-Jones knew all about the Awads' servant. Aziz had pumped him for the information that had made tonight's adventure possible—including the rooftop layout and the signs that pointed to another all-night drinking bout by his employer—and had advanced the scurvy fellow some small funds for the low entertainments that would keep him out of the way this night.

"I can't wait, my love," Hamid-Jones said hoarsely, trying to pry her loose and failing. Locked together in an awkward tangle of intertwined legs and clinging arms, they staggered in an off-balance union toward the bedroom.

She was snoring gently and rhythmically, with a set of identical back-of-the-throat clicks at the end of each long-drawn exhalation. Hamid-Jones raised himself cautiously on one elbow and looked at her face under the violet night-light. Her puffy little lips were slightly parted, to show the white gleam of an incisor. There were dewy beads of moisture on the light down above her upper lip. She looked as if she were really out this time.

It had taken longer than he had thought it would. Every time he had thought she was asleep and had attempted to leave the bed, she had stirred drowsily and pulled him back for another bout of acrobatics. The orange star had already set, and it could not be more than an hour or two till the first blush of primerise.

Gingerly he slipped from beneath the sheets and swung his feet to the floor. Mrs. Awad moaned in her sleep but did not open her eyes. He pussyfooted to the bedroom door, holding his breath all the way.

The harem was at the end of a long hallway, past Mr. Awad's

own bedroom door. The lock was formidable: a combination voice and five-finger identilock that required Awad's living presence. Voicelocks alone could be fooled by synthesized sound, but the five recessed slots would accept nothing but flesh-and-blood fingertips with the right whorls. The cleverest plastic molds could not trick such a system, nor even Awad's own severed hand, had someone been willing to go to such appalling lengths. A sixth recess had been disconnected when the harem had been converted to its present purpose.

The system had been inherited from a previous tenant, according to Aziz's information. The Awads were a liberated couple, though Awad, at his pay scale, could easily have afforded the four wives permitted to him by law, with a concubine or two thrown in for good measure.

Instead, the harem had been remodeled into a private sanctum for Mr. Awad—a home office where he could keep secret files.

Hamid-Jones sweated as he bent to the lock. What he was about to do was no longer merely a personal transgression, but a breach of government security.

He removed the large, showy ring that had been provided by Aziz. Mrs. Awad had complained that it scratched her. The oversize synthetic ruby and the heavy gold mounting contained a miracle of compressed electronics. It must have cost a fortune on whatever black market it had been obtained—but the Christian Jihad had plenty of funds, thanks to Colonel Ish-Shamaal.

The door frame was massive and deeply incised. The *bab* itself was heavy steel plate painted to look like bronze, with a thick ornamental boss centered in each panel.

Hamid-Jones passed the ruby ring over the door, frame, and moldings until a tiny diode flashed green at him. The *bab*'s brain was about where he expected it to be, behind one of the intaglio ornaments near the lock. He made smaller and smaller circles with the ring until the little light was at its brightest, then slapped it down over the spot to cling magnetically.

He inserted his fingers and thumb in the slots. He sweated some more. He hoped that Aziz and the Jihad had their information right. If it didn't work, he was about to lose his fingertips.

He cleared his throat. "Open, *al-bab*," he said softly.

The door swung open. The electronic skeleton key had performed as anticipated. It was no good trying to mimic fingerprints and the characteristic mixture of body oils, sweat, and skin flakes that went with them. Nor had there been the time or opportunity to steal Awad's words from him, one phoneme at a time, and to reassemble them with the right synthesized timbre. Instead, the tiny computer and two-plate magnetron in the ruby ring had corrupted the door's own electronic brain, resetting it to accept the voice and living fingerprints of Hamid-Jones. Awad was going to have trouble getting into his own harem after this. He'd have to send for a locksmith. But if all went well, there would be no evidence of an intrusion; the lock's failure would be put down to product fatigue.

Hamid-Jones crept into the room and swung the heavy door shut behind him. There were no secondary defenses. He made sure the drapes were pulled tight, then turned on a lamp. Awad's computer console was an elaborate one, with wall-size holo window, a triptych of flat displays, and enough peripheral equipment to run a starship. He settled himself in the contour couch. There were all sorts of controls within easy reach—keyboards, joysticks and joystrings, light-styli, a helmet for providing artificial realities, and feedback gloves that would allow Awad to put himself inside the display and interact with it. There was even a full-size bodysuit folded neatly on a rack, presumably incorporating the same flexion and abduction sensors and tactile feedback devices as the gloves, but on a grander scale; it would have to be tailored to Awad's exact measurements and could be worn by no one else.

Hamid-Jones pulled a keyboard over to lap position and turned on the power. All the screens around him promptly lit up, and he was faced with his first problem. He could feed data into Awad's system all day long—except, of course, for potentially infectious programs rejected by the computer's immune sysem—but he couldn't take anything out of it unless he had the password.

He peeled off his false thumbnail and took out the first of the small stack of paper-thin gigachip wafers that had been concealed beneath it. His hand trembled as he inserted it into Awad's machine. It was a capital offense even to possess the high-powered search program it contained, provided the court could prove intent to bypass government security systems.

There was no alarm or lockdown. He was past the first of the hurdles. The screens around him blurred with text that whipped across them at speeds too fast to be seen.

It took all of two minutes to hit paydirt, even at the tremendous gigaflop rates executed by the wafer. The screens jerked to a stop. Centered in each screen was a single phrase in classical Arabic:

Guide us to the right path.

Hamid-Jones shook his head in disbelief. With a whole universe of nonsense syllables and scrambled characters in scores of languages available to him, the unimaginative Awad had chosen the totally obvious sixth line from the opening surah of the Koran—surely one of the most familiar phrases in all the Arabic language. Although the gigachip program had taken as long to ferret it out as it might have taken to randomly duplicate any other possible code, the famous line might have occurred to any sneak thief, without benefit of a sophisticated search program.

He fed it back via the keyboard, and when the computer gave him the green light, he called up Awad's menu. A second gigachip wafer from the thin pad on his thumbnail gave him a weeding program to help him identify the files that were called up most often.

One file went by the promising heading of "Eyes Only: Project Blue." He punched it in, and a life-size nude woman, making obscene gestures of invitation, sprang up in the holo window. The datagloves flexed, and the woman gave a theatrical groan of pleasure. Awad, it seemed, had a taste for adult interactive holoporn. Hastily, Hamid-Jones shut it off. The image disappeared, but not before the feedback suit sat up in its rack.

He tried again. This time he got a set of mathematical tables showing the relationship between the size and mass of black holes. The Earth, if squeezed into a black hole, he learned, would have a diameter of two centimeters. The sun would be condensed to a diameter of three and three-quarters miles. Ten suns would make a black hole with a diameter of thirty-seven miles—the density kept going down with size, evidently, and in this case would amount to ten-to-the-fifteenth-power grams per cubic centimeter.

He riffled through the file and got another set of mathematical tables. Now it was the relativistic mass of various objects traveling at different fractions of the speed of light. A starship traveling within one hundred millionth of one percent of the speed of light—ninety-nine percent followed by a decimal point and eight more nines—multiplied its mass some seventy thousand times. Add another nine after the decimal point and the spaceship multiplied its mass by a factor of approximately two hundred and twenty-four thousand.

After that, the figures became unreadable—Awad had substituted a symbol of his own to do away with the proliferating nines.

Clipped to the file in the form of an expandable window was a set of rough engineering sketches. They had something to do with the Harun drive, and Hamid-Jones, remembering the surmise of the Christian Jihad terrorists that the Sultan might be planning a starship flyby, with the Harun drive turned on, that would sterilize Mars, felt the hairs on the back of his neck prickle.

The sketches, as far as Hamid-Jones could tell from Awad's scribbled marginal notes, had to do with modifications to the drive calibration safety system—the feedback "valves" that limited the infall of hydrogen and antihydrogen from adjacent universes to a rate that would maintain a comfortable one-gravity acceleration. The modifications, in effect, would open the floodgates of Creation. Such a ship would have no brakes.

But what did black holes have to do with it?

With a sinking feeling, he ran once more through Awad's menu. Sure enough, there was a file with the rather cute label of "The Black Swallower." Awad had substituted a *zay* for the *sin* in the word for "black" to make an awkward Arabic pun on the word for "wife."

Hamid-Jones scanned the material as rapidly as he could, trying to make some sense of it before he ran out of time. The file was voluminous, but it was bits and pieces of a larger file that Awad had smuggled home from work so that he could pursue one aspect or another of the Sultan's secret project after hours. Awad's scrawled shorthand notes to himself were confusing, but after a while the material started to organize itself into a number of broad headings.

Hamid-Jones sucked in his breath. This was no abstract discussion of black holes in general, but a lot of nitty-gritty data about one black hole in particular!

It had a size: one and one-half solar masses. That was puzzling. A black hole found in nature—if it were the remnant of an ordinary collapsed star—had to be at least twice that mass. Otherwise it would be a white dwarf or a neutron star.

And it had a particular position in space—somewhere beyond the orbit of Pluto, in the Solar system's Oort Cloud.

Hamid-Jones knew about the Nemesis theory—that the death of the dinosaurs and the other periodic mass extinctions of the distant past were caused by a remote companion star to the Sun that regularly pelted the Earth with comets torn from the Oort Cloud. The theory still had its supporters a thousand years after it had been propounded, though no such killer star had ever been detected.

Was, then, Nemesis actually a black hole?

Hamid-Jones scratched his head. There was something ambiguous about the reference. Though the black hole had a particular position and a particular mass, it did not have a particular *time*. Some of Awad's scribbles had been cribbed from a *zij*—an astronomical table—and they showed the inner planets at different places in their orbits. To judge by the various relative positions of Earth and Mars, the window of uncertainty was at least half a Martian year wide.

As if Awad—or the project astronomer he'd cribbed the *zij* from—were trying out various times for the black hole to come into existence.

But that was patently ridiculous.

Or was it?

One of the subfiles had the troubling title of *al-Kindusah*—the Condenser. Awad's specialty was ballistics, and in his notes he was working out variations in the trajectory of the black hole according to the moment it came into being. It was an insanely complicated problem, because he had to take into account a quantum twitch in Einsteinian time contraction as the black hole collapsed into existence from a somewhat larger mass, and because the relativistic speed at which the hole was traveling distorted space itself, making a sort of furrow along an Einsteinian geodesic. Apparently the hole would be traveling like a bat out of hell from the very moment of its birth.

The implication was that the black hole was somehow being—he hardly dared form the word in his mind—*manufactured*.

Manufactured in a vast secret installation in the cometary wilderness beyond the orbit of Pluto.

But that was so fantastic that Hamid-Jones dismissed the idea out of hand. He had misinterpreted the data, that was all, he told himself. A black hole had been floating around in the Oort Cloud for eons, and the Sultan's scientists—lucking into a discovery that had always eluded Earth's astronomers—had simply happened to find it.

He returned to Awad's orbital diagrams. One of them appeared to show the black hole intersecting the orbit of Earth and swallowing up the planet, Mecca and all. The Sultan wouldn't want that. Someone—Awad or the astronomer who had made the calculation—had crossed the sketch out so vehemently that the stylus had ripped a hole in the original paper now shown on the screen. In the margin was another diagram that showed the Earth safely tucked behind the Sun, while the black hole whizzed harmlessly by. Written large in someone else's handwriting—possibly the Sultan's himself—was the laconic comment: "Better."

Hamid-Jones found that his hands were shaking. He got himself under control and searched further. A computer simulation went with the file. He had to use the holo window for that. It was trickier, but he set it up for viewing.

The simulation was clearer than the rough sketches had been. It showed a number of alternate scenarios in ballistics, including the prohibited one that would have made the Earth disappear.

He settled back in his contour couch and ran them through, one after another. The simulation didn't specify how one could move an object that had a mass one and one-half times that of the Sun. You could scarcely toss it a few comets, for example, and coax it out of its orbit that way.

But the thing was being aimed nevertheless. The scenarios didn't make sense otherwise. That's why the simulation had been set up as a ballistics problem.

It wasn't the whole ballistics problem, though. It was only the phase that Awad's notes called "exterior ballistics." The earlier phase involving the Einsteinian twitch as the hole suddenly was born was called "interior ballistics." Apparently the stage that described the actual impact of projectiles on targets was a separate branch of the science called "terminal ballistics." Awad hadn't gotten that far in his work yet.

As a result, the little black ball in the animation rolled inward from the Oort Cloud, crossed the orbit of Pluto without incident, and came to an abrupt halt somewhere in the vicinity of the orbit of Neptune. Then the problem started over again from the beginning, with a different set of parameters.

The ball was *supposed to* penetrate the inner system, dive past the Sun, and head outward again at very nearly the speed of light. That much was clear from the preliminary rough sketch on which the Sultan had written his big red "no-no." And the holographic scenario that matched the forbidden Earth-erasing preliminary sketch in fact had a red tag attached to it, though it hadn't yet been edited out.

It didn't matter. Hamid-Jones didn't need to know any more. There could be only one reason for the Sultan to send a black hole hurtling toward the inner Solar system.

To swallow up Mars.

It would be the perfect crime. There would be no corpse of a planet to be picked over by the coroners of Islam—no evidence of a starship flyby that had fried a world to death with the awful radiation of the Harun effect—no one able to point a speculative finger at the Sultan of Alpha Centauri.

Instead, Mars would simply disappear.

And with Mars would disappear the Sultan's only serious rival for the Caliphate of Islam.

Fingers trembling, he wiped the display. A sense of dread settled over him like a pall. He used his remaining blank giga-chips to make copies of the entire file.

A salmon-colored light was leaking around the drapes when he finished. He put everything in order, trying to cover his tracks as much as possible, then closed the door softly behind him.

He got back to the bedroom in the nick of time. Mrs. Awad was yawning, stretching, her eyes half open. "Where were you, *ya* Abdul?" She pouted. "I reached for you, and you weren't there."

"Sorry."

"You don't have to wash after each time, you know. Just once, at the end. We follow the Reformed version of the *Hadith* here."

"I'd better be going. It's almost daylight."

Her arms snaked out and caught him as he tried to get by her to his clothes on the chair. "There's still time for once more," she purred. "He never gets home till after the morning prayer."

It took too long this time; Mrs. Awad was sated by the long night of lovemaking. Hamid-Jones, with gritted teeth, silently willed her to finish. He was just feeling her final, long-drawn shudder beneath him when a door at the other end of the apartment opened with a rattling of security chains and a whine of abused servolocks.

Mrs. Awad sat right up, knocking Hamid-Jones over. "It's Izzat! Get out of here, quick!"

Her face was ashen with fear. The penalties for adultery still obtained, even on Alpha Centauri.

"No, not that way!" she gabbled in a panic. "You can't go through the hall!"

He was only trying to get to his clothes. She wouldn't let him stop to dress, either. He scooped up his clothing into a bundle, with her pushing at the small of his back.

"Where, then?" he said.

"The window!" she gasped, pushing him toward the French door that opened onto the bedroom balcony.

"Oh no!" he said, resisting the push. It was a twenty story drop. He tried to remember the emergency escape routes he had worked out with Aziz. They had gone over the blueprints of the building together. "Where are the maid's quarters?"

"Through there." She had mistaken his meaning. "You can hide in the linen closet. Oh my God, he's at the door! It's too late!"

By that time Hamid-Jones had managed to find the little beeper in one of his pantaloons pockets. It was another of Aziz's black market specials. The button was only a goosebump on the plastic ovoid. He scraped at it with his thumbnail, hoping that Aziz was within range, just as Awad finished fumbling at the door latch and burst into the bedroom.

He was a pudgy, pale little man, still drunk as a lord and none too steady on his feet, but he looked dangerous. When he saw Hamid-Jones his face turned red with sudden rage, like a light-bulb going on.

"I've seen you before, you snake!" he shouted at Hamid-Jones's fleeing back.

He lurched toward a dressing table drawer. Mrs. Awad screamed and tried to block his way, but he pushed her aside.

"No, Izzat, don't!"

A little pink gun from the dressing table had appeared in the engineer's hand and was making erratic circles in Hamid-Jones's direction. Hamid-Jones tripped over a footstool at exactly the right moment. A tiny missile whined over his head like a mosquito. He picked himself up off the floor and kept running.

The maid's room was another amenity that had been made obsolete by building services. Mrs. Awad had turned it into one huge closet. Hamid-Jones fought his way through shoeracks and racks of clothes, looking for the laundry chute. Behind him he heard floundering sounds, like a wild boar crashing through canebrake. Mrs. Awad was hampering her husband's progress by hanging onto one leg and making him drag her along. Another mosquito zipped over Hamid-Jones's head and burst with a tiny flash of flame against the wall.

He located the linen closet through a forest of clothes trees. The laundry chute had to be next to it. Piles of soiled sheets and undergarments dumped carelessly on the floor marked the spot. He lifted the lid and flinched at the steepness of the dark shaft within. The square opening was just big enough to take him. Screwing up his courage, he put one leg through. A muffled roar of rage at close range made up his mind for him, and he tumbled through.

Then he was sliding down a stainless steel chute while an angry bellow echoed from above: "Come back and take your medicine, you defiler!" There was the splat of another microexplosion overhead, but the corkscrew turns of the chute kept any missile from reaching him.

He managed to get his pants on during the giddy ride down, but the friction burns he had sustained would make it uncomfortable for him to sit down for some days to come. He erupted through the bottom of the chute in a cascade of dirty laundry he had picked up along the way. A chambermaid wearing a starched veil with the building services monogram on it dropped a hamper she had been loading and gaped at him.

He ran barefoot across the cement floor of the utility room, past a long table where blue-smocked laundresses sat folding linen, and out a side door at ground level. Aziz was waiting outside, at the tiller of an electric service cart.

"Sorry, master," he said as Hamid-Jones climbed in beside him. "The engineer sobered up too quickly. One of the bartenders must have been watering the drinks."

Izzat was shouting at him from a balcony twenty flights above, a gnat-size figure waving a red speck. "I'll find out who you are, you serpent! I got a good look at you! And then your life will be mine to dispose of, by all custom and law!"

Too late, Hamid-Jones remembered the slipper he had left behind on the balcony. It was red leather, curl-toed and expensive, with his monogram and the label of a fashionable shop in the Triangular City. An aggrieved husband with the weight of the law behind him would have every right to demand store records.

But Izzat might have to stand in line for his revenge. If the application for a husband's warrant alerted the court investigators to a possible computer break-in, Hamid-Jones might face a death penalty for espionage first.

"Where are your slippers, master?" Aziz said. "What's that he's waving at us?"

Hamid-Jones slumped in his seat. Faces were starting to appear at the windows. "Never mind that, you misbegotten lump! Just get me out of here!"

There was time to go home to shower and change. The *issayida* Yordan gave them a big breakfast, frowning her disapproval of Hamid-Jones's red-eyed condition and the alcohol on Aziz's breath. When little Meryem tried to hang around, she shooed her away. One or two of the other boarders made jocular remarks about them being in the doghouse but desisted and confined themselves to shoveling food when they saw how glum Hamid-Jones was.

The call from the palace came about midmorning. Hamid-Jones was summoned to the Sultan's presence forthwith.

"This is it," Hamid-Jones told Aziz. "Here, you'd better get these gigachips to the Christian underground immediately. And you'd better get out of sight yourself. I'll hold out as long as I can, but I don't know how long I can avoid implicating you under torture."

"Master, master," Aziz chided him. "This is not Mars. The Sultan is an enlightened and benign ruler."

"Enlightened? Benign? When he's plotting to commit worldicide so that he can become the Caliph of Islam?"

Aziz had been shaken when Hamid-Jones told him about the computer simulation. Now he wore a sick grin as he said, "Don't jump to conclusions, master. You're no expert. Black hole physics and orbital mechanics aren't your game. Wait till the Christian Jihad's intelligence analysts have a chance to work on the material.''

"It's no use," Hamid-Jones groaned. "Why would the Sultan send for me? I haven't seen him in the six months since we arrived.''

"If you were going to be arrested for espionage, the palace wouldn't have sent for you. They'd have come to take you away in fetters.''

"They haven't gotten around to uncovering everything yet. If you ever return to Mars, tell Lalla that I died thinking of her.''

"Stay cool, master. Remember that Izzat isn't going to be in a hurry to admit taking classified material home against security regulations. He'd be in as much hot water as you. With luck it'll stay just another case brought by a silly little cuckold. The magistrate may be merciful and let you off with a hundred lashes. Offenders often survive that.''

"It'll all come out once a security investigation is started. Izzat's high up in this black hole project. Espionage'll be the first thing they'll suspect. They'll have an expert dust his computer for evidence of intrusion. And it won't be some little civil court investigator, either. Centauran intelligence is very thorough. I ought to know.''

"You're too pessimistic, master. It goes with having an overactive imagination. Wait till the boat leaks before you bail it, as the saying goes.''

"You're very reassuring," Hamid-Jones said sarcastically.

"Think nothing of it, master. It's a good servant's job to comfort his employer.''

Meryem was waiting to waylay him when he emerged from the house. She tagged along at his heels, keeping up with his long strides, till he gave in and noticed her.

"What are you doing, following me? Go home, before your mother misses you.''

She regarded him gravely. "Is it true they're going to flog you?''

"Have you been eavesdropping again? What have I told you about that?''

"I thought they threw stones at you. That's what they did to Mr. Alhabbal.'' She added thoughtfully, "He died.''

"You're too young to know about such things. Go home. I haven't time for you right now."

"Is Mrs. Awad prettier than your lady friend on Mars?"

Exasperated, he made a grab for her. "I'm going to take you home myself, even if it makes me late for my summons."

She skipped nimbly out of his reach. "I hope you don't die, ya Abdul," she piped after him before she disappeared into the crowd."

"I'm told you've been up to all sorts of mischief," the Sultan said coldly. "I wonder if you understand how much of a hornet's nest you've stirred up."

He gave Hamid-Jones a stare of bleak severity, his eyes like chips of stone. Piles of work surrounded him, and he could not have been too happy about being called away from it. He was dressed more regally than the last time Hamid-Jones had seen him, in a tall turban emblazoned with a star ruby, and a long pelisse of royal purple. There was only one secretary in the office with him this morning, a hard-faced military-looking man who'd switched off a monitor screen as soon as Hamid-Jones had entered the room.

Hamid-Jones swallowed the lump in his throat. "I'm sorry your Majesty had to be bothered by an unimportant matter like this."

"Don't toady to me!" the Sultan said sharply.

"I'm sorry, your Majesty."

"As it happens, the man you cuckolded *is* important to me. He's an essential cog in a vital project that is under my personal supervision." Thunderclouds gathered on the imperial brow. "Such men are to be kept happy. You, on the other hand, are a foreigner of no consequence who has broken the law. Mr. Awad's complaints can't be ignored, even if I were so inclined. Do you agree?"

"Yes, your Majesty," Hamid-Jones said miserably, bracing himself for whatever unpleasant medicine was coming next.

"Your life at this moment is not worth an infidel's foreskin. Awad doesn't know who you are—yet! But there is no way to keep it from him. In any case, the security office has been instructed to comply with any court order obtained by Mr. Awad for the release of information, up to and including the mug shot file for everyone on the Triangular City payroll with your general description. Mr. Awad is used to absorbing data at a high rate of speed, and he's very diligent. I'd give him a day or two to root you out, once he gets started.''

Hamid-Jones licked dry lips. ''If . . . if Awad hasn't named me, how did this come to your Majesty's attention?''

The Sultan didn't seem to regard the question as impertinent. He stroked his square beard and said, ''The shopkeeper where you bought those accursed slippers had the wit to stall Awad and inform the palace. Luckily he was on the security office's *baksheesh* distribution list. Luxury retailers, bank clerks, and such are under standing instructions to report potential problems in the Triangular City—but usually it's a matter of some official on a spending spree, or making the kind of large unexplained withdrawals that signal trouble.''

So the matter *was* in the hands of the security *wallahs*. Hamid-Jones's hopes sank another foot or two.

''There are those of my advisors who are howling for your head,'' the Sultan went on, looking at Hamid-Jones as if he were a piece of meat that had gone bad. ''Give him to Awad, they say; it's the simplest way of disposing of a security problem. And to tell you the truth, *ya* Abdul, I'm tempted to throw you to the dogs, as they suggest.'' He shot a mollifying glance at the stiff-faced aide, who was putting a bunch of microfiles back in their covers and stacking them with the labels turned out of sight. ''Though there's no telling where things might end up if they are allowed to proceed independently, eh, *ya* Abdul?''

Hamid-Jones's hopes slid further. He had the distinct impression that the Sultan suspected everything. Suspected everything and didn't care. He groaned inwardly. That could only mean that the matter was settled in the Sultan's mind, that his fate was sealed.

The Sultan scratched at an ear. ''Well, there's no way to keep you out of harm's way here in the Kingdom of the Triple Suns. Awad is entitled to his vengeance. We can't deprive him of that, can we?''

''I'm sorry, your Highness,'' Hamid-Jones said. He tried to be philosophical about his fate. He hoped it wouldn't be stones. He hated the idea of stones. He would much rather have Awad saw at his throat with a rusty knife.

''No, there's only one way to get you out of harm's way.

You've got to leave the system entirely. It's back to Mars for you.''

"I beg your pardon, your Highness?''

The Sultan was wearing a satisfied smile. He rubbed his hands together and said, "Too bad, young man. You only arrived here six months ago, and now it's another two years out of your life. But it can't be helped.''

A death sentence was waiting for him on Mars, too, but at least it was not imminent. Hamid-Jones stammered his thanks.

The Sultan waved a hand in dismissal. "It's a way for me to solve two problems at the same time. At this stage I can use someone with a broad knowledge of Mars who is able to act at his own discretion, without slavishly following out-of-date instructions from Alpha Centauri. There's no way to know what's been happening on Mars for the last four and a third years, and four and a third years from now, there'll *still* be that gap. In the meantime, certain political elements of my long-range planning may be coming to fruition.''

"Your . . . your Majesty knows that my life is forfeit on Mars. If I'm to move around freely—''

"Oh, that! You'll just have to take your chances, won't you? After twelve years, the heat may be off. And you'll be a younger man than anyone is looking for. You'll only have aged a bit more than four years by the time you get back—eight years younger than you ought to be.''

"What . . . what is it your Majesty wants me to do?''

"Help the Ambassador with the political process. The poor man's embassy is stuffed with Colonel Ish-Shamaal's agents— most of whom have the quaint idea that he doesn't know who they are. But Colonel Ish-Shamaal has his limits. He's very good at financing terrorists and supplying bombs and military ordnance and getting one group of *mujahidin* to cut the throats of another group, and all that. But now the time has come to deal with the respectable elements who'll have to be reconciled to an al-Sharq victory. The sort of people who always run things under any regime. We'll need their support if al-Sharq is to consolidate his power. It's one thing to win—quite another to govern. They'll have to be reassured—persuaded that al-Sharq is not a wild man, and that they can do business with him. As one of al-Sharq's former freedom fighters, you're uniquely qualified for the job.''

Oh, the Sultan was good, all right, Hamid-Jones had to admit.

Sincere, forceful—without the slightest hint of black holes, planetary billiards, the destruction of Mars waiting in the wings in case his political machinations didn't work out.

Hamid-Jones could do nothing but go along with the fiction. Perhaps he could do something when he got to the scene, he thought. Even warn the false Emir's dreadful regime, if it came to that! In any case, he was now committed—somehow he had become a double agent for the Sultan and the Christian Jihad.

He looked the Sultan forthrightly in the eye. "I'll do my best, your Majesty," he said. "When do you want me to leave?"

"Tonight," the Sultan said without a flicker. "There's a starship casting off at midnight."

"I'll keep your things for you, *ya* Abdul," Mrs. Yordan said, biting her lip. "I'll lock them up in the storeroom, and they'll be waiting for you when you get back."

"That's not necessary, *ya sayyidati*," Hamid-Jones protested. "Just sell them and keep the proceeds. It would be twelve years before I returned at the earliest—if I return at all. Who knows what Allah's plans for any of us are? Life must go on."

"I'll keep them," the *is-sayida* said firmly. "We'll all miss you, *ya* Abdul."

Impulsively, she raised herself on tiptoe and kissed him on the cheek. Hamid-Jones was so flustered, he didn't know what to say. The *nisrani*, he told himself, had different customs.

"I think Meryem's going to miss you most of all," Yaqub Yordan laughed. "She won't have anyone to moon over."

"Oh, Father!" Meryem said, making a face.

"I'll miss you, too, *ya* Meryem," Hamid-Jones said gravely, turning to the little girl. "You're going to grow up while I'm gone—into a fine lady like your mother. Obey your parents, and stop this wild running around in the streets. That's for little children. And you're not a little child anymore. On Mars you'd be almost old enough to get married."

Abruptly she colored and fled from the room.

"She'll get over it," her mother said with a slight frown. "She's been acting very strange today."

Yaqub Yordan clapped Aziz on the shoulder in the overfamiliar way that *nisrani* men had. "We'll miss you, too, you old so-and-so. Stick close to Abdul and keep him out of trouble."

Aziz winced. "The master's not going away because of any

trouble," he said, trying to match Yaqub's hearty smile. "He's been given an important assignment by the Sultan himself."

"Of course," Roxane said. "I always knew he'd get recognition someday."

"When do you leave?" Yaqub asked.

"The starship leaves orbit at midnight tonight," Hamid-Jones said. "I've got to be on the last shuttle—that's right after sunset prayers."

"I'll make you an early dinner," Roxane said. "It'll be ready about noon. Your favorite—roast lamb, with eggplant and stuffed vine leaves."

"And the Prophet won't mind a farewell toast," Yaqub said. "I've got a bottle of wine I've been saving."

"No, no, that's very kind, but I've got to pack. And then I've got to go back to the Triangular City to pick up my passport and other travel documents," Hamid-Jones said.

"And I've got to say good-bye to Zubeideh and the children," Aziz said. He seemed on the verge of tears.

"Of course," Yaqub said. He patted Aziz awkwardly on the shoulder.

As soon as the landlord and his wife left the room, Aziz turned to Hamid-Jones with a tragic expression on his face. "It's too much to bear, master," he wailed. "To be separated from my treasure for twelve years, maybe longer! A hot-blooded woman like that doesn't wait around very long, let me tell you! There'll be plenty of parasites hanging around, hoping to get their hands on her property. And the children will be all grown up when I get back—if I ever get back! That little boy I took to mosque school only a few weeks ago will have come of age as a young gentleman, without my guidance!"

"All the more fortunate for him," Hamid-Jones said roughly, out of habit, but his heart wasn't in it.

"Even if she waits for me, she'd be twelve years older," Aziz said despairingly. "I'd have gained only about five years. It's true that I'm seven years older than her at present, and we'd be matched in age, but a man should be older than his wife, don't you think? How else is he to have authority over her? Oh, my darling Zubeideh! My rose, my gem! How can I leave you?"

"You don't have to go if you don't want to, you know," Hamid-Jones said. "The Sultan said nothing about you. Why don't you stay behind?"

"What, and leave you to face danger alone? What would Allah say to me on the Day of Decision? Aziz, he'd say, you have the liver of a chicken. Paradise is not for you!"

"I insist. I won't tear you away from your Zubeideh."

Aziz began to backtrack. "On the other hand, what's twelve years out of a lifetime? A mere ten percent. The *zakat* of Allah. True love can survive a separation. Absence lends spice to the reunion, as the saying goes."

"You have business of your own on Mars, don't you?"

"What, me? My only business is to serve you, master." Aziz was all righteous indignation. He brightened. "Of course a clever man can always turn a profit on an interstellar trip. Doesn't the Prophet tell us to make profits by mutual trade? Centauran recreational chips fetch a high price on Mars. They're easily smuggled past customs in personal electronics items."

"Are you insane? There's enough danger in getting *ourselves* past customs."

Aziz was aghast at the suggestion. "What do you take me for? I'd use a commission mule. There are always a few professional mules aboard a starship, and on a long voyage there's time for two mutually interested parties to seek each other out and make certain of each other. The usual commission's forty percent, but the mule takes all the risk and their professional ethics prevents them from betraying you if they're caught."

"I forbid it."

Aziz sighed. "As you wish, master. I'd rather spend as much as possible of my last day with Zubeideh, anyhow."

"You'd better go, then. I'll finish the packing. Give me a drop of your blood before you go. I'll pick up a passport for you in the Triangular City. Colonel Ish-Shamaal has drawers full of them—all it needs is your DNA sample, and they can run it through in about five minutes. Your holo's already on file." He smiled sourly. "Sometimes it helps to know the right people."

It was late afternoon by the time Hamid-Jones returned from the Triangular City. His new passport described him as a junior attaché, assigned to the Centauran embassy for a five-year tour. Aziz was going back as a Martian—his elongated physique didn't fit well with a Centauran identity and might have encouraged unwelcome scrutiny at the port of entry, even though there were plenty of Centauran citizens who had grown up in Mars-strength gravity on the smaller planets of the triple-star system. Colonel Ish-Shamaal was helpful and affable, and before Hamid-Jones departed he took him aside and proposed that, even though he was traveling to the Sol system under Foreign Office auspices, he work undercover for the clandestine department as well. "Nothing operational for now," the colonel had assured him. "Just keep your eyes and ears open around those diplomatic stuffed monkey jackets, that's all. I need a reliable man in place." Hamid-Jones agreed readily. He didn't see that it much mattered if he upscaled himself from double agent to triple agent.

The house was cool and silent when he entered through the parlor. The blinds had been drawn against the afternoon sun, and he walked through dimness toward the stairs. The other boarders were out, and Yaqub would be somewhere around back, doing the outside maintenance work at this hour. Hamid-Jones heard faint noises from the kitchen that indicated that Roxane was making preparations for supper.

He crossed the upstairs bridge to his quarters and went into his bedroom. A figure with its back to him was leaning over the bed.

"Aziz, is that you? What are you doing back so early? I'd have thought you'd want to squeeze every minute you could with—"

Aziz snapped around quickly, a dagger in his hand. There was an odd expression on his face. When he saw that it was Hamid-Jones, the coiled tenseness of his body relaxed, and his face regained its usual lines of craven duplicity.

"Master, finished your errands so soon?"

"What's that you've got there?"

Aziz tossed the dagger back on the bed with the other two objects. A flat cake sent an odor of spice into the room. Lying next to it was a sheet of parchment.

"No cardamom," Aziz said. "It's just a love letter this time."

Hamid-Jones picked up the parchment and read:

> *Remember, Death is at your shoulder,*
> *Though he may not press his claim.*
> *Keep your covenant with the Cold One,*
> *For he eats distance as he eats lives;*
> *But is lenient to those who serve.*

"The Assassins?" Hamid-Jones said in disgust. "Again?"

"It's nothing to worry about, master," Aziz said. "They've put you on probation. It's just their reminder of whose side you're supposed to be on."

CHAPTER 7

The Emir's head was on every street corner, mounted on a holopedestal and twice as large as life. A golden alms basin was in front of it, into which hurrying pedestrians dropped coins as they passed. A flashing sign on the plinth proclaimed the *"Emir's Feast Day Fund."* Last week it had been the *"Ring Around Mars Fund,"* the week before, the *"Widows and Orphans Fund."* It was all in addition to the regular *zakat* and the other proliferating taxes. The Emir's treasury was mad to raise money by any means possible, or so it seemed.

"Hey there, brother, what's your hurry?"

Hamid-Jones stopped in his tracks. The challenger was a man in the shoddy gray uniform of the God's Loan police, a large shambling brute with a low forehead and loose lips.

"What's the trouble, officer?" Hamid-Jones said, his belly turning cold. These scurvy cops, a new development since he'd left Mars, had the power to take people in for questioning, and though his Centauran identification had held up so far, Hamid-Jones didn't care to push his luck.

"Funny how it's always you rich swells who walk by the collection bowl without tossing in a few dirhens. The ordinary stiffs always cough up. Whassamatter, you too good to contribute your fair share?"

He stared insolently at Hamid-Jones's tailored cloak with its silver trim, part of the wardrobe provided by the embassy. It was the cloak that had drawn his attention. Native Martians

107

tended to look shabby these days, after twelve years of Bobo's unbridled rule.

"I'm sorry, I must have had my mind on something else. I wasn't paying attention." Hamid-Jones fumbled at the cloak's fastenings to get at his purse.

"Yeah, yeah, and that's why you was coming out of a side street," the alms cop said sarcastically. "You wasn't walking the long way round to get out of passing all the Golden Wells on the main drag."

The God's Loan police were drawn from the lowest elements in society, and they enjoyed humiliating their betters. But as Hamid-Jones opened his cloak, exposing the Centauran haberdashery underneath, the cop checked himself and said reluctantly, "Oh, you're a foreigner. I guess you don't know any better."

"That's all right, I'll be glad to contribute," Hamid-Jones said with false cheer. He dropped a five-dinar note into the well. "Happy *Iid al Fitr!*"

The cop watched narrowly as Hamid-Jones walked away. But his attention soon returned to the well—the *puits d'or*, orwell, as Moroccan Arabs called it; the name had caught on. The little vignette had not been lost on other passersby; more of them were slowing down to toss money in the bowl. The oversize head projected at the top of the pedestal followed each approaching donor with a steely programmed gaze, smiling at the hefty contributions and intimidating the cheapskates with a scowl.

Hamid-Jones had walked barely half a block when he encountered a Gigabaksheesh lottery booth. He felt safe in bypassing that one; there was a willing crowd surrounding it, shoving their hard-earned dinars at the attendant. That was another symptom of deteriorating conditions on Mars—people without hope are more likely to buy lottery tickets than those who are better fixed.

Where was all the money going? Hamid-Jones had been on Mars long enough to be appalled at the ruinous extravagance of Bobo and the Chamberlain—the new orbital palace that Bobo rarely used, the insane public spectacles and feast days that drained the treasury every time Bobo became bored, the impractical public works projects that were launched on a whim and then abandoned when the fanfare died down.

Hamid-Jones involuntarily lifted his eyes to the rock ceiling of the thoroughfare. The Ring Around Mars was a good example. It had somehow come to Bobo's attention that Saturn's rings attracted droves of tourists and honeymooners from all over the system, so he had decided that Mars should have rings, too. The project was disastrously expensive, but Bobo kept insisting that it would "pay for itself in new revenues." He went on repeating the same platitude despite all evidence to the contrary. So ice hauled from Saturn, badly needed by irrigation projects, was diverted to the Ring extravaganza and locked in orbit. On a clear night, if you strained your eyes, you could see the beginning of a tenuous hairline in the sky, but it would never amount to anything.

And then there was the cost of the Emir's election campaign. It had been going on for eight years now, ever since a date had been fixed for the next Caliphate Congress. The Chamberlain was ingenious in soaking the populace for "contributions." He started with weekly auctions of personal memorabilia from the palace—a pair of shoes that had been worn by the Emir himself, bottles of the Emir's bathwater, a chair that the Emir had sat in. And woe to the unenthusiastic bidder! The bottles of bathwater started at a thousand dinars each. It was a calamity to be invited to the auctions—but no excuses for nonattendance were accepted. To judge by the number of items sold, the Emir sat down in a new chair every five minutes and took a hundred baths a day. But the auctions were only the beginning. Rich businessmen who were slow to contribute to the campaign fund, or whose contributions fell short of what was expected, found themselves denounced for treason by some anonymous informer. They were then arrested and all their property confiscated. This had a salutary effect on slackers. There was a rush to contribute. But this did the unfortunate donors no good—it only got them on the list of those to be squeezed, including those who hadn't been thought wealthy enough to be put there before.

Hamid-Jones's eyes fell on one of the Emir's election posters, fixed to a shopfront. Bobo's crafty, puffy face, a perfect match for the old Emir, turned to follow the onlooker, no matter what the angle. Glowing script reminded all and sundry that campaign contributions were tax deductible. This too was a double bind for those trying to buy off future trouble from the *zakat* collectors and the professional informers; it only put them on the contributors' list, to be squeezed dry later.

"Hey brother, have pity on the unfortunate," said a voice at waist level. "How's about sparing a few dirhens for a fellow what's down on his luck?"

Hamid-Jones looked down and saw a legless beggar sitting on a little electric roller platform. The man looked fairly able-bodied otherwise.

He reached for his purse. "Why don't you grow yourself a new pair of legs?" he said sternly. "Surely you can scrape up the nominal fee for one of the charity clinics."

"I'm working on it, brother, I'm working on it. But it's hard to get a few dinars ahead, with the tax and all."

"Tax? What are you talking about? People like you are supposed to be beneficiaries of the *zakat*, not contributors."

The beggar's eyes roved over the Centauran cut of Hamid-Jones's shirt and compared it with his Martian accent. "You must have been away a long time, brother," he mumbled. "Just give me my money and I'll be on my way."

Hamid-Jones dropped a twenty dinar note into the beggar's cup, which buzzed and lit up at the amount. "There you are," he said with a rush of pity. "That ought to get you into the clinic."

"What about the tax? That's another fifty percent."

"You want me to pay a tax on the handout I just gave you?"

"You don't expect *me* to pay it, do you? Have a heart, brother!"

"Look, why do you have to turn in a tax at all? There can't be anyone keeping tabs on people like you."

Pure terror showed in the panhandler's eyes. His gaze darted in all directions to see if anyone had been close enough to hear. "Brother, you *have* been away, haven't you?" he said in a strained voice. He took a little memocalc from his rags and, holding it up ostentatiously for the benefit of anyone who might be passing, he punched in a figure. "Never mind, I'll pay it myself," he said.

He gave Hamid-Jones a look somewhere between fright and reproach, and with an electric hum rolled quickly out of sight.

Hamid-Jones walked on. There was no Golden Well at the next street corner. Instead, there was an object lesson: six dangling bodies hung from portable aluminum gibbets, their faces black and rotting under a clear plastic coating that kept the smell in. A hortatory poster stretched over the gibbets said: *"Remember, tax evasion is treason."*

Hamid-Jones gave the bodies an unintimidated glance as he passed by. After checking to make sure that the God's Loan cop posted at the next corner was facing the other way, he turned down the first side street he came to.

It wouldn't do to be late for the meeting. Birds as nervous as these were might fly away.

"The situation is now impossible," the first conspirator said. "Even as recently as a year ago it was possible for a prudent man to lie low, take his losses, pay lip service to the Emir, and survive. Survive as a pauper, perhaps, but stay alive. Now, with the best will in the world, even a pauper's life is worth nothing if he's thought to have a few dinars squirreled away."

He had no name. The three frightened men had been introduced only as "Mr. Yaa'," "Mr. Waaw," and "Mr. Zaay." The go-between hadn't given Hamid-Jones's assumed name, either. He had been introduced only as "our friend from abroad."

The second conspirator, Mr. Waaw, nodded agreement. He was a cadaverous individual who kept his face muffled as much as possible in the trailing end of his headcloth. "They took away poor Badri last night," he said. "In the last few months they stripped him of his villa in Xanthe, his town house in Tharsis, his businesses, his bank accounts and stock holdings, and even his wife's bride money, which strictly speaking didn't belong to him. They were reduced to living in poverty with an in-law, when Badri thought he'd remove any remaining suspicion that he was hiding assets by voluntarily giving up one last safe-deposit box in a bank in Boreosyrtis that the assessors had somehow missed. It had exactly the opposite effect. It whetted their appetites. They accused him of having more safe-deposit boxes secreted elsewhere, and they refused to believe him when he said he didn't." He shuddered. "Now he's strapped to a surgical table somewhere while the eunuchs question him."

The third member of the alphabet, Mr. Zaay, uttered a low growl. "And what about Farid? He thought he'd curry favor by disinheriting his wife and children and making the Emir his heir. All that got him was to be executed on some trumped-up charge so that all his property could be confiscated in one swoop instead of piecemeal. Worse still, the damned fool gave the eunuch bloodsucker ideas. Now a law's been passed making the Emir *everyone*'s heir. He can pick us off at his leisure.''

''All of Mars will be plucked clean before he gets to the end of his list,'' Mr. Yaa' said with a scowl. ''Next month they're raising the intercourse tax.''

Hamid-Jones heard them out patiently. They had a lot to get off their chests, and for soft-living businessmen and unadventurous pillars of their communities, they'd shown a lot of courage in coming here to meet him.

The back room of the wholesale warehouse was gloomy. Heavy drapes over the barred windows trapped stray light. Net bags of dried truffles hung from the rafters like shrunken heads, and cases of imported goods were stacked against the walls to ceiling height. The go-between waited patiently in the shadows. He was a sober-faced, intelligent man in his thirties—someone's tool, a throwaway. Hamid-Jones wondered who he really worked for. Someone very rich and powerful, to whose advantage it was to put together these three staid burghers and the young fellow from the Centauran embassy who had been sounding out key businessmen and other paragons and dropping a discreet bribe here and there. Whoever he was, he would be insulated by two or three layers of cutouts in case something blew up in everyone's face. People like him never took the rap.

''The eunuchs form an insulating wall around the Emir,'' Mr. Waaw elaborated. ''Sensible men can't get near him anymore. Al-Sharq's propaganda claims that the Emir's actually a spin-off, made from one of the spare heads, and I believe it. The original Emir was greedy, but he took care not to kill the goose that lays the golden eggs. He gave us breathing space. But not this inexperienced reproduction of him.''

''The eunuchs have gotten completely out of hand,'' Mr. Zaay said tightly. ''They have no sense of restraint. This Ismail creature's built himself new palaces all over Mars, and his juniors are feathering their own nests as well.''

Hamid-Jones commiserated with them at length. ''Mars can't go on this way any longer,'' he said at last. ''The deficit's twice the size of the entire planet's net worth. But your suffering hasn't gone unnoticed. I represent a Certain Personage who's willing to help bail you out—after there's a change of leadership and a return to the principles of sound government.''

He didn't have to specify who the Certain Personage was. His

Centauran dress told the story. The three conspirators looked at one another. "Excuse us," Mr. Yaa' said. The three of them withdrew to a corner of the warehouse and whispered among themselves. The whispers rose and fell, like the hissing of snakes having a spat. Then they all came to an agreement and approached Hamid-Jones once more.

"This . . . change of leadership you referred to," Waaw said, frowning. "You're referring, I take it, to al-Sharq."

Hamid-Jones shrugged. "Who else is there? He has the organization, a broad base of popular support, and he's forged alliances with the most important of the other *fedayeen* groups— who otherwise might be expected to make trouble for a victor. Moreover, he has some legitimate claim to the throne—he's of royal blood, after all—and so claims the loyalty of the desert tribes."

Waaw nodded reluctantly. "But is he . . . reliable?" he said with a cough.

"If you're asking if he'll respect private property, I can assure you that the answer is yes. Al-Sharq's a thoroughgoing moderate, not a wild-eyed zealot like some of the other *fedayeen* leaders. He's interested in governing, not tearing things apart. That's why the Legitimists are for him. They don't want an extremist in the saddle—they want a return to public order, same as you."

"But can he win, that's the question?" Mr. Yaa' broke in. "We're staking everything on this gamble. If he loses, and takes his supporters down with him . . ."

"Now's not the time for cold feet," Zaay reprimanded him. "We agreed, remember?" He turned to Hamid-Jones. "You personally fought with the Shining, we were told?"

"Yes, I did," Hamid-Jones confirmed. "He's well-equipped, he has the fighting tribes ready to rally behind his banner, and I'm in a position to tell you that he's being lavishly supplied for a final push." He looked at each one of them in turn. "You said you were worried about what would happen to his supporters if he loses. Maybe you'd better ask yourselves what happens if he wins."

That decided the fence-sitters. "All right," Mr. Waaw said with a nervous glance at his coconspirators. "You can tell your friends that we're in."

The go-between came out of the shadows to interrupt. "My telltale registers a police patrol two blocks away and coming closer. We've been here too long. Leave one at a time, at least two or three minutes apart.''

Hamid-Jones was the last to go, and he might have cut it too fine. He was only halfway down the back alley, with barely enough time to hide behind some bales of nylon, when the patrol turned the corner and stomped toward the warehouse as much as Martian gravity allowed one to stomp. There were three of them—a three-striper in a uniform keffia and two flatfoots in hard hats, all carrying assault rifles.

The warehouse did not appear to be their specific destination; as they approached, the sarge consulted a little hand-held squawker and made the other two stop. He stuck a cone-shaped charge to the door, stepped back, and when the door blew, all three rushed inside.

Hamid-Jones took the opportunity to slip around the corner. He joined the crowds on the main drag and worked his way obliquely out of the neighborhood.

So one of the three alphabet men had planted a short-range fink somewhere in the warehouse! Which of them could it have been? Or could it have been the go-between?

He resolved to find out. It looked like a case for the Assassins. If only someone from the underground would get in touch with him.

"Why haven't they contacted us?" Hamid-Jones fumed. "We've been on Mars over a month."

"Patience, master," Aziz said. "They're very cautious men."

"Patience go to the great satan! With every day that passes, that black hole out on the fringes of the Solar system comes closer to being created. Perhaps it's being made right now, this instant!"

"Relax, master. The underground here knows all about it. Your information was encoded and piggybacked on Centauran commercial message traffic before we left. The organization here on Mars has had a year to look into it. They'll contact you in their own good time."

"And in the meantime," Hamid-Jones said bitterly. "I'm wasting my time playing Oliver for the Sultan."

"Don't take it so hard, master. You're doing useful work. If the Sultan can be convinced that an al-Sharq coup will be successful, the black hole may never be used."

"Al-Sharq had better make his big move soon. The Caliphate Congress is less than a half year away. Time's running out."

"There are rumors of a pitched battle in the desert. They say that a huge Emirate force was wiped out somewhere to the north, in Arcadia. Al-Sharq's on the move. People here in Tharsis are waiting to see which way the wind blows. If they're given a clear enough sign, there could be a general uprising. And that would settle the matter."

"Don't count on it. If that bunch I met with last night is any sample, the sky would have to split and the sun fold up, as foretold in the Koran, before the people rise."

Aziz looked at him curiously. "And yet that's exactly what you say may happen, in a manner of speaking, isn't it, master?"

"You show unexpected facets, *ya* Aziz. I didn't know you were a Koranic scholar."

"A little piety never hurts—in the right quarters," Aziz said. He composed his expression to offer a quote. " 'When the sun folds up, and the stars darken, and the mountains move . . .' From the eighty-first surah, master. It's in the eighty-second that the sky splits and the stars scatter."

"That's enough. The Prophet's words weren't meant to issue from the mouth of a scoundrel like you. What have you found out for me regarding those matters we discussed?"

"The Royal Stables? I've made the acquaintance of a number of the juniors who frequent a certain coffee shop—the younger element who weren't there when we left Mars twelve years ago and wouldn't recognize me in any case—and I've come up with enough gossip to make my head spin. Your old rival Rashid is still in charge—"

"He was never my rival."

"Just as you say. At any rate, he must have shown a great talent for licking boots, because they've combined the Palace and Stables cloning departments and put Rashid in charge of the whole shooting match. He's become a great favorite of the Chamberlain."

"I didn't think Rashid had it in him to get so far."

"He and the Chamberlain understand one another. They both know how to cater to that patchwork abortion who now calls himself the Emir. Rashid's heading up a project to create head-less clones that won't be a threat to his Jigsaw Majesty. He's very sensitive about his own origins, and he's afraid the eunuch will replace him someday. Still, he can't do without clones for medical repairs and the next rejuvenation, so he's planning to replace them with the headless variety whenever Rashid succeeds. There's to be a general slaughter of the clones then.''

"Acephalous clones can't survive,'' Hamid-Jones said. "There isn't enough brainstem to sustain the vital functions. The old Emir once had the same idea. Everyone must have forgotten about it.''

"They think they can keep the bodies going with a mediating computer hooked to the nervous system. No head—just a little box the size of a domino sitting on top of the spinal cord. Rashid's gotten as far as headless chickens so far. He's tried it with dogs and primates, but it hasn't worked.''

"And it never will,'' Hamid-Jones said firmly. "It's Rashid who'll find himself without a head when Bobo realizes that.''

"Don't be so sure of that, master. The eunuch's been successful in stringing Bobo along so far. And even if Rashid succeeds, he'd find some way of keeping a few head clones in reserve, just in case Bobo becomes unmanageable.''

"What else have you found out for me? On that other matter.''

Aziz became uncomfortable. "Now master—''

"Out with it! Don't keep anything from me. I'm strong enough to bear anything.''

"Well, master,'' Aziz said, casting down his eyes, "soon after we left Mars, that strutting dandy Thamir who took out a contract on you had his way with the Lalla woman.''

"I knew it!'' Hamid-Jones cried in anguish. "The scoundrel!''

"And after he grew tired of her, he abandoned her . . .''

"Oh, my poor Lalla!''

"Look at the bright side, master. You're off the Assassins' hit list. The Assassins gave Thamir a partial refund. The news of your readjusted status still hadn't reached Alpha Centauri by the time we left, but now that you're back on Mars, you're home free.''

"I don't care about all that. What about Lalla?''

"Never fear, master. She's a very practical woman. She landed on her feet right away. She had a whole string of protectors, one after another. She's a very wealthy woman now. She got rid of Murad and that whole crew of eunuchs so as to give herself a free hand. She keeps one or two tame eunuchs around for show, but they know where their bread and butter comes from. I understand Murad had his genitalia recloned, and he's gone out of the business.''

"Oh, how my poor darling must have suffered. I don't believe anything you say.''

"Please, master, don't carry on so. She's doing all right for herself. In fact she has a steady relationship with a well-to-do protector now. She has him wrapped around her little finger.''

"Who? Who is the swine?''

Aziz became evasive again. "An old admirer.''

"Out with it!''

"It's Rashid.''

Hamid-Jones turned purple. "Oh, the ungrateful blackguard! To think that I stuck my neck out to get him released by the Department of Rectitude—that I even paid to have his eye re-grown!''

"Don't take it so hard, master. It's all water under the bridge.''

"I must go see her!''

"No, master, don't do anything rash! Nobody's supposed to know that you're on Mars!''

"Out of my way!''

"Master, think! You've hardly aged, and it's been twelve years. It'll be a dead giveaway.''

Hamid-Jones glowered dangerously. "Are you suggesting that Lalla would betray me?''

"At least let me put a little gray in your beard.''

Hamid-Jones gave the bellow of a wounded animal. Aziz quickly backed off. "All right, master, but remember, it isn't just your own skin anymore that you're risking.''

"I'm foolish to see you, *ya* Abdul,'' she said coyly. "I should send you away.''

"Don't do that, Little Candy,'' he begged, pressing her plump little hand to his lips. "Let me feast my eyes on your beauty.''

There was more of her beauty to feast on than there had been twelve years before. In fact, even Hamid-Jones could see that she had grown a bit tubby—pigeon-breasted, a neutral observer might have said. Makeup could not quite conceal the crow's-feet at the corners of her eyes; she was biologically older than he was now. But to Hamid-Jones, the soft flesh that bulged at her waistline and spilled in creamy profusion over the top of her gown was still enticing, the greedy little pouter lips still a temptation.

"You haven't changed at all," she said with a giggle, and Hamid-Jones could see that she thought she hadn't, either. "Except for the beard."

He had been too impatient to be off to let Aziz color his beard, but in the end he had allowed himself to be prevailed on to at least comb the beard out and to change out of his Centauranstyle clothes. There had been no problem about getting in to see Lalla. The new eunuch who had answered the door had smirked and simpered, and ushered him right upstairs, as if gentlemen callers were an ordinary occurrence. Lalla had let out a little shriek when she had recognized him, but she had quickly recovered and had been receptive. Extremely receptive, in fact.

"I didn't know what had happened to you after that awful time—I didn't think I'd ever see you again," she said breathily.

"I . . . I lived in the desert for a while."

"Oh," she said without curiosity.

Hamid-Jones was happy to leave it there. It had been a long time since he had become a wanted man. Perhaps Lalla thought that since he was still alive and walking around a free man, it had all somehow blown over.

"Forget the past," he said, forgiving her for blowing the whistle on him. They had already been caught by Murad, he told himself reasonably; a girl had to protect herself. "All that matters is that we're together again, and that my heart aches with love for you."

"Oh, ya Abdul!" she said, breathing faster. She allowed him to kiss her arm up to the elbow, pulling back the wide sleeve of her gown to assist him.

There was no screen of tassels this time, no miniature Cerberus to come between them. When he had to take a breather after Lalla coquettishly stopped him from proceeding any further up her arm, he looked around for the little beast and was relieved to find that he was nowhere in sight. How long did two-headed toys like that live, anyway? He tried to gain a point with Lalla by expressing concern.

"Oh, I had to get rid of him," she said with no apparent distress. "He was getting to be a terrible nuisance, always in the way. I only keep cage birds now. See?"

She stretched out the bared arm and lifted the slipcover on

what turned out to be a large cylindrical cage on a floor stand. A small brownish bird immediately began to sing with heart-breaking sweetness, meanwhile flashing on and off like a fifty-watt lightbulb.

"A lightingale!" he choked.

"Isn't it marvelous? It sings me to sleep every night, and I don't need a night-light, either."

The bird, with its mixed nightingale and firefly genes, was a Palace prerogative. It could only have come from one place—the Royal Stables cloning department. Rashid!

"These are not easy to come by," he said, trying to hide his anger.

"Everything's easy when you have influential friends," she said smugly. She noticed his frown. "Why, *ya* Abdul, is something wrong?"

"No," he growled.

"I know what the trouble is. You're embarrassed because you didn't bring me a little gift. Never mind, you can bring me something next time."

"Next time? Is there going to be a next time? Won't your protector object?"

"How can you be so cruel?" She began to weep. She stopped long enough to say, "I'm entitled to a little life of my own, aren't I? You can come sometime in the afternoon. I can send word when."

"Afternoon, eh?" Hamid-Jones said, smoldering. "Like to-day? Is that why your eunuch was smirking when he showed me up here? Because you reserve your afternoons for come who may?"

The weeping grew louder. "Oh, *ya* Abdul! Why must you be so cold and unfeeling. Can't you show a little pity for a poor girl who's alone in the world and must make her own way? You have no right to be so merciless! You're the one who's responsible for my present position. You led me on when I was helpless and confused—took advantage of my feelings—and then you ran away! Where were you all those years when I needed you? How can you blame me?"

Hamid-Jones's smoldering temper fizzled out, to be replaced by guilt. "I'm sorry, Little Candy," he said awkwardly. "I'm a brute."

Then she was in his arms, and they were kissing passionately.

She reached out with one arm to pull down the lightingale's cage cover, and the singing stopped.

The gown was tight as a sausage casing. Peeling it off her was a difficult chore; she wriggled and made little sounds of protest. "How can I resist you?" she sighed. "You're strong, and I'm only a helpless woman." But somehow all the wriggling seemed to work toward the goal of helping to shuck her out of her clothing, and when at the last he had trouble with a fastening, she undid it for him. Then, when his trembling fingers were slow at divesting him of his own garments, she whisked off his djellaba as deftly as she had removed the bird cage cover.

"Oh, Little Sugarplum!" he groaned, daring to use the sobriquet for the first time.

A half-hour later, as drained and hollow as an eggshell, he raised himself on one elbow to watch her at her dressing table. She was brushing and teasing her hair back into shape, restoring it from the ruin their tangled strivings had made of it. With each stroke of the brush, her pale opulent flesh rippled. Hamid-Jones found he was not as depleted as he had thought.

"Come back here, Little Candy," he said lazily.

"*Mumtaz*, what a tiger!" she said. But she went on brushing her hair.

"Come on, *ya* sweet one. Don't torture me," he pleaded.

"That was enough for today," she said complacently. "It's getting late. You must get dressed and leave. Besides, you'll muss my hair again."

"To the great satan with your hair! I'm burning up!"

That was not strictly true. The fact was that Hamid-Jones was not as ardent as he pretended to be. At best, what he was feeling was the uncomplicated appetites of a young and healthy body. But the encounter had left him with a sour taste and an unaccountable sense of depression. What should have been the realization of his heart's desire had been somehow flat, mechanical. Lalla had been adequately responsive, but he had felt he didn't have her full attention—as if she were ticking off the minutes, rationing her time. He blamed himself. There had to be some flaw in him—the coldness of feeling that she had accused him of. Still, for the moment, the automatic stirrings of his flesh were sufficient to conceal his emptiness and insincerity from her, and he went on protesting as a matter of form.

"Please don't be difficult, *ya* Abdul," she said, a little crossly.

"You can't stay here now. You can come back tomorrow afternoon if you like." She put on a wrapper, hiding herself from view.

Grumbling for the sake of appearances, he put on his clothes. He was just looking around for a shoe when a remembered and despised voice rang out downstairs.

"Hi, it's me, Little Sugarplum! The Chamberlain let me off early!"

"Now look what you've done!" Lalla hissed. "It's Rashid. Quick, get that shoe on. I'll think of something to tell him."

There was some kind of altercation on the stairs. "Get out of my way, you grinning idiot. What do you mean, madame is indisposed?"

A moment later, Rashid barged into the room. When he saw Hamid-Jones, his face turned the color of corned beef. His sandy mustache twitched.

"So this is how you live up to all your sweet talk!" he accused a defiant Lalla. "Making a fool of me behind my back again!"

He turned in a rage to confront Hamid-Jones. Anger suddenly gave way to puzzlement as he peered more closely into Hamid-Jones's face. He hesitated. "I say, *ya* Abdul, is that you?" he blurted.

Hamid-Jones took a step backward and tripped over his shoelace. He threw his headcloth across his face and fled. Upstairs, Lalla had begun to gabble shrilly at Rashid.

The underground caught up with him two days later. He was walking down a crowded street, on his way back to the embassy after another meeting, when a man bumped into him from behind. The man muttered something at him and hurried ahead. When he got over his surprise and digested what the man had said—a terse summons—he followed him around the next corner. He saw the man disappear into a shop and followed him inside. No one was there except the proprietor, who scrutinized him from beneath racks of hanging leather goods but said nothing as he proceeded down the single narrow aisle toward the rear. When he passed through the burlap curtain there, strong hands seized him and hustled him out a back door to a waiting car.

The car sped off as soon as he was inside. He turned to look at the man who had been waiting in the backseat for him, and got the shock of his life. It was his old neighbor from the lodging house in the Street of the Well, Kareem, the foppish desk clerk at the Tharsis-Savoy.

"Hello, *ya* Abdul," Kareem said softly. "You've been a damned fool, haven't you?"

"Kareem!" Hamid-Jones exclaimed. "What, you, a Christian?"

"Surprised?"

"But when . . . how . . ."

"Let's just say I saw a great light in Tharsis." The mocking tone that Hamid-Jones remembered from his rooming house days was absent. This new Kareem seemed serious, hard, controlled.

"You've got a lot of people awfully mad at you, *ya* Abdul," Kareem went on. "There are those who want to cut your throat for endangering our operation. But luckily for you, we have a use for you."

"I . . . I told the Christian *mujahidin* on Alpha Centauri that I'd help if I could. What do you want me to do?"

"Go to Pluto."

CHAPTER 8

As Kareem had warned, they were furious with him. The leader, a grizzled, burly Christian named Paul, gave him a tongue-lashing.

"You were told to lie low until it was safe for us to contact you! To do your political chores for the Centauran embassy and stay out of trouble as far as it was possible for you to do so! Instead, you deliberately allow yourself to be seen by someone who is able to recognize you!"

It was a grim tribunal he was facing. A dozen bareheaded men sat behind a long, felt-covered table in what seemed to be some sort of back-room social club. Tough-looking *fedayeen* with automatic weapons guarded the doors, occasionally taking turns to don headcloths and have an unarmed look outside. Two men in black robes and flat turbans sat to one side, contributing nothing to the discussion. Hamid-Jones didn't have to be told that these were observers from the Assassins' faction.

"All right, I may have been recognized," Hamid-Jones said defensively, "but that wouldn't tell anybody anything. My cover wasn't broken, they don't know where to find me or what I'm up to." He gave Paul a resentful stare. "And even if I *am* caught and taken in for questioning, I can't tell them anything about what *you're* up to."

"You're a fool," Paul said bluntly, and there were low growls of assent from the other men present. "Your apparent biological age tells the whole story. The security police are quite capable

123

of working it out that you must have made a round trip to Alpha Centauri.''

"Lalla's not a police agent," Hamid-Jones said, reddening.

"You were recognized by the Clonemaster himself. That's about as bad as it can get. You may be sure that he took the information directly to his overlords at the Palace.''

Hamid-Jones was taken aback by the mention of the Clonemaster, but after a double take he remembered that Lalla's father was irrevocably dead and that Rashid was the Clonemaster now. Mars had indeed become a topsy-turvy place when the likes of Rashid were elevated.

"And that's exactly what he did," put in another of Hamid-Jones's inquisitors, a square man with a chest-length black beard. "There are stakeout vans covering the Centauran embassy now. We saved you from walking into a trap—and taking us down with you.''

Hamid-Jones's first thought was for Lalla. "I've compromised her, haven't I? Why didn't I think of that? I've gotten her into trouble.''

"Don't waste any worry on the vixen. She's fine. She's busy denouncing you nonstop.''

"Er . . . let's not be too hard on the lad," said a third man, a thin-necked, white-haired patriarch in combat fatigues. "He, uh, *did* risk his life for us on Alpha Centauri after he was told of the enormity being planned by the Sultan. And he was willing to turn double agent for us . . .''

"Unless he's turned triple agent," rumbled another Christian, a great slab of a man who had a heavy caliber pistol lying on the table in front of him.

Hamid-Jones flinched, recovered with a show of unconcern. He remembered how he had allowed Colonel Ish-Shamaal to recruit him before he left. It hadn't seemed to matter very much at the time. But if the Christian organization's intelligence was as good as it seemed to be, and it ever came to their attention that he was working for the Colonel on the side, there would be no way he could explain it.

The patriarch passed over the interruption. "The information you uncovered on Alpha Centauri was of immense importance," he said, speaking directly to Hamid-Jones. "It confirmed what we already suspected. The transmission preceded you here by a year, and we've been very busy ferreting out information on this end and making preparations. We don't know exactly where in the Oort Cloud the black hole installation is—but we know how we can plant an agent in it. He'll need Centauran credentials, of course. So I'm afraid that you're elected."

His eyes were almost pleading.

"I'll do it," Hamid-Jones said. "Of course."

"And don't get any fancy ideas," snarled the unpleasant fellow whose gun was lying on the table. "You're convenient but not indispensible. We can get rid of you and find another way to penetrate the Oort installation if we have to."

"I said I'd do it," Hamid-Jones returned evenly. He and his antagonist locked eyes.

"Now, now, Timothy, I'm sure we can depend on young Hamid-Jones," the white-haired man said smoothly. "We've worked with infidels before for the common good." His eyes roamed to the pair of Assassins, who sat motionless and impassive. "After all, we have a mutual interest in preventing the annihilation of Mars, don't we." He turned a crocodile gaze on Hamid-Jones. "You understand you can't return to the embassy now. It wouldn't be prudent for you even to be seen on the street. Comrade Kareem will give you a place to stay until it's time for you to go."

"I can't just disappear," Hamid-Jones protested. "What will the Ambassador think?"

"You're not working for the Ambassador anymore," Paul said, leaning across the table. "Or that lunatic Ish-Shamaal. You're working for us. Kareem, he's your responsibility. Don't let him out of your sight until we get him off the planet."

"It's an antimatter bomb," the armorer said. "Very tricky to handle—that's why the military and amateurs alike prefer to stick with ordinary nukes. Its virtue is that it can be very small—smaller than your run-of-the-mill knapsack bomb, and yet be made as powerful as your usual military ordnance." He smiled a thin professional smile. "A bigger bang for the dinar."

He was a pale, wiry, fair-haired man who had been introduced by Kareem as ibn Wil and had immediately and with some asperity let it be known that he styled himself as Wilson. Wilson was a full-blooded Englishman and unreconstructed Unbeliever who somehow contrived to make Hamid-Jones feel as if the Arab half of his ancestry was worth less than the English half.

"Gram for gram, we can get about a thousand times as powerful an explosion out of antimatter as we can out of a fusion reaction," Wilson went on dryly. "In other words, we can make an antimatter teraton bomb about the same size as a gigaton fusion bomb. But there's no point in it. There's a shortage of rational targets even for gigaton bombs. Now, this little baby here is designed to yield only a ten kiloton explosion, but it ought to be big enough for you to wreck any conceivable installation, as long as you place it within a mile or two of your target bull's-eye."

He patted the device fondly. It was a thick disk about the size of a pair of cymbals, and it was surprisingly lightweight.

"There's practically no metal in it," the armorer explained. "It's made mostly of composite materials, including the superconductors, the insulators, and the superflywheel that powers it all and keeps it from blowing up in our faces."

The heart of it, he explained, was a minute gob of frozen metallic antihydrogen, trapped in a vacuum chamber by the magnetic field generated by the superflywheel. "And it's a *perfect* vacuum, I might add," he said. "The antimatter cleaned out every last molecule of air while it was settling down. The radiation killed two of our couriers while we were getting it here. Don't look so alarmed. It's safe now. The only radiation we get is from the occasional stray cosmic ray that penetrates the casing and encounters its mirror image, and that's quite infinitesimal."

"Safe?" Kareem yelped. "When there's a ten kiloton explosion in there waiting for the magnetic field to fail?"

"That can't happen until the flywheel runs down. And it's a quite good commercial variety—the same kind used for powering small short-range passenger vehicles—with enough stored energy to keep it spinning for another ninety days. After that, of course, it better be off-planet somewhere. But of course you'll have used it before then."

"How do I set it off?" Hamid-Jones asked.

"You brake the flywheel. There's a timer you can set, to get yourself out of the vicinity. Or you can crack the inner case—about a ton of pressure would do it. When the antihydrogen encounters the dollop of hydrogen contained in the outer shell, that's when the fireworks start. Or when the antihydrogen encounters *anything* outside its vacuum—air, anything. But then it would tend to fizzle a bit. You could lose up to half of your ten kilotons.''

"A five kiloton explosion," Hamid-Jones said. "Great!"

Kareem mopped his brow. "Try not to drop it, *ya* Abdul. Until you're out of Tharsis City. I'll keep it locked up in a cabinet till you leave my rooms."

After the armorer left, Hamid-Jones turned to Kareem and said, "How am I going to get into this installation in the Oort Cloud if you don't know where it is?"

Kareem looked smug. "You'll be escorted there. By the Centaurans themselves."

"Huh?"

"You're going to be a visiting VIP from Alpha Centauri. An engineer. No one on Pluto or Charon knows him by sight. He's never been in the Solar system before. His starship is due to arrive in a day or two—there's a little Doppler uncertainty. He'll be met by a team of Assassins who'll take him into custody and relieve him of his identification. Our forgery section will replace his holo and DNA prints with yours."

"What . . . what will happen to the engineer?"

"He won't be killed, if that's what you're worried about. He may make a useful hostage. He'll simply be a guest in the Assassins' paradise until it's all over." The old, mocking Kareem peeped through for an instant. "I believe you know him—or his wife, at any rate."

"Who is he?"

"His name's Awad. Izzat Awad."

"Wake up, *ya* Abdul. It's time to go." Kareem was shaking him out of a deep sleep.

"Wha . . . whazzat?" Hamid-Jones sat up blearily, rubbing his eyes. It had been two days since the armorer's visit. He looked at the glowing holo window of his watch. It was the middle of the night.

"We've got an ascent vehicle waiting for you in the desert," Kareem said. "An old three-man chemical job. Paul doesn't think it's wise for you to risk going through Martian customs on Deimos just to pick up a ferry there—but your visa stamp and the rest of it ought to hold up all right on the other end. Anyway, there'll be other passengers making direct rendezvous with the blowtorch, so nobody'll think anything of it, and once you're aboard, you'll be safe—it's flying under the Plutonian flag.''

Blowtorches weren't allowed to dock at Deimos or Phobos— or any other moon in the Solar system, for that matter. Unlike starships—which made their antimatter as they went along and which represented no threat to inhabited moons and planets once the Harun drive was turned off—blowtorches carried a substantial quantity of live antimatter in their magnetic storage tanks.

The antimatter was collected, milligram by milligram, in factories beyond the orbit of Neptune, using the same principles that made the Harun drive possible. Antimatter drives were the only practical way to get to the outskirts of the Solar system at a constant one-G acceleration. Ten grams of antimatter were enough to take a spacecraft from Earth to Mars; a couple of decagrams would take it to Pluto.

The odd milligram of antimatter could occasionally be diverted by a well-bribed insider; bulk shipments of a gram or more were always a tempting target for hijackers. A radioactive splat in deep space usually announced the attempt. Wilson's dab of antimatter doubtless had come from some such source, with better luck than most.

Kareem held the awful black disk out to him at arm's length. ''Take it, *ya* Abdul,'' he said with a shudder. ''You'll find a false bottom in your duffel bag—the thing's transparent to ultrasound and muon-scopes. It's already had two days to run down. I'll be glad to see the last of it.''

CHAPTER 9

Charon hung motionless overhead, a smudged white ball against utter blackness. A tiny sun, hardly more than a pinhole in the sky, was still bright enough to give the frozen moon a glinting crescent edge and pick out the lumps on its surface.

Hamid-Jones trudged across a field of methane snow, methodically picking up one encumbered foot and placing it in front of the other. The snowshoes were thick pucks of sandwiched superinsulator and the borrowed suit was a collection of bulky spheres that made him resemble a snowman with strings of beads for arms and legs. The outfit was clumsy but not heavy; Pluto's weak gravity, only a tenth of Earth standard, made it seem as light as Styrofoam.

"Sorry about the walk, mister," his driver said. "The dang snowmobile hadn't oughter throwed a tread like that—I just had it checked out. I could've radioed in for a ride, but it would've been an hour's wait at least. Every hack and jitney in Plutopolis is busy ferrying passengers from the hoppers."

He swore as a snowcab careened past them, sending up plumes of methane frost and spattering them with slush. "You'd think one of them would stop and give a fellow hackie a lift, but no, they're all after the fast dinar. That was Yahya Gordon from Green Crescent Cabs that just passed us—he had room in back for a couple more. I suppose his passenger promised him a big tip. I'll have a word with him later."

"It's all right," Hamid-Jones said feebly. "It's a good way to see the sights."

He had to give an extra tug to the rope of the little sledge that was carrying his luggage; one of the runners had become stuck in a rut from the previous traffic. It was hard for him to tell, not being used to the gravity yet, but it seemed to him that he was doing more of his share of the pulling than the cabdriver.

"Well, I can't charge you for the taxi ride, that's for sure," the driver said cheerfully.

"That's nice of you," Hamid-Jones said. The fare he had been quoted had seemed exorbitant—ten dinars for the two mile ride from where the little landing craft had come down.

"Have to charge you for the rental of the snowsuit and the duckfeet, though. How does five dinars for the suit and five for the snowshoes sound?"

"Fine," Hamid-Jones said. He didn't want to antagonize the man, in this hellish environment where even helium liquified and collected in pools during the three-day Plutonian night, and a pratfall could turn the unwary pedestrian into a statue of solid ice within seconds.

The cab driver was a recent import from one of the more uncivilized American or Canadian satrapies—he had switched to English without a by-your-leave as soon as he realized that Hamid-Jones was fluent in the language. The trans-Plutonian frontier had attracted a lot of roughneck types from North America—prospectors, comet miners, ice wildcatters, lumberjacks. They all dreamed of staking a claim on a comet of their own. In the meantime there were plenty of jobs for them in the Oort Cloud, boosting cometary ice toward the inner system or harvesting cometary cedar. What they had in common was a kind of loud, crude vitality, sloppy personal habits, and the fact that their Islamic roots ran shallow.

This fellow, for example, who went by the name Maq-duwal, had neglected the sunrise prayer, though there wouldn't be another one for six Earth days, and wore a greasy cap instead of a proper turban or headcloth. Hamid-Jones was guiltily aware that he was probably being unfair to the man, but he felt that he could not depend on the comity that one Believer always owed to another.

"Watch it!" Maq-duwal said sharply, coming to an abrupt stop. Hamid-Jones was caught off-balance and fell to his bowling-ball knees, though without any damage. He bounced upright again, leaving two small depressions of melted methane that froze again instantly.

"What is it?" he asked.

"Goosebumps," the driver said.

He pointed to a quicksilver blob about the size of a soccer ball that lay in their path. They had almost run it down with the sledge. Trailing behind it were a dozen smaller blobs, about the size of golfballs. The big one and the little ones alike were crowned by a sort of ribbed fin that fanned out into a semicircle. And, with his eyes adjusted to the stygian gloom, Hamid-Jones could see that the fins glowed a dull red.

"Mama and her babies," the driver said. "Leading them to a shady spot where they can hole up before the day gets too hot."

By looking closely, Hamid-Jones could see that the quicksilver spherules were indeed moving, oozing along the snow about as fast as the minute hand on an analog watch.

"Pluto's native life-form," the driver explained. He seemed as proud as if he personally were their creator. "Chemistry based on lipids dissolved in helium II. It only becomes a superfluid at minus four hundred and fifty-six degrees Fahrenheit. That's only four degrees above absolute zero. The little critters get rid of their excess heat through those radiators on top."

"It was considerate of you to stop for them," Hamid-Jones said. He had banged one of his knees hard enough for it to feel sore.

"Oh, nobody on Pluto would hurt a goosebump. A fellow could get himself lynched that way. They make fine mascots out here. I've met prospectors who swear goosebumps saved their lives—warmed themselves over a clutch of 'em in a cave till help came, times they'd been stranded or something. Sometimes a few degrees difference'll take just enough of a load off a life-support system to make all the difference."

"How do they live?" There had been passing references to Plutonian goosebumps in Hamid-Jones's old biochemistry texts—something about superconductivity and the transfer of heat via paramagnetic effects at supercooled temperatures. He hadn't paid much attention at the time; it had very little to do with ordinary biochemistry.

Maq-duwal misunderstood his meaning. "Oh, on the frostflowers and other Plutonian plant life.'' He waxed enthusiastic. He must have given the same spiel many times to other newcomers, in order to increase his tip. ''You know, this slow-motion ecology we've got here is the only life ever found in the Solar system, except for what we brought with us from Earth.'' He gestured at the suspended moon. ''The first expeditions found goosebumps and frostflowers on Charon, too—different species but definitely related. Some say it suggests that Pluto and Charon were once one—a moon of Neptune that broke into two chunks when it escaped. There're others who think Pluto's not a planet or moon at all—that it's just the granddaddy of comets. Sure as hell, it's mostly ice of various kinds.'' He squinted at Hamid-Jones through the goggle eyes of the frosty ball on his head. ''Say, you a scientist?''

''Engineer,'' Hamid-Jones said, remembering his Centauran persona in time.

''Thought so. You don't look like the kind of comet rat we usually get out here.''

The little procession of silvery lumps inched past, leaving a groove in the methane snow. The littlest one at the end hurried to catch up, moving fast enough so that Hamid-Jones could see the small creeping puddle of itself on which it flowed. He and the driver leaned into the ropes and got the sledge moving again.

A mile behind them, the hopper leapt into the sky on a sudden plume of blue flame, heading for the orbiting blowtorch to take on another load of passengers. Hamid-Jones turned his head to watch. The spidery form dwindled, winked out. It would coast most of the way. You didn't need much escape velocity to get off Pluto.

The blowtorch was halfway to Charon and invisible. If it had been an ordinary vehicle it could have orbited a couple of miles up, for all the atmosphere Pluto had to hinder it, but even on a frontier planet like this, the port authority didn't want a load of antimatter within five thousand miles of the surface. Hamid-Jones could see the blowtorch in his imagination, though—a long titanium tube bearing the shielded disk of the passenger quarters before it. The disk didn't have to spin for gravity; its floor always gave you planet-strength gravity at the blowtorch's constant one-G acceleration. The trip from Mars had taken only twenty-one days.

Twenty-one days. Hamid-Jones shivered and sneaked a glance

at the duffel bag lying on top of the load of luggage on the sledge. That was twenty-one days out of the useful life of the flywheel that kept that deadly dollop of antimatter at bay. He still had to get it to the secret Centauran installation in the void beyond Pluto. Izzat's travel documents, seized by the Assassins who had intercepted him, had suggested that the doomsday base was within 400 AU, and that made sense. There were still plenty of stray comets at that distance, on the thin margins of the Oort Cloud. There would have been no point in the Centaurans' setting up their base in the cometary halo proper, at distances of half a light-year or more. In that case, they might just as well have worked from the Centauran system itself, since the boost times were almost the same. He'd have needed a flywheel with a year's worth of life in it.

He shivered again, more violently this time. If the armorer's estimate was wrong, he was going to have to find some way to jettison a duffel bag from a ship traveling at a respectable fraction of the speed of light.

He was too lost in thought to duck as another snowmobile whizzed by, spraying him with methane slush. Frost sizzled as it hit his snowsuit, sending up clouds of hydrocarbon steam. He used the flat edge of a waldo mitten to wipe fog from the goggle ports of his helmet.

"That was Yahya Gordon again!" Maq-duwal fumed. "Going back for another fare. Too money hungry to stop and help us out, the son of a dog!"

From the tone of his voice, Hamid-Jones knew he was going to be stuck for an exorbitant tip. With these devious American *dhimmi*, every transaction had to be greased with *baksheesh*.

They topped a rise. "There's Plutopolis," Maq-duwal said proudly. "What do you think of it?"

The capital city was spread out no more than a thousand yards away, a miserable collection of makeshift hovels set out in streets of methane slush. Flexible tubes connected many of the insulated cubes and domes, riding out the day-to-day variations in the level of structures that floated on melting methane, hydrogen, ammonia ice and Allah only knew what else. Water was about the only thing you could count on to stay solid, even with all the leaking heat from the works of man. There were a few larger structures among all the plastic huts and frosted bulges—a multitiered branch of the Bank of Neptune, a highrise hotel called the Ice Palace, a tremendous igloo bearing the crystalline logo of the interplanetary ice consortium, a massive cube made out of giant logs that could only be the headquarters of Cometary Lumber Multicorp. There were no large mosques on the scale one saw in every civilized capital—only a few smallish domes with ice minarets, all of them dwarfed by the rather modest capitol dome at the center of the city.

"Uh, very impressive," Hamid-Jones said. "What's the population?"

"Twenty thousand and growing," Maq-duwal informed him with chamber of commerce fervor. "The future of the Solar system's out here. Trillions of pieces of real estate waiting to be developed. 'Gateway to the Comets'—that's the official slogan of Plutopolis!"

Hamid-Jones gave a polite murmur of acknowledgment. He cast a dubious eye over the grimy frosted layers of the Ice Palace and hoped he could get a fairly decent room there. Then, tugging at the rope, he helped Maq-duwal coax the loaded sledge down the slope.

It was a rather seedy lobby with worn carpeting and overstuffed chairs occupied mostly by men in rough work clothing, some of them still wearing their snowboot liners. Hamid-Jones surrendered his passport to a tired-looking Lebanese clerk with the droopy face of a basset hound. The clerk checked him in and returned the passport. "Have a nice stay, Mr. Awad," he said, and rang his bell for a porter.

"Uh, I'll be taking the ferry to Charon in the morning. Can you wake me in time?"

"Certainly. There's plenty of time. The Charon ferry doesn't leave until midmorning, hexaday time. We'll arrange ground transportation."

"Thank you."

The porter arrived, a great frostbitten lout in a plaid flannel shirt and shiny green pants, who began to tuck Hamid-Jones's luggage under his apelike arms.

"I'll take the duffel bag," Hamid-Jones said hastily, grabbing for it.

He followed the porter to the elevators at the rear. In Pluto's low gravity, they turned out to be dangling glassite booths at the end of long booms that rotated in Ferris wheel fashion within a shallow circular recess that took up the whole width of the hotel's back wall. The abutting corridors on each floor were by necessity pushed farther and farther out until midpoint at the twentieth floor, where they then started to close in again. The circular recess had been left entirely open, as what was probably supposed to be a striking architectural feature back in the palmy days when the hotel was new and some hotshot architect from Earth was trying to make a Statement, but to Hamid-Jones's jaundiced eyes it looked as if someone had left the machinery exposed to save money.

His room was on the twelfth floor, with a small insulated porthole looking out across the desolate Plutonian landscape. He could see small yellow points of light here and there across the frozen wastes—isolated cabins of settlers—and on the close-up, sharply curved horizon there was a cluster of bright actinic flares that probably signified a mining operation.

The room was small and dingy, with faded chintz slipcovers to protect the furnishings. Previous tenants had left scratches in the wood surfaces and paneling—wood was cheap and plentiful out here, and it had replaced plastic for many traditional uses, Hamid-Jones had noticed. He sighed and gave a one-dinar tip to the porter, who looked at it skeptically and left without a thank you.

He stowed the duffel bag in the narrow closet and piled the rest of his luggage over it until it was buried out of sight. It would be an industrious thief who bothered with it. He washed his face in a cracked ablutions font and changed out of his travel clothes into comfortable Centauran trousers and frock coat, then went downstairs via the rotating buckets to look for a restaurant. Outside, it was still early in Pluto's extended morning, but it was already evening in the twenty-five-and-a-half hour day that Pluto's transplanted human inhabitants observed. It was not too different from Mars's slightly stretched day and had the virtue of putting the sunrise and sunset prayers in synch with astronomical rhythms every sixth day.

He ate dinner in a restaurant whose English name, in quaint Barnum letters, was the Loggers' Paradise. The menu featured such items as a "Prospector's Special"—an indigestible heap of fried meat and potatoes, from the look of a neighboring diner's plate—and "Iceman's Comets," a snowy mound of white rice with a tail made of minced lamb. He ordered the "Lumberjack's

Blue Plate''—something called flapjacks, which turned out to be a kind of pancake or *fatir*, covered with a sweet syrup that the waiter informed him was made from the sap of a tree. Plutonians were very fond of the syrup, which was a by-product of lumbering operations in the cometary halo.

It was too early to go back to his room, so he explored the limited resources of the hotel arcade, which ran heavily to souvenir shops and other tourists traps, now mostly shuttered for the evening. He found a dim grotto called O'Ryan's Bar next to the brighter, noisier nook that billed itself as the Wildcatters' Room and opted for the former. The place was some decorator's idea of what a pre-*Nadha* refreshment shop looked like, with a long, dark mahogany counter in back, a brass rail, and an ornate gilt mirror. The name O'Ryan was evidently a throwback form of ibn Ryan, a common North American name.

Feeling adventurous, he sat down at one of the small wooden tables. Alcohol was sold openly here. Pluto was indeed infested with *dhimmi* and backsliders; at dinner the waiter had actually offered him bacon with his flapjacks. It was all the North American blood in the Pluto-Charon system, he supposed. Even after a thousand years of *Nadha*, the Americans had not assimilated as well as his own British ancestors.

The drink list suffered from the same kind of forced quaintness as the dinner menu, offering such alcoholic concoctions as a "Lethe Cocktail," a "Styx Pickup," "The Comet's Tail," and "O'Ryan's Belt." Many of them seemed to be decorated with little paper parasols. Fortunately, the place also sold nonalcoholic beverages. Hamid-Jones was relieved to find the traditional Ramadan thirst-quencher, Moon of Religion, on the list and ordered one.

He had hardly taken a sip of the tangy apricot slush when a young man in many-pocketed corduroy coveralls and snowboot liners came over to the table, drink in hand.

"*Salaam aleikum.* Do you mind if I sit down?"

A caution light went on in Hamid-Jones's brain. The fellow was wearing a Centauran-style headdress—a turban wrapped in two lobes around the central core of a tarboosh. But this couldn't be his contact. He was supposed to meet his connection on Charon.

"Go right ahead."

The young man settled down. "My name's Sherkan. I saw

the Centauran togs and couldn't resist coming over. Do you mind?''

''Not at all,'' Hamid-Jones said. ''Though I'm not really—'' He shut up. Perhaps it would be better not to reveal too much about himself until he knew more about Sherkan.

''Let me buy you a drink,'' Sherkan said. ''What's that you're having?''

''A *qamar al-din*,'' Hamid-Jones said. ''Don't trouble yourself. I haven't finished this one.''

''You'll have to try the house specialty.'' Sherkan indicated his own drink, an unappetizing dark liquid in a squat heavy glass. ''O'Ryan's Belt. That's *dhimmi* for a stiff drink. It's made with three-star brandy.''

''No thanks,'' Hamid-Jones said hastily. ''I don't drink alcohol.''

The young man took a swig. From the flush in his face, Hamid-Jones guessed the drink hadn't been his first.

''When among the *dhimmi* . . .'' the young man offered. ''Though I shouldn't use that as an excuse. I've only been here two days. You come in on this morning's blowtorch?''

''Yes.''

''You didn't happen to see a fellow named Izzat on board, did you? Izzat Awad.''

Hamid-Jones almost choked on his apricot slush. He got himself under control after a small coughing fit.

''You all right?''

''Yes. I just swallowed the wrong way.''

Sherkan smiled impishly. ''See? A Moon of Religion can be more dangerous than one of these Unbeliever drinks of perdition. Izzat ought to love it out here. He's quite a naughty man that way.''

Hamid-Jones found he had gone numb and cold. The Christian underground had assured him that there was no one on Pluto or Charon who knew Izzat by sight. They had missed out on the recent arrivals.

''I rode out with Izzat from Centaurus on the starship,'' Sherkan said. ''Very congenial traveling companion when he isn't having one of those black moods of his. He was doing a survey in the cometary belt, he told me. Something to do with orbits—not my field. I thought I was going to be able to count on the company of a fellow Centauran at least as far as Pluto. We were supposed to ride out together on the same blowtorch." He frowned. "But he disappeared."

Hamid-Jones took a sip of his slush. "Maybe he'll show up later," he said.

"Yes. Perhaps he was detained on Mars. Not the best place to be stuck in these days, with all the unrest." He cocked his head. "What did you say your name was?"

Hamid-Jones breathed a silent prayer of thanks that he hadn't given the Izzat name when Sherkan had introduced himself. It couldn't hurt, he decided, to give his real name. Mars had no writ on Pluto, which was governed more or less loosely from Neptune. Besides, he was only going to be here for one night.

"Abdul," he said. "Abdul Hamid-Jones."

"You're not a Centauran, are you? I mean, you're wearing Centauran clothes, but your accent . . ."

Hamid-Jones cursed himself for letting his accent slip. He'd have to do better than that when he met his Centauran contact on Charon, posing as Izzat.

"That's right. I'm a Martian. But I lived for . . . some time . . . on Alpha Centauri Alif."

Sherkan showed distress. "I hope you didn't mind . . . my remark about conditions on Mars?"

"No. Not at all. I don't care for conditions there myself. That's . . . that's why I went to Alpha Centauri."

"Political refugee?" Sherkan inquired sagely.

Hamid-Jones nodded, leaving it at that. "You said orbits aren't your field. What are you doing out here?"

Sherkan had been waiting for the chance to talk about himself. "I'm a forestry expert," he said with boyish eagerness. "I was sent out by the ministry to study the Solar system's forestry project in Sol's cometary halo. We've been backward in that regard in the Kingdom of the Triple Suns. We've got an enormous Oort Cloud of our own—tremendously complicated by the gravitational vagaries of a multiple star system, of course—but we've been slow to exploit it. I suppose that's because we've had no need to until now. Not while our population was still low and we had empty planets to grow forests on. But the day will come when our natural resources run out, as they did on Earth, and we'd better plant a viable ecology among the comets before then. After all, there are trillions upon trillions of comets. We'll never run out of them. They're individually small, but they add up to thousands of times the surface area of a planet like Earth. And they've got all the basic constituents of life—water, carbon, nitrogen. Plus the heavy metals, silicates, and other useful materials in their cores. Some day the bulk of the human race will live among the comets, not on planets and moons.''

His young face was suffused with enthusiasm. Hamid-Jones let him run on.

"So far I've only been talking to people from the forestry service here. They've been very helpful. Tomorrow I have an appointment at the research department of Cometary Lumber Multicorp. They're going to show me around their experimental farm. They've developed a new type of seedling that's even more efficient at conserving water in the vacuum of space. The leaves incorporate a biological mirror that focuses starlight for improved photosynthesis. Later I hope to wangle a field trip to one of the nearby comets. What's your line of work, ya Abdul? You don't have something to do with ice mining, do you?''

Hamid-Jones answered without thinking. "No, I'm a biologist.''

"I knew you were an educated man. Oh, then you must be here to have something to do with the lumber consortium's bioengineering department—perhaps we could go out to the Cedar Palace together tomorrow.''

"No, I'm . . . I'm here to study Plutonian life.'' He improvised hastily. "I'm traveling out to Charon tomorrow to have a look at the native species there.''

"Oh, the goosebumps?''

"Yes.''

"Oh well, maybe we'll get together later. I may go out to Charon myself after I'm finished here. There're some well-established logging tracts there—stands of cryocedar, mostly—though of course in Charon's gravity, the trees can't grow as tall as they do on a comet.''

"Uh, certainly. Though I may be away on a field trip of my own.''

"Field trip?'' Sherkan's eyebrows lifted.

Hamid-Jones tried to correct his slip. "Um, you see, there are reports that Plutonian goosebumps may have been seen on vagrant comets nearby . . . as if . . . as if the comets were debris of a Pluto-Charon breakup.''

"Really? I hadn't heard.''

Hamid-Jones spent the next few minutes fielding questions about Plutonian life that he couldn't answer, before turning the conversation back to vacuum-grown trees. It wasn't hard—the young forester was absorbed in his own topic. Hamid-Jones endured a couple of hours of statistics and rambling encomiums to space-based lumbering before managing to pry himself loose. Before leaving, he was persuaded against his better judgment to try an O'Ryan's Belt. He didn't care for it. The proper use for alcohol, as far as he was concerned, was to preserve specimens.

The Charon ferry was a ramshackle collection of fuel tanks, piping, antennae, cargo racks, passenger module, and randomly placed engines, all mounted on an open framework. It stood on four widely spaced skeleton legs wearing spherical shoes. Hamid-Jones looked at it with some dismay. He had to cross twelve thousand miles of space in the thing, and it looked as if a sneeze would blow it apart.

"Better get going," the hotel's jitney driver said. "He doesn't like waiting."

Hamid-Jones tipped the driver, then followed the other passengers through the narrow accordion tunnel that was fitted to the jitney's airlock. There were only about a dozen of them, mostly ice prospectors and lumberjacks returning to Charon after a binge in the Plutonian fleshpots. It was hard to imagine, but Charon was even more primitive than Pluto.

He shouldered his duffel bag and ducked through the low tube. His luggage had already gone aboard, he had been assured. He hoped it was in the passenger cabin and not in an outside rack; he could visualize some clumsy porter dropping a suitcase and having the supercooled contents shatter like glass.

The ferryman was stationed at the entry lock, an old geezer with a white beard. He wouldn't let them aboard until they paid. Hamid-Jones had his fare ready, as he had been warned to do— a one hundred–dinar gold piece that civilized persons found too heavy for daily commerce. The ferryman didn't trust bank chips and other forms of credit transfer. Too many dubious characters out here in the Solar system's badlands. He accepted Hamid-Jones's coin with a sour look, then dogged the outer hatch and cast loose the accordion tube.

"Find yourselves seats and strap yourselves in," he told the passengers. "You there, Billy, what did I tell you about glass bottles in the cabin the last time you came down here on a toot?"

Billy, a grizzled ice rat with breath that lacked only an oxidizer to put him into orbit on his own, solved the problem by draining the bottle in a couple of long swallows and handing the empty to the ferryman.

"Trip'll take about an hour," the ferryman announced as a grudging concession to Hamid-Jones and the other tenderfoot passenger aboard, a middle-aged Tritonian clutching a briefcase. The ferryman turned and climbed a ladder and disappeared through an overhead hatch.

"Think the old *Persephone*'s going to make it this time, Billy?" said one of the passengers.

"Always has so far," the ice rat replied. With a sly grin, he produced another bottle from under layers of baggy liners and offered it all around. Hamid-Jones and the Tritonian declined.

After a wait, ancient chemical rockets—good enough for a planet that had no escape velocity to speak of—wheezed into life. The ferry rose unevenly on a cloud of hydrogen steam. Hamid-Jones grabbed at his armrests. The *Persephone* and its crabbed old pilot did not inspire confidence. In a surprisingly short time, the engines shut down and the rickety spacecraft floated free. Almost immediately the ferry rotated a full one hundred and eighty degrees to point its landing legs at its destination—there was no nonsense about coasting sideways during the middle journey to give the passengers a scenic view of the locked moon. But before Charon's refrigerated face sank below the rim of the porthole, Hamid-Jones managed to have a look anyway. Since the previous hexaday, the hard cold light of the faraway Sun had advanced to illuminate another sixth of the moon's surface. It still wasn't much to look at—just a grimy snowball. Hamid-Jones thought he could pick out patches of green here and there in the fully lit crescent portion—the experimental forests getting out of hand. He wondered if the biological warmth they generated bothered the goosebumps.

They landed an hour later, as the ferryman had promised, in a snowy waste demarcated by a few makeshift utility buildings constructed of water ice and rough-hewn wood. Charon hadn't entirely escaped the *dhimmi* propensity for waggishness. A rustic wooden sign planted in front of the spaceport's arrival shack said ELYSIAN FIELD. The Charonians were proud of their frozen hell.

Styxville was like Plutopolis, only less so. There was only one street in what passed for the moon's capital, with nothing larger than an eighty-foot dome. Two long rows of dilapidated wood or plastic hovels fronted on a thoroughfare that the snow-mobiles had stirred into slush. The messy backyards behind the main street were dotted with even cruder outbuildings and lit-tered with junk—broken-down snow vehicles, scrap metal, gi-gantic log skidders, obsolete mining equipment. Clusters of frosted spheres that were men in cryosuits strolled along the duckboard walks like snowmen come to life. It seemed to be some sort of a Charonian fashion statement to wear a woolen scarf between the large sphere of the torso and the smaller sphere of the helmet. One dapper fellow had a battered stovepipe hat perched atop his helmet.

The saloon that Hamid-Jones entered appeared to have been carved out of a single tree stump some forty feet in diameter. The bioengineered bark, a better insulator than most commer-cial materials, was still on it, and it had been roofed over with a curving slab of more tree.

Inside was a hollowed-out chamber of random shape and an irregular floor covered with sawdust. The massive bar had been carved in one piece out of the floor. The bartender worked in his long-sleeved thermal undershirt and a neckerchief that ought—Hamid-Jones thought disapprovingly—to have been his headcloth. The place served no fancy drinks as the Ice Palace's bar had done—the Charonians had not yet grown effete. Instead of cocktails with fruit garnishes and paper parasols, the clientele stuck to plain whiskey, beer, or one hundred–proof gin frozen into slush by the liquid nitrogen in the glass's hollow stem.

Hamid-Jones hung his rented snowsuit on a hook; its coating of hydrogen frost immediately went up in vapor without having time to drip to the floor. He made the mistake of touching the outside surface with his bare flesh and jerked his hand away with a frostburn on his fingers.

The bartender looked at him oddly when he ordered a Moon of Religion but poured it out for him without comment. He took it over to a corner booth and sat nursing it while he watched the door.

All the Assassins had been able to gather from Izzat's travel papers was that he was supposed to show up on Charon, where someone would make contact. The Centaurans maintained no official presence on Charon—or on Pluto, for that matter. The nearest Centauran consulate was on Neptune's giant moon, Triton, and that was only manned by a chargé d'affaires. But of course there would be an unofficial presence—a clandestine agent or two fitting into the local life and keeping tabs on any situation that might tend to jeopardize the black hole project.

Eventually the Centauran agent would find him. It wouldn't be hard to do. Styxville was small—most of Charon's population was out in the boondocks. There were only a few rooming houses and public gathering places to keep tabs on. Stumpy Pete's, as this wooden rat hole was called, was Styxville's most popular watering place.

He looked out across the sawdust expanse at the assortment of ice rats. They were a rough and ready bunch. Their simple pleasures included arm wrestling over a sizzling lump of hydrogen ice that was busy shrinking to nothingness; the loser got a bad frostbite. There was also a table of card players and a group of music lovers harassing a shirtsleeved synthesizer player who was bawling out dirty songs in English, French, and Russian. The *dhimmi* music was simple and foursquare, without the intricate vocal arabesques of a decent *maqam* song.

One of the ice rats at the bar caught him staring and scowled back at him. Hamid-Jones quickly averted his eyes; he didn't want to get into an argument here. But to his dismay, the fellow came swaggering over, drink in hand.

"What're *you* lookin' at?" he demanded. He was a great big bruiser with curly black hair and a quarter-inch of stubble on his face.

"Nothing," Hamid-Jones said, wondering if he was going to have to fight with his fists. North Americans did things like that and considered hitting someone a form of combat, not a deadly insult.

"What kind of a hat is that?" the iceman said, pointing at Hamid-Jones's Centauran tarboosh.

"Now see here," Hamid-Jones said, starting to get up.

"Sit down," the big man said, reaching across to give Hamid-Jones's shoulder a push. "I didn't mean no harm." He pulled up a chair and sat down himself. "You're all right, son. Feisty."

The miners at the nearby tables, seeing that there wasn't going to be a fight, lost interest and turned away.

"Your name's not Izzat, by any chance?" the man said so softly that Hamid-Jones wasn't sure for a moment that he had heard correctly.

"Uh, yes, I—"

"We don't have to go into it now." The big man swiveled around in his chair and raised his voice to its previous level. "Hey, Pete, a whiskey for my friend!"

"I don't think—"

"You're not gonna refuse to drink with me, are you?" The man scowled.

"No, I—"

"Good man!" the ice rat said, reaching around to clap Hamid-Jones on the shoulder. The bartender brought over a glass of a pale brown liquid that splashed when he set it down, despite an inner lip and mouthpiece designed to baffle Charon's low gravity.

Any remaining interest from onlookers quickly melted away at this new show of amity. When the bartender left, the man said in a casual undertone, "Stay here and finish your drink. Wait at least twenty minutes. Then meet me at the end of the street, over past the snowmobile stable."

He drained his glass in a giant gulp and stood up.

"But—" Hamid-Jones began.

"Nice talking to you, son," the man boomed out. "Sure sounds interesting, that planet you come from. Like to hear more about it some time."

He walked away without a backward look.

Hamid-Jones tried the whiskey. It had an astringent taste and burned his throat. But it produced a curiously pleasant warming sensation in his stomach. He finished the glass, making it last twenty minutes, as the Centauran agent had ordered. Then he got to his feet and went to the chilly alcove where his suit hung. It had warmed up enough to be touched. He climbed into the lower half, shrugged his way into the upper part of the suit, then screwed both hemispheres of the big ball together in the threaded hoop that joined them. He stretched the belt gasket over the waist connection and headed out into the Charonian cold.

Nobody paid any attention to him in his rented suit. Quite a few people were abroad, despite the fact that Styxville still lay in a slice of night. The people thinned out as he got toward the end of the street, a walk of a couple of miles. The snowmobile stable was a big shadowed shed. No one seemed to be around. He clumped past it on his thick-soled snowshoes to where the street petered out in a snowy hollow strewn with forgotten trash. The ruins of an earlier generation of shacks and sheds stood here and there throughout the vale—twisted metal structures cannibalized for their materials, collapsed domes, sagging plastic cryocabins with gaping holes in the walls and roofs.

A voice spoke in his helmet. "Get in."

He turned around. He hadn't sensed the snowmobile pulling up behind him. Charon's layers of different ices, constantly subliming and recondensing in Pluto's creeping shadow, tended to damp out vibrations at the interfaces. The driver had spoken to him via a modulated infrared laser that triggered the cheap voice synthesizer in his own helmet—a rough-and-ready communications system that was Charon's practical answer to the problem of cluttering up the universal frequency with short-range conversations.

The driver was a typical prospector—grimy, stubbled face showing through the goggle ports of his helmet, plaid scarf tied around what passed for the neck of his suit. Another ice rat sat beside him: the curly-haired man Hamid-Jones had spoken to in the bar.

A door was open. Hamid-Jones climbed into the rear compartment of the little ovoid cabin, using the broad snowtread as a step. The door slammed down. The snowmobile scooted off into the white void, quickly leaving the lights of Styxville behind.

The cramped space was filled with his luggage. Someone had been in his room at the lodging house he had checked into. His blood ran cold as he saw the duffel bag lying among the other pieces. But the trick zipper—the one that jammed if someone tried to open it the wrong way—seemed to be undisturbed.

"We checked you out of your room," the curly-haired one said. "No fuss. The suit's paid for, too. Long-term rental."

"Thank you."

"We spread around a little cover story for you, in case anyone asks. You hired a couple of prospectors to take you along with them. You're studying comets for one of the Centauran ministries."

The man at the steering yoke spoke without turning his head. "We've used that one before," he said.

"That'll explain your absence in case anyone's interested," the other said. "But I don't think anyone noticed you except your landlord and a few of the customers at Pete's. Not that it matters much, but on general principles it isn't good business to have people wondering what Centaurans are doing in this neck of the Solar system's woods."

The snowmobile bucked and veered as its forward skis encountered a dip. Hamid-Jones and his luggage bounced and floated in midair before a burst of acceleration crowded them against the rear bulge of the compartment.

"Better hang on," the driver said. "It gets rough from here on out."

He cradled the duffel bag in his arms. He wondered how many G's it took to interfere with the superflywheel.

Outside the oval ports the landscape had grown more rugged. They were crossing a desolate frozen field where jagged blocks of ice pushed up through the methane surface. Every gas froze at its own temperature, and when a low temperature ice like hydrogen melted under the influence of a summery Charonian noon, it floated layers of more recalcitrant ices like methane and left tilted edges of ice floes exposed after it refroze. It could get worse, though. It could get cold enough to turn liquid helium into helium II, which never froze at all at any temperature, and which had zero viscosity and crept. A snowmobile that encountered a pool of helium II was in real trouble.

Pluto was low in the sky, shining palely by Charon's reflected light. Since Pluto and Charon never moved in each other's skies, the rising of Pluto was a pretty good indication of distance traveled on Charon's surface. A snowmobile with a reckless driver could completely circle Charon in about twelve hours. Hamid-Jones dozed. When he woke up again, Pluto was halfway to zenith.

The snowmobile was slowing down. They were in the middle of a forest. Gigantic trees rose all around them, mostly the cedars of Lebanon that were the mainstay of the interplanetary lumber business. This tract hadn't been clearcut yet, and some of the trees rose several miles high. They weren't allowed to get much higher than that before cutting; it was too uneconomic to haul the logs out of Charon's gravity well. But on a comet, where the gravity was infinitesimal, there was no limiting factor. A tree might grow to a height of fifty or sixty miles before sucking the comet dry. Then, trimmed to save mass, it could be given a boost to send it on an elongated orbit to the inner system for harvesting. The newer varieties of bioengineered trees didn't have to be coddled anymore or grown from cultivated seedlings. They propagated themselves through seeds that were adapted to the rigors of space and sent on their way by puffs of gas or by tiny gossamer sails that caught the pressure of light as earthly seeds had once caught the wind. Eventually, biologists thought, they would seed the entire cometary belt by themselves and then spread from star to star where adjoining clouds mingled. With the trees would go an accessory ecology that would someday make the entire galaxy inhabitable by man. It would no longer be necessary to find hospitable planets; the comets would provide a friendlier environment for humanity.

"Here we are," the bogus ice miner said. "Next stop, Project 'Allah's Will.' "

A skeleton spaceship stood before them in a clearing, a tower of open girders that had been stripped of everything but reaction mass tanks, engines, and a life-support module. It looked as if it were built for speed. It could only be an illegal blowtorch, docked on an inhabited world by people who thumbed their noses at Solar authority. "Allah's Will," indeed!

"How . . . how long will it take to get there?" Hamid-Jones asked.

His knuckles whitened on the duffel bag containing the antimatter bomb. There couldn't be more than about seventy days worth of spin left in the flywheel.

"They're going to boost you at one and a half G's," the agent said. "You won't like it, but your Centauran build can take it—these stringbeans you see out here would break in two. You'll be there in sixty days."

CHAPTER 10

From space, the comet looked like an ice cube garnished with sprigs of parsley. Except that the sprigs were gigantic evergreen trees rising miles high. The tallest of them had to be at least twenty miles from root to crown—a runaway growth that was already dwarfing the frosted iceball it would someday consume, to become free-living in space. Moored to its upper branches was a tiny pearl onion shape that, when Hamid-Jones's mind adjusted the scale, became a starship a mile in diameter.

"There it is, *ya* Izzat," the blowtorch pilot said. "Your project. 'The Will of Allah.' How does it feel to be actually seeing it firsthand?"

Hamid-Jones stammered a protest. "It's not really *my* project . . . I'm only a small cog in the machinery . . . I did some of the calculations, that's all. They got along very well without me . . . I really don't know why I'm here."

The pilot chuckled at Izzat's modesty. "You could have knocked me over with a feather when they told me I was going to have a passenger this run. And the famous Izzat, at that! You should hear some of the younger engineers talking about your simulations. It's you younger fellows who do all the work while the old camels take all the credit."

The pilot could not have been more than five years older than Hamid-Jones himself. He was a balding roué in his early thirties. Hamid-Jones knew he was balding because he had the impious habit of lifting his fez to scratch the bald spot.

148

"They're going to have all sorts of questions for you," the pilot went on. "I hope you're prepared to be pestered."

Hamid-Jones's heart did flip-flops in his chest. "I'm only here as an observer. Anyway, I'm wrung out from the high-G trip. A month of weighing an extra ninety pounds takes it out of a man. I intend to spend the next couple of days in bed."

The pilot laughed at the joke. "They've got the red carpet out for you. The reception committee's been on the radio. They can't wait. They asked me what you looked like."

"I really need a little rest first," Hamid-Jones said, fighting down his panic. Izzat's notes had been marvelously detailed about things like the translation of angular momentum into the rotation parameter at the moment of the black hole's formation, the gravitational harmonics caused by the vibration of space-time at the moment of collapse, and so forth. But there wasn't a single clue as to how the black hole would actually be *made*. And besides, Hamid-Jones didn't know enough physics to be able to flounder through the kind of shop talk he was sure to be drawn into.

"Nonsense," said the pilot. "A little G never hurt anybody. I've got supplies in the cargo hold that are more delicate than you. Some of that fanciful Umbrian crystal for Hamza's table, for instance, that he arranged to have trans-shipped from Uranus."

"Hamza?"

The pilot gave him a surprised look. "Sheik Hamza al-Din. The project chief."

"Oh. Right."

The blowtorch, its awful motors off, drifted in toward the comet on puffs of hydrogen steam. There was all the hydrogen and oxygen one could want in a comet's snows. And with a starship's Harun drive to draw on, there would be plenty of antimatter available, too, for people who were reckless enough to want to handle the stuff.

They were close enough now for Hamid-Jones to make out enclosed walkways and small surface structures tucked among the great gnarled roots of the trees. The greater part of the installation, of course, would be buried out of sight. Nobody was likely to come visiting—the next nearest rogue comets would be on the order of tens of astronomical units away—but if some prospector equipped with a blinker program did happen to come blundering by, all he would see would be a piece of property that some other developer had got to first.

"Here we go, *ya* Izzat," the pilot said. "You don't have to hang on to your duffel bag like that. There'll be somebody to take your luggage for you."

"We're so glad to see you, *ya* Izzat," Sheik Hamza al-Din said with impeccable courtesy. His smile, past the neat black mustache and goatee, was correct but frosty. "But I'm afraid you won't find much to do. We've run our tests. The countdown begins in seventy-two hours."

"Oh, it's your show," Hamid-Jones said hastily. "I just came to see the thing come to fruition."

Out of the corner of his eye he watched helplessly as his duffel bag disappeared down a long corridor with the rest of his luggage. He had tried to hang on to it, but when the sheik had insisted with aggressive benevolence that everything would be taken care of, he'd had no choice but to surrender it to a porter. Now, with the shocking news that doomsday was only seventy-two hours away, he was desperately aware that time was running out for him to learn the layout of the installation and plant the antimatter bomb.

To say nothing of finding some method of escape.

"Then you got here just in time, *ya* Izzat," Sheik Hamza said, giving the knife of courtesy an extra twist. "When the *hegira* starts, all star travel will be disrupted, of course. Yours, I imagine, was the last ship to be sent out from Alpha Centauri, but I pity those poor devils caught in the void during flights originating in the Solar system. They couldn't be warned in advance, of course." He shrugged. "It will be our duty as humane Moslems to gather them back to safety."

What was that about a *hegira*? Hamid-Jones struggled for comprehension. The thing hinged on some kind of flight. But of what or whom? And why would it interrupt all interstellar travel between Sol and Alpha Centauri? The gulping down of Mars by a black hole might be an event of some moment in human affairs, but it would scarcely make a ripple in the greater cosmos beyond the Solar system.

Hamid-Jones was appalled at the cynicism and hypocrisy of the man, talking about being humane while plotting the destruction of a world.

"But I'm being a poor host," the sheik continued in a tone

that contained not the slightest hint of apology. "Come, we'll have coffee."

Hamid-Jones followed the great man down a half mile of prefabricated corridor, trailed by a bevy of about two dozen men of various ages whom the sheik had not found it necessary to introduce. One of the men, a chubby young fellow in laboratory coveralls, kept nodding and smiling at Hamid-Jones. Hamid-Jones, feeling awkward in the circumstances, nodded and smiled back. Immediately a second chubby young man caught his eye and began smiling at him, too. He seemed anxious to say something. Hamid-Jones returned a strained smile and hurried to keep up with the sheik, who had turned his head impatiently to see what was holding Hamid-Jones up.

After a number of turns and an elevator ride, Hamid-Jones found himself in a large suite that was fitted out with barbaric splendor. Billowing canopies recreated the ambience of a Bedouin tent, though in the comet's microgravity every random draft of air tended to punch out large hollows that took their time about settling back in place again. The floor was ankle deep in thick rugs, and the furniture tended toward large, plump cushions in bright geometric patterns.

The sheik motioned Hamid-Jones to sit beside him on a platform made of mattresses covered with more rugs. The other guests disposed themselves around on cushions. The party had shrunk considerably at the elevator, but the two chubby young men were still there, still smiling shyly at Hamid-Jones.

A servant brought a bowl and ewer for Hamid-Jones to wash his hands with. Sheik Hamza was personally pounding coffee beans with a mortar and pestle. A brass tray as big as a tabletop had been brought, and on it was a graduated row of ornate coffee pots, so that the first brew could be distilled and redistilled until it yielded a tiny cup of ritual mud.

The sheik looked every inch the proud Bedouin aristocrat as he went through the traditional rigamarole of hospitality, though the flowing robes must have been an inconvenience in a comet's gravity and though it had been a thousand years since his forebears had seen a goatskin tent in the desert. But his patrician face, with its proud beak of a nose, betrayed nothing but the most profound seriousness as he bent over his self-assigned task, and no one in the canopy-draped room would have dared to laugh.

When everyone had been served in descending order of rank,

a little conversation was evidently allowed. The ritual welcomes were gotten through, and Hamid-Jones began to learn the names of those present.

The two chubby young men in lab coveralls were somewhere near the lower third of the lineup, but they introduced themselves eagerly.

"I'm Hossain."

"And I'm Hassan."

They both laughed together, and Hamid-Jones laughed politely along with them. An older, dish-faced man of somewhat seedy eminence, who had introduced himself only as Gamal, leaned over to Hamid-Jones and said, "By Allah, they're not brothers, but you can't tell them apart. We call them the binary twins around here."

The two technicians laughed uproariously at what must have been a familiar sally. It wasn't true that they were identical; they just gave that impression at first sight. Hossain had a little pointed beard, Hassan a forked goatee; Hossain was a little more rotund; Hassan had great wooly eyebrows.

"But the project couldn't have gone forward without them," Gamal said good-humoredly. "They're brilliant engineers. At least, one of them is. He does the work for the other. The only trouble is, we can't tell which."

There was another round of amiable laughter, then Hossain became serious. "We've been working with your simulations, *ya* Izzat. They're pure artistry. They say you can get to know a man by the game of chess he plays, and we feel that we've gotten to know you—"

"But we have a few questions," Hassan broke in.

"Yes," Hossain said. "Now, take the division of the collapse into matter and antimatter components that merge *after* they've both acquired their own event horizons, and then settle down into a single black hole whose circumference at the equator can be derived by the ordinary Kerr solution—"

"Not that it matters," Hassan piped up. "A black hole has no hair."

"Yes, a black hole has no hair," Hossain agreed.

They chuckled in unison. Both looked at him expectantly.

"Er, yes . . . precisely," Hamid-Jones managed.

Hassan nudged Hossain. "See, what did I tell you?"

Sheik Hamza interrupted. "That's enough shop talk. You can

bother Izzat all you want to later. Right now, he must be tired from the trip, and we mustn't breach the rules of hospitality by making him work.''

The two technicians fidgeted like puppies, but they relapsed into a hair-trigger silence. The prescribed number of tiny cups of coffee were consumed in a murmur of small talk, and then Gamal, the senior guest in this company, overturned his cup decisively in his saucer and stood up. As if a whip had been cracked, everyone else stood up, too. A ceremony of leave-taking began. Hamid-Jones turned his cup upside down and rose to his feet. He was a little too abrupt in the microgravity and suffered an embarrassed moment of hanging in midair with his feet a foot off the ground till the comet tugged him gently to the rug again.

"I'm so sorry you must leave now, *ya* Izzat," the sheik said graciously. He clapped his hands for a servant. "Rafi will show you to the quarters that have been prepared for you."

Hamid-Jones found himself being eased toward the door. Hassan and Hossain, looking like puppies that had been deprived of a bone, waved a shy good-bye at him. "We'll see you later, *ya* Izzat," Hassan called.

His duffel bag was intact. That was the important thing. He'd had a bad moment when Rafi had ushered him into the Spartan room that had been assigned to him. Somebody was already there, unpacking his luggage and laying out Izzat's things. He hadn't gotten to the duffel bag yet. Hamid-Jones told the valet that he'd finish unpacking himself, and the man had bowed his way out with Rafi.

He lay on the narrow bed, thinking.

His quarters were a long way from the center of things. Sheik Hamza wanted to keep him at arm's length. That was all right with Hamid-Jones. The long trek through the corridors had given him a chance to gain some impression of the comet's layout.

He hadn't seen anything heavy-duty. Nothing that smacked of a great industrial enterprise. But that wasn't surprising. The black hole itself would have to be manufactured a safe distance away. A distance measured in the millions of miles. How it could be done, he could only imagine. He'd done some reading before leaving Mars. The Christian underground had loaned him some of the fruit of their own research. He'd been briefed on possible clues to look for. A low-mass black hole in theory could be formed by compressing a small amount of matter with really tremendous pressures—say a hydrogen bomb several miles in diameter built around a pond of heavy water. The only trouble was that, if it worked, you'd have a black hole about the size of a proton.

That wasn't the kind of black hole predicated in the Izzat simulations. Izzat's black hole had been big enough to gulp down Mars in one swallow and then flee from the Solar system at almost the speed of light, like the thief it was. It had the mass of a star.

There was no way around it. To make a black hole that big, you had to have enough mass to begin with. And there simply wasn't an extra star rattling around out here.

And if there were, how would one go about squeezing it? A thing to squeeze a star would be bigger than the star. So you'd be back to square one again.

Certainly there was no evidence of anything on that scale here at the sprouting comet. The biggest thing Hamid-Jones had seen was the starship moored to the granddaddy tree. Otherwise, the comet seemed to be nothing more than a base for no more than a couple of thousand men—and most of them support personnel at that! There were living quarters, life-support systems, warrens of the modest cubicles that are seen in any scientific enterprise, whether it be theoretical physics or statistical biology. There was a small astronomical facility, appropriate to a third-rate university, a labyrinthine ecology works to extract air and water from the tree roots, a basic chemistry plant to make things out of the trees' sugars, garages of scooters needed for getting around the comet and the trees, docking facilities for the larger vehicles.

And there was one hell of a communication facility. You needed lots of power to reach all the way to Alpha Centauri. That was how the base had started. All of the Centaurans' clandestine radio traffic originating in the Solar system was squirted through this place.

Maybe that was the kind of clue the Christians had told him to look for. If you had a holemaker hidden somewhere out there at these trans-Plutonian distances, you had to be able to send a message to it. And the communications facility was certainly powerful enough to do that.

But what *was* the holemaker?

Still wrestling with the problem, Hamid-Jones fell asleep.

* * *

"Well, this is our nerve center, such as it is, *ya* Izzat," Hossain said. "I know it doesn't look like much."

"But of course we can't do much from here except initiate the automatic sequence," Hassan contributed. "With a radio delay of five seconds, it's pretty much out of our hands once we start."

Hossain gave a theatrical shudder. "And even at that, a million miles is closer to a Harun drive than we want to get, even though we've taken care not to have the business end pointed in our direction."

"Not pointed in our direction if everything works *right*!" Hassan amended, giving a little shudder of his own.

"Well, what do you think, *ya* Izzat?" Hossain said.

They waited for his approval with anxious faces.

Hamid-Jones looked around the operations center that—evidently—contained the heart and soul of Project "Allah's Will." There wasn't a lot to see. It was a crescent-shaped gallery of moderate size, with walls that were painted a pale institutional blue. Workstations sprouted from the floor like mushrooms. There was a glass loggia on an upper level for observers, but it was empty. A couple of dozen technicians were wandering around, not doing very much. Somebody had left the remains of his lunch on one of the nearby consoles.

"It looks just fine," he assured them.

Both of them beamed.

"It's part of the old message center," Hassan said. "We just moved in our stuff."

"Mainly it's just telemetry for the starship," said Hossain. "You'd be surprised at how many subsystems there are to keep track of."

"And that's just while we're jockeying it to the starting line with the fusion drive," Hassan said. "After the Harun drive goes on, it's all automatic."

"We *hope*!" said Hossain. "Even with all the engineering studies, we can't be one hundred percent certain how well things will hold up after a thousand G's."

Hamid-Jones was getting confused. But at least he had learned that the creation of the black hole had something to do with the starship he had seen moored to the tree. "A thousand G's," he repeated in a flat tone that did not turn it into a question that he should have known the answer to.

Hossain reacted with distress. "We hope that's all right, *ya* Izzat. We know that your specs called for a shorter period of infall delay before the quantum jump to black hole formation, but the structural engineers told us that the old starship just wouldn't hold up under more acceleration, even with all the added internal bracing. And it's got to hang together until the last moment."

"But Gamal did the recalculations, projecting your original simulations on a logarithmic spiral based on a curve generated by the gamma factor for relativistic effects," Hassan said. "It works out exactly the same, only stretched."

"So Gamal did the recalculations?" Hamid-Jones said, attempting to look judicious.

"Yes. Naturally you couldn't have known about it, since it's only within the last four years that he undertook the task, and the signal wouldn't have reached Alpha Centauri until after you'd already left."

"Oh, naturally," Hamid-Jones said.

"Perhaps you'd like us to show you?" Hassan said.

"Don't bother Izzat with that stuff," said Hossain. "It's all irrelevant now. The important thing is that the terminal velocity is the same."

"That's all right, I'd like to see it," Hamid-Jones said.

"See, what did I tell you?" Hassan hissed at Hossain.

Hamid-Jones found himself in front of a large holo window, looking at unfolding three-dimensional geometric shapes generated by the math. None of it made the slightest sense to him.

"Nice job," he said. "Very elegant."

"Of course it's elegant." The words came from Gamal himself. The seedy old gent had come up behind the three of them while they were watching the display.

"Oh, *ya* Gamal, we were just showing Izzat your amended solution," said a flustered Hassan.

"And do you approve, *ya* Izzat?" Gamal said amiably.

"Oh, yes, er, of course," Hamid-Jones said.

"Did you notice the appearance of the Mandelbrot set at the moment of the quantum jump?"

"Ah, yes. Very nice."

Gamal's beady old eyes bored into him. "And what do you think it signifies, *ya* Izzat?"

"Well—" Hamid-Jones temporized.

Hossain jumped in eagerly. "Obviously the Mandelbrot images come from the complex numbers generated by the square root of minus one in the gamma formula where it interacts with the logarithmic spiral! At least that's what *I* think!"

"Very reasonable," Hamid-Jones said.

Gamal kept his unwinking stare on Hamid-Jones. "It was interesting enough so that I tried it out on some of the early assumptions that led to the project, and the Mandelbrot images always appeared no matter what the origin of the hole or its final mass. Would you care to see?"

"Uh, yes, of course."

It was a fantastic piece of luck. Gamal moved to the console, and in the next minute, Hamid-Jones was being shown how the Centaurans expected to manufacture a black hole. He didn't have to ask any questions that might have revealed his ignorance—the binary twins, as Gamal had called them, vied with each other to impress him and Gamal.

"Let's take the simplest case," Gamal said, punching routines into the console. "A star of more than three point six times the mass of the sun collapses and becomes a black hole. For convenience's sake, I made our hypothetical star ten solar masses."

Vivid abstract shapes roiled and writhed in the holo display. Hamid-Jones risked a general comment. "I see," he said.

"I knew you'd appreciate it, *ya* Izzat!" burbled Hassan.

"Now," Gamal said, "let's collapse a cloud."

More of the incomprehensible abstractions appeared in the display. This time Hamid-Jones recognized a sort of striped caterpillar that extruded infinities of striped pseudopods into a jewel-like continuum.

"That's at the moment of collapse, too," Hossain volunteered. "Of course the time scale had to be condensed, or we'd be sitting here for a year."

"Quite," said Hamid-Jones.

Gamal turned his dish-shaped face in his direction. "When the Sultan's father asked *my* father how one could go about making a black hole, my father gave him a somewhat facetious reply, I'm afraid. 'Turn on the hydrogen spigot of a starship's Harun drive,' he said. 'Leave it on until you have enough gas to make a star of more than three point six solar masses. Then wait until it condenses into a protostar and kindles. Then wait several billion years more until the star exhausts its fuel and can no longer support itself against its own gravity. And then, your Majesty, we can present you with a black hole.' ''

Hamid-Jones laughed politely. Hossain and Hassan went into hysterics, slapping their knees and whooping, though they must have heard the story before.

"Amusing," Gamal said. "But he spoke more truly than he realized at the time. Because the remark contained the seed of the great insight that led to Project 'Allah's Will.' Though credit for the insight must be given not to my father or the Sultan's father, but to the Sultan himself. A remarkable man, the Sultan, when you think that he has no scientific training."

The mismatched twins sobered up. "Yes, the Sultan's a re-markable man," Hassan chimed in piously. "Intuition is every-thing. It's not given to all of us."

Gamal's face twisted in self-deprecation. "It only remains for others to do the dog work that turns the notions of the mighty into reality. My father devoted the rest of his life to chasing down that particular whim, then passed the task along to me."

Hamid-Jones was surprised at the glimpse of bitterness that Gamal had allowed to escape from behind his amiable mask. He had already begun to suspect that Gamal was not the shabby old hack he had appeared to be at first glance, but a man of the most powerful intellect and of a seething pride that he disguised with a show of indifference. He had the feeling that Gamal was the real brains of the project, not Sheik Hamza.

Gamal recovered his sangfroid. The dish face contained noth-ing but the mild didacticism appropriate to an academic.

"The second great insight, of course, was that you don't have to *wait* billions of years for a hydrogen cloud to condense to a star in the black hole range, burn itself out, and collapse. In theory, an object of *any* size can become a black hole if it's dense enough. But you know all about that, eh, *ya* Izzat?"

Hamid-Jones was saved from having to reply by Hossain.

"The concept may seem strange to a layman, *ya* Izzat, but Gamal explained it all to the Sultan in simple language when the Sultan was only a boy who was in the process of inheriting his father's ambitions. That the Sun, for example, is below the mass range that would turn it into a black hole, but that it would become a black hole all the same if you could somehow condense it to a diameter of three and a half miles. The Earth would have to be shrunk to two centimeters—the size of a cherry. And if we squeezed this comet to a black hole, it would be the size of an atomic nucleus.''

Hassan took up the theme. ''So the Sultan must have grown up with the basic notion in his subconscious that the key to creating a black hole was to compress a required mass into a small enough volume within critical time limits. His father had never made the hajj, either, but the Sultan's ambitions must already have been surpassing those of his father, and he knew he would someday have to find a way.''

''And then came the Mizar business,'' Gamal said.

''Ah, yes, the Mizar business,'' Hamid-Jones echoed, as though he knew what he was talking about.

''It's an amazing dynasty, isn't it?'' Gamal said. ''They've always seen the big picture—made long-range plans that wouldn't be realized in their lifetimes, but would be passed on from generation to generation.''

Hossain nodded reverently. ''It was Malik the First who united Alpha Centauri Alif Prime and left it to Malik the Second to consolidate the whole Alif system . . .''

''And then Malik the Third founded the Kingdom of the Triple Suns as we know it today,'' Hassan finished for him.

Gamal waited out the interruption, then resumed. ''The Sultan's grandfather, Malik the Sixth, was the first to look out to Mizar, though. It wasn't possible to expand to any of the nearer stars—they'd all been taken. And Sol lies nearer to virtually all of them anyway. But we're four light-years nearer to Arcturus and Gamma Virginis—and beyond them lies the tantalizing prize of the Mizar group. It must have made his mouth water. A binary pair circling another binary pair, and, orbiting both of them at a distance of only three light-months, Alcor—five stars all in a single grand slam, waiting for one bold player to sweep them in.

''Never mind that they were fifty-six light-years away—sixty light-years from Sol—and that they'd be impossible to administer with a message round-trip of a hundred and twelve years! Malik the Sixth had plenty of sons. At least he could keep Mizar in the family.''

''If he could get there,'' Hamid-Jones said, then closed his mouth. It was the first he'd heard of the Sultan's grandfather's crazy dream, and he wasn't sure how much he was supposed to know.

"Precisely," Gamal said. "Every ship that had ever been sent to Mizar from Sol had vanished. At sixty light-years it was just past that strange barrier that's kept the human race within a sphere with a radius of forty light-years or so. The colonists stopped trying after the first two hundred years of relativistic spaceflight."

"The Sphere of Allah," Hassan said, tracing the sign of the crescent on his forehead and chest.

Gamal continued, "And then the Sultan's grandfather heard that the Gamma Virginians, only twenty light-years from Mizar, were casting their eyes in that direction. But their own colony at that time, of course, was young. It would take them at least two more generations before their industrial base became large enough to afford an expendable starship and mount what might become another suicide expedition. So Malik the Sixth made his magnificent gamble. He risked three of his starships on a race to Mizar, hoping that at least one of them would get through, and varying their rates of acceleration by a small fraction so they wouldn't all get there at once. They would have left, let me see—"

"One hundred twenty-two years ago," Hossain supplied.

"Hmmm, indeed. And they vanished, just short of their goal, some sixty-six years ago, during the reign of Malik the Seventh. But of course you know all that, *ya* Izzat. That was the germinal event that ultimately led to the birth of this project."

"Yes indeed, very germinal," Hamid-Jones agreed promptly.

Gamal turned inquisitive eyes on him. "You would have been—how old?—when the information arrived at Alpha Centauri and reached our present Sultan. Not yet out of school."

"Yes," Hamid-Jones said, hoping he'd got it right.

"I was with his Majesty when the news arrived." Gamal was subtly letting Hamid-Jones know who was who around here. "He was magnificent. The tragedy might have broken a man of lesser stamp. But his Majesty recovered his composure quickly. He asked one or two searching questions. And then—layman though he was, and not very good at mathematics, if I'm to believe the tales my father told of tutoring him as a youngster— he noticed the anomaly."

Hamid-Jones felt that a comment was expected. "Ah yes, the anomaly," he said.

Gamal was staring at him curiously. "The fact that the starships had all disappeared at different distances, and that in fact the first ship to disappear was the last one—the one that had been accelerating at a slightly faster rate to catch up to the others. He immediately grasped the significance of this, and asked me to run the figures through for him. But the basic insight was his. '*Ya* Gamal,' he said, turning that noble brow in my direction, 'it's clear that the vanishing ships have nothing to do with the boundary of an imaginary Allah's Sphere at some fixed distance, but have something to do with the velocity of the ship itself.' "

"Yes, *ya* Gamal, but you were the one who worked it out!" Hassan cried.

Gamal did not deign to acknowledge the flattery. "His Majesty had grasped the fundamental notion that a ship accelerating at a constant rate by means of the Harun drive *never* turns off its boost until turnover time, and that since an Earth-bred race tends to accelerate always at one gravity, the critical moment *seems* to arrive at some arbitrary distance, give or take a few light-years."

"Yes, yes," Hassan said, beside himself with the need to show off. "That you don't need to collapse mass per se in the form of a hydrogen cloud or any other agglomeration of matter. You can *store* the 'mass' of a hydrogen cloud that would have been big enough to condense into a protostar in the form of kinetic energy. And when the starship gets going fast enough— when it's crawled with increasing difficulty to within the final hair of the speed of light—its Einsteinian mass turns it into a black hole!"

"And," Hossain said, competing with Hassan, "since we can fine-tune the acceleration at that final point, and the starship does, after all, occupy a relatively small volume of stretched space, we can manufacture a black hole that's considerably smaller than the ordinary starting point of three point six solar masses!"

"Please," Gamal said with a grimace. "Would you teach your grandmother to suck eggs? It was Izzat here who refined the original projections to a hole of only one point five solar masses—just big enough to do the job, but not so unwieldy as to . . . inconvenience . . . us afterward."

All at once, the horror of the discussion caved in on Hamid-Jones and left him flat. He'd been so caught up in abstractions that he'd allowed himself to forget the ultimate purpose of the hole—to ingest Mars and all its people and to carry the evidence out of the Solar system at the speed of light, before astronomers had time to notice any gravitational anomalies.

He was still reeling from the shock of that sudden raw emotion as Hossain, his pudgy young face bland and guileless, began burbling more nonsense to impress him.

"The Sultan didn't realize it at the time, but actually, as a sort of appendix to his insight, he solved the Fermi Paradox. Hassan and I think it's only right to give him a credit in the paper we're writing on the subject."

"And Gamal, too," Hassan made haste to add.

"You can keep your credit and a plague on it," Gamal said with a smile that was perhaps just a bit too tight. "All of this will be top secret for some time to come. The Sultan will want to keep it under security wraps as long as possible, so he can use the trick again. Until some astronomer, somewhere, has the wit to figure it out."

Use the trick again . . . Hamid-Jones recoiled at the impact of more horror. So Izzat was to be commended for limiting the black hole to a size that would not "inconvenience" this gang of world-killers after the crime. He supposed that meant that a very large black hole stood a greater chance of giving away its existence through gravitational effects and bringing the condemnation of all Islam down on the Sultan's head.

But he would put a stop to this enormity even if he died in the attempt!

He thought of the antimatter bomb in his duffel bag. Now he knew where to place it.

Hossain was explaining all about the Fermi Paradox. Hamid-Jones hadn't been listening.

". . . and it's been a thousand years since the *ferengi* scientist Enrico Fermi asked the question: 'Where is everybody?' What he meant was that if life exists elsewhere in the galaxy, and if at least the earliest races to arise have had billions of years to spread out among the stars, why hasn't anyone ever visited us? And now we know the answer."

Hassan nodded vigorously. "Earth has never been visited by extraterrestrials because there don't happen to be any within a

few hundred light-years, and those who come calling from farther away turn into black holes before they get here.''

"We almost lost a star or two when our three inadvertent black
holes went whizzing through the Mizar group," Gamal said
humorously. "But fortunately the velocity of the black holes was
the terminal velocity of the ships at the moment of their collapse—without the additional increment of delta vee that the
navigators had assumed—and the stars had all moved further
along in their orbits. But you must have seen the original studies—the sanitized version that turned the Mizar incident into a
hypothetical case?"

"Er, yes," Hamid-Jones said.

Hassan wanted to show off how much he was privy to. "Fortunately none of the three ships had quite reached their turnover
points. It might have been a different story if they'd been accelerating at substantially less than one G and had gotten past turnover safely, or if Mizar had happened to be a few light-years
closer. Then we'd never have known."

"But we'd have gotten to Mizar, *ya* Hassan," Hossain countered.

All at once, Hamid-Jones remembered the sad, lonely little
man he'd bumped into at the Emir's diplomatic function on Mars
four years earlier—no, it would be closer to twelve years of real
time, unadjusted by all the relativistic travel that had mixed up
his personal chronology.

The little man was the unlucky ambassador from Gamma
Virginis B, exiled from his own culture by an eighty-year round-
trip. He'd brought news from his own vicinity—news that had
not yet become general knowledge on Sol or Alpha Centauri,
though the two intelligence communities must have known.

Hamid-Jones squinted, doing arithmetic in his head. "It's academic now, though, isn't it?" he said, "when the Sultanissimo
of Gamma Virginis A planted his colony ship only four years
later. By now they've had three generations to propagate."

Gamal looked at him sharply. "So his Majesty took you into
his confidence?"

Hamid-Jones said nothing. For all he knew, Izzat might very
well have been told by the Sultan. Scientists were always kept
ignorant of political matters, but this wasn't the sort of secret
that could be kept forever.

Gamal became gruff. "Let the Virginians have Mizar—for now! The Sultan's won an incomparably greater prize."

Hamid-Jones had to agree with the cynical assessment. From a practical point of view, winning the Caliphate of all Islam *was* a greater prize than gaining empty title to a cluster of stars that were so far away that news from them was only ancient history.

And, so the Sultan believed, learning the trick of making black holes had given him the key to the Caliphate. Even if it involved the destruction of a planetful of innocent people.

Hamid-Jones's lips tightened. Somehow he had to find a way to get to the starship tethered to the branches of the comet's gargantuan tree. He'd have to cross miles of empty space to do it.

Gamal was still poking at the sore spot of old injustice. "There'll be plenty of credit to go around after we succeed," he said. "I don't begrudge Hamza his directorship of the project. It's only natural that his Majesty would feel more comfortable putting his own kinsman in charge. '*Ya* Gamal,' he said to me at the time, 'you're too important to the project to waste your time on administrative details. Sheik Hamza al-Din's a good manager and a fine scientist in his own right. He can take that burden off your shoulders.' "

Al-Din. The Faith. Even the director of the "Allah's Will" project had a vainglorious name. The Sultan, thought Hamid-Jones, must be a megalomaniac to think that he had been fore-ordained by Allah to become the first Caliph in a thousand years!

"And *did* he take the burden off your shoulders, *ya* Gamal?" Hamid-Jones said.

A shadow of bitterness crossed Gamal's face, contrasting with the light tone he attempted. "Oh yes, *ya* Izzat, he has a finger in everything."

Hossain and Hassan were becoming agitated, and when Hamid-Jones looked around, he saw why. Sheik Hamza himself was striding imperiously—God knew how, in the low gravity—into the control center, his robes swirling about him, his keffia flying, a golden dagger thrust dramatically in his sash. Hamid-Jones decided that the sheik was wearing sticky sandals and that he had lead weights sewn into the hem of his robes. He passed an icy gaze over Hamid-Jones and spoke directly to Gamal.

"I've decided to move the countdown up twenty-four hours."

Gamal's skin turned a shade darker. "I wish I'd known. Station B—"

"I've already notified Station B. They're making laser re-alignments now."

"I'll do the readjustments," Gamal said mildly. "It will mean working all night."

Hamza turned to go. Hossain and Hassan fluttered in his path like moths.

"Yes?" Hamza said.

"If the ship's to be sent on its way a day earlier, then we ought to make a final inspection of our modifications to the Harun drive," Hossain said. "We'd planned to scooter out there to-morrow, but—"

"I'll notify security that you're going out a day early," the sheik said impatiently.

Hamid-Jones spoke up before the sheik could turn away again. "I'd like to go out with them," he said.

Hamza turned a magisterial stare on him. "Why is that?" he said. "You're not involved in the nuts and bolts of the opera-tional hardware."

Hamid-Jones returned a steady gaze. "I've come four light-years as the Sultan's observer to see 'Allah's Will' launched. I'd like to get a feel for the actual, physical part of it."

"Let him come with us, ya Hamza," Hassan begged. "Poor Izzat's been four years removed from the final stages of this project. He deserves to be a part of it now."

"Oh, very well," the sheik said. "Make sure you keep an eye on him while he's out there. I wouldn't want to have to report to the Sultan that anything had happened to him."

He strode off, his weighted robes sweeping the deck. This time Hamid-Jones could see the tacky footprints he left, as they dried out and evaporated in his wake.

"Meet us at the outside lock in an hour, ya Izzat," Hassan said. "The scooter lock at the end of the corridor near your quarters. You can get a space suit from stores."

"Fine," Hamid-Jones said.

An hour would give him just enough time to retrieve the an-timatter bomb from his quarters and figure out some way to conceal it in his suit's equipment.

CHAPTER 11

"**H**ang on, *ya* Izzat," Hossain said to him through the suit radio. The scooters flew up the trunk of the tremendous tree like a pair of fluttering forest birds, using conservative bursts of their thrusters. Even so, Hamid-Jones wouldn't have wanted to slam into one of those giant twisting branches at any speed. He hoped Hossain was a good pilot.

Tightening his grip on the handhold of the saddle in front of him, he ventured a downward glance. It was amazing how "downward" seemed such a long way to fall when the scooter's one-tenth-G thrust was added to the comet's feeble gravity. Actually that primitive sensation of dangerous height was only an illusion caused by pseudoweight plus distance. If, despite the tightly cinched safety belt, he were somehow to fall out of his seat, he would continue to fly upward at a far greater speed than the comet's insignificant escape velocity and sail forever into the eternal night.

From twenty miles up he could see all of the comet—an irregular chunk of ice and hoarfrost sprouting trees in all directions. It was as big as Halley's. But this comet would never swing near enough to the Sun to grow a tail. It would remain a frozen lump of matter, forever circling the outer darkness.

He shifted uncomfortably in his bulky space suit. Sweat trickled down his forehead, maddeningly out of reach. The flat, round canister of the antimatter bomb was squeezed into a pocket of the canvas cover to his cumbersome backpack, along with some loose tools to disguise its contours. He'd had to sacrifice a repair kit containing patches and spare connections to make it fit, and he hoped the suit was in good condition.

He felt a new discomfort. He told himself it was crazy, but though he couldn't possibly feel any part of the hellish disk with his skin through all the layers of fabric and hard casing, it was making him itch between the shoulderblades. He couldn't shake off the sensation that the cryogenic hub of that spinning fly-wheel, with its spoonful of antihydrogen sherbet trapped unreliably in a magnetic field, was boring into his spine.

Above him, Hassan's scooter spat a tongue of blue flame and turned a cartwheel. Another brief jet halted its slow revolution. Hanging upside down in the saddle, the roly-poly space-suited figure waved.

"Ready? Here we go," Hossain said, and a moment later the scooter that Hamid-Jones was riding performed the same maneuver. A few discreet puffs of reverse thrust brought both vehicles to a halt relative to the tree. Then the two scooters began following a branch wider than an eight-lane highway out to where the starship rode at the end of its tether.

The tremendous wooden hull was a mile wide, an immense polished acorn. Like an acorn, it wore a cap that Hamid-Jones had not been able to see from below. The cap was of some dull metal, and obviously it was meant to take the place of the more fragile superconducting parasol. A parasol would not have withstood the inconceivable acceleration the vessel was going to be subjected to. There would be no people aboard, true, but you didn't want to fry the equipment.

Hamid-Jones decided to risk a comment. "It must have been a job getting all that armor plating in place."

Hossain immediately became defensive. "I'm sorry, *ya* Izzat. We had to use solid lead instead of the steel plate you specified. The extra mass helps, though—Gamal figured it into the recalculations. In the final few picoseconds, the mass will be multiplied by a factor of about an octillion, and with a spin to bring the rotation parameter up to point ninety-nine, that will hold the static limit far enough above the event horizon to allow the finishing touches of hydrogen and antihydrogen infall. We figured in the mass of the added internal bracing, too."

"We?" Hamid-Jones said.

"Gamal farmed out the dog work," Hossain said miserably.

"Don't blame us, *ya* Izzat. But your original calculations were his starting point—his canvas, so to speak."

"Gamal's an artist," Hamid-Jones said dryly.

Hossain brightened. "That's it, *ya* Izzat. He has to put his signature on everything."

The great starship loomed closer. They were under the curve of the hull now. Hamid-Jones could see details of the planking. There were the rough slabs of old meteor repairs, loose strands of the superfilament cables that stitched the ship together, great scabrous patches where the varnish had flaked away.

This was a ship that had been ready for the boneyard before the Sultan had converted it to his new purpose. It would be no loss.

The two scooters drifted toward a lock just below the equator. It was a service lock. A few degrees of longitude away, he could see the stupendous copper knobs with which the Harun drive parted the veils of adjacent universes, and the mouth of the enormous funnel that was part of the valve assembly. The other valve would be on the opposite side of the ship, as far away as it could be placed.

"Which valve is this, *ya* Hossain?" he asked.

"The antihydrogen valve, *ya* Izzat," the answer came. "But don't worry. Any atoms of antihydrogen that might have been left floating around in the vicinity have long since gone to their reward. This may look like vacuum out here, but there are always a few stray products of tree respiration hovering about—traces of unconserved oxygen and carbon dioxide. You should have seen how it looked for a few hours after the static tests—sparkles of blue fire outlining the ship and the branches. A beautiful sight!"

They arrived at the lock with a gentle bump. Hassan was already there, tethering his scooter. Hamid-Jones undid his safety belt and followed them inside.

The first thing he saw in the yellow light of the hand torches was the colossal bracing that had been added to the ship's internal spaces—raw girders of some superalloy, ceramic-organic pillars as thick as houses, monumental honeycomb cliffs to replace interior bulkheads that had been ripped out.

Starships were built to be flexible. They had to be—that's why they were stitched, as were Arab ships of old, instead of made with rigid fasteners. But this one had to be protected from the unnatural acceleration that would have snapped its timbers and squashed it to flatness before it had a chance to metamorphose into a black hole.

It presented a new problem for Hamid-Jones.

The ten kiloton bomb he was toting on his back ordinarily would be powerful enough to totally destroy a mile-wide starship. But the tremendous mass of all this internal buttressing—much of it doubtless composed of advanced temperature-resistant materials like titanium-matrix composites—would surely absorb the effects of the explosion and prevent it from reaching the opposite side of the ship. He remembered the lecture on obsolete starships he had heard aboard the *Saladin*. One of them had relied for propulsion on megaton bombs exploding behind pusher plates of 5×10^{12} grams of copper. His antimatter bomb was a hundred times less powerful, and it had more mass to contend with.

He thought it over. At first he considered trying to plant the bomb in the center of the ship. But that might mean that both of the creation valves on opposite sides of the hull might escape damage. Then he decided that all he had to do was to make sure that only one of the valves was destroyed. It didn't matter which one—hydrogen or antihydrogen. The Harun drive wouldn't work without both.

"This way, *ya* Izzat," Hassan said.

The three of them floated through the vast doughnut-shaped cavern that once had been the observation lounge at the ship's waistline. They hardly needed to use their suit jets in this forest of pillars and girders with so many surfaces to push against. There was no net drift toward the walls, which led Hamid-Jones to believe that the mass of the bracing was pretty evenly distributed.

Inside, the ship had been cannibalized of everything valuable. The great lounge had been thoroughly stripped, except for a few overlooked chairs that had not been uprooted. No, Alpha Centauri's passenger fleet would not miss this obsolete vessel.

They alighted at a jumble of equipment bolted around the perimeter of the central shaft. Some of the housings were quite huge, with conduits disappearing through the floor and ceiling. Hossain and Hassan unpacked their electronic paraphernalia and set to work.

At first they tried to involve him in their checklist, but he fended them off.

"No, no, I can't contribute anything. I'm just a spectator here."

He waited until they were deeply involved in some particularly tricky calibration, then yawned into his suit radio and stood up.

"I think I'll have a look around," he said. "These old liners are magnificent dinosaurs. I almost hate to see it go."

"Don't get lost, *ya* Izzat," Hossain said without looking up.

He kicked himself up the central shaft to the next level so that the two technicians wouldn't see what direction he was heading in, then made his way in what he hoped was a straight line toward the outer skin of the ship. This deck had been devoted to passenger facilities. Hamid-Jones drifted past the ravaged heath of an indoor golf course, a drained and cracked pool with a deflated rubber raft resting on the bottom, rows of steam baths with their fixtures ripped out, demolished tennis courts with frayed nets still hanging.

He came out in a curved corridor with a stairwell leading to the same lock he'd entered by. The inner and outer doors were still open to space. Without using his suit jets, he levered himself outside and skimmed along the hull toward the great copper knobs of creation, looking for a place to plant his bomb.

The comet's surface was ten miles below, and there were plenty of branches in between. Even through a telescope, he'd only be a flyspeck. Still, it didn't pay to take chances. Hossain and Hassan hadn't shown any interest in inspecting the outdoor hardware, but one never could tell.

The hull's dilapidated condition helped him. Ordinarily he'd never have been able to budge these thirty-foot-wide planks, a yard thick with dovetailed edges. But some speck of space debris had caught the vessel with its parasol down, and no one had ever bothered to repair the damage. He found a crack with splintered edges, big enough to stuff a goat through.

His hands trembling at the enormity of what he was about to do, he extracted the antimatter bomb from the wide canvas pocket of his backpack. A small wrench drifted loose, but he made no effort to retrieve it. He set the bomb's timer as the Christian armorer had shown him.

He'd wangled a copy of the countdown schedule from Hassan,

and made sure that the chronometer function of his wristcomp was set to comet time. First would be cast-off. The ship would drift outward. At a safe distance the first-stage fusion drive would ignite and point the ship toward the inner system at the one-G acceleration it was designed for.

Then the redesigned Harun drive would kick in. Fuel consumption was no object—not when you had unlimited quantities of hydrogen and antihydrogen from adjacent universes to call on. Very quickly, the ship would claw its way to a peak acceleration of thousands of gravities. In hours it would do what ordinary starships took a year of acceleration to do—brush the speed of light to within a fraction of one percent. The Harun drive would not quit at that point. It would keep striving for smaller and smaller increments of that unreachable goal. And within days thereafter its Einsteinian mass would reach that fatal point at which errant starships always stretched the skin of the universe into black holes.

Hamid-Jones could not take the chance of allowing the Harun drive to switch on. God knew what would happen if the antimatter bomb went off while the engines were sucking virtual particles out of other realities!

He set the bomb to go off after the first hour of travel at one-G acceleration. That would put the ship at a distance of about forty thousand miles. It was cutting it a little fine, but antimatter explosions put out a lot of gamma rays, and forty thousand miles ought to be far enough to insure the safety of the personnel on the comet. He had no intention of becoming a murderer.

He didn't want to think about what would happen if the countdown were delayed.

With a muttered prayer to Allah, he wedged the pie-plate shape of the antimatter bomb as far into the crack as it would go. He tugged at it a couple of times and it stayed put. He was satisfied that Hossain and Hassan wouldn't notice anything when they came out. He looked again at the enormous knobs and funnel of the antihydrogen-making apparatus, not more than a hundred yards away. The bomb was placed right where it ought to be. He had no idea of how much of the ship the bomb would vaporize, but whatever the size of the bite it took, the antihydrogen component of the drive would go with it.

Hassan and Hossain were still at it when he returned. They'd hardly noticed his absence. ''It's a bigger job than we thought,''

Hassan remarked. "We've got a couple of more hours here, and then we'll be working late at the operations center." He yawned happily. "Big day tomorrow, *ya* Izzat!"

The corridors were dimmed for the night by the time Hamid-Jones was able to break away from Hossain, Hassan, and the other diehards in the control center. A lot of the younger men in particular were too keyed up to want to think about sleep tonight. Plans were afoot for a celebration tomorrow if everything went off all right—Sheik Hamza had even promised to sacrifice a sheep from the supply pens—but when Hamid-Jones, pleading fatigue, finally escaped, some of them were already raiding the buffet table of the less perishable items that had been laid out under plastic wrap and preparing to stay up all night talking.

Two portly men in elaborate Centauran costume brushed by him in the narrow passageway and apologized. "*Ismahlee*—excuse me," one of them said. "Can you tell us the way to the tent of Sheik Hamza?"

He actually used the Bedouin form denoting the sheik's abode as a house made of goat hair, though Hamza's quarters were made of wood and industrial materials like everyone else's. Like Hamza, they wore the antique curved knives of a desert past and for further adornment had bedecked themselves with jeweled cartridge belts. The aristocracy was big on tradition.

Hamid-Jones gave them directions, and they thanked him.

"We've had a long ride out from Uranus to see the show," the man said. "But Hamza says it will be worth it."

So much for security, Hamid-Jones thought. Hamza had been inviting Centauran VIP's from the satellites of all the outer planets. Two blowtorches had arrived in the last twenty-four hours, and another was on the way.

"Are you one of the scientists?" the other desert warrior asked.

"Er, yes," Hamid-Jones said.

"Bless your hands, brother. This is a great day for Islam."

They bounced and floated down the corridor, having trouble with the low gravity. Hamid-Jones made the turn to his own corridor. Everything was buttoned up tight. Sensible men had turned in long ago. In terms of the comet's arbitrary day, it was about two o'clock in the morning.

Using the key he had been given, he let himself into his quarters and turned on the overhead light. The first thing he saw was his luggage scattered over the floor where someone had been digging through it. The second thing he saw was his duffel bag disappearing under his bed to join the man who had been stealing it, who had dived for a hiding place when he heard the key turning in the lock.

Hamid-Jones didn't bother with niceties. The bed was bolted to the floor. He grabbed a protruding ankle and yanked. The man, light as a bag of feathers in the microgravity, came flying out after it with a yelp of surprise. Hamid-Jones swung him against the wall with a bone-crunching crack.

"Don't kill me, master, I can explain!" the burglar cried, raising his arms to ward off the next blow.

It was Aziz, trying to put on a servile expression and not quite succeeding. In the moment before Aziz had overcome his surprise, Hamid-Jones had seen a quite different expression cross his face—the look of a determined man about to defend himself and then by an effort of will suppressing his instincts. Over black skintights, Aziz was wearing a stolen lab coat that must have helped him to get through the corridors unchallenged.

"Explain what? Why you were trying to steal the antimatter bomb? You're too late. I've already planted it."

"No, master!" Aziz groaned. "Where exactly did you place it? We've got to get rid of it!"

"How did you know which compartment was mine? Never mind, don't bother to tell me—there was a direction-finding bug in the duffel bag, wasn't there? Tell me something else. How did you get to this comet? How did you even find it?"

"We followed the duffel bag to your takeoff point on Charon," Aziz said unwillingly. "We tracked the blowtorch by telescope to get its course bearing, then trailed it by its exhaust products."

"We? Who's we?"

Aziz didn't answer, but Hamid-Jones saw the involuntary flick of his eyes toward the pocket of his lab coat. Holding Aziz an inch off the floor by the scruff of the coat, he plunged his hand into the pocket and came out with a wadded length of black fabric.

"An Assassin's turban!" he exclaimed. "You're an Assassin! You've been one all along!"

"No, master, let me explain. I was with them in a manner of speaking, true. You see, they debriefed Izzat, and—"

"And they wanted to defuse the antimatter bomb, is that what you're telling me?"

"No, they still want to blow up the holemaker."

"But you don't?"

"No. I'd do anything to prevent it." He looked Hamid-Jones squarely in the eye. "You see, things have changed . . ."

"Changed? You've changed your loyalties, you mean. They've always been for sale to the highest bidder, haven't they? You've decided to go over to the Centaurans. In fact, you've probably been working for Colonel Ish-Shamaal ever since we left Alpha Centauri."

Aziz's expression turned defiant. "No, I haven't. But if there's no other way, I'll warn the sheik that you've planted that bomb."

Hamid-Jones, still holding on to the lab coat, could feel Aziz's muscles bunching. "Don't try anything," he warned. "You may have become stronger since your stay on Alpha Centauri, but you were born on Mars and I was born on Earth."

Somebody in the corridor outside rapped on the door. "Can you keep it down in there, brothers? I'm trying to sleep."

Aziz, opening his mouth to call out, took a swing at the side of Hamid-Jones's head with the duffel bag. Hamid-Jones got a slam that made his head ring. But still holding tight to Aziz's lab coat to conserve the momentum of the punch, he clipped Aziz on the jaw.

"What's going on in there?" the man in the corridor demanded.

"It's all right, brother, go back to sleep," Hamid-Jones said. "There won't be any more noise."

He got Aziz trussed up with torn laundry, stuffed a wad in his mouth for a gag, and wound his lower face round with the Assassin's turban, then shut the limp form up in the closet. Grimly, he prepared to sit up the rest of the night. Despite his resolutions, he dozed off toward morning. The sound of feeble movement in the closet jerked him awake. He opened the door and found Aziz half loose of the strips that bound his arms. He clipped him again, tightened everything, and locked the closet door.

He was just in time. Less than ten minutes later, there was a discreet tapping at the door. He opened it to find Hossain and Hassan standing there, looking bleary-eyed.

"Oh, you're already dressed," Hassan said. "Would you like to join us for the dawn prayer? There's just enough time. The bird flies at sunrise."

The countdown was going smoothly. Sheik Hamza was in high good humor. From where he had been placed, at a spare console down on the floor with a bunch of flight controllers, Hamid-Jones could see him in the glass-walled observation booth, gesturing animatedly to his VIP guests, a broad smile on his aquiline face.

The small screen in front of Hamid-Jones showed a somewhat blurred teleholo view of the stripped starship, taken from a remote camera about five miles up the trunk of the tree it was docked to. This was the general view the sheik's guests were now seeing in the big holo bay that had been set up facing the booth. The picture suddenly sharpened as the sheik pampered his guests with a computer enhancement. The better picture contained no additional information, however; it was simply a fiction that would not have shown anything the remote couldn't make out. Hamid-Jones stuck with the view—he could punch in any of the other concurrently running displays, but most of those were of no interest to anyone except the individual technicians monitoring them.

Hassan slid onto the empty stretch of bench next to him. "Nothing more for me to do for a while. They're checking out the fusion drive verniers now. All Hossain and I have to do from now till cast-off is maintain a live signal. Then we interface with the fusion team to assure lineup at the moment of Harun ignition. But between you and me, it's pretty much up to the pre-set timers. With a ten-second radio round trip, there wouldn't be much we could do from here if anything went wrong."

Hamid-Jones remembered the disagreeable little scene between Sheik Hamza and Gamal about the changed deadline—something about Station B and laser realignments. Station B, he supposed, was parked somewhere out along the line of flight, closer to the point at which the switchover would be made.

"Well that's what Station B is for," he said with what he hoped sounded like professional camaraderie. "That's their job."

Hassan turned to him with a puzzled frown. He opened his mouth to say something, but at that moment Sheik Hamza's voice came through a loudspeaker.

"While we're waiting, perhaps it won't be amiss to review the whole maneuver. We've all been drowned in technical details so far this morning, but the idea behind 'Allah's Will,' like all great inspirations, is simple. In fact, we might liken it to a cosmic billiards game."

A golden ball appeared in the holo bay, replacing the varnished spheroid of the starship. In the twinkling of an eye, it grew a smiling face and spiky, stylized rays straight out of a medieval astronomical treatise.

"Our friend the Sun," Hamza proclaimed. *"Ash-shams."*

"He's grandstanding for the VIPs," Hassan whispered. "He asked Hossain and me to do the animation—'simulation,' he called it. What do we know? We plugged in a graphics program. Luckily there's a guy in the hydroponics section who's a pretty good artist."

The golden ball shrank to a dot and the field of view grew to show the orbits of the inner planets as a series of hairline rings, appropriately colored: yellow for Mercury, white for Venus, blue for Earth, red for Mars. Each planet flashed, grossly out of scale, as the circle of its orbit appeared, then quickly dwindled to a colored dot to show its present position in its orbit.

"Our calculations are very precise," the sheik went on. "What madman would take the chance of disturbing the orbit of the Earth, bearing the holy jewel of Mecca?"

What madman indeed, thought Hamid-Jones. Only the same kind of madman who would contemplate using a black hole to sop up Mars, like a sponge absorbing a drop of water!

The holographic cartoon ballooned in scale rapidly. Now the entire inner system was an undifferentiated disk. So that his distinguished audience could keep track of the positions of the inner planets, the sheik had provided a sort of accessory zoom that floated like a halo above the enlarging view. For those who might not grasp what they were seeing, a ghostly cone of light provided a pointer from the halo to the shrinking center of the main diagram.

Jupiter appeared, then fell behind. Then Saturn, Uranus, Neptune, and Pluto. Sheik Hamza did not fail to name them all. Now the entire Solar system floated in primordial darkness, like a delicate diadem bearing its fake, colored jewels. On the far side of the hologram, the artist had provided a poetic impression of the Oort Cloud as a distant bank of spectral vapor. Though inaccurate, it was all immensely impressive. Hamid-Jones had to admire the talent of Hassan's friend from hydroponics.

"And here *we* are," Hamza said.

A little toy comet with sprouting trees and a tethered starship winked into existence. All pretense at any kind of accuracy of scale had ended. It was now obviously a dog and pony show for the benefit of the visitors. Few of the technicians were bothering to watch.

"Now we're ready to play our game of billiards," the sheik said. "Carom billiards, as a matter of fact—a particularly apt simile, since, like carom billiards, we use three balls. At least at this end."

What is the man talking about, thought Hamid-Jones.

"First our cue ball," the sheik said.

The toy ship detached itself from the tree and floated outward. A sparkler ignited behind it and it began to pick up speed, heading inward toward the orbit of Pluto. Before it got there, the sparkler turned into a brilliant pencil of light, and the animation provided a trailing-edge blur to show that the ship was moving faster.

"The Harun drive is on," the sheik explained. "Now we begin to approach the speed of light very quickly—much more quickly than our passenger traffic between the stars does. We can never reach the speed of light, of course—before we got there our ship would weigh as much as the universe. But we keep shaving thinner and thinner slices off that final bit. It gets harder and harder to do. But on the other hand, as we narrow the gap, the relativistic effects grow by leaps and bounds. At ninety-nine percent of the speed of light, the ship weighs only seven times as much. But at ninety-nine point nine, it weighs twenty-two times as much. Add just one more nine after the decimal point and you have a ship that weighs seventy times its rest mass. And so on. By the time you've put a string of *nine* nines after the decimal point, your ship has multiplied its mass by almost a quarter-million . . ."

In the holo, the outline of the ship dazzled and, like a deflating balloon, abruptly shrank to a dot. Thoughtfully, the artist brought it up to size again so that it could be seen. Now it was a black ball with the number 8 whimsically painted on it surface.

"This is our first black hole," the sheik informed his audience. "We've arranged the moment of collapse so that it weighs exactly one point five solar masses."

First black hole? Hamid-Jones began to have the feeling that something was horribly amiss.

"If this were the only hole," the sheik went on, "it would skim through the plane of the Solar system and exit through the other side, never to be seen again. Unfortunately, it would be going too fast. It wouldn't give Uranus enough time to get out of its way. Uranus would lose its outermost moon, Oberon, and possibly Titania as well. They're small bodies, but people are living there."

An audible gasp of horror from the VIPs came through the loudspeaker. Hamid-Jones became more bewildered. This show of concern didn't jibe with the picture of a Sultan blithely contemplating worldicide.

"So we'd better hope that Station B has done their job properly," Sheik Hamza continued briskly. "Even if we wanted to correct their alignment by radio or laser, they wouldn't get the message for days. And by the same token, they must have gotten off their own shot that long ago. By now, it's already crossed Pluto's orbit on the other side of the Sun."

The hologram obliged with a second black ball rolling across the playing field of space. Its origin, as shown by the trail of ghostly balls it left, was a comet on the opposite side of the Solar system at about the same distance as Hamza's command center.

Station B.

"If he told *them* about the change in the countdown then, I don't see why he waited until the last minute to tell *us*," Hassan grumbled. "I think he just wanted to make Gamal jump."

No wonder Gamal had been so miffed, Hamid-Jones thought.

And no wonder Hassan had been so puzzled by his own remark about Station B correcting the alignment of Hamza's "cue ball." It wasn't a matter of light-seconds—it was a matter of light-days! He hoped Hassan had forgotten the remark. If not, he'd have to claim some kind of misunderstanding.

On the holographic pool table, the two black balls were hurtling toward each other in what looked like perfectly straight lines. Their enormous masses and velocities largely exempted them from the gravitational force that curved the paths of the Sun's family of planets. In fact, since they outweighed the Sun, the gravitational influence would be the other way around if they ever slowed down enough.

And they were going to do just that. The two holes were on a collision course, and the point of impact looked to be somewhere in the vicinity of Neptune's orbit.

A moment later, Hamza confirmed it. "Our cue ball is traveling at very nearly the speed of light—too fast to capture the Sun and planets at this period, but able to cause some very serious mischief indeed. It must be slowed down—and kept outside the orbit of Neptune to avoid distorting the orbits of the inner planets."

Hamid-Jones remembered that Izzat's simulations—the ones he'd stolen and that had so upset the Christian underground— always stopped at approximately the orbit of Neptune, then went back to the starting point. Now he knew why. Izzat's end had only been hole number one. Station B provided the second hole.

"The holes are flattened almost to disks by relativistic contraction along their direction of movement," the sheik was saying. "Black hole physics says that can't happen—and indeed it can't. In their own frames of reference, the holes are obeying the rules. Black holes are flattened only by their own rotation, and the shape of a hole is determined only by its mass and its rotation parameter. And even then their behavior is very peculiar—a flattened hole doesn't change the size of its waistline, for example. But it's pulling space-time out of shape in all sorts of complicated ways. So that when you add the distortion caused by the relativistic contraction, some very queer things must be happening in space-time indeed!"

In the holo cartoon, the two billiard balls had in fact flattened, and now they smacked together and became one.

"When two black holes bump, it's not like an ordinary collision," Hamza said. "They can't bounce and they can't shatter. They swallow each other up, and merge into a single black hole whose event horizon, oddly enough, has a cross section whose area is greater than the sum of its parts. The new hole contains the mass of the holes that went into it, plus the sum of their angular momentum and electric charge. Nothing else matters. 'A black hole has no hair,' as we like to say. So, for example, it doesn't make any difference if one is made of matter and the other of antimatter. They can't explode, as would be the case in an ordinary situation. The explosion couldn't get beyond the event horizon in any case."

He gestured at the object in the holo bay. With momentum almost canceled, it had reverted to a spherical shape again—a black ball slightly larger than the two that had disappeared.

"The combined mass of the two holes is three solar masses. In actual fact, just a bit less than that to provide a small net motion toward Alpha Centauri and to satisfy the requirements of orbital mechanics as we worked them out. The mass of the second hole was slightly less than that of the first, though its velocity was identical. We might have done it the other way round, of course—same mass, different velocities—and arrived at the same vector sum. The result would be the same—the capture of the entire Solar system by a mass greater than itself."

In the holo bay, the Sun and inner planets had started to do a slow dance around the black hole. The two outer planets, however, had been torn from the Sun's grasp, and were now circling the black hole on their own.

"The hole will strip Pluto and Neptune away from the Sun, and Uranus may settle into a crazy figure-eight orbit," came the sheik's confident voice, "but the Sun will manage to hang onto the rest of its family of planets. And that shouldn't be a hardship. After all, for the human race over thousands of years of its history, there were only five planets in the sky."

Somebody was interrupting the sheik with a question. Hamid-Jones heard Hamza say, "What's that?" and then some background noise, and then the sheik's reply.

"Ah, yes, what about the inhabitants of Pluto and the moons of Neptune and Uranus. They won't suffer, I assure you. They're getting virtually no heat from the Sun anyway, and their populations have been doing fine with their own energy sources. They should be able to hang on very well until we can evacuate them. But an exodus may not be necessary—I shouldn't be surprised if most of them elected to stay. Especially when they find they have three tiny suns in the sky instead of one."

Hamid-Jones was beginning to form a fantastic surmise. He wasn't at all surprised at the sheik's next words.

"Now for the next carom in our game of billiards. We can wait a hundred thousand years for our new binary system to drift into Alpha Centauri's neighborhood, or we can speed up the process . . ."

In the outer darkness beyond the comet, a new black hole was taking shape. It was bigger than the composite black hole that was waltzing the Sun around, and it was racing toward it on a course that put the comet directly in its path.

"We had to back up a bit to get this one going," the sheik said. "It's ten times the mass of its target—thirty solar masses."

There was a frantic buzzing of questions in the control booth. Hamid-Jones could see one of the VIPs he had bumped into the night before. He looked quite agitated.

"No, no," the sheik soothed. "It won't gobble us up. It's still quite far off. By the time it gets here, the comet will have moved along in its orbit. I'm going to help it along with a push from the blowtorches that brought you here. We'll feel the wind of its passage, so to speak, but it will be gone at almost the speed of light."

The hologram confirmed his words by moving the toy comet, and the VIPs settled down.

"Thirty solar masses and three solar masses splash together to make a new black hole of thirty-three solar masses," the sheik went on. "Their momenta average out. The combination black hole is now moving toward Alpha Centauri at approximately ninety percent of the speed of light. And carrying the Solar system with it."

In the blackness of the holo bay, Hamid-Jones could see two orbital diagrams, dancing an unequal dance around each other. The massive hole, with the two wire hoops that denoted the orbits of Pluto and Neptune, swung its smaller partner around in a wide circle, wobbling itself a little in response.

"We have here a perfectly ordinary double star system," Hamza said, "in which one of the stars happens to be a black hole. The third hole stretched the orbit before it snapped back, and as a consequence of its much greater mass, the Sun is obliged to speed up and move further outward. That puts the entire system's center of gravity far beyond what used to be the orbit of Pluto—about seven hundred AU's, or four light-days—so the two partners should settle down to a fine life together. We won't even have rattled the teacups in the cupboards of Earth and Mars."

There was another question from the VIPs—one that put a frown in Hamza's voice.

"What would happen if the second hole missed? In that case we'd be left with a thirty-one point five solar mass departing for Alpha Centauri at ninety-nine percent of the speed of light—too fast to capture the Solar system. We'd only have failed. It would be much more serious if something happened to the *first* hole. Our cue ball. If the first hole were to be canceled, its momentum would not be added to that of the thirty-sol hole. The thirty-sol hole would encounter only the second hole, going in the opposite direction with its momentum intact. It would be slowed sufficiently to linger in the neighborhood, and at a point closer to Sol, long enough to disrupt the orbits of the inner planets. Earth might roast. Or freeze."

What have I done? thought Hamid-Jones in an agony of remorse. At the very least he had assured the ascendancy of the evil clone of the Emir over an enlightened Sultan. At worst, he had put the entire populations of Earth, Mars, and the inhabited moons in peril!

In the observation booth, the sheik was winding up his presentation, blithely unaware of the ticking time bomb that would turn the Sultan's brilliant conception into the most terrible disaster the human race had ever known.

"But we won't miss," he smiled with aristocratic confidence. "Nothing will go wrong. We're not relying only on simulations—the Sultan insisted on a successful test before authorizing this project, as a result of which there's a black hole sitting halfway between Alpha Centauri and Ross 154 which the astronomers will discover some day."

His voice took on a ring of command. Even the hunched, inattentive technicians sat up and took notice. "So, my friends, very shortly the Solar system will be taking a trip to Alpha Centauri, where its momentum will be canceled by a final carom shot. Both the Solar system and the three stars of the Alpha Centauri system will take up residence around a black hole of sixty-six solar masses, in a multiple system which will rival Mizar for complexity. And the Sultan will have Earth—and Mecca—in his own backyard!"

Eyes flashing, he paused to savor the triumph to come.

"The Will of Allah is fulfilled," he said. "If the Sultan cannot go to Mecca, then Mecca must go to the Sultan."

CHAPTER 12

Hamid-Jones sat stunned for the moment. Around him, technicians and guests were applauding.

Little by little the numbness of his senses went away. He knew he had to get his wits about him—fast! There wasn't much time left to do something about the antimatter bomb. Already, the technicians were turning back to their consoles, preparing to cast off the starship.

He stood up, trying to be unobtrusive about it. The bomb's timer could be turned off; the Christian armorer had shown him how. But the flywheel that kept the magnetic field going was running down—it had days to go at best. He would have to jettison the bomb—give it a good shove into space. What was the escape velocity of a comet this size? His muscles could handle it, he was sure. A good pitch, and the bomb could be thousands of miles away before the explosion came. It wouldn't matter if it got into the path of the onrushing 30-sol juggernaut—a mere ten-kiloton explosion wouldn't bother a black hole.

"Where are you going?" Hassan asked.

"I'll be right back," Hamid-Jones evaded.

"But you'll miss the launch."

"No I won't. It'll take a while for the cast-off routines."

"I know, but—"

"Excuse me," he said, squeezing past a technician. Up on the big holo monitor the display had reverted to a closeup of a loop of monofilament hawser in the automatic release mechanism of a docking cleat. The holo bay divided itself into four windows to show three such closeups plus the original long shot from halfway up the tree trunk.

He made it almost all of the way to the exit before Hossain intercepted him. "*Ya* Izzat, guess what? A friend of yours just arrived on the blowtorch from Pluto. They told him he'd find you here."

He was beaming happily. The man who stood beside him was a nightmare come to life. It was Sherkan, the forestry expert he'd met on Pluto, who had ridden out with Izzat Awad from Alpha Centauri, and who had wondered why Izzat had disappeared on Mars.

Sherkan peered at Hamid-Jones, his mouth open in a frozen greeting. Then he said, "This isn't Izzat!"

"What?" Hossain said, the foolish smile still in place.

"His name's Hamid-Jones. He's a Martian."

"Excuse me," Hamid-Jones said. He pushed past them and started walking fast. This was a mistake. His feet left the floor, and he was pedaling in midair for several beats until he could get traction again.

"Spy!" Sherkan yelled, snatching at his sleeve. Hamid-Jones broke free and started running—this time in long flat pushes that kept him in contact with the floor between five-yard strides. Behind him he could hear Sherkan gibbering an alarm toward the control booth. Someone shouted, "Get him!"

He got about eighty feet down the corridor before a man who had been attracted by the hubbub popped up in front of him. Someone else tackled him from behind. A pair of large, solid men in fashion-tailored versions of Bedouin robes—the kinsmen who served as Sheik Hamza's bodyguards—hauled him to his feet.

Sheik Hamza himself came down the corridor, a small mob of VIPs and momentarily unoccupied technicians at his heels. "What is all this?" he demanded.

"He told me he was a biologist, come to study life on Charon!" the young forester babbled excitedly. "I checked with the desk later—I was waiting for Izzat to show up—and they told me he'd checked in, stayed one night, and checked out again. I thought there was something fishy—I didn't see how Izzat could have come through without my seeing him!" He faced Hamid-Jones, his face red and accusing. "What have you done with Izzat?" he demanded.

"Lock him up somewhere," the sheik said. "We can't let this disrupt the countdown. I'll deal with this later."

"No, listen, you mustn't proceed!" Hamid-Jones cried desperately. "There's a—"

One of the bodyguards struck him a blow that jarred all his teeth. "Shut up!" he said.

Hamid-Jones shook his head doggedly and tried again. "Listen to me, *ya* Sheik Hamza . . . I came here to stop the launch, but—"

This time the blow was less measured; it rattled the brains around in his skull and gave him a bloody mouth.

"What did I tell you?" Sherkan twittered. "He's a Martian agent . . . his confederates back on Mars must have kidnapped poor Izzat!"

"These fanatics," the sheik said sorrowfully, and turned on his heel. The mob of people followed him back to the control room.

"No, wait, you've got to listen to me!" Hamid-Jones called after the departing backs. The large kinsman gave him an offhand smack, and they dragged him away. A few minutes later he found himself locked in a small lavatory, with one of the guards stationed outside.

Hamid-Jones inspected his surroundings without hope. There wasn't much here to help him—only the usual lavatory fixtures, soap, towels, a hot air blower for the fastidious. There was a small closet with cleaning materials. Somebody had parked a cleaner's dolly here, with a fifty-gallon trash drum and a sheaf of plastic liners for it. A mop and bucket were leaning against the wall.

There was no way out. Outside the locked door was a very muscular man, armed and competent. There was little hope of besting him with a mop handle, even if Hamid-Jones could somehow smash the lock. On the other side of the opposite wall was naked space.

Hamid-Jones thought it over and after a while began to get a small idea.

He had been aboard Station A long enough to know how things worked. A comet was not a space habitat or ship with a complex recycling system. The plumbing was very simple and direct. On the other side of the outside wall was a large cesstank where wastes collected. Periodically its contents were dumped into the vacuum of space. There was no point in recycling when there was a comet to provide all the water a smallish human installation could need. The wastes exploded into space; after a while the water and organic molecules came drifting back and the trees eventually reused them. It could, presumably, be called a recycling system of sorts—a long-range organic one.

Behind a service panel he found a lever that opened the outside lid. There were safety latches so that a cleaner could swab out the bin to prevent the buildup of fungus or bacteria—he had just done the job, in fact, to judge by the disposable swabs enclosed in plastic bags in the trash drum.

Could a man survive the vacuum of space for a minute or so? One occasionally read of those who had—they turned up on newscasts, ruddy with burst capillaries, expounding on their experience.

If he could think of some way to keep his eyeballs from freezing! And would a minute be long enough? He seemed to remember that all of those lucky survivors he'd heard of had lost consciousness after the first few seconds—there had always been someone right on the spot to rescue them.

His eyes fell on the sheaf of spare plastic trash liners on the cleaner's dolly, and he had an inspiration.

He peeled one off and unfolded it. It was a nice stout transparent sack, industrial size. Man size, in fact.

Using the mop handle, he broke the glass in front of the outside lever. He paused, holding his breath, but the guard in the corridor did not respond. He pulled the lever, opening the outside hatch to flush the storage tank, just to be sure, then closed it tight again. If there had been an explosion of frost outside, it had been silent.

He had to force the inside safety latches, but he finally got them undogged and swung open the inside panel. His heart sank. The cleaner had not done quite as thorough a job of swabbing out the bin as a fastidious Moslem would have liked, and though vacuum had instantly sucked out the last traces of moisture, the abstract idea of crawling into the fluoroglass-lined bin was not inviting. He consoled himself with the thought that he would be encased in plastic.

He climbed into the trash bag and hopped over to the hot air blower. With a little squatting and twisting, he contrived to fit the neck of the sack around the nozzle and, with a fist holding it in place, fill it with hot air. Quickly, before he spilled too much air, he everted the neck of the sack and closed it, topologically inside with him, with a twist and a knot. He hopped back to the wall panel, blundering about in the low gravity, and opened the outside lid again. It wasn't easy, manipulating the lever through the half-inflated plastic, but he managed.

He hesitated.

Nothing but raw vacuum was waiting out there for him. Only a thin wall panel separated him from it now. He had no idea how long he could survive in space. He had a pretty good diagram in his head of the comet's layout, but he didn't know how many minutes it would take him to get where he wanted to go.

One thing was sure: there was nothing to be gained by waiting. With every passing moment he was losing some of the margin of warmth he'd trapped inside the sack with him.

He got hold of the mop handle through the plastic and, wielding it with both hands, he pried open the safety latches he had previously forced. An alarm went off. "Hey, what are you doing in there?" a shout came from the corridor.

He had himself wedged as tightly as possible behind a lavatory fixture when the last latch gave way and the air whooshed out. There was a hurricane of towels and other loose objects, but Hamid-Jones was able to resist the tug. The hammering on the door faded as the air disappeared. They wouldn't be able to open the door now, with the corridor air pressure pushing it shut. For that matter, they wouldn't want to—not with vacuum on the other side. They would assume that he had gone to great lengths to kill himself and hope to recover his corpse somewhere in the vicinity of the comet later.

He unwedged himself and, using the mop handle as a boat hook, levered himself through the yawning panel into space. In vacuum, the air-filled bag puffed out into a taut balloon, but he'd already had a firm grip on the mop handle, and he was able to wriggle along like a Mexican jumping bean.

He half rolled, half squirmed across the outer skin of the station, using the mop handle to get himself across obstacles and trying to avoid any violent movements that would make him lose contact with the station. About a hundred twenty feet away, he saw the bright yellow-painted outline of a small airlock. You could always open them from outside; safety regulations required it.

He humped along, making painful progress. Already he had gulped three or four searing lungsful of air, and the bag was getting stuffy. And the temperature was dropping fast enough for him to see frost with each breath.

He might not have made it if he had not been half-Martian. The sojourn with the Bedouin had toughened him. He was used to walking between tents on a lungful of air, or dashing outside shelter to do a chore in fifty-below-zero cold without bothering about protection. But by the time he got to the airlock, he knew another fifty feet would have finished him.

He fumbled with frozen hands through ballooning plastic to work the airlock's outer handle. He couldn't get a good enough grip on the spokes, and he knew that he couldn't hold out for more than a few more seconds. With a convulsive poke, he tore through the plastic and thrust his bare hands outside. All the spent air puffed out, and he felt his ears pop. The cold metal burned his hands but he spun the wheel and the door opened. He tumbled inside and managed to tug the door shut after him. His lungs on fire, he gave the inner wheel a spin and collapsed to the floor. Air automatically started to fill the lock immediately. Hamid-Jones took a shallow draft, his chest heaving.

After a few minutes he was able to stand. He shed the remnants of the plastic bag and cautiously opened the inner door for a peek inside. No one was around. Everyone who wasn't engaged in some absolutely essential duty would be in front of a screen with his friends, watching the launch.

There were only two serviceable space suits in the robing chamber. One was hopelessly elongated—meant for a citizen of a low-gravity moon. But the other looked as if it might fit. It had better!

Hoisting the bulky suit and backpack to his shoulders, he skulked through empty corridors back to his own quarters, like an ant toting a dead beetle.

He hoped it wouldn't occur to anybody to search his room for a while. There would be no reason to. At this moment, a lot of men would be milling confusedly around the door of the lavatory he had just quit, trying to figure out what to do. After all, a body might still be wedged inside. At some point they'd get word to Sheik Hamza in the control room. But everybody would be too occupied with the launch to worry about putting an outside patch on the breached room or otherwise trying to sort things out.

The door to his room stood ajar. Hamid-Jones kicked it all the way open, lurched inside, let the space suit slide to the floor, and pulled the door shut behind him. A sour taste rose in his throat.

Aziz was missing from the closet he'd been locked up in. The door hung open, and the strips of cloth that had bound him lay scattered on the floor.

What was he up to now, and was he ally or enemy? And where were his playmates, the Assassins?

Hamid-Jones shook his head to clear it. He couldn't worry about that now.

He hoisted the space suit back to his shoulders. It wasn't heavy—in the comet's feeble gravity it weighed less than a quarter-pound—but the flopping arms and legs made it an awkward burden. As an afterthought he tucked a set of long johns under his arm to use as a suit liner.

He was still lucky. He encountered nobody on the way to the vehicle airlock that Hossain and Hassan had used getting back the day before. As he came close to the parking garage, he heard voices.

". . . adjust the trim. Ready to cast off now . . ."

It was Sheik Hamza talking. His voice was coming over the comm system. The holemaker's tethers were about to be loosed. Hamid-Jones found it hard to believe that time had crawled so slowly. It couldn't have been more than twenty minutes since he'd been unmasked by the forester.

The voice was coming from the open door to the parking garage. Hamid-Jones edged close enough to see the broad back of a single attendant sitting in front of a pocket holopane that he had propped up on a shelf.

He estimated the size of the man and the distance to his desk and wondered if he'd be able to rush him and overpower him. He still felt shaky from his trip outside and the two blows to the mouth that he'd sustained. Centaurans were just as strong as he was.

Perhaps it wouldn't come to that. He hoped so. Right now he was a dead man, but a trussed garage attendant and a missing scooter would give him away.

He waited until he was sure that the man's attention was fully engaged, then slipped past the door frame. Another hundred feet of low-gravity shuffle took him to a small service airlock that he knew was positioned near the vehicle airlock on the other side of the garage wall. He'd used it the day before.

Another swift look up and down the passageway, and he let himself into the small chamber. He hoped that no warning light had gone on near the attendant's desk or, that if one had, he hadn't noticed it.

It was difficult getting into the space suit in the cramped quarters with no one to help him, but he managed. He made a bundle of his clothing and crammed it under the straps of the backpack. It wouldn't do to leave it behind.

He cycled the lock, and with a silent prayer opened the outer door. His luck was still with him. One of the scooters from the previous day's expedition was still tethered outside. Hossain and Hassan, casual about everything, hadn't bothered to check them back in.

Hamid-Jones allowed himself a moment to go weak with relief. What if the garage attendant had collected them? Or if there had been another person indifferent to rules who'd borrowed the unattended second scooter, as someone seemed to have borrowed the first.

He climbed into the saddle and kicked the scooter away from the comet with his foot. The controls were idiotproof. That was the trouble. He wasted about a minute and a half trying to figure out how to activate the attitude jets without pushing the big red ignition button.

Using only the attitude jets, he coaxed the scooter around the trunk of the enormous tree. It was more than a mile across at the base, and he had to keep stabbing at the attitude buttons to keep the scooter from settling into the snowdrifts around the great gnarled roots.

About a mile into his circuit, he judged that he was safely out of the line of sight of any cameras clustered at the operations base. He was on the opposite side of the trunk from the camera he *knew* was mounted five miles up the trunk. If there were cameras on this side, he was cooked.

He took a sighting past the edge of the trunk to where the starship hung from its branch like a *ferengi* Christmas ornament.

And now there was a new reason for alarm. A minuscule drift downward told him that the ship was floating free. It had dropped its mooring cables. As he watched it began slowly to roll over on its side.

They were aiming it now. The countdown held at this point so they could trim the ship and compensate for the downward drift. But it would begin to move outward at any minute.

He jammed the throttle of the scooter forward and zipped up the side of the trunk at reckless speed. The first branches were about four miles up. He dodged the first one with a twitch of the handlebars, had to fire the belly thrusters full force to miss the second. The corrugated bark of the trunk whipped by in a blur. He had no idea what his turnaround point was; he'd forgotten to punch a destination estimate into the computer. He eyeballed it. At what he judged to be halfway there, he killed the engine just long enough to horse the scooter around without squirting off sideways, then fired at full blast again

He'd guessed pretty well. He only overshot the branch by a quarter-mile. He corrected, re-aimed the scooter, and followed a path above the branch where he'd be invisible from below.

He parked at a tremendous stanchion where a monofilament cable as thick as an elephant's thigh hung limply from the branch. He could look over the edge now without fear of being seen. The ship itself offered a mile-wide eclipse.

It was alarmingly far away—a quarter-mile drop, at least. An open airlock at its equator was only a black speck. The knobs of creation that had been at the ship's waist were now facing topside. Which ones—hydrogen or antihydrogen—he couldn't tell.

He nudged the scooter over the edge and let it drop, with a small extra push from a steering jet. The black square of the airlock rose toward him. He recognized a meteor scar etched in the wood. Allah was with him. This was the side of the ship where he'd planted the bomb!

He cut his fall with a sneeze of his belly jets. The scooter settled to what had been the inner bulkhead of the lock. He tied it to a cleat, just to make sure, and climbed a wall to stick his head out the door.

He started to crawl across the outside planking and found himself adrift, without an ounce of weight to hold him down. Free fall is free fall, no matter how slow the rate of drop. He floundered for a nonexistent handhold, and then something grabbed his ankle and pulled him back into the airlock.

He struggled, helplessly clumsy in the bulky suit, but found himself being pulled like a toy balloon through the inner door of the lock and into the ship.

His captor released his ankle and backed away, a weapon in his hand. He was wearing a lightweight suit with sleeve garters at the elbows and knees to give him mobility without the need for stovepipe joints and bleeder valves—a practical design for someone who didn't value his comfort or life. A lean, ascetic face showed through the inflatable helmet, beneath a black turban.

An Assassin.

There were three of them—all Martian stringbeans with the moderate elongation of the natives of the Solar system's second-heaviest inhabited body. The third man, floating against the wall with his arms folded and staring coolly at him, was Aziz.

The Assassins didn't seem to regard Hamid-Jones as a threat—only a minor nuisance. They motioned him to stay out of their way and keep out of trouble.

One of them carried a flat satchel whose soft outlines revealed a familiar discus shape that brought Hamid-Jones's heart up into his throat.

He tried to talk to them, but one of them made a savage gesture indicating that he was not to use his suit radio. They waited in a no-gravity crouch, their heads cocked in anticipation.

The kick came, a gentle chemical boost that lasted about twenty seconds and sent the ship moving outward. It was followed by a series of adjustments—little shoves of steam jets from various angles to correct the alignment.

Hamid-Jones looked through the yawning doors of the airlock at the dwindling comet. When it was several miles away, Aziz indicated to him with a hand sign that he could use his radio now. Hamid-Jones searched through the frequencies till he found the one they were using.

"What is this?" he demanded. "What's going on here?"

"The Christians never trusted you, *ya* Abdul." Aziz wasn't calling him 'master' anymore. "They used you as a decoy. If you got caught, then you'd draw attention away from the backup team."

He nodded toward his two companions. One of them, the

ascetic-looking cutthroat who'd pulled Hamid-Jones into the ship, grinned at him engagingly.

"But I've already planted the bomb."

"So I've informed them. It doesn't matter. You were always insurance . . . just in case you *didn't* get yourself caught, and something happened to the real demolition team. They're going to set off their own bomb anyway. They're taking no chances that you've done the job properly, that the timer sets off the bomb before black hole formation starts, that your bomb works, and so forth."

"You have a way to get off the ship?"

Aziz smiled. "No. There's only the lifeboat that brought us here—we approached from above, as you did, to avoid detection. The blowtorch that carried us from Pluto is a long way off. But even if the lifeboat got us far enough away from the antimatter explosion in time, we're shortly going to share this ship's tremendous delta-vee. We couldn't hope to overcome *that* with a lifeboat engine. We'd only be lost in the stars till the air ran out. In any case, my colleagues have no intention of going off and leaving our bomb unattended. They want to be absolutely sure that nothing can go wrong."

"But you'll all die!"

"Assassins are quite prepared to die, *ya* Abdul."

"I never figured you for a fanatic."

"Death is a boon devoutly to be sought," Aziz said piously. "The Old Man of the Mountain has promised paradise to those who die while faithfully carrying out his missions."

The grinning Assassin nodded vigorously at his words.

"But have you told them it's not necessary anymore to blow up this ship? It isn't intended to swallow up Mars, as we all thought. It's part of an engineering plan to move the Solar system—in furtherance of the Sultan's political aims. With Mecca within easy travel distance, he can complete the hajj . . . win the Caliphate . . . depose the Emir's clone, and install al-Sharq in his place. The Sultan's reins are light. It'll be a better world for everybody, including the Assassins. They're only throwing a monkey wrench in the works."

"They know all that. The Old Man debriefed your friend Izzat. He was a stubborn nut to crack. Otherwise we'd have had the information before you left."

"Well, then?"

"The Assassins don't care all that much about installing a satrap of the Sultan of Alpha Centauri. He's too tolerant—they're afraid the Christians will be in ascendency. They're not all that fond of al-Sharq, either. They were willing to deal with him when they thought Mars itself was in danger. But now they'd rather deal with the satan they know."

"But don't they realize the danger of interfering with this black hole three-shot?" He struggled to recall Sheik Hamza's warning. "If the ship's blown up, it won't be able to cancel the momentum of the *second* hole. The second hole will slow down the third hole by five percent. There'll be a black hole with a mass thirty-one and a half times greater than the Sun lingering too close to the inner planets. It could pull Mars out of its orbit."

"I explained that."

"For Allah's sake, why are they going ahead, then?"

"These are simple God-fearing men, *ya* Abdul. They know nothing of astrophysics. They *do* know that any attempt to turn them from their purpose might be a trick. A ruse by an enemy to confuse them. You or I might be the unwitting carriers of misinformation. Or we might be their enemy."

The grinning one grinned more widely in approval of Aziz's analysis.

"Of course, I'm honor bound to bring these matters up and lay them out for their consideration," Aziz said. He smiled back at the Assassin.

"Oh, God!" Hamid-Jones said.

"It could be even worse than that, *ya* Abdul. Have you thought about what might happen if only one half of the Harun drive were destroyed, and the hydrogen and antihydrogen were not able to annihilate each other?"

"Yes. That's why I placed the bomb to destroy the antihydrogen valve. It might be dangerous to have an antimatter cloud drifting around the Solar system where a spaceship might encounter it."

"Precisely the point that occurred to my friends. An Assassin is not without conscience, you know. So they're determined to set off their bomb on this side of the ship, too. One bomb or the other will do the job, and the bomb that goes off first will release the antimatter in the other one, to augment the size of the explosion. Some thought was given to planting the bomb in the center of the ship, but with all this massive shielding—whole cliffs of superhard alloys and composites—such a bomb might fail to reach *either* side, and we'd have a Harun effect enclosing a vaporized core contained by a shell of melted materials.''

"I'm glad they had that much sense, at least," Hamid-Jones said.

His tone wiped the grin off the Assassin's face and brought a scowl. But it looked more like a case of hurt feelings than anger.

"As much sense as you have, *ya* Abdul," Aziz said. "Are you familiar with the Christian fairy tale about the magical salt mill at the bottom of the sea?"

"No."

"It wouldn't stop grinding out salt. When the person who had unwittingly called up the magic spell became inundated with mountains of salt, he got rid of the mill by throwing it into the ocean. And that's why the sea is salty. And presumably why it will become saltier. What do you think will happen if the damaged Harun drive keeps pouring out hydrogen without end—if the rift into the adjacent plenum widens with time?"

The Assassin was over his sulk. As Aziz had said, he was a simple-hearted fellow. He sat back, his automatic weapon resting on his knees, enjoying seeing Aziz put Hamid-Jones on the spot.

"The Solar wind would push hydrogen clouds away. Eventually the hydrogen would reach equilibrium."

"A happy thought. But there are computer studies that indicate that when such a hypothetical cloud reaches some critical density—perhaps several hundred hydrogen atoms per cubic centimeter—it begins to exert its own pressure on the Solar wind shock front. In such a case, the shock front would be forced back to well within the orbit of the Earth, and the Earth and the planets beyond it would be wrapped in blankets of hydrogen."

"You seem to know a lot about astrophysics," Hamid-Jones said.

"I've studied it," Aziz admitted. "There are many things about me that you don't know, *ya* Abdul."

"What about your damned hydrogen blanket?" Hamid-Jones growled.

"There are theories that past encounters with hydrogen clouds triggered the ice ages on Earth. Too much hydrogen in the upper atmosphere would react with radicals and produce water vapor which would turn into cloud cover. Of course, that's just a moderate amount of hydrogen—perhaps two hundred atoms per cubic centimeter. But what happens if our salt mill in the heavens keeps grinding away?''

"Go on," Hamid-Jones said grimly.

"Hydrogen's light. It's supposed to ride on top of the atmosphere, like oil on water. But suppose this blanket gets heavier and heavier, piling up—attracted by the Earth's gravity. Or Mars's gravity, for that matter. At some point the lower layers start to mingle with thicker air. The hydrogen combines with oxygen—think about why such great pains are taken to keep hydrogen and lox apart when chemical rockets are refueled! With the top of the atmosphere on fire, the heat draws more oxygen up. Earth would go up like a tennis ball soaked in gasoline.''

"I don't believe you! At some point the rift in creation would seal itself. Otherwise the universe would keep expanding.'' He stopped and bit his lip.

"Perhaps. But where is that point? When a protostar is formed? When a galaxy is born?''

Both Assassins were grinning hugely now. They were pleased at Hamid-Jones's statement of disbelief. They, too, had resisted the devil's arguments.

Aziz sighed. "Perhaps the human race could get along without Earth. We've managed to spread ourselves across a host of worlds that aren't blessed with oxygen-rich air. Titan does very well with an inflammable atmosphere. But I haven't mentioned the worst-case scenario.''

"Get on with it then," Hamid-Jones said irritably.

"Suppose the Earth *didn't* go up in flames. The hydrogen cloud keeps growing and growing. It rains on Jupiter and provides enough extra mass to kindle Jupiter into a star. But before that can happen, it rains on the fires of the Sun. The Sun might simply become hot enough to boil away the oceans of Earth, boil away the atmosphere of Jupiter. Or it might get indigestion. All that extra hydrogen that it couldn't handle might cause it to grow into a giant. It might suffer a core collapse without waiting to exhaust its fuel supply and explode as a supernova. With all that mass, the remnants of the Sun would certainly become a black hole. Or, contrary to the usual order of black hole evolution, snuff out its fires and become a black hole without bothering to explode first. Or become a black hole with a supernova explosion at the center—an explosion which would never be able to escape—which would amount to the same thing.''

Hamid-Jones gritted his teeth. "Can't you get through to your friends?''

"I don't wish to. The Old Man of the Mountain promised me paradise, too. As a reward for volunteering my services to join the demolition team and track the direction finders I planted in your luggage.''

A shudder went through the ship. The Assassins raised their heads like hunting dogs. A moment later there was weight as the fusion drive kicked in. Weight grew rapidly toward one gravity. Hamid-Jones found himself standing on his feet instead of hanging like a picture on the wall. The squatting assassins settled to the floor, too, and stood up.

They were very serious now. Without rancor, they gestured with their weapons at Hamid-Jones to get him moving.

"Where are you taking me?" Hamid-Jones asked.

Aziz had become businesslike, too. "It's time to lock you up out of harm's way, *ya* Abdul. They don't want you getting in the way.''

"But the bomb I planted is set to go off one hour from now.''

"They know that, *ya* Abdul. They want the honor of having their bomb go off first.''

It was a small cubbyhole that had served as a service kitchen for the deck's *farash* when the ship had plied the stars as a passenger liner. Hamid-Jones lay on his hip, tied to a heavy zinc fixture that had been the *farash*'s sink and stovetop. A row of battered coffeepots that no workman had bothered to abscond with during the conversion was still on the shelf, along with a bag of ancient coffee beans that vacuum had sucked dry.

Hamid-Jones shifted his position and tried once more to get to his feet. But they'd tied his ankles together, too, and under a full gravity in a heavy space suit it was impossible. He had no way to explore his bonds, either, even if he'd been able to pluck at knots with his clumsy gloves. They'd bound his hands behind his back, which with the hump of his life-support equipment and the general stiffness of the suit meant that his arms were pulled straight back and his wrists lashed together across the backpack.

He "listened" in the airless environment for any telltale vibrations that would give him a clue to what was happening. How much time had gone by? It felt like hours. But that couldn't be. In one hour, he would have ceased to exist.

The door to the pantry opened, and a space-suited figure squeezed inside. It was Aziz. He had a knife in one thick mitt. He raised a finger in front of his helmet to warn Hamid-Jones not to talk, then reached out to disconnect Hamid-Jones's radio antenna and insert a small input jack. A length of fine wire connected the jack to Aziz's own antenna.

He bent down to sever Hamid-Jones's bonds, talking quickly as he worked.

"You may be wondering what I am besides a dilettante in astrophysics, *ya* Abdul. Aziz is only a part of my name—I'll introduce myself properly later. If there *is* a later. I'm a prince of the Royal House of Mars—the true Royal House, not the false line of the usurpers and that cursed severed head that's propped up on the throne now. I'm not a very important prince, but al-Sharq is my kinsman. I've been working for him all along." He smiled with one corner of his mouth. "When you replaced the Clonemaster, it seemed like a good idea to have me attach myself to you."

The ankle ropes parted, and Hamid-Jones struggled to a sitting position. Aziz started working on the wrist ropes.

"Al-Sharq doesn't mind ruling Mars as a satrap of the Sultan. It's not a bad arrangement. Al-Sharq is a realist."

Hamid-Jones started to speak, but Aziz said, "Questions later. There isn't much time. I wasn't in a position to prevent the Christian underground from sending you to Charon to sabotage the hole project, but I was able to manage to follow you here, thanks to the Assassins." He tapped his helmet to indicate the black turban. "I don't know how, but the imam who serves as the current Old Man of the Mountain somehow got the idea that I was a stray member of the sect. Most Assassins are good family men, you know, and are rarely called upon to do their bit, except to lend their support to operations. The important jobs go to those with the talent for them. I hitched a ride to Charon by offering to help track you from there."

The wrist ropes gave way to the knife. Hamid-Jones said, "What are they doing now?"

"They're saying their final prayers. They're going to set off their bomb in the airlock. They figure that ought to put it close enough to the antihydrogen fixtures.''

The only weapon Hamid-Jones could find was a coffeepot. He took the largest of those on the shelf, a heavy brass urn with a flaring spout. He had no illusions about his ability to best a trained Assassin while wearing a near-inflexible heavy-duty space suit in gravity, especially when the Assassin was in a lightweight suit built for action and was carrying an automatic weapon.

The same thought must have occurred to Aziz, because the last thing he said before pulling the plug out of Hamid-Jones's helmet was, ''We can only try.''

At that moment all weight disappeared as the fusion drive turned off.

Hamid-Jones and Aziz looked wordlessly at each other. Then, simultaneously, they dived through the door. They bounced off a corridor wall, tangled up in each other. They sorted themselves out in midair, flopping like fish to make contact with a solid surface. Then, pushing off violently, they hurled themselves down the airless passageways toward the airlock.

The Assassins had just finished commending themselves to the imam. One was getting to his feet, his weapon in his hand. The other, still prostrating himself, had bounced his forehead too hard off the floor and was floating an inch above his prayer rug.

When Hamid-Jones and Aziz burst through the door frame, they turned immediately to meet the threat. The floating one had left his gun leaning against the wall, but with no wasted motion he got a knee and the heel of one hand under him and, drawing a thin knife from a sleeve scabbard, started for Aziz. The other had whirled around too fast, and while he was trying to stop his spin and get his gun up at the same time, Hamid-Jones hurled the coffeepot. It struck without damage, carrying the Assassin backward.

Hamid-Jones saw the soft satchel with its telltale pie-plate outline lying in a corner. In the moment of respite his diversion gave him, he made a dive for it. He got hold of it by the handle, slung it around twice, and chucked it out the airlock door into space.

The recoil knocked him backward. The first Assassin had reached Aziz and was raising his knife for a slash across his air hose. Hamid-Jones floundered into him, helpless. For a moment he saw the lean abstemious face poised over him, its teeth bared in a snarl, and he expected a stab or a slice that would finish him.

But the Assassin wasn't looking at him. He was staring after the disappearing satchel. Without a moment's hesitation, he jumped out into the void after it.

Instantly, the second Assassin jumped out after him.

Hamid-Jones got to the gaping doorway. Horrified, he watched the two twisting bodies, tumbling end over end through the dark.

Aziz picked himself up, shaken but unhurt. He plugged in the suit radios.

"There's a story," Aziz said, sounding unnerved, "that the Old Man's predecessor in the tenth century demonstrated his power to Henry of Champagne by ordering a number of his followers to jump to their deaths from the ramparts. They haven't changed a bit. They still do things like that without stopping to think."

"The first man, yes, but—"

"The second man sacrificed himself to provide reaction mass for his friend."

"May Allah have mercy on him!" Hamid-Jones exclaimed in horror.

"So that he could get back to the ship with the bomb," Aziz finished.

Fascinated, Hamid-Jones watched the unfolding of the grim tableau.

The first Assassin had caught up with the bomb. He writhed violently and managed to snare it. Man and bomb continued to sail outward.

The second Assassin must have given a mighty kick at the airlock, because little by little he was gaining on the man with the bomb. The two of them were as big as fleas now against the blackness, but Hamid-Jones saw it all with dreadful clarity. The two stretched toward each other like trapeze artists. They caught each other by the wrists and hauled in. The second man transferred his grip to the other's ankles and carefully placed his feet against his chest. They adjusted their positions, the one putting himself in a tight crouch, the other drawing up his knees to place his center of gravity where it would do the most good. Then, the bomb tucked under his arm, the first Assassin kicked out convulsively.

The volunteer launching pad went sailing away, his velocity redoubled. The other seemed to have checked his outward fall. He hung against the stars, and Hamid-Jones waited to see a slow net drift back to the ship.

But he didn't have enough net momentum. He might have been a little heavier than his friend. Or the mass of the bomb, which Hamid-Jones had pitched outward with great force, might have untilted the equation.

Little by little, the flea-size figure receded. The Assassin shook a tiny fist. Then, in what must have been a rage, he threw the bomb at the starship.

He had given himself the coup de grace. He shrank even more quickly against the darkness. But the satchel started to come back to the ship like a yo-yo.

"Oh no!" Hamid-Jones cried. "What do we do now?"

"Nothing."

"But if he set the timer to go off before it reaches the ship, we won't be able to turn it off . . ."

"The Assassin's bomb *has* no timer," Aziz said. "It's set to go off as soon as the button is pushed. It didn't. It was a dud. That must have been what made him mad."

"A dud? But how . . ."

Aziz lowered his eyes modestly. "It wasn't easy. They never let the damned thing out of their sight. But I had weeks aboard a blowtorch with them to find a way. I finally improvised a two-plate magnetron and fried the circuitry with radar through a wall. It couldn't have affected the flywheel, of course."

"Then why did I throw the bomb away?" Hamid-Jones said ruefully.

"It got rid of the Assassins, didn't it? Come on! They can't interfere with us now! Show me where you hid the other bomb!"

They crawled out on the wooden skin of the ship. The Assassin was a tiny mote among the stars, just barely man-shaped. The mote had assumed the position of prayer.

Hamid-Jones retrieved the bomb from its hiding place in the cracked plank. The digital timer blinked doom at him. There were scant minutes left to go. With Aziz looking over his shoulder, he switched off the timer.

Nothing happened. The ruby figures continued their inexorable march toward zero.

"Well, *ya* Abdul," Aziz said softly, "it seems they were afraid you might get cold feet."

Hamid-Jones braced himself to pitch the bomb into space, but Aziz touched his shoulder.

"No, it's too late for that. You can't possibly throw it with enough velocity. If that thing goes off anywhere within a hundred miles, the gamma flux . . ."

He left the sentence unfinished. Both of them had the same thought. They scrambled across the rough planks back to the airlock. Together, working with deliberate speed in the taffy hindrance of weightlessness, they wrestled the scooter outside. While Hamid-Jones stuffed the fat dish into a saddlebag, Aziz did things to the controls.

"This isn't meant to accelerate at more than a G," he said, "but I goosed it up. If it holds together, it'll keep boosting at twice that till the fuel runs out. Keep your fingers crescented!"

They held the scooter down while Aziz started the main engine and all the attitude jets on one side, then jumped out of the way as the scooter leapt into the night, heading out at a tangent.

"Come on, we'd better get inside!" Aziz said.

As Hamid-Jones turned to follow, the second bomb, the dud, arrived, fat and slow. Aziz caught it and, with an indifferent glance, tossed it back along the line of flight. Someday soon the flywheel would run down by itself, and a new star would flare momentarily in the local sky.

They headed toward the interior of the great ship, swimming like minnows past the clifflike braces and thick pillars, pushing themselves off by any surface they could reach.

"Far enough," Aziz said. "We'd better hide."

They found a cozy cave between two twenty-foot slices of superalloy and buried themselves deep inside.

"How long has it been?" Aziz said.

"Three or four minutes," Hamid-Jones said.

"If the scooter's fuel held out, it should be traveling at over five thousand miles an hour relative to the ship by now. Another few minutes, and it could be covering a couple of hundred miles per minute, even after burnout."

They waited, counting out the seconds on their helmet clocks. Presently, the interior of the ship was flooded with a brilliant white light. It lasted a few seconds and began to fade. The flash must have been awesome to have reached them there through seams, airlocks, and bounced light coming round corners.

"A thousand miles away, at least," Aziz whispered.

"The Assassins?"

"Cooked. Maybe the poor fellow who got tossed further could linger a while, but if Allah is merciful, he won't."

Hamid-Jones said a silent prayer, a brief, private *du'a*. Aziz held his tongue. Hamid-Jones suspected he was doing the same.

"We'd better sit it out here for a while," Aziz said, as Hamid-Jones started to get up.

But they didn't have that luxury. A trembling began around them, and Hamid-Jones felt weight pressing him to the floor. It built up rapidly.

"The Harun drive," he said. "The flight controllers back on the comet must have seen the antimatter flash and tried to save the situation by turning on the creation engines ahead of schedule."

He was getting heavier and heavier. The acceleration was going to reach thousands of G's in very short order. But by the time it got to a small fraction of that, he and Aziz would be crushed to the floor, unable to move.

He didn't have to express that thought to Aziz. The prince's face was ashen.

They were trapped on a runaway spaceship that was on its way to turning into a black hole.

CHAPTER 13

$H$is first impulse was to run for it—jump mindlessly into space. That might have gained him a few extra seconds of life, until the virtual particles of the Harun drive caressed his body and dissociated the very atoms of his being into their fundamental quanta before he even had time to char.

Aziz grabbed his arm. "This way!"

"Where to?"

"The north pole of the ship. That's where we hid our lifeboat."

Hamid-Jones didn't see what good a lifeboat would do in the long run, when the ship's crazily multiplying acceleration would eventually put it so far ahead of any conceivable lateral separation that the drive exhaust, despite its pencil-tight focus, would eventually fan out wide enough to paint them with death. But the self-preservation urge, stronger than logic, was willing to snatch at any brief reprieve. He followed Aziz deeper into the ship, feeling his weight grow by the minute.

"I hope the elevator's still working," Aziz said tightly. "Otherwise we'll have half a mile of stairs to climb. I don't think we'd get very far after we passed the one-G mark."

Floundering after Aziz through the caverns of trusses, Hamid-Jones tried to estimate his weight so far. It felt like about half a Mars gravity—maybe Moonweight. How long did it take a starship to reach a full Earth/Centauran G after the Harun drive was turned on? He thought he remembered that it had been about ten minutes aboard the *Saladin*. But the holemaker was not going to be that tender to the sensibilities of passengers.

"There it is!" Aziz panted.

Together they crowded into the stripped cage of the elevator. The ship's internal power was still on. Hamid-Jones punched the button for the top deck. The cage surged upward, adding its modicum of G.

By the time they stumbled out into what had been the topmost atrium, full Earthweight was dragging at Hamid-Jones's knees and calves. Despair grabbed at his consciousness. There were still acres of deck to cross, a semicircular wasteland littered with the twisted shapes left by salvage.

"The lifeboat's in one of the polar garages," Aziz wheezed. "Head for exit *baa'*."

They made it through a fire door, and were confronted by iron stairs leading upward. Aziz's face looked like yellow putty. It was much worse for him; Hamid-Jones remembered that he had been born under Mars gravity and that despite the toughening stay at Alpha Centauri and the weeks aboard high-G blow-torches, he was laboring under a weight that was almost three times what was normal for him.

"Can you make it?" Hamid-Jones said.

"I'll get there, *inch'allah*," Aziz replied through gritted teeth.

Hamid-Jones draped Aziz's arm around his shoulder and grabbed him round the waist. He climbed the iron treads one at a time, in a series of straining hoists. Aziz helped all he could, half walking and pushing with all his might. By the third landing, each lift was a nightmare. At several steps, they fell back and had to try again before they could make it.

At the last landing, Hamid-Jones could no longer stay upright. He sank to his knees, lungs heaving. A red warning light was flashing in his helmet.

"One short flight left," he puffed. "What do you think? About a G and a half?"

"Feels like I weigh about a ton," Aziz said with a sick grin.

Below them, the stairs and first couple of landings suddenly crumpled. A portion of deck collapsed, leaving open space all around them. The ship's lighter interior structures, unbraced, were starting to cave in.

It was a great incentive. Hamid-Jones got Aziz under the armpits. Together they humped their way up the few remaining steps, like a pair of linked inchworms.

"Get the hangar door button," Aziz gasped, lifting his chin toward a short post about twenty feet distant.

Hamid-Jones crawled to it, heaved himself to a half sitting position and, with an arm that felt like lead, stabbed at the button on top. At first nothing happened. Then, reluctantly, the door mechanism strained against a weight it had not been designed to handle. With the door only a quarter of the way open, it ground to a halt and refused to go further.

"Keep trying," Aziz told him.

Hamid-Jones punched repeatedly at the button, trying to get a rocking rhythm started. Little by little, in a series of jerks, the recalcitrant door retreated about two thirds of the way down its tracks, then froze for good.

"That ought to be enough," Aziz said in a strained voice.

The lifeboat was a small one, about sixty feet in length. But more than half its cylindrical length was given up to its engines. A blowtorch's escape vehicles had a lot of delta-vee to kill before hope of rescue became even remotely possible—the intrasystem ships could build up to ten thousand miles per second by midpoint of an Earth-Pluto run—and even so, passengers had better hope nothing happened between the orbits of Saturn and Neptune.

But none of it was going to help them ultimately, Hamid-Jones realized. Any push still remaining in the lifeboat after its trip to the comet was going to go for lateral separation from the hole-maker. They'd still be sharing the starship's forward velocity at the moment of separation, and that would take them on a chord through the ecliptic and out of the system into interstellar space at a speed too great for any conceivable rescue.

If the Harun drive exhaust didn't get them first.

He crawled back to Aziz and hooked a loop of webbing through the spindly man's harness. Amazingly, Aziz had managed to crawl several yards on his own before Hamid-Jones reached him, inching along on his belly.

"What does it feel like now?" he said.

"Like about three G's," Aziz grimaced. "But we both know that's impossible. I'd be nothing but a pinned butterfly."

Hamid-Jones had to admire his spirit. Even he, with his more muscular build, was finding it tough going. He must weigh over a quarter-ton by now. And he had another quarter-ton of Aziz to drag.

Like injured beetles, they belly-dragged themselves across the hangar floor. A junked vehicle that looked as if it might once have been the captain's pinnace dropped to the floor with shocking speed as its spindly landing legs, meant for nothing more taxing than a quarter-grav moon, buckled under it. Cracks radiated from the depression it made in the floor, and Hamid-Jones thought he could feel the floor itself begin to sag.

"Almost there," he grunted.

A new problem presented itself. The lifeboat's airlock doors had been left open by the Assassins, and the boat itself rested on its belly. But that left a threshold about three feet high that Aziz was going to have to climb over. And at this point he could barely lift his head on its scrawny neck.

"You go on without me," he said.

"The hell!" Hamid-Jones retorted.

He grabbed the lip of the airlock and with much grunting and effort dragged himself upright. He got himself seated on the edge, overbalanced himself, and fell inside like a ton of bricks.

It was only a one-foot drop inside, but with the weight he had acquired, it knocked the stuffing out of him. He lay there awhile, hurting. He didn't seem to have broken any bones, and his suit's life-support seemed undamaged. He moved as soon as he was able. He was gaining pounds with every passing minute.

"Try to sit up," he told Aziz.

Groaning, straining, the slender Martian rolled over on his back and propped himself to a sitting position against the boat. For one bad moment, Hamid-Jones was afraid that one of Aziz's skinny arms would snap as he levered his torso upright, but Aziz let himself fall back before that happened. Aziz's backpack was a flat one, Assassin-style, so Hamid-Jones was able to wrap his arms around the narrow chest and lock his hands together. He heaved with all his might. Aziz, with his remaining strength, helped by pushing his heels against the hangar floor. With an inch to go, Aziz almost slipped away, but Hamid-Jones let himself fall backward, taking Aziz with him. He got a quarter-ton thump that bruised his ribs, even through the thick space suit. It must have been worse for Aziz.

Somehow they got to the controls and flopped down on the crashpads. The thick gel mattresses rose around them like billows. It was better, but Hamid-Jones's chest was so compressed under its own weight that each breath was an enormous labor.

Two padded consoles the size of fists dropped to Aziz's sides where he could play them by touch without having to raise his arms, and a gel mask that projected displays plopped down over his helmet faceplate like a cream pie.

"Congratulations, you now weigh over a thousand pounds," Aziz gasped. "Better not try to lift your head. You could break your neck. Better keep your eyes closed, too."

Hamid-Jones was glad to comply. At that point he couldn't see very well anyway. With his eyeballs flattened by five or six G's, everything was a farsighted blur. Aziz's displays, he supposed, compensated for focal length, even though the gel mask was plastered over his faceplate, several inches above where it ought to be.

"Can you take ten G's?" Aziz said thickly. "I can goose the thrust up to that till the fuel runs out or the nozzles burn out. The ship's up to six G's already. At that rate, it'll take two point nine seconds for a mile of ship to slip past us. I want to get us as far away from the exhaust beam as possible before then."

"Go ahead," Hamid-Jones croaked.

"Hold on!"

An enormous force slammed Hamid-Jones all the way into the jellybed. He hit bottom with a jar. His ribs creaked. He couldn't breathe at all. Behind his closed eyelids he saw a pink curtain.

Three seconds later a great light turned the pink curtain into a brilliant sheet of radiance. That would be the pencil beam of the Harun drive drawing a line several miles behind him. The flash couldn't have lasted for more than a thousandth of a second before the lifeboat ports opaqued, but it left a dancing afterimage of red glare.

An elephant was standing on his chest. He tried to speak but couldn't get out a word. He could feel his face stretching, the corners of his mouth drawing back into a lizard's gape. The elephant was pressing him to death. He must have passed out.

Abruptly it was over. He sat up, feeling no weight at all. Aziz was grinning at him, his eyes spectacularly bloodshot and rimmed by purple bruises.

"We got six minutes worth of thrust out of the leftover fuel," Aziz chortled. "Praise Allah that our suicidal friends were in too much of a hurry to blow up the lifeboat as they originally intended! That took us forty thousand miles out—those G's really add up! And we're still coasting at our terminal velocity—about twenty-two miles a second.''

Hamid-Jones looked backward through a darkened port. Nothing could be seen except the long, incandescent scratch of the Harun drive, as bright as the port would allow. There was still no noticeable fanning out at this distance. But he could see the forward tip of the line drawing itself at an ever-increasing rate as the holemaker's acceleration mounted.

He turned back to Aziz. ''Are you all right?'' he asked as he saw the sudden grimace of pain.

''A couple of broken ribs, I think. You can help me bind them up after we pressurize the boat and get these suits off. How long till hole formation?''

Hamid-Jones thought back to his briefing at the comet. ''A few hours. Not long after it bumps up against lightspeed. We'll still be following in its wake, but it'll be at planetary distances by then.''

''Suns grab their planets at planetary distances,'' Aziz said. ''And this will be a sun and a half.''

The moment announced itself by the instantaneous clearing of all the ports as the Harun drive was snuffed out by the black hole. Hamid-Jones and Aziz turned with one accord to see the incredible event that was taking place some millions of miles to starboard.

Space itself had crumpled at the moment of the black hole's creation. At the end of the fading stardust trail left by the ship's exhaust, the constellations rippled like something seen through wavy glass. Though the collapse had happened in a blink of time, the optical effects, because of the finite speed of light over the distances involved, took some seconds to play themselves out. Hamid-Jones could see the surrounding stars elongate and run into the locus of the hole like water swirling down a drain, as their light was swallowed. A halo of runny stars circled the empty spot that contained the hole.

The spot was not quite empty visually, though. As Aziz punched up the magnification still more and the scene through the port jumped several million miles closer, Hamid-Jones could see a tenuous glow, pale as spiderwebs, as ambient hydrogen atoms and other matter plunged toward the hole's event horizon and gave off X rays with a little visible light thrown in for good measure.

The whole strange distortion was moving across the sky at what had been the starship's ultimate velocity, visibly puckering the field of stars, which ironed itself out again as the hole passed. The swallowed stars reappeared as smears of light that shrank once again to points in the hole's wake.

"If you look closely, you can see an accretion disk of sorts starting to form," Aziz said, bringing up the magnification again. "We've got a Kerr hole here, even though the ship wasn't rotating. But a starship isn't perfectly spherical and there are irregularities of mass distribution; if something weighing a star and a half hits bottom and bounces a few times before settling down to a regular shape—black holes bounce when they form, you know—you're bound to get a wobble going. So when all that virtual mass snapped down to within the event horizon, equivalence concentrated the angular momentum just as if it had been something star-size that shrank. The singularity stayed put—you can't undig a hole—but the event horizon will have bounced back to the normal size for a hole of one and a half solar masses. Maybe about six miles in diameter. The hole's rotation will be wrapping space-time in a vortex around it." He shuddered. "That's one whirlpool you don't want to get caught in."

Hamid-Jones peered and managed to make out the ghostly brim of the accretion disk. It grew brighter as he watched, then settled down to a foggy luminescence. There wasn't much to nourish it out here, but if it ever ran into a rich H II region or started to rob a star, the X-ray flux could get dangerous.

But the black hole itself remained invisible, a ball of nothingness wrapped in gauze.

"We have a problem, ya Abdul," Aziz said. He was scanning the lifeboat's regular instrument board with a worried look, his fingers darting over a keyboard as he fed calculations into the computer.

Hamid-Jones tore his gaze away from the shriveled area of sky. "What's that?"

"What I feared. That's an immense gravitational field. It's captured us. We're falling."

The lifeboat's instruments were not very sophisticated. They didn't have to be. Hamid-Jones held his tongue, fidgeting, while

Aziz tried to get a better reading. They were falling, all right, but free-fall is free-fall. It felt the same whether you were drifting like a feather to the surface of an asteroid like Eros, or orbiting the Earth, or were about to slam into Jupiter at thirty-eight miles per second.

Aziz at last turned a face toward him that was covered with a sheen of sweat—whether from the pain of the broken ribs or the knowledge of their predicament, Hamid-Jones couldn't tell.

"How long will it take us to fall?" Hamid-Jones asked.

"Forever," Aziz replied. "The difference in velocity between the hole and the lifeboat is on the order of the speed of light—our piddling delta-vee hardly counts in that league. If we were within a few diameters of the hole, it would be a different story, but it's separating from us faster than we can fall toward it."

Hamid-Jones wiped away some of his own sweat with the sleeve of his long johns. "That's a relief," he said. "I had visions of being sucked into that thing like a strand of spaghetti."

"But the tug it gave us might be enough to make us fall into the Sun," Aziz went on. "We need an orbital velocity of about fifty miles per second out here. But we're pretty much standing dead in the water."

"Great!" Hamid-Jones said.

"I wouldn't worry about it, *ya* Abdul," Aziz said. "Our air would give out long before we hit the Sun."

"That's a great comfort."

"What I'm really worried about is something else."

Hamid-Jones groaned. "What's that?"

"Have you forgotten that another black hole is on the way from the opposite direction? When they splash together, we'll be in the grip of a gravitational pull that's twice as strong. And this time it won't be fleeing from us faster than we can fall—it'll be stopped in its tracks. A mass three times as great as the Sun, and a lot closer." He licked his lips nervously. "It won't be a very long way to fall."

"Maybe hole B won't show up for a while—long enough for hole A to pull far enough away from us. It's traveling at almost the speed of light. Another hour and it'll be inside the orbit of Uranus. Maybe it won't capture us."

"*Ya* Abdul, *ya* Abdul," Aziz said gently. "Didn't Izzat's simulations always show an intercept at about the orbit of Neptune? It's going to capture the whole Solar system."

"Then we're done for."

"Maybe not."

Hamid-Jones lifted his head. "What do you mean?"

"We might go into an independent orbit around it. Neptune and Pluto will."

"Oh, wonderful," Hamid-Jones said, venting his despair in the form of sarcasm. "Fall into it, go into orbit around it—what's the difference?"

Aziz gave him a long, serious look. He was a far cry from the craven creature Hamid-Jones had known as a servant. "Being in orbit around a black hole is no different from being in orbit around any other body, ya Abdul, though relativistic effects begin to apply as you approach ten radii. We'd be in free-fall, subject only to ordinary orbital mechanics—as long as we didn't approach close enough to be torn apart by tidal effects."

Hamid-Jones was unable to tear his eyes away from the rippling patch of sky that had doomed them. Now, beyond it, another winking star caught his attention.

"Here it comes," he said.

You could trace its progress and direction by the blinking of the stars whose light it bent. It appeared to be making a beeline toward them. It was still very far away, but as it closed the gap, the angular separation between it and the first hole decreased.

Aziz took a sighting and calculated angles. "A hundred million miles away. It'll take nine minutes to get here." He paused for second thoughts. "In fact, it's already hit. It'll take nine minutes for the light to reach us."

As the seconds ticked by, the isolated blinks that marked the hole's flight across the starfield turned into a second crinkled patch of sky. The distortion grew until it was visible as a distinct circle of spattered stars that soon would match the first one in size.

"One minute," Aziz announced. "Eleven million miles apart."

"But if they're *both* traveling at the speed of light . . ."

"One minute," Aziz said firmly. "Remember your relativity."

The two circles of stars touched and suddenly there was only one.

That was all there was to it, except that Hamid-Jones's retinas carried the memory of a figure eight of stretched stars snapping into a single circle. The circle hung motionless in space, the product of canceled forces. The new hole didn't even look particularly bigger than the two holes that had poured themselves into it.

"Did you feel anything?" Aziz asked.

"Like what?"

"Oh, a tingling sensation. A sensation of falling a millimeter or two, then falling again."

"Now that you mention it, maybe."

"I thought so," Aziz said with satisfaction. "Gravity waves. When the two holes merged, they would have sloshed around for a microsecond before settling down. That's three solar masses twanging the strings of space-time."

Aziz's abstract air irritated Hamid-Jones. "For Allah's sake, don't you care about what's happening to *us*?" he snapped. "Or your family on Mars?"

Aziz was imperturbable. "As for the people on Mars and the inner planets, nothing's happened to anybody. Didn't your Sheik Hamza tell you that?"

"He said it wouldn't even rattle the teacups in the cupboards," Hamid-Jones admitted.

"What happened, happened on an astronomical scale. It will take a while for the Solar system to realize it, but now it's been captured. The Sun is now part of a binary system, dancing to the tune of a rather heavy partner."

"Allah have mercy! I've been shot at, asphyxiated, and almost blown up, but I wasn't prepared to be lectured to death!"

"As for us," Aziz went on composedly, "that remains to be seen."

He busied himself with the lifeboat's meager array of instruments. Presently he looked around at Hamid-Jones again.

"It's reached out for us," he announced in a less cocky tone. "We're falling twice as fast, and this time it's standing still waiting for us. We'll be picking up speed at an enormous rate now. Eventually we'll be falling at some millions of miles an hour."

"H-how fast will we be going when we hit?"

"Don't be morbid, *ya* Abdul. *If* we reach the gravitational radius, we'll fall to the singularity at the speed of light. In our own time frame, of course. Do you want to know the mathematical formula for the time of the final fall? It's very simple. You divide the gravitational radius by—"

"The satan take your mathematical formula!" Hamid-Jones growled.

"But we wouldn't feel a thing at that point, *ya* Abdul. Once we pass the event horizon, we'd be torn apart so quickly that the nerve impulses wouldn't have time to move even an angstrom along our synapses."

"By heaven, I liked you better when all your conversation was about thievery and bribes," Hamid-Jones said.

Aziz gave up his banter. "Somewhere in the universe it must be time for prayer, *ya* Abdul," he said simply.

They strapped themselves to the jellycouches to keep from floating around the cabin and waited out the fall. At some point, Hamid-Jones's imagination gave him a case of vertigo, and he angrily shook his head to clear it of the notion that he was about to smash into a brick wall.

For the first few million miles, the patch of puckered sky remained about the same size, then started noticeably to grow. Hamid-Jones instinctively clutched the armrests as it filled the forward screen.

"I can't get a reading," Aziz said. "The boat's instruments weren't meant for this. I think we're dropping at about twenty-five million miles an hour."

The hole had finished its meal of available hydrogen. Its gauzy nightgown was gone. Now it was really black—blacker than anything Hamid-Jones had ever seen, so black that it showed against the inky background of airless space as an optical illusion that kept changing from a dimple to a bulge to a bottomless well. There was no flashing of borderline stars that Hamid-Jones could discern, and that meant that their approach was not vectored in the slightest degree. They were rushing straight toward it.

"We're not seeing it, you know," Aziz said. "We're just seeing the difference between *something* and nothing."

The hole yawned at them. Hamid-Jones's fingers dug into the armrests. Somehow he had imagined that the hole would be perfectly round, but it wasn't. By dint of a few crushed stars that gave it a partial outline and that queer impression of a blackness blacker than black, he could see that it was flattened at the poles. It was shaped more or less like some enormous stygian hassock meant as a seat for the great satan himself.

"It can't be spinning all that fast—otherwise it wouldn't be sheared off so neatly at top and bottom," Aziz said. "It would have some wild non-Euclidean shape that our eyes wouldn't make sense of. The rotation parameter shouldn't be much more than about point eight six. That means that the whirlpool it's making in space-time will be a bit tamer, and the static limit won't be so far above the event horizon. We may have a chance after all.''

At that moment a single star flashed and gave Hamid-Jones back the hope that had been taken away from him during the plunge.

The open pit of darkness was only thousands of miles away now. It slid sideways out of the forward viewport and flashed past a side port. A fraction of a second later, it flashed *up* the port on the opposite side of the cabin and appeared in the front viewport again.

There it shrank with incredible rapidity until it was only a pinprick in space once more. Just as rapidly, it swelled to a devil's hassock.

Aziz exhaled. His voice shook as he spoke. ''We're in a long elliptical orbit around the hole. I think we're going to settle down to a period of a second or two. We're far enough away at peribarythron not to be torn apart by tidal forces, but I wouldn't be surprised if we dip in and out of relativistic effects. Help me time the starfall.''

There was a rain of stars outside the ports. The black hole bobbed up and down in the forward viewscreen like a yo-yo. When the hole grew, the stars rained down. When the hole shrank, the stars rained up.

Hamid-Jones didn't need to use the chronometer function of his wristcomp to time the effect. It was apparent to the naked eye. Every time the black hole grew large enough to fill the viewscreen and slide past them, the shower of stars speeded up into a sudden downpour. Then, just as suddenly, the downpour subsided and the shower decreased more steadily until, when the hole was tiniest, it had slowed to a drizzle.

Hamid-Jones relayed his impression to Aziz.

Aziz nodded. ''You'd expect things to speed up at the small end of our orbit. But not that abruptly. You notice that nothing like that happens at apbarythron. But every time we pass through the region of space that's stretched by the black hole's gravitational field, the outside universe speeds up for us like a crazy cartoon.''

Hamid-Jones's mouth was dry. He had noticed something else.

"Is that why I'm feeling this . . . sort of flutter?"

"No. No matter how powerful the gravitational field of a black hole is, you can't feel it as long as you're in orbit around it. A fall is a fall, whether you're falling at Mars gravity or at the worst a superdense object like a black hole has to offer. What you're feeling is the tidal effect. It's trying to pull you apart. Fortunately, the hole is large enough, and we're distant enough, so that you're experiencing only the weakest suggestion of a tide—the sort of pull you'd get if you were hanging by your hands and a mouse jumped on your boots. Or rather, if a mouse were bouncing up and down on your boots on a little pogo stick. If we were passing within a couple of radii of the static limit, though, the hole would be trying to tear every lineal centimeter of your body away from every other lineal centimeter with a force of about ten million Gs."

Hamid-Jones gulped. "Oh."

"You'll get used to it. After a while it won't seem any worse than a heartbeat."

It took a couple of hours before Hamid-Jones's queasy stomach settled down. He learned to ignore the tiny rapid-fire jolts—it was rather like getting used to riding a loping camel in a weak gravitational field like that of Mars, provided you assumed that the bumps came in two directions at once. It helped if you didn't look at the jumping-jack universe that flickered back and forth outside the ports.

They broke out the lifeboat's supplies and had a small uninspired meal of rehydrated hummus and thermostabilized kibba with flatbread. Hamid-Jones was just brewing tea when something made him look out the big front port. By then the extreme precession of the orbit had brought them around to face what had been rear in the previous line of flight.

Against the black night, a circle of rippling stars was growing.

Aziz looked up too, a mouthful of kibba forgotten in his hand. "It's the third black hole, *ya* Abdul," he said. "The one that's going to bump the Solar system to Alpha Centauri."

Hamid-Jones stowed the gravityless kettle in a safe place. He didn't need to add to the disaster by getting scalded.

This was the black hole that weighed thirty solar masses. It dwarfed the other two by a factor of ten.

"Aziz, my dear brother," he said, making his peace with God. "Can you tell me what the size of a hole of that mass would be, compared with the size of the composite hole it's about to strike?''

Aziz was already down on his knees. "The radius of its static limit will be about five times larger, *ya* Abdul. Big enough to swallow us, too.''

CHAPTER 14

The thing bore down on them, widening like the pupil of a gigantic demon eye—a blinking eye that sparkled with radiation from the bruised atoms it was impacting at the speed of light. The black orb's apparent dilation gave Hamid-Jones the uncomfortable sensation that it had taken a personal interest in them.

"It can't be more than ten million miles away," Aziz breathed. "It will be here in less than a minute."

"Allah have mercy," Hamid-Jones said. "We're between it and its target."

"Don't give up, *ya* Abdul," Aziz said. "There's still the peribarythron shift."

"What new babble is this?"

"We're in a *very* long and stretched out elliptical orbit, *ya* Abdul. You can tell by the way our captor hole keeps expanding and contracting like a balloon. But the orbit itself is pivoting around its gravitational focus like an eccentric gear. All orbits do that to some degree, because of the dent in space-time caused by a gravitational mass. The precession is almost unnoticeable in the case of the Sun and planets. But close to a condensed mass like a black hole, the shift is tremendous. We go completely around the merry-go-round every ten or twelve orbits!"

Hamid-Jones could see the truth of this now, with the onrushing giant hole as a reference point. It swung minutely to one side, was eclipsed briefly by the hole that had snared them, then emerged again in a series of bobbing advances timed to the oscillations of the smaller hole.

218

"God is great," Hamid-Jones said. "Where will we be when it hits?"

"There's no way of telling. We've already made three or four circuits while we were discussing it."

That was all the time there was for talk. The onrushing black ball seemed to fill the universe. Hamid-Jones felt all his joints and teeth ache. Then the thing shot by in a blur. For its passage to be visible at all as motion, at more than ninety-nine percent of the speed of light, that final sprint had to encompass a distance of tens of thousands of miles.

"God is great, indeed," Aziz said in a voice that shook. "We were almost exactly at apbarython."

They couldn't have seen the splash. It would have happened too quickly. But their vision's memory retained the imprint of separate images and shuffled them together in a jerky imitation of motion.

At that, the brain would have slowed down the action to a manageable frame of a thousandth of a second or so. The event horizons of the colliding holes, snapping together at the speed of light, would have needed only a ten-thousandth of a second to fall some fifteen or twenty miles and merge; in that time, nerve impulses from eye to brain would have traveled less than half an inch.

What Hamid-Jones thought his eyes saw was two enormous dead-black rubber balls squeeze together until one was suddenly inside the other and the remaining ball jumped in size.

Simultaneously, his brain told his eyes that, no—what they were seeing was two hemispherical pits. The edges of the pits crumpled and suddenly there was only one pit, a scoop of emptiness in the void.

There was the familiar flutter that Aziz had told him was gravity waves. And a wash of coruscating sparks swept over the surface of the pit, turned it into a ball again, and vanished.

Aziz leaned forward tensely. "I hope we were on the downcurve," he said. "Otherwise . . ."

They were taking that crazy plunge again. The upward rain of stars seemed much faster. They whipped around the enormous mass and looped out to a distance once more. Hamid-Jones's brain adjusted for comfort. The lifeboat was solid as a rock. It was all Creation that was whirling round his head. About once every second, something black and ominous flapped by.

Aziz busied himself with his instruments again. "We're in a new orbit around the combined mass," he said. "The mass increase speeded us up and moved us outward. And the hole itself is larger, so the volume enclosed by the event horizon averages less dense—the area of the event horizon formed by two merging black holes is always greater than the sum of the areas of the event horizons of the contributing holes. So we're pretty safe from it."

"What about the Sun and planets?"

"Same thing happened to the Sun as happened to us. When the mass of the black hole suddenly jumped by a thousand percent, Sol speeded up and moved outward in its orbit, too, taking the inner planets with it. But since the Sun and the inner planets, considered as a single orbiting mass, were already in free-fall around the hole, nobody felt a thing."

"Except that all those people are on their way to Alpha Centauri."

Aziz showed his teeth in a yellowish grin. "It's the best way to travel, *ya* Abdul."

Hamid-Jones retrieved the teakettle and let the tea steep in a dumbbell-shaped zero-G pot that he set spinning. While he waited, he activated the pantry computer and began to take inventory of the lifeboat's supplies.

He didn't like what he saw.

"How long will it take this whole traveling circus to reach Alpha Centauri? Subjectively speaking, that is."

Aziz considered the matter, whispered a few sweet nothings to the data entry mouthpiece of the control board's brain.

"Black holes are very simple, *ya* Abdul. Take a hole with the mass of thirty suns traveling at practically the speed of light, carom it into a hole of three solar masses that's just hovering there, and the averaging of momentum works out to ninety percent of the speed of light. We can ignore the Sun's previous minuscule drift toward Alpha Centauri, which it will share with its new partner. Hmmm, at nine-tenths of the speed of light, relativistic time dilation works out to a factor of two point two nine four. So we'll arrive in the vicinity of Alpha Centauri in about one point nine years. Call it twenty-three months. Why? What's the problem?"

"Assassins make lousy storekeepers. They don't replenish their stock. Our air will run out in half that time."

CHAPTER 15

Aziz, visibly shaken, made him run through the figures again. He could handle cosmic disasters, but air was always an intensely personal subject to a Martian.

"One way or another, we're going to use about a pound and a half of oxygen per day apiece," Hamid-Jones told him. Aziz might have the edge on him in astrophysics, but Hamid-Jones knew his biology. "Maybe we could shave it still further by reducing all physical exertion to a minimum, but in seven hundred days, we're still going to run through about a ton of it. A lifeboat's recycling system isn't big enough for peak efficiency. Sure, we'll make oxygen by electrolyzing our waste water, and we'll make more water by combining our waste carbon dioxide with the leftover hydrogen. But we're going to lose two thirds of a pound of oxygen a day through overboard leakage. Ordinarily we'd make that up through reserves. But your murderous chums didn't leave us very much."

"A lifeboat like this is supposed to be able to support eighteen men for a year," Aziz said, shaking his head. "There were only three of us in it for a week, coasting most of the way. I never thought—"

"Water's short, too," Hamid-Jones said harshly. "We can either breathe it or drink it. But there's plenty of food. We can gasp out our last breath in style, stuffing ourselves with rehydrated pigeon pie."

Aziz made no reply. Hamid-Jones took his silence to mean that he was crestfallen. But presently the raffish princeling was taking a keen interest in the spectacle outside the viewport. He seemed to be timing the yo-yo motion of the new, monstrous hole. After a while he began to doodle eggs on the computer screen. The eggs grew more and more elongated until they were spindle-shaped.

"What are you doing?" Hamid-Jones asked.

"Plotting our new orbit around the hole. I think I've got a pretty good approximation now. It's a very peculiar ellipse. We ought to be sweeping out equal areas in equal intervals of time—if we want to obey the laws of orbital mechanics, that is. But we aren't."

"Has your reason snapped, entertaining yourself with geometry at a time like this? Haven't you grasped the fact that we're going to draw our last breath halfway to Alpha Centauri?"

Aziz, making some final calculations, suddenly brightened. "Maybe not, *ya* Abdul, maybe not. Allah is truly wonderful. After all, He gave us Albert Einstein."

"What do you mean?"

Grinning broadly, Aziz explained.

Proxima was a sixth of a light-year behind them, a dim red ball whose surface crackled with flares. Ahead was a jolly orange sun and its yellow companion, the main Alpha Centauri pair. The lifeboat's great speed as it drew abreast made the orange sun appear to move visibly to eclipse the other. The in-and-out relativistic effects, as the boat whizzed around the black hole, turned the motion into a series of short darts.

"Shouldn't they be blueshifted?" Hamid-Jones asked.

"I told the boat's computer to fiddle with the filter sandwich in the ports," Aziz replied. "I figured that if we've come this far, we deserve a truer view. There's a little lag, though—this pea brain isn't quite up to the job. You'll notice the color pulses a little at each peribarythron of our orbit."

"I don't care. It's a beautiful sight."

"Never thought you'd live to see it?"

"No."

"Black holes are time machines, if you can keep them from ripping you apart. We were lucky in our orbit. We dip within the zone where the tremendous gravitational mass creates its own relativistic effects, aside from the time dilation we're already enjoying because of our velocity. But not within the three to nine radii where we'd be shredded or sucked in. It helped that this hole was so huge—twenty-two times the mass of the original hole, the cue ball, that grabbed us. It gave us a much larger safety zone above the event horizon.''

''You've explained all that. Several hundred times.''

Undaunted, Aziz went on. ''So the time we spent in the hole's gravitational field slowed our clock by an additional factor. The people on Earth, Mars, and the other worlds had their time compressed by more than half. They've taken a four year trip in two years. But here *we* are, only a few months later, and we're still alive, with air to spare!''

He took another chomp of his rehydrated pigeon pie, then reached for the thermostabilized caviar. Hamid-Jones had broken out the special rations for their celebration. There was even a bottle of alcohol-free champagne with a mullah's seal on it.

''I wonder what's been happening on Earth during those two years. Do you think the All-Islam Caliphate Congress was postponed?''

They had received stray scraps of radio transmissions from the Solar system over the past months but hadn't been able to make any sense of them. The constant bouncing in and out of squeezed time had made it impossible to hang on to any frequency, and the black hole tended to swallow radio waves anyway, just as it swallowed visible light.

''The Solar system's orbit around the hole will have wreaked havoc with the eternal swing of the stars,'' Aziz speculated. ''Even the man in the street would notice that the fixed stars now have a planetary motion, and that he can't find the familiar constellations where he's used to seeing them anymore. That would make it a very inauspicious time to be deciding the destiny of Allah's kingdom. What can this new portent mean? And then, when the astronomers began to explain that the Solar system is rushing toward Alpha Centauri, that would seem a portent indeed! You can be sure that the Sultan's agents on Earth are making the most of the situation.''

''Yes . . .'' Hamid-Jones agreed. He remembered the name of the Sultan's stupendous project. Allah's Will.

''More to the point, I wonder what's been happening on Mars those two years. How al-Sharq's revolution is going. The sky show would have helped him—unnerved the opposition, won the support of the uncommitted desert tribes, loosened the purse strings of the rich fence sitters. If he's deposed the Emir by now, then that son of a psoriatic skin scraping is no longer a contender for the Caliphate anyway. The Sultan will be a shoo-in as soon as he assuages the faithful by performing the hajj."

The orange sun was falling astern. A large luminous object shot by, close enough for them to see it as a disk the size of a grape pit, with a thin ring around it.

"First he's got to brake this hole. We're going too fast to capture the Triple Suns. We'll be shooting past the outer limits of the system soon. That was one of Alif's gas giants—Antar, I think."

"There's time, *ya* Abdul. The hole's lengthened its reach. The Twins will be orbiting the center of gravity of a much larger mass—one that includes the entire Solar system as a very minor component. And Proxima may decide to orbit the whole she-bang instead of just the Twins—though it will probably take a few hundred years to settle down."

The first warning came a couple of hours later by the lifeboat's slowed-down clocks. Arcturus disappeared. Arcturus was more or less on the same line as Sol's old position and Alpha Centauri.

Hamid-Jones strained to focus on the spot where it had been. The bracketing stars seemed a little displaced. Between them he could just make out a dot of dead nothingness against the more vibrant black of space. It was just hanging there, showing no proper motion and not growing, either.

"That's the three-solar-mass hole, stopped dead in space," Aziz said. "Counterpart of Sheik Hamza's first combination shot. By itself it could only slow us down by nine percent. It needs a thirty-sol bump at the speed of light in order to match our momentum."

"Where's the other hole?" Hamid-Jones cried. "I don't see it."

Aziz frowned. "They're cutting it awfully close. If the shot's perfectly lined up, then it could still be eclipsing the thirty-sol hole. But since the thirty-sol hole is bigger—"

At that moment the hole seemed to grow around the edges.

"There it is, coming up behind it," Aziz said.

The larger hole swallowed the other without a pause and kept coming. It grew with alarming swiftness.

"Please, God, let it strike at apbarythron!" Hamid-Jones prayed aloud.

"And at the farthest precession," Aziz amended.

Hamid-Jones watched his own personal black hole separate from them on its invisible rubber band. At the end of its stretch it seemed to pause. The distances were too vast for detectable parallax, but in that half second of forever, the counterpart hole, perfectly matched at thirty-three solar masses, covered the last hundred thousand miles and slammed into its target.

The whole universe seemed to vibrate. On either side, the sun and the twin stars of Alpha Centauri, though they were not within the circle of distortion, rippled. Hamid-Jones felt a strangeness pass within his body.

A mass equivalent to that of eighty-five suns—the relativistic increment of two objects traveling at ninety percent of the speed of light—had abruptly been canceled at the moment of collision, leaving only the combined rest mass.

Gravity waves lapped at the shores of the plenum. The curvature of Einsteinian space vibrated like a plucked violin string. When it was all over, an enormous mass, the equivalent of sixty-six suns, sat beneath them, waiting.

"Here we go again!" Aziz said.

They fell. Aziz waited out a few orbits, then turned to Hamid-Jones, the relief plain on his face.

"We're all right," he said. "We're in a more comfortable orbit, in fact, Farther out, because of the greater mass. Probably hitting a quarter million miles or so at apbarythron."

Hamid-Jones inspected his sensations. The tidal flutter was reduced to a tenuous ghost of its former self. And the view out the port, though still rather like being inside a spinning hoop of stars with a black spot in it, was not quite so disconcerting.

"Doesn't a mass this great pose a threat to traffic between the two systems?" Hamid-Jones said.

"Oh, there are stars in a comparable mass range," Aziz said. "Rigel, or Y 380 Cygni, for instance. There ought not to be any problems. In fact, even when the hole's between the two systems it might be a help slingshotting ships back and forth. Otherwise, folk will hardly know it's there, except that their new neighbors across the way will occasionally make loops in the sky and exhibit retrograde motion. Let me show you."

Aziz used the navigational display system to draw a sketch on the forward port's LCD sandwich.

"Start with the black hole—that's the real center of gravity of the whole multiple system. Or at least a barycenter very close to it."

He drew a couple of glowing green circles around the dot he had placed in the center. "Neptune and Pluto. Now they orbit the hole itself. It doesn't make any practical difference to the folk there. The Sun's about the same distance it always was, and it rises and sets with their rotation. Except that the Sun is orbiting around *them* instead of the other way around—or at least orbiting their epicycle." He thought it over and drew a couple of additional concentric circles. "The hole will also snare the outermost planets of Alpha Centauri Alif and Baa' when they make their closest approaches on their own epicycles within epicycles. It may be a century or two before *that* picture is clear."

Now Aziz drew a wide dotted circle around the black hole's personal family. On its perimeter he drew a little sun.

"This is the Solar system's orbit, with the Sun as *its* center of gravity." Around the little sun he drew six small concentric circles. "More epicycles—right out of Ptolemy. He would have loved this. The orbits of Mercury, Venus, Earth, Mars, Jupiter, Saturn. I don't know what's going to happen to Uranus. It may become a commuter."

At that point the sketch resembled a target, with a smaller target centered on the dotted outer rim of the big one. Next, Aziz carefully drew an even larger dotted circle that enclosed both. He marked a point on this new dotted rim with an X and drew an egg around it. He placed a smallish sun at one end of the egg and a larger sun opposite, between the X and the eggshell.

"That's the Alpha Centauri main pair," he said. "There's a little wobble here, because Alif outweighs Baa'. And of course it's a little more complicated than I've drawn it, because even though the Solar system–black hole pair probably outweighs the whole Alpha Centauri system by some thirty times, they share that common center of gravity close to the black hole, and the Centauri system, considered as one orbiting mass, is able to make *them* wobble a little, too. You can see that there are a lot of different gears going around. It ought to make for an interesting sky, when you count the rotation of the planets themselves and the axial tilt of the seasons."

There wasn't much room left on the viewport. At the extreme edge he enclosed the whole diagram with another dotted circle. With a flourish, he added a red dot to the perimeter.

"Finally, here's poor Proxima, with its nose still pressed against the glass. It has more to look at now—three star systems instead of two. Four, actually, if you count the black hole and its kidnapped gas giants as a system.''

Abruptly he shrank the whole whorl-like design to a tenth of its size and generated a lot of random dots around it.

''As for the cometary shells, I don't even want to make a guess. They'll eventually be commingled in one huge Oort Cloud. One thing's for sure—the inhabitants of all the planets and moons in the middle are going to see a lot more comets in their skies from now on.''

He yawned and switched off the display. ''But the Sultan's purpose has been accomplished. Earth and the Centauran worlds are now only light-hours apart instead of light-years apart. He's reduced interstellar travel to planetary distances. He'll be able to reach Mecca by blowtorch in less than a month. More important, now he can *rule*! He has the basis of an interstellar empire. With radio communication a matter of only a half day or so, he'll never be out of touch.''

He helped himself to the remaining caviar on a piece of flat-bread. The caviar was somewhat dried out by now, but that didn't seem to bother him.

The months of being cooped up in the lifeboat with Aziz had gotten on Hamid-Jones's nerves. He watched with mounting impatience as his former servant, now with the insouciance of minor royalty, munched his way through the sticky morsel. Finally he exploded.

''That's all very well for the Sultan! But what about us?''

Aziz paused to lick a crumb from his beard—another of his annoying habits. ''Oh, that? The Sultan will have all sorts of observer vehicles in the vicinity to check up on the mass and spin of the final hole. They may be in radio range already. Here, I'll turn on the lifeboat's distress beacon.''

Hamid-Jones's fingers itched to get themselves around Aziz's scrawny neck and shake him till he rattled. He restrained himself.

''How can any rescuer extract us from the gravitational field of a black hole weighing as much as sixty-six suns?'' he said tightly.

Aziz was unfazed. ''I admit it will take some doing,'' he said. ''The orbital mechanics involved are going to be awfully complicated by the gravitational time dilation we experience at peribarythron. The timing will have to be exquisite. But on the other hand, the Sultan will have his best experts on relativity and black hole physics out here as observers. They'll have fought for the chance to go. We'll have to help them—from inside the well, so to speak. Come on, we'd better get started timing the orbital shift.''

CHAPTER 16

Hamid-Jones crouched in naked space, watching the hole's black shadow whip by his head time and time again. He and Aziz had been out here hanging from the hull for about ten minutes in their own recurrently stretched timeframe. But to the would-be rescuers on their hyperbolic orbit millions of miles away, the elapsed time would have been much longer.

"One chance," Aziz reminded him. "That's all we get."

"I know," Hamid-Jones snapped.

"Just don't freeze."

Aziz's stick figure, like some enormous black praying mantis in the skimpy Assassin's space suit, crawled away from him to the other end of the hull, dragging the huge cannisters that contained the lifeboat's arresting gear, while Hamid-Jones played out cable. It had been a job getting the cannisters out of their housings; they hadn't been meant to be dismantled. Hamid-Jones and Aziz had worked all through what would have been their night, straining their backs, skinning their knuckles, and cursing the wrenches from the lifeboat's inadequate tool kit. Only the absence of gravity had made it possible for them to move the equipment.

Hamid-Jones watched the precession of the lifeboat's orbit wind round and round its hub at the black hole like the second hand of a clock. The tumbling stars, imprisoned in their spinning hoop, had a secondary motion that you could see plainly from out here on the hull with the whole universe around you—a slower, more stately advance that cut through the edges of the starstream. After the first 360-degree shift, it was possible to visualize the shape of the orbit as a cigar whose tip traced the circle of the precession.

"Tell me again why we're not going to get jolted into our constituent molecules when we get snapped up by something traveling over a hundred thousand miles a second," he inquired of Aziz.

"You know the answer," Aziz said patiently. "The hyperbolic orbit of the rescue ship has been very carefully calculated—even taking into account the dragging effect of the space-time whirlpool above the ergosphere. *Their* orbit goes out to infinity, and its closest approach to its focus is *our* apbarythron, hundreds of thousands of miles from the black hole. Orbital motion in both cases is in the same direction. So the difference in velocity will only be a few miles a second."

"That's difference enough," Hamid-Jones said nervously.

"The arresting gear has a stretch ratio of thousands to one. It's the same monomolecular elastomer they use in orbital rope tricks, like mail satellites and the Deimos space elevator. And there's hundreds of miles of it. They weren't sure it would handle the mass of the lifeboat without snapping, but it won't have any trouble handling us."

"*If* they catch us at the top of our orbit," Hamid-Jones fretted.

Aziz was nervous, too, and he covered it up with a laugh. "We've got at least a fiftieth of a second's leeway, *ya* Abdul. Don't worry. Have faith in the Sultan's experts."

After that, there was nothing to do but wait, with the coils of line between them, and stare at the wheeling stars.

"Fire your rocket!" Aziz yelled.

"I don't see anything."

"Fire!" Aziz screamed at him.

He aimed the heavy launcher outward and up and squeezed the trigger. The rocket leapt forward with a silent whoosh of flame, carrying the pencil-thin line with it. Aziz's rocket hurtled out of sight at a widening angle. Before the flames winked out, Hamid-Jones saw the twin sparks halt their increasing separation as the ladder rungs between them jerked taut.

"Jump!" Aziz shouted.

There was nothing in sight, but Aziz had the cesium timer. Hamid-Jones jumped clear. He didn't want to take the risk of being dragged across the hull at several hundred miles an hour, or have his line snag a projection.

He drifted among the circling stars, hugging the cannister. It was as big around as a barrel. The lifeboat dwindled beneath him. He could see a tiny stick figure swimming through space at a distance—Aziz. Embracing his cannister, Aziz waved with a free hand.

Something flashed by overhead. Amazingly, Hamid-Jones had time to make out its shape before it disappeared. It had the typical candlestick configuration of a blowtorch, but with extra bulges round the shaft and forward disk.

Then line was uncoiling from his cannister at a furious rate. The cannister emptied itself out and was torn from his grasp. Then he felt himself jerked like a fish. It knocked the wind out of him, but it wasn't too bad. There was the illusion of weight as the line stretched, doling out the momentum of the rescue ship. A tiny mite, lost among the stars, came swinging back toward him, gaining size. Aziz, on his own leg of the fifty-mile-wide rope ladder. They would have slammed together with bone-crushing force, but Aziz fired a reaction pistol past him and kept firing until they collided with a gentle bump.

The next bump was not so gentle. After a couple of hundred miles, the line stretched to its limit, and they hit bottom with a lurch. The line tightened on his harness, and the ship began to reel them in.

"Tea, *ya sayidi*?" the wardroom *farash* said, his voice tinged with awe at being in the presence of two men who had been extracted from a black hole.

"Yes, thank you," Aziz answered for both of them, leaning back in a swivel chair with his legs stretched out, the very picture of princely nonchalance despite the fact that he was in his stocking feet and stretchies, and stinking to high heaven after months in a lifeboat and hours in a space suit whose limited 'fresher capabilities had been under a severe strain.

Hamid-Jones, equally disreputable in the malodorous long johns he'd used as a suit liner, sipped the hot mint tea gratefully. He was still getting used to being alive. It had been only a few minutes since a couple of petty officers had helped to shuck him out of his space suit and turned him and Aziz over to the officer of the deck.

The two of them had been whisked immediately to officers' country, thwarting a gaggle of overexcited civilian scientists who were crowding about hoping to get at them. The *Prophet's Arrow* was a Navy vessel, and its captain had strict ideas about military discipline.

Hamid-Jones looked over at the wardroom door. A pop-eyed young ensign jerked back out of sight and hurried on his way. There was a constant parade past the door of junior officers pretending errands and hoping to get a glimpse of their new passengers. The whole ship was agog. But evidently strict orders had been issued to stay out of the wardroom. Aziz and Hamid-Jones had it to themselves.

It was frustrating. They were bursting with questions, but the crewmen who had hustled them here had maintained a tight-lipped discretion when asked about events on Alpha Centauri and Mars.

Aziz turned his attention to the *farash*. The mess attendant, a fresh-faced kid who could not have been long in the Imperial Navy, was overwhelmed at the responsibility of serving two men who had been important enough to warrant the sending of a blowtorch to rescue them.

"You'll be a hero when you get back, sailor," Aziz remarked genially.

"How's that, sir?"

"Member of the intrepid crew that dived into a black hole's gravity well and lived to tell the tale. This is going to become the stuff of legend."

The boy flushed with pleasure.

"I don't suppose they told you who we are?" Aziz probed.

"No sir."

Hamid-Jones and Aziz exchanged glances. As far as Sheik Hamza knew, Hamid-Jones was an imposter and a saboteur, and Aziz was an Assassin. The Centauran embassy on Mars would know nothing except the fact that Hamid-Jones, who was supposed to have been in the Sultan's confidence, had disappeared one day and shown up on Pluto. It might have discovered by now that he had been mixed up with Christian terrorists. The intelligence community would certainly be eager to pump them both.

But as far as Hamid-Jones could tell, he didn't seem to be under arrest. Under seal, yes, but not under restraint. Of course there was nowhere he could go on a blowtorch. The captain might simply be waiting to deliver the two of them.

"What are you going to do when you get back?" Aziz queried the *farash*.

"Well . . . I suppose I'm going to celebrate the Feast of the Sacrifice with my family."

"Ah, the Feast of the Sacrifice! Then the hajj must be over. More time must have passed than I realized while the black hole slowed things down for us. I suppose it must be a month or more since Mecca arrived in the Kingdom of the Triple Suns."

"Yes sir," the crewman said, lifting his brows in bewilderment. He obviously didn't have the faintest idea what Aziz was talking about.

"That must have been quite an event."

"A special feast's been proclaimed to celebrate the accession of the Caliph."

"Then a Caliph *was* chosen! Who—"

A smartly uniformed lieutenant appeared in the doorway, and the *farash* immediately became busy with his pots and warming tray. The lieutenant stared balefully at Hamid-Jones and Aziz and said: "You gentlemen are to come along with me. The captain wants to see you now."

Hamid-Jones rose. The slight gravity—about asteroid strength—was taking some getting used to. The *Prophet's Arrow* was starting gradually to pour on steam, preparatory to breaking out of its hyperbolic orbit.

"Uh . . . we'd appreciate the chance to clean up first. If we could borrow some fatigues—"

"Later," the lieutenant said.

Aziz spoke up. "Has the captain received any instructions with regard to us?"

"I wouldn't know about that, mister. Come along."

The captain's quarters were neat and bare, except for all the framed honors hanging on the walls. He would have had to have been the best to have been chosen for a mission like this. The captain himself was a square, stolid man with heavy features and thick wiry gray hair showing under his uniform cap.

He spoke without rising. "So you two are the ones that all the fuss has been kicked up about."

Hamid-Jones was acutely aware of how they must look to the

captain in their unwashed and scruffy state. He felt like a prisoner in the dock.

"We'd prefer to do without the attention, captain," he said weakly.

"So? You're not going to have much choice about that. You'd be Hamid-Jones, I guess. The Palace is taking a particular interest in you. They're awfully anxious to know what happened after you dropped out of sight on Mars. They traced you to a cell of Christian terrorists."

"He can explain that," Aziz said helpfully.

The captain gave him a bleak and humorless stare. "The Sultan's been in communication with Sheik Hamza," he said to Hamid-Jones. "It's only a few hours either way by radio now. The Sheik had quite a tale to tell. Some engineer kidnapped by Assassins and you taking his place. Antimatter bombs planted in the holemaker—they monitored two explosions in nearby space. They were sure you were dead, you know, when they found you gone and the lavatory you were locked up in full of vacuum."

"Captain," Hamid-Jones said, "I made a terrible mistake—"

"Save your explanations for the Sultan," the captain said. "I'm not your judge and jury."

"May I sit down?" Hamid-Jones said. The unaccustomed gravity was beginning to get to him.

"Go right ahead," the captain said, smiling with tombstone teeth. "The Palace instructed me to deliver you both in good condition."

"They did?" A wave of dizziness overtook Hamid-Jones as he sank to a padded bench by the wall.

"They picked up one of the Assassins you tossed out of the starship," the captain said, the smile getting wider. "Naturally they had a chase ship out."

"Naturally," Aziz interposed.

"Took him about three days to die from the dose of radiation he took, but while he was still able to talk, he gave them an earful. Cursed the two of you to hell and gone. Told them how you ruined their plans to sabotage the holemaker. Of course Hamza's people knew *something* of the sort must have happened when they detected the antimatter explosions and the starship went sailing on, but they didn't know you were the ones who saved it.''

"Well, what happened was—''

"*Ya* Abdul,'' Aziz said, waving him to silence. "The captain doesn't want to know the details of how we infiltrated the terrorist underground and tracked the Assassins to the comet. That's a security matter.''

"You're right there, by Allah,'' the captain said fervently. "The less I know of such matters, the better off I am. All I have to know about the pair of you is that you saved the day for the Sultan. He's said in public that he owes the Caliphate to you. When you land on Alif, the worlds are going to be your oysters.''

It was noisy in the Triangular City. The clatter of jackhammers and the rumble of heavy construction equipment split the once-peaceful air. Looking about as the stretchbubble limousine took a roundabout route to the palace, Hamid-Jones saw giant cranes looming above the ancient tiled walls, new excavations where polymer was being poured for foundations and pools. The lovely avenues were being torn up. Lying along the wide boulevard leading to the Golden Dome and blocking traffic was an enormous space-grown timber a mile long, meant for some colossal building project or other—it must have been a job getting it down from orbit in one piece.

"The Caliph is building a new Elliptical City to intersect the Triangular City,'' the driver volunteered. "The Black Mosque is going to be at its focus. You can see it going up there.''

Hamid-Jones followed the driver's gesture to the enormous dome rising above the rubble of demolition beyond the base of the triangle. It was going to dwarf both the golden dome and the orange dome when it was finished. Right now it was still an inflated plastic bubble on which mitelike workmen were spraying a permanent shell of glistening black liquid ceramic.

The marine officer who was their official escort frowned at the breach of protocol. Hamid-Jones didn't care. He was starved for conversation. The officer had been an impossible clam during the entire ride from the spaceport, speaking only to answer direct questions with a military courtesy that was indistinguishable from brusqueness.

"What's the timber for?'' Hamid-Jones asked.

"It's going to be carved into a lintel for the gateway joining the triangle and the ellipse," the driver informed him. "I tell you, the Caliph thinks big."

"Indeed he does," Aziz murmured.

"Every ruler in the Solar system has been coming to pay homage to the Caliph," the driver went on. "Kings, presidents, pashas, satraps. The courtyard of the audience hall's like a garden of peacocks. You've never seen such a parade of satin and silk."

Hamid Jones looked down at his own costume. He was respectably but not ostentatiously dressed in a well-tailored tunic and pantaloons with felt slippers. Somehow Aziz, in a display of his former talents for improvisation, had contrived to have two proper outfits waiting for them when the blowtorch's tender alighted at the spaceport. "I'm not showing up for an audience with the Caliph in navy dungarees," he had said.

Hamid-Jones saw more changes as the limousine passed through to the palace grounds. The Sultan's private park was being relandscaped. Dominating the approach was a tremendous monument—a pylon and sphere sitting on an island in the middle of an artificial lagoon. The pylon, a gleaming mirror-bright spike, was a thousand feet tall; the greenish-black ceramic sphere was a third as high.

"That's the Caliphate's new symbol," the driver said proudly. "It's going up everywhere."

The officer turned Hamid-Jones and Aziz over to a deferential palace official with great puff sleeves and a mushroom turban, who ushered them past the glittering throngs in the gardens and courtyards of the audience hall.

"It looks as if the high and mighty didn't waste any time coming to pay their respects," Aziz remarked.

"Oh, it's been a madhouse," the official said fussily. "We're trying to make do with the old palace till the new one can be built. All of a sudden, half the universe is descending on us. I don't know what we'll do when the news reaches Barnard's Star and Sirius. We're putting up a lot of partitions and inflatables in the meantime."

"Well, the Sultan seems to have hit the ground running, at any rate."

"Please!" The official screwed up his face. "The *Caliph.* The Commander of the Faithful. Defender of the Faith. Oh, it's

going to be so hard getting people used to the new titles. You have no idea what the Protocol Section's been going through.''

"Work must have started even before he was invested with the Prophet's mantle.''

"Oh, it was all cut and dried before he left for Earth. He had radio messages from the Caliphate Congress. The Emir of Mars was out of the picture soon after the Solar system started its hegira, of course, and al-Sharq immediately threw his support to the Sultan. That tipped the scales. Once the Sultan reached Earth, it took no time at all. First he had to complete the hajj, of course, omitting nothing—the day of the standing, the stoning of the pillars, the final *tawaf*. He attended the Caliphate Congress session the following day, still wearing his humble *ihram* garb, with one shoulder bare. By sunset, Islam had a Caliph.''

"What's next?''

"The Ingathering. But I expect he'll tell you about that himself.''

When they entered the audience room, it was obvious that walls and a ceiling had been ripped out to make a more imposing chamber. The interior decorators had done wonders with temporary hangings—great sheets of drapery making a plastic architecture that created an impression of great splendor. Hamid-Jones got a peek round the edge of one waterfall of brocade and saw scaffolding and plasterers' tools. Ranks of guards and court officials made a maze that had to be threaded before reaching the raised dais that held the Caliph's throne, and the throne itself was concealed behind an arrangement of gold filigree screens that the fortunate were allowed to pass.

Nine years had not aged the Sultan at all. He was still the same bluff, hearty red-bearded person Hamid-Jones remembered. But the informality was gone; he was wearing rich jewel-frogged trappings that befitted the Caliph of all Islam, and his turban, no longer a simple wrapped Centauran tarboosh, was out of a storybook past. He was in the process of dismissing a delegation from one of the Solar system's lightweight moons—nine-foot-tall stick-men who wore powered exoskeletons to allow them to move around in Centauran gravity. There had been a slight mishap: the joints of one of the power frameworks had become locked when a delegate had tried to prostrate himself before the throne, and the Sultan was helping the man to his feet with his own hands, while court officials looked on in distress at the Sultan's careless disregard for the dignity of his new office.

His eyes lit on Hamid-Jones and Aziz. "Ah, there they are— the two fellows who almost got themselves turned into a black hole for my sake. I'll be with you in a minute."

He patted the stick-men on any convenient part of the arm he could reach, gave them a blessing, and dismissed them. An appointments secretary started to read from a scroll on which the names were written in fiery holographic letters, while Hamid-Jones's escort pushed him and Aziz forward, but the Sultan said, "Never mind all that nonsense. Come on, let's get out of here."

To the further distress of his officials, he led Hamid-Jones and Aziz back to a private office behind the dais.

"Needed a break," he said as he shucked off the heavy jewel-encrusted overgarment and set his turban down on a stand. "Let those fellows out there earn their pay for a change—shuffle things around till I get back."

A double-ender that had been lying under the desk got up and sidled over, wagging its heads. The Sultan ran his hand down the graceful curve of its back, and the animated plant crooned in pleasure.

"Hmm, this one's about to sprout," the Sultan said, pointing out the broccolilike buds at the bases of the necks. "I'll have the gardener send you a couple of sprigs as soon as he gets them started. This one is good racing stock."

"That would be too kind of your Majesty," Aziz said.

Hamid-Jones wondered what he was going to do with a double-ender. You couldn't give away a royal gift, and you couldn't neglect it, either. Double-enders, with their finicky dextrarotary biology, were expensive to care for.

"Well, let's hear the whole story," he said, sitting down. He rang a bell, and a servant brought refreshments.

Aziz did most of the talking. He spun a highly colored tale, with the emphasis on fanciful deeds of derring-do by Hamid-Jones. He evaded any mention of the way Hamid-Jones had been recruited by the Christian underground on Alpha Centauri to work against the interests of the Sultan. Even the Sultan would have found it hard to forgive that one. Instead, he left the impression that Hamid-Jones, mindful of his undercover commission from Colonel Ish-Shamaal, had cleverly infiltrated the

Christian cell. He didn't mention the fact that Hamid-Jones had planted one of the antimatter bombs, either. The Assassins could safely be blamed for both of them now.

"These Christians are a troublesome lot," the Sultan said, shaking his head. "Still, they're my subjects, and I'm responsible for their welfare. I can't punish the loyal many for the actions of a few. Even though these communities of Unbelievers are breeding grounds for unrest."

"Is Izzat Awad safe, your defendership?" Hamid-Jones asked.

"Yes, the Assassins released him unharmed. He wasn't very happy when he found out you'd been impersonating him. But Colonel Ish-Shamaal calmed him down by pointing out that you were on an undercover mission for the Palace, and that you'd saved his life."

So Colonel Ish-Shamaal was moving to take credit for everything. That was all to the good. The colonel was a whiz at covering up inconvenient facts.

"The colonel wants me to decorate you, *ya* Abdul," the Sultan continued. "And you'll certainly have all the medals that can be struck. But I have a more substantial reward in mind. A pashaship, for example. Think it over carefully. Anything I can grant is yours."

Hamid-Jones mumbled his thanks.

"You might wish to be Pasha of Triton, or a moon of one of our own gas giants. It would almost be like being a sovereign in your own right—these barbarous places are difficult to govern, and when I can install a man I trust, I like to leave him alone. Or you might prefer to be made pasha of a district right here on Alif, closer to the center of things. You'd have less independence, but you'd be assured of access to me."

"Th-thank you, your Highness," Hamid-Jones stammered.

The Sultan turned to Aziz. "And you, *ya* Prince Aziz. What can I grant you?"

Aziz flashed the familiar roguish smile that Hamid-Jones remembered from the old days. "I have no talent for ruling, your Highness. The family found that out about me a long time ago. I'll take cash."

The Sultan laughed. "It shall be done."

"Your Majesty," Aziz said boldly, "will my kinsman al-Sharq be coming here to pay his respects to you, now that Mars is only a few weeks away?"

"No, he offered but I wouldn't hear of it. All this ceremony and sycophancy may be necessary to hold an empire together, but it's a lot of nonsense. He's needed much more urgently on Mars. I want him to consolidate his power, mop things up, get Mars humming and prosperous again."

"What . . . what happened to the Emir, your Defendership?" Hamid-Jones said. "We still haven't heard the full story."

"The Emir's excrescence, you mean? It was separated from its host body and put on display at the Bab al-Dahub. As were the heads of the forty-nine other clones still surviving, all in a row for the populace to see. I want there to be no doubt in the minds of al-Sharq's subjects that the rule of the Emir is gone forever."

Hamid-Jones shuddered a little at the hardness in the Sultan's tone. It was a reminder that, however genial their manner, all monarchs were capable of being ruthless when they had to be.

"And the Chief Eunuch, Ismail?"

"Captured alive. Hiding under his bed. I'm leaving his punishment to Rubinstein. It's his prerogative, after what he suffered at the eunuch's hands. I have no doubt that Rubinstein will think of something inventive."

"Rubinstein—alive? After all this time?" Hamid-Jones was stunned.

"Oh yes. Al-Sharq's troops found him in a cage in the basement. He was in terrible shape. Dehydrated, encrusted with filth, covered with scars. At one point he'd been blinded. But Ismail had his eyes recloned. He couldn't bear the thought of Rubinstein not being able to see his own degradation. Then he more or less lost interest in him. Kept him alive and out of sight against the day when some new cruelty might occur to him. Rubinstein kept his mind active—did sums in his head, wrote a book about political power that he's going to call *The New Machiavelli*. I can hardly wait till he sets it down on paper so I can read it. I'd like to appoint Rubinstein as my own Grand Vizier, but that will have to wait for a while. At this point, al-Sharq needs him more than I do."

He turned again to Aziz. "Speaking of which, you'll have to earn your reward, Prince Aziz. I need you to go to Mars to do some errands for me."

"What—spy on my kinsman?" Aziz exclaimed.

The Sultan laughed heartily—too heartily. "Of course not.

Just a little necessary liaison work. There are many things left to settle, and it's hard doing it at long range, even when that long range has been reduced to a few hours by radio. I need an intelligent man—a native Martian—for the job, and it won't hurt that you're a member of the new royal house. Call yourself a minister plenipotentiary. The job shouldn't take more than a few weeks. You'll be briefed before you go."

"I'll be happy to serve the Commander of the Faithful," Aziz said gravely. "There can be no conflict of interest among the sons of Islam in this."

"Good," the Sultan said, and their eyes met in understanding.

"I'll go with you," Hamid-Jones said abruptly.

"That's fine," the Sultan said. "I would have suggested it. Rubinstein is most especially anxious to see you."

Aziz was giving Hamid-Jones a worried look. "*Ya* Abdul, you're not still thinking about that woman? After she deceived you and betrayed you to the authorities? Forget her. You're going to be a pasha. You can start a new life with a clean slate."

"I just want to go to Mars," Hamid-Jones said gruffly.

Aziz stared at him a moment, then shook his head. "All right. But you'll have to wait a week or two. I'm not leaving for Mars until I see my Zubeideh." His eyes grew starry. "We have a lot of catching up to do. I know she still cares for me. But I'll have to begin my courtship again from scratch."

"That's fine, then," the Sultan said. "You'll both leave in two weeks."

He strode to a wall switch and turned on a floor-to-ceiling holo map of the nearby stars. It had been brought right up to date. In its center was a cluster of multicolored jewels—the nucleus of his new empire, with Sol's bright yellow sparkling next to Alpha Centauri's orange, yellow, and red.

"There is still much to do," the Sultan said, a far-away look in his eyes. "I pray to Allah to give me a hundred years for my work, so that I may hand over to my successor a true interstellar empire, where no world is more than a few weeks away from any other world."

Aziz cleared his throat. "Then you plan to add more stars to your crown, your Majesty?"

"More?" The Sultan's eyes burned with his inner vision. "I

plan to draw in *all* the inhabited stars. Allah's children have strayed too far. I propose to gather in the Faithful."

"That's a very big dream, your Highness," Aziz said quietly.

The Sultan adjusted the scale of the holo. The field expanded to show a teeming universe of stars, glinting like dustmotes in sunlight.

"And my heirs will continue the work," he said. "The new stars will be *brought* to us to be colonized. There are four hundred G-type stars within a hundred light-years of the Sol-Centauri system, and sooner or later they'll all be Ingathered."

The motelike stars balled up in response to some preloaded program. "The cluster of Allah," the Sultan breathed fervently. "A gathering of stars, close enough to be ruled, with the Caliphate at the center."

"I beg your pardon," Aziz said irreverently, "but won't it have a black hole at the center?"

It was like watching a puppy nip at a mastiff. Hamid-Jones waited for the Sultan to bite Aziz's head off, but nothing happened.

"I mean, it's already up to sixty-six solar masses," Aziz went on, "and that's just from pulling in one small sun. If you have to double it every time . . ."

The Sultan shook himself back to the present. "We won't have to do that anymore, *ya* Aziz," he smiled tolerantly. "We've already got a large mass to absorb momentum, and we can match up our future stars in pairs—send them careening in from opposite directions to cancel each other's impetus. Besides, the need for haste is gone, now that the crisis is over, so we can afford to give them a smaller push in the first place and wait for them to come drifting in. That way we won't need to add more than three or four solar masses to our black hole for each new star. In the fullness of time, we may end up with a black hole of one or two thousand solar masses as our anchor in the universe, but what of it? That's nothing compared to the black hole that's already sitting at the center of the galaxy."

He paused to scratch one of the heads of the double-ender. It responded with a vegetable yawn that showed a double row of thorns meant for tearing small animals apart and a velvety pink lining meant for absorbing the result. Hamid-Jones shuddered. The motile plants were good for blood sports, but he found it

hard to understand the mentality of people who liked to keep
them around as pets.

"What suns will you draw into your orbit next, your Highness?" Aziz asked.

"Tau Ceti and Ross 128," the Sultan said, pointing to two
stars on the opposite sides of Alpha Centauri. Ross 128 was a
red dwarf, in about the same league as Proxima. "They're not
evenly matched, I know, but we'll give Ross 128 a faster push
to make up for it. Tau Ceti is absolutely vital to the Ingathering.
It was the oldest established colony after us and Epsilon Eridani,
and I've got to move quickly to counterbalance its influence. We
have a team of black hole engineers already in place in its cometary halo. It should arrive twelve years hence, and by then
Sirius and Barnard's Star will be clamoring to join us."

Hamid-Jones was numb with the marvel of it all when the
Sultan dismissed them. "Can Allah have intended this?" he
asked Aziz as they walked out through the courtyard. "This
cozy dominion that the Sultan is arranging."

"It's not for us to say what Allah intends, *ya* Abdul," Aziz
replied. "Leave that for the mullahs."

"Wait, where are you going? We haven't even fixed up anything about lodgings yet."

"I'm going to see Zubeideh. I don't dare delay, with a prize
like that. She must be under siege by suitors. I wonder if she's
still as beautiful as ever."

"But where shall I go?"

"I suggest you go to the Unbeliever's Quarter. There'll be
someone there who'll be glad to see you."

"Oh, Abdul! I can't believe it's you! Let me have a good look
at you! You haven't changed at all! Meryem will be thrilled!
She's missed you so much! We've all missed you! You do us
great honor, coming to our poor place! I've saved your old rooms
for you! They're just the same as when you left them! Nothing's
been changed! Just give me a few minutes to get fresh bed linen!
Will Aziz be coming?"

Is-sayida Roxane looked flushed and pleased. Nine years had
added some roundness to her figure and some gray to her hair,
but she was still a trim, pretty woman. To Hamid-Jones's con-
sternation, she stood on her tiptoes and kissed him.

There was a sound of a throat being cleared in the doorway.

"Well, if it isn't Abdul. This is a great day. Welcome back, Abdul. What adventures you must have had. Do you know the Sultan—the Caliph, I mean—mentioned you and Aziz in a holovision interview after he came back from Mecca? You're celebrities here in the Quarter. And we're celebrities, too, because you lived here. I can't even pay for my own drink anymore when I go to the tavern."

It was Yaqub Yordan, burly and blue-jawed, a little more grizzled than the last time Hamid-Jones had seen him. He had a welcoming grin on his broad, honest face. He didn't seem at all scandalized to find his wife kissing another man. Hamid-Jones would never understand *nisranis*.

He took hold of Hamid-Jones's hand and pumped it, *nisrani* fashion. "You don't look a day older," he said.

"That's what I told him, Yaqub," Roxane said.

"It's the time dilation," Hamid-Jones explained. "I've only lived three years of my life since I last saw you—I have so much to catch up on." He was met by blank stares. The Yordans were simple folk; they didn't know what he was talking about.

"Yaqub, go fetch Meryem," *is-sayida* Roxane said. "Tell her we have a surprise for her." As Yaqub lumbered off, she turned to Hamid-Jones and said, "I've got to get dinner started. It's going to be a real celebration. I'm going to make all your favorites—lamb and stuffed vine leaves, roast eggplant with tahini, yogurt and cucumber with garlic. For dessert, a real Moslem recipe—Ali's Mother with raisin sauce!"

She bustled off, leaving Hamid-Jones in the parlor. In a little while he became aware of a silent scrutiny from the door to the hall. He turned and saw a stunning young *nisrani* woman standing there. She was tall and leggy, with huge dark eyes and beautifully sculpted cheekbones. The only flaws in her beauty were a faint dusting of freckles across the bridge of her nose, and the fact that she was a little too slender. She reminded him of a younger Roxane.

"Meryem?" he said with a start.

She gave him a cool appraisal. "Hello, Abdul." She stepped forward and took his hand with perfect self-confidence. "I knew you'd come back someday."

"You've grown up," he said inanely.

"That's what little girls do," she said. Was she being her old impudent self? He searched her face suspiciously for some trace of the brash, skinny tomboy with scraped knees and smudged face that he remembered. But he saw only a poised, serious young woman, willowy in a *ferengi*-style dress that nevertheless was reassuringly modest with its long sleeves and ruffled bodice.

Abruptly she gave him a big, generous smile, and his heart melted within him. "But you haven't changed," she said. "You're just as I remember you."

"I hope you remember my advice about *mish-haram* behavior," he said gruffly.

She wrinkled her nose. "And you're still as stuffy as ever. Come over here and sit down, so we can talk."

She was gratifyingly eager to hear all about Mars. She listened attentively as he described, in lengthy detail, the political situation as it had been in the last extravagant days of the Emir's sinking reign, and he was flattered by her breathless absorption in his adventures with the Christian underground.

He thought he had successfully skirted the subject of Lalla, but she interrupted to ask: "And did you see your lady while you were there?"

As curtly as possible, he admitted paying Lalla a visit.

"And was she glad to see you?"

Lalla had been all too glad to see him—till she found she was about to get caught. Then she had screamed blue murder. But that was not the sort of story one told a respectable young woman, even if she *was* a *ferengi*.

"No, she has a new friend now," he said brusquely.

Meryem gave him an unfathomable look. "Oh, poor Abdul!" she said sympathetically.

Was she mocking him? He felt himself starting to glower, and made an effort to smooth over this queer conversational trap he'd somehow gotten into. "It doesn't matter," he said in as flat a tone as possible. "All that was more than four years ago, as time is counted on the surface of planets."

Then he realized that wasn't so in the case of Mars and the other planets of the Solar system. They'd been carted off to Alpha Centauri at ninety percent of the speed of light. With the time dilation factor, less than two years had elapsed for Lalla. And she was within reach now. He could travel to Mars in weeks—*was* going to travel there with Aziz!

"Don't be sad, Abdul," Meryem consoled him. "She's probably old and fat by now, anyway."

"That's enough!" he exploded. "You haven't grown up at all! You're still as impertinent as ever!"

"You still care for her, don't you?" Meryem said with a trace of asperity in her voice.

"Enough, I say! This is unseemly!" He got hold of himself. "Can't we be friends?"

She sat quietly with her hands in her lap. "Of course, Abdul," she said composedly. "Tell me about the Assassins and about how you rode a black hole back here. We all know you did something heroic to help the Sultan become the Caliph, but so much of it is classified. A holovid news crew came here to take pictures and interviewed all the neighbors. They wanted to take pictures of your bedroom, but mother wouldn't let them."

He expanded again under her warmth and launched into an only slightly censored account of his impersonation of Izzat and the thwarting of the Assassins' sabotage attempt. She hung on his every word, and soon his tongue was getting ahead of itself.

"The Christians are a dangerous lot," he said. "They were a thorn in the Emir's side, and now the problem's been dumped in the Sultan's lap."

As soon as he realized what he'd said, he became flustered and contrite. "I didn't mean all Christians," he apologized. "I only meant . . ."

But Meryem was not at all offended. "I know. Most of the nonturbans here in the Quarter don't approve of terrorist tactics, either, even though people pay lip service to the freedom fighters and are afraid not to give contributions when they come to the door. They make life harder for us. They cause us trouble with the authorities, they cast suspicion on the whole community, and they make it that much harder for us to be a normal part of society." She shivered. "And their gunmen kill people here, too. But most Christians—and the other nonturbans—are loyal citizens who work hard and pay their *zakat*—and the special nonbelievers' tax, too."

Hamid-Jones was so relieved to be off the hook for his thoughtless remark that he hardly noticed that he was having a serious political discussion with a woman. "Very true," he hastened to agree.

She thrust out her dainty chin defiantly. "But we have our

legitimate aspirations all the same," she said. "There are dozens of national groups here in the Quarter alone—from a score of inhabited worlds and some of us tracing our lineage back to Earth itself—all of them trying to hang on to their own languages and beliefs. But we'll always be outsiders."

Hamid-Jones tried to hide his embarrassment. "No you won't. The Sultan—the Caliph—is a just man. He told me himself, only this morning, that he regards most *ferengi*—nonbelievers—as his loyal subjects, and that he considers himself responsible for their welfare."

He did not add what the Sultan had said about the communities of Unbelievers being breeding grounds for unrest.

Meryem turned to him with her eyes shining. "Oh, Abdul, did he really?"

"Yes." He gave a small cough.

"We *are* loyal—but the Sultan needs to know more about us. He has to understand our needs and our aspirations. Abdul—you have his ear. You could help us!"

"Uh, well, naturally I'd put in a good word if I could . . ."

"That's what Father said. He said that there are hints that you'll be named to a very important position. 'Abdul's a good friend,' he said. 'He's a very decent sort. *He'll* let the Sultan know how things are.' "

"Well, I'll, uh, certainly do what I can. But you mustn't expect too much . . ."

"Will you let me take you around the Quarter?" she asked eagerly. "Introduce you to some people?"

What had he gotten himself into? "Yes," he agreed. "Of course."

So it was that he found himself, a quarter-hour later, talking to a shriveled old crone named Mother Bashdi, who was sitting cross-legged among her wares in a stall at the market, swathed in black like a crow, with her face dimly visible through black netting.

"We Zoroastrians were hounded out of Iran a thousand years ago, along with the Bahais, the Sufis, and everyone else who didn't suit," she said. "We settled on Triton, and there's still a colony there, but Triton was far from the light of Ahura Mazda, so six hundred years ago those who were brave crossed the great dark and settled here, under the Yellow Sun. The Sultan is tol-

erant and wise, and we are no longer hounded here, or perse-
cuted for our customs. But the Moslem population here doesn't
understand us or our beliefs any more than the Terrans and Tri-
tonians did. Our burial customs, for example—exposing our dead
on the Towers of Silence.'' She shook her shrouded head, and
the brass ornaments strung across her forehead and face jangled.
''What we have to go through to get a burial permit . . .''

''That's why I brought Abdul, *Um* Bashdi,'' Meryem said.
''He wants to be our friend at court. The Sultan plans to elevate
him to a great station. He can intercede for us.''

The old woman's face seemed to glow through its veil. ''Bless
you, sonny,'' she said.

After they left, Hamid-Jones said, ''But she's not a Christian.''

''No—not all nonturbans are Christians, you know,'' Meryem
said. ''Come on, I'll take you to one who is.''

Next, he found himself outside a wholesale vegetable warehouse being introduced to a member of an obscure sect called
Episcopalians. There was a moment of confusion during the
introduction—Hamid-Jones started calling him ''Mr. Bishop,''
but it turned out that that was not his name, but a title.

''Oh, that's all right, Mr. Hamid-Jones,'' the bishop said to
him in excellent English. ''People often make that mistake.
Bishop *is*, after all, a fairly common North American name.''
He laughed. ''The early holders of that office must have been
diligent about increasing their flocks.''

He picked up another of the crates of vegetables he had been
loading when they interrupted him and swung it aboard a waiting truck. He was a lean, wiry man with overdeveloped fore-
arms, pale-skinned and beginning to get a bad sunburn on his
back and shoulders. He was stripped to the waist except for a
curious neckband that looked like a turned-around collar, and
despite the active nature of his work, he wore a very large gold
cross on a chain that slapped against his chest when he straightened up after bending over.

''Abdul wants to know some of the problems of being in a
religious minority,'' Meryem said.

The bishop scratched his head. ''Well, let's see. I suppose it
all starts with the *jizza*—the head tax paid by the unconverted in
place of military service and other obligations. Now don't get
me wrong, Mr. Hamid-Jones—I don't have any objection to

having the *jizza* withheld from my paycheck. We *dhimmi* recognize our obligations. Render unto Mohammed, and so forth. But it does tend to set us apart from our neighbors. They tend to resent us for—so they think—evading our responsibilities. For simply standing aloof from the great enterprise of Islam. And it shows up in big ways and little ways.''

"For example, *ya* . . . er . . . . Bishop?'' Hamid-Jones said to humor him.

"Jobs, for one thing,'' the bishop replied promptly. "We do all the menial jobs—all the work that society needs done, but that nobody else is willing to do. I'm talking about unskilled labor—cleaning, gardening, agricultural work, kitchen work. The lowest-paid clerical jobs. Factory assembly work that could be better done by nanomachines.''

He hoisted another crate of vegetables, then stared ruefully at his callused hands. "I have a doctorate, you know. From a theological seminary on the third planet of Baa'. But it isn't recognized.''

"There are *dhimmi* with good jobs,'' Hamid-Jones protested.

"Sure, thanks to the Sultan's antidiscrimination laws. But have you noticed how *dhimmi*s always seem to get passed over for promotion? The really top jobs—the policy-making jobs—always go to Believers.''

"There are *dhimmi* in the Sultan's cabinet. The Minister of Charity and the Minister of Cometary Development.''

"Showcase jobs. The house Christian and the house Jew.'' The bishop looked embarrassed. "I don't mean to be contentious, Mr. Hamid-Jones, but you Faithful just can't understand what life is like for those of us who are essentially outside of society—the poverty, the daily slights, the lack of access. For example, to make ends meet, a man may have to send his wife to work as a menial among the Faithful—that's where the maids, the cooks, the scullions in those fine houses outside the Quarter come from. Can you imagine what it does to his manhood? And then the respectable people criticize the crime, the drinking, the lack of ambition they profess to find among us.''

It was the usual alibi. Hamid-Jones could not even pretend to be sympathetic.

"And then there's the lack of schooling for the children. For one thing they don't get the head start they'd have if they went to mosque school.''

"But public education is guaranteed," Hamid-Jones said.

The bishop snorted. "In segregated schools. Where they get an inferior education that holds them down for the rest of their lives. And even there, they're hampered because of language barriers. *Dhimmi* children, many of them, grow up not speaking one of the recognized second languages at home—English, French, Russian. It's more apt to be—oh, Armenian or Albanian, or one of the North American dialects. And their Arabic is often atrocious. So they're held back. I myself was lucky in that I grew up speaking English as well as Arabic. And look at me."

Hamid-Jones, conscious of Meryem's attention and her expectant *I told you so* expression, did his best to hold down the exasperation he felt rising. "What is it you people *want*?" he said with an artificial smile.

The bishop's sunburned face took on a wistful expression. "My flock is scattered over this entire planet. I hardly know the priests in my diocese, let alone the laity. As for getting off-planet to confer with my fellow bishops, that's an impossibility. We've been trying to settle the succession of the archbishop for years by mail and radio. It would be nice if there were a little moon set aside somewhere for Episcopalians, or at least some cohesive community where we could make our clout felt—like the various satrapies and republics the Sultan allows within his own empire. And we're not alone. Other ethnic and religious minorities doubtless feel the same—I know that Meryem's people would like to be joined with their brethren on the piece of moon they share in the orange star's system."

"Yes," Meryem said, "that's exactly right." She turned to Hamid-Jones. "If the Sultan could be made to *see* . . ."

"Good luck, young man," the bishop said. "We appreciate your efforts."

They all seemed to be taking him for granted. Hamid-Jones groaned inwardly. None of these people outside the feast of power seemed to have any idea of how things *worked*.

A hairy individual in an undershirt and a filthy turban came out on the loading dock and glared at the bishop. "Whaddaya taking, a vacation?" he chivvied the bishop. "C'mon, get back to work. Hump it!"

The bishop apologetically picked up a crate of vegetables.

"My foreman. He's a Yezidi—a devil worshipper. They're fine people, but they have little regard for a man of the cloth."

Meryem seemed to know an astonishing number of people in the Quarter, both turbans and nonturbans, and they all knew her. Hamid-Jones, trailing in her wake, soon got over being surprised at her ease with either sex. Many of these people had known her since her street urchin days and had watched her grow up. She seemed to have a word for every basket seller, leather worker, sherbet vendor. The proprietor of a *ta'miyya* stand, after inquiring about her family, offered them both a sample and was offended when Hamid-Jones tried to pay.

She seemed to know all the shadier characters, too. There was one old man, hidden away behind piles of junk, whom Hamid-Jones was sure was a fence, and another furtive character with a cast in his eye whom he suspected of being a pickpocket or worse.

Meryem was his passport to them all. "Meryem darling, you never come to see me anymore," said a blowsy woman sitting with her neighbors outside the street door of a blank-walled tenement, looking suspiciously at Hamid-Jones's tarboosh.

"Abdul's all right, he's a friend of ours," Meryem told the woman, and in short order Hamid-Jones was getting an earful of the grievances of the Coptic community.

As the afternoon wore on, he learned about the special problems of Maronites, Druses, Baptists, Buddhists, Tritheists, American Catholic Eclectics. Some of them were special indeed. He was introduced to a close-knit Mormon family. They had run into trouble because Islam allowed a man to have only four wives, and they were over the limit. They might have gotten away with it if they'd been willing to call the two extra wives "concubines," but Mormons were too moral. Besides, that would have led to its own legal problems in such matters as inheritance.

It all added up to a liberal education in what it meant to be an Unbeliever in the Sultan's wide-flung domain. It wasn't really a pluralistic society—just a tolerant one.

"Do you think you're beginning to understand, Abdul?" Meryem said.

"Yes," he replied truthfully.

"And can you make the Sultan understand?"

"I don't know. I'll try."

They walked side by side down the crowded lane, their hands not quite touching. Hamid-Jones remembered vividly taking her by the hand when she was a little girl and leading her home; he could feel the small, warm clutch now, and he felt an unaccountable sense of warmth and closeness. But he reminded himself that she was a grown woman now, that they had nothing to do with each other, and that he would be on his way to Mars to see Lalla before he had hardly had a chance to get settled in at the Yordans.

"Perhaps I should take you home now," he suggested. "It's getting late."

"Oh, Abdul." She laughed. "You haven't changed at all."

Dinner was a delight after lifeboat rations and four weeks of Navy food. It was the first real meal Hamid-Jones had enjoyed since he had left the Solar system on his wild ride. "Have another helping, Abdul," Roxane kept urging him. "You're so thin."

Aziz did not show up for dinner. "We understand," Yaqub said with a wink. "He can't tear himself away from his rich widow. A skinny little fellow like that is always attracted to a woman with meat on her bones."

"Yaqub!" Roxane scolded him. "They're two people in love. They have a lot to catch up on." Turning to Hamid-Jones, she said: "I have Aziz's room ready for him. He can let himself in any time he comes. Just think—a prince, and in our home!"

The Yordans had only one other lodger at the moment, a sales manager for atmospheric mining equipment who was away on a business trip to Jupiter now that it was so close, so it was a family meal. Roxane sat down with them to peck at her plate between trips to the kitchen, and Meryem, when she was not helping her mother to serve, was seated disconcertingly opposite Hamid-Jones. It was very strange, eating with two women and including them in serious conversation, but in a peculiar way, Hamid-Jones found it very pleasant.

"So Meryem took you sightseeing this afternoon," Yaqub said, spearing a slice of roast lamb. "What did you think—has the Quarter changed much since you've been away?"

"No, it's stayed exactly the same," Hamid-Jones said. "Except that I think I got to know it a little better than when I was here before.''

"I took Abdul to meet the bishop," Meryem said. "And a few other people."

Yaqub put down his fork. "I'm sorry," he said to Hamid-Jones. "You shouldn't be bothered with our problems."

"That's all right," Hamid-Jones said. "It was an eye-opener."

He didn't know why he should be feeling so guilty. He had nothing to do with such discrimination as still remained in the system after a thousand years of *Nadha*, like the water that remains in the bottom of a tank after draining. He was not a *dhimmi* himself, but somewhere in his ancestry—and not too far back, at that—there were *mawali* forebears. These people, after all, could always do what that distant Jones had done—embrace Islam and become a part of the greater society.

Roxane, standing at Hamid-Jones's shoulder with a serving dish, said, "Abdul has a good heart. If he becomes a pasha, he's sure to have communities of nonturban subjects under his jurisdiction. It can't hurt to know more about them."

"I don't know if I want to become a pasha," Hamid-Jones said.

He got a round of shocked looks from the others and hastened to explain. "I mean, I don't want to go to some frontier moon and run the lives of the people living there. Maybe I'd be better off closer to home."

"You're right, Abdul," Meryem said with a look of understanding and relief. "I wouldn't want to see you go far away. We've lost you once already. If you had a position in the Sultan's court, you could be an advocate for *everybody*, not just your own subjects."

Yaqub nodded slowly, chewing the idea over.

Hamid-Jones looked around the table, frowning under the weight of a new thought. "The Ingathering's going to change things drastically, you know. A safety valve will be gone. Populations that have been developing independently for generations are suddenly going to be part of a Greater Caliphate. Militaristic societies like the one that's taking shape on Mizar aren't going to like finding their star suddenly on a course for Alpha Centauri. The Sultan will have to exercise all his diplomacy to avoid conflict. He'll have to undermine the diehard regimes—we'll have the story of Mars repeated on a grand scale."

"But there's going to be a new golden age, even greater than the *Nadha* itself," Yaqub protested. "That's what all the holovid commentators are saying. And with the general prosperity, some of it's bound to trickle down to the nonbeliever populations."

"Sure, there'll be a renaissance lasting for centuries as new energy is pumped into this society, and easy travel leads to a rush of cross-fertilization. But eventually social entropy has to set in as a hermetically sealed Islamic empire crusts over—with no place to go."

Two pairs of astonished eyes fixed on Hamid-Jones, as Meryem and Roxane took in what he had said, but wisely they said nothing. Hamid-Jones was a little astonished himself at the disloyal thoughts his tongue had found swimming around in his brain. The bishop and the Zoroastrian woman and the others must have affected him more deeply than he had thought. He bit off further comment and concentrated on his dinner.

"What God wills, will be," Yaqub said.

He let out a comfortable belch. Roxane went to the kitchen and set a dish of Ali's Mother, piled high with whipped cream, in front of him, and he fell to.

After dinner, as the women cleaned up, Yaqub rose and stretched. "I think I'll go to the tavern for a little while," he said. "Abdul, would you care to come with me?" He grinned guiltily. "I'd like to show you off."

Roxane paused with her hands full of dishes. "Yaqub, don't you dare let anyone offer Abdul wine."

"Of course not," Yaqub said indignantly. "Everybody to his own customs, I say. The tavern has a mixed clientele anyway—there's coffee and other beverages for Believers."

Aziz came sneaking in past midnight, climbing the outside entrance so that he wouldn't have to wake anybody up. But Hamid-Jones was awake anyway; his day exploring the Quarter with Meryem and his evening in the tavern with Yaqub had given him much to think about, and after tossing and turning for an hour he had given up and turned on his light to read.

Aziz saw his light and tapped on his door. "I'm in paradise," he announced. He was flushed and talkative, and he had a fading red mark on the side of his throat.

"What happened?"

"She still loves me. She says she'll marry me—I'll have to scrape up the purchase price, and we'll have to ask the permission of her son. He's fifteen now, the little boy I took on his first day to mosque school—can you imagine that? He's grown up into a fine lad, with a head for the law. That will come in handy some day, having a *qadi* in the family! I'm going to adopt him and her other children. She had two more while I was gone—adorable little girls."

"Two more—" Hamid-Jones almost choked but quickly concealed it.

"She remarried and was widowed again while I was away. I can't blame her. She's a passionate woman, and shouldn't be alone. Her second husband was a respectable, older man, and I was pleased to learn that he strictly observed the laws of *halal* and *haram*—that took a load off my mind. He was very wealthy, and when he died, he left her twice the fortune she had before."

"Does she know you're an impecunious Martian princeling?"

Aziz drew himself up to his full weedy height. "I have the family homestead on Mars with a well and a few acres of desert, though it's true there's not much income in it. But I'll have the Sultan's reward—that will set me up for life. And anyway, she loved me just as much before she knew I was a prince. I'm going to manage the export-import business for her. You don't understand these things, *ya* Abdul. When you're truly in love, money doesn't matter."

"I beg your pardon. I wish you every happiness."

Aziz was bubbling over. "She was worried about the age thing, I don't mind telling you that. But I told her not to worry; everything worked out for the best."

"She's older than you now?"

"No, not at all. That's the beauty of it. It's true she aged eight and a half—let's face it, nine—years while we were away chasing black holes, while I aged only three. But I was six years older than her to start with. Now we're evenly matched. *Ya* Abdul, I'm no young satyr any more, chasing dancing girls barely out of their training veils. I feel more comfortable with a woman my own age. That's a sound basis for a marriage, don't you agree?"

"Yes . . . you surprise me again, *ya* Aziz. I never thought I'd hear such words from you."

"I have hopes of some day persuading her to emigrate to Mars, where I have a position in society. After the political situation stabilizes there, of course, and life returns to normal. She could sell out the business—or even run it from a distance, with the help of a factor here on Alpha Centauri. But that's for the future."

"When is the happy day?"

"As soon as we get back from Mars. I don't want to embark on a marriage and then go away on a trip again. Zubeideh doesn't like the idea, but she understands that it's only for a couple of months this time. We'll all have to get used to the idea that star systems are only a short hop away from one another now. Your British ancestors took longer than that to trade with India—and yet they managed to keep a great empire ticking, didn't they?"

The innocent reminder of his *mawali* ancestry hit Hamid-Jones with unexpected force. He realized it had been hovering just below the surface of his mind all day. The bishop, slaving away on the loading platform, the burly porters and laborers he had met in Yaqub's pub—any one of them might have been him if an obscure Britisher named Jones, so many years ago, had not uttered the *shahada*, the declaration of belief.

They had shown a touching belief in his ability to help them— in his willingness to do so—despite the *tarboosh* he wore, the Arabic cadences of his speech, the admixture of desert genes that showed in his hawk's visage. Perhaps they had looked past these things to the Jones within.

"They're all good lads," Yaqub had said as they walked home together. "Don't worry, Abdul. They don't expect too much."

The trouble was that he expected too much of himself. He had responded to their trust, to their simple belief in his fairness and good will. And worse, to their belief that he somehow had the power to help them with a word or two to the Sultan. It had struck some mysterious responsive chord within him. Something wild was beginning to grow in the perfect garden of his faith—he could feel it taking root there.

"Yes, empires have their moment in the sun," he replied to Aziz's remark. "But they don't care who they run over."

The two weeks passed quickly—too quickly. Aziz disappeared into the recesses of the Foreign Ministry for briefings on his mission to al-Sharq and spent the rest of his time with Zubeideh. Hamid-Jones had a few palace sessions himself, about the little errands *he* was supposed to do. But he found himself, during his free afternoons, thrown together more often than not with Meryem.

He looked forward to being with her—found himself talkative with her—and wondered at his own responses. It was like having a friend—a friend who was improbably a woman, and even more improbably, an Unbeliever.

In an unguarded moment, he tried to express that thought to Meryem, and she said, "Poor Abdul, you have a lot to unlearn. Of course a man and woman can be friends—when you don't lock a woman away behind a harem door and treat her as property. And I don't mean 'friend' the way you use the word when you talk about that pampered Kewpie doll on Mars you used to moon about."

Hamid-Jones opened his mouth to rebuke her for her outspokenness, then realized that this was exactly the sort of thing he had been loftily disavowing. Instead he made a weak riposte.

"Aziz and Zubeideh don't regard *her* as *his* property, and they're both followers of the rightful way. If anything, she's the one who's going to have the upper hand in their marriage. And besides, the Koran guarantees a woman the right to her own property—and that's more than I can say for other faiths through the ages."

"Aziz and Zubeideh are commonsensical people, and they're very fond of each other. Human nature will always find a way. But you—you're preserved in amber! Sometimes you talk like one of those old, musty antediluvian mullahs the Sultan's been trying to sweep out of his society along with the rest of the cobwebs!"

He could see they were heading toward an argument—one of those sudden squalls of foot-stamping fury that so terrified him, in spite of the fact that they were almost always over as quickly as they had begun—and he moved hastily to defuse her.

"I'm sorry, I'm not used to the ways of nonbelievers," he said, "but I'm learning. Let me take you to tea in one of those fashionable restaurants in the New City where men and women sit together. And afterward"—he remembered that she liked music—"we can go to a concert."

"You're so transparent," she said. But then she became sunny again. "But you're trying, and you're nice all the same."

Tea went very well. Meryem wore her best outfit, a smart but modest ensemble consisting of an ankle-length gown with a swirling, ruffled hem, and a patterned overblouse, worn open, that reached her knees. She did not wear a veil, but Hamid-Jones was relieved to note that she had curbed her progressive ideas to the extent of covering her hair with a dark foulard scarf whose pattern matched the overblouse. There were lots of other unveiled women in the restaurant, which was filled with modernized young government officials and executives showing off their wives, and chic travelers from some of the more liberal societies in the Solar system. But Meryem, Hamid-Jones thought, was by far the most attractive woman in the room. The waiter must have thought so, too; he hovered over the table, treating her with the utmost deference and calling her "*Madehm*," and neglecting some of his other tables. Meryem responded with graciousness and dignity; one would never have believed that she was a *nisrani* innkeeper's daughter from the Unbelievers' Quarter. Hamid-Jones was proud to be seen with her.

The concert was not a success. It was a recital of classical songs, with a small ensemble of lutes, violins, and tambourines accompanying an earnest singer. Meryem had to sit in the gallery, among veiled women, and though Hamid-Jones was unable to see her through the grille, he could imagine all too well the stares and nudges from the others as she sat there, straight and defiant, refusing to drape a corner of her scarf over her lower face. He steeled himself for her anger when he went round to collect her afterward, but unaccountably she was not angry but rather . . . amused, might have been the word. He tried to draw her out, but she would only say, "It's all right, Abdul, I didn't mind in the least. It was a lovely concert, and the acoustics were very good up there." Then he found that *he* was getting angry on her behalf. But that was ridiculous; a society must have order, standards, traditions.

All the same, he resolved never to put her in that position again. In spite of himself, he found himself fantasizing: what if there were a *ferengi* world, a whole planet, where social relations between men and women were as free and easy as in the Unbelievers' Quarter? But he snapped out of the nonsensical daydream immediately. Islam had monopolized space travel in the twenty-first century, and those *ferengi* who made it to other

worlds got there in the ships of Allah. That would be the state
of affairs forever; the great turning points of history could never
be undone.

In fact, the fist of Allah would have an even tighter grip on
the universe in times to come, as the Sultan's dream of Ingathering became a reality. Though other suns might be added to
that compact sphere of stars, there would be no traveling beyond
it.

"Why are you frowning so, Abdul?" Meryem said. "You
look as if you're having a bad dream."

"Was I? I guess I didn't like what happened in there. But I'm
waking up."

The time they spent together did not go unnoticed. One afternoon, while Hamid-Jones was letting himself through the parlor on his way upstairs to the bridge to his quarters, he overheard
a conversation Roxane was having with her frowsy neighbor, a
neo-Nestorian woman whose husband was a tile worker.

"Roxane, you'd better have a talk with Meryem," the woman
was saying. "If you don't watch out, you're going to have a
turban for a son-in-law. Or worse yet, a pregnancy without re-
course to the courts. You can't leave one of them alone with a
woman for three minutes—especially one of our women. They
think it's their prerogative to have their way. Yesterday she was
seen with him at the thieves' market, showing him off to a bunch
of Proximan Separatists—and *that's* fine company for a girl to
be seen in, let alone a turban!"

Roxane replied, in a voice tight with anger: "Abdul's a fine
person. He's like one of the family. I can't think of anyone I'd
rather trust my daughter with. And Meryem goes her own way
and does what she pleases. I have absolute confidence in her.
And I think you'd better have a talk with that son of yours. He's
been bothering those young girls who belong to the sherbet-
maker's widow across the way."

Hamid-Jones tiptoed up the stairs, hoping they hadn't heard
him. He found Aziz, stopping off briefly between visits to the
Foreign Ministry and Zubeideh's house.

"Three more days," Aziz said. "How are you coming along
with your packing? Don't you have some shopping to do? Have
you forgotten what the climate's like on Mars?"

"I'm fine," Hamid-Jones said. "Everything's under control."

"You're spending all your time with Meryem. But you're like a stallion stomping in his stall and not getting anywhere."

"What, you, too? By Allah, is the whole world minding my business?"

"*Ya* Abdul, I have your best interests at heart. You can't let it go on this way. It isn't fair to Meryem. Have you spoken to her yet? Seriously, I mean. And have you spoken to her father?"

"There's nothing to speak to anyone about, especially you. I've known Meryem since she was a little girl, and we enjoy each other's company. Like any good friends. But you wouldn't understand that—you don't have any appreciation of *ferengi* ways. You're the type who thinks—" He struggled on for something cutting. "—that if you're left alone with a woman for three minutes, you're entitled to jump her!"

"Friends, eh? Have you seen her eyes when she looks at you?"

"What is this? You're the one who always opposed my getting married."

"*Ya* Abdul," Aziz said quietly, "for each of us in this universe of tears, Allah places a special treasure. Some people never find theirs, and go to the Day of Decision unfulfilled. I've found my treasure, and I knew it right away. You don't let it get away. Allah has placed yours right under your nose. But your neck is too stiff to bend."

"Don't be an ass. Meryem would laugh you to scorn if she could hear you now."

Aziz shrugged and finished tucking in the folds of the turban he was changing into. On the way out he paused at the door and said, "All the same, you'd better have a word with her before we leave for Mars. You're making everyone nervous. But I suppose you haven't noticed that."

On the night before his departure, Hamid-Jones took Meryem to a kind of social event the *ferengi* called a *shindy*. It was to celebrate the engagement of a rich ethyllegger named Suleivan, who had invited the entire Quarter to the festivities. Roxane had fussed at the late hour of it, but Yaqub had said with indulgent good humor, "It'll be all right, the whole neighborhood will be there, and the street will be lit as bright as day. Suleivan's going to have torchbearers standing ready for anybody who needs one, and you know as well as I do that this is thugs' night off—nobody would dare pull anything where Suleivan's involved.'' He squeezed Hamid-Jones's arm and said, ''Take good care of her, Abdul, and try not to get her home too late.''

The *shindy* was as festive, in its own way, as a Ramadan celebration. There was a lot of drinking, of course—Hamid-Jones had to make sure that he was imbibing from one of the punchbowls that hadn't been spiked—and there were games and songs and *ferengi* folk-dancing, dances with names like the *waltz* and the *reel* and the *square* and the *fox-trot* and the *rigadoon*. Suleivan himself, a rough-looking customer with a laser scar on his cheek, took a turn round the dance floor with his bride-to-be. Hamid-Jones was scandalized to see a man embracing his fiancée in public—some of the dances were very close—but after a while he began to relax and enjoy himself. Some of the Yordans' friends, whom he had met around the Quarter, urged him to dance with Meryem, but Meryem, blushing, fended them off for him. After a while, when the party settled down to sentimentality and songs, and lots of toasts, Hamid-Jones found a quiet alcove where he could sit and talk with Meryem. He turned to her and was surprised to find that her eyes were moist.

''What's the matter?'' he said.

''Oh, nothing. I suppose I'm sentimental. I was just thinking about the two of them. Do you think their life together will be happy?''

''Why not? They seem well matched. This Suleivan, you wouldn't think a man like that would have affections, but you can see the way the two of them keep looking at each other.''

''Yes,'' she said, and fell silent. After an interval she said, ''This trip of yours to Mars, is it really important?''

''The Sultan's entrusted me with his messages to the Vizier,'' he said sententiously. ''The Vizier, Rubinstein, asked especially to see me.''

She knew a little of Hamid-Jones's history. ''Will he offer you a job?''

''I suppose so.''

''Will you take it?''

''I don't know. I don't have very fond memories of Mars. First I have to return to Alpha Centauri to claim the Sultan's favor.''

"The pashaship?"

"That remains to be seen."

"Is there a pashaship available on Mars?"

"No. Al-Sharq's not a man to let power slip through his fingers. The nearest pashaship's on Pallas. But that's always been run through Greater Arabia."

"But you could have it if you wanted it?"

He couldn't understand what she was driving at. "Nobody says no to a Caliph," he said uncomfortably.

She toyed with the lemonade he had brought for her. "Will you be seeing your family when you go to Mars?"

"There's nobody there. My father divorced my mother when I was eleven—clapped his hands three times and said, 'I dismiss thee,' after some silly argument about a women's service she'd gone to during the Feast of Ali with a female mullah presiding. I think he regretted it immediately afterward. But she went back to her family. She died a few years later. Her family's not very friendly. I don't see them. My father died while I was at university, getting my bioengineering certificate."

"So there's nothing to hold you on Mars?"

"Well . . . uh . . ." He hesitated.

"As a matter of fact, there's no real reason for you to go to Mars at all, is there? The Sultan can exchange messages with this Rubinstein perfectly well by radio. And Aziz is carrying the Sultan's instructions to al-Sharq."

He gathered the shreds of male dignity around himself. "You don't understand these things . . ."

"I understand perfectly well. You're going to Mars to see that woman—the one with the big *bizzaz* under her harem gown and the simpering expression on her silly face! You saved her holopicture, didn't you? I saw it in your room one day when you'd forgotten to switch it off!"

"Meryem . . ." He tried to frame a reply that would allow him to regain the upper hand—something about it being improper for her to be in his room—but she didn't give him a chance.

She stood up. "Please find a torchbearer to take me home," she said. "I don't think I'm enjoying myself anymore."

Rubinstein was the same little cricket of a man as always, unshaken and unchanged, so it seemed, by his horrifying experiences. The only difference that Hamid-Jones could see was that the eyes in the wizened old face were younger. The recloning physician had done a first-rate job, and the Vizier's eyes twinkled mischievously as Hamid-Jones fiddled with his teacup.

"Well, *ya* Abdul, it's kind of you to come and visit an old man," he said, stroking the three heads of the Cerberus puppy on the divan next to him in alternating impartiality. "You've come up in the world since I last saw you. How does it feel to have a Caliph obligated to you?"

If the Vizier intended to rattle him, he succeeded. "I'm sure his Defendership isn't indebted to me in any way," he stammered.

"No?" Rubinstein fed a fragment of scone and jelly to each of the three puppy heads in turn. "That's not what he told me in his messages. He knows he would not *be* Caliph if you and Aziz had not safeguarded the reverse hegira that brought Mecca to him. He's a fine and honorable monarch who pays his debts. Think it through thoroughly before you claim your reward, *ya* Abdul."

"Oh, he doesn't have a practical bone in his body, your Mightiness," Aziz said.

"Well then," the Vizier said with an impish smile, "he must claim an impractical reward."

"Like a universe of his own?" Aziz joked.

"Why not?" Rubinstein said blandly. One of the puppy heads nipped at his fingers and he reproved it gently. "That's not nice, Tartarus." He looked up at his guests again. "I might have forgiven Ismail many things," he said, "but I could not forgive him for having my pets slaughtered. Fortunately there was a tissue sample from my old faithful Pluto, misfiled in the DNA banks, and this little fellow is growing up just like him, including his bad habits." His voice turned grim as he added, "And I'll tell you this, this is the only clone that will ever be seen around here."

Hamid-Jones looked into Rubinstein's new eyes and shuddered. "What did you do to Ismail, your Mightiness?" he said.

"This is an enlightened Emirate," Rubinstein said. "We don't allow eunuchs here anymore."

Hamid-Jones shuddered again. Whatever the form of the Vizier's revenge, it had been good riddance.

The Vizier gave him a wicked smile. "I sentenced him to

have his missing parts recloned. He'll never rise to a position of influence again.''

Aziz laughed. "That's a fate worse than death for the likes of Ismail. But won't he be tempted to . . . take matters into his own hands? Reverse your sentence?''

"Undoubtedly," Rubinstein said, the smile growing broader. "We're prepared to restore him to wholeness as often as it takes.''

Aziz helped himself to some grapes. "Now I see why the Caliph is so anxious to have you for his own Grand Vizier, your Mightiness.''

"I have work to do here," Rubinstein said. "The Caliph and I have discussed it fully. I'm to remain with al-Sharq as long as he needs me.''

Aziz popped a grape into his mouth and chewed it thoughtfully. "You could take Abdul in hand in the meantime, your Mightiness. Give him a vice-viziership. Show him the ropes. Then, when your Mightiness moved up . . .''

"Anything," Rubinstein said. He turned to Hamid-Jones. "Is that what you want?''

"I don't know," Hamid-Jones replied. "Maybe I'm not cut out to be a Vizier.''

He was itching to be off. It had been good to see Rubinstein again, but the tête-à-tête had been going on a long time. The thought kept intruding that Lalla was only a tube ride away.

But Rubinstein was as talkative as ever. "Perhaps you're wise. You can have a great future in the center of things. Within the Caliph's gathering of stars, the human race will attain new heights in the centuries ahead. As the cluster grows and a synergy sets in, the Caliph's court will be a glittering place where a young man like yourself can have a brilliant career. Mars will become a backwater by comparison.''

The Vizier's tone was kind, but Hamid-Jones felt compelled to defend his rebuff of Rubinstein's offer. "Islam may reach new heights, but there'll always be those who'll never share those heights. Perhaps one could do more good at the center, where policy is made.''

Aziz flicked a glance at him, then said to Rubinstein: "Abdul is in love with a *nisrani* girl, only he doesn't know it yet. He's become caught up in the concerns of the community of nonbelievers.''

Rubinstein's eyes lit up with interest. "So—you don't think all will share in this new triumph of Islam? Perhaps you're right. But what could be done about it?"

"I don't know," Hamid-Jones said miserably.

"I'm pleased at your generosity of spirit, *ya* Abdul," Rubinstein said. He leaned back on his divan. The squirming three-headed puppy started climbing all over him and he set it firmly back in place.

"The Sultan's starting with about twenty of the nearest inhabited stars," Hamid-Jones said. "But eventually he hopes he and his successors will pull in all the uninhabited G-type stars within a hundred light-year radius. Now that we've discovered why starships disappear at fifty light-years or so, it can be done by stages, or by coasting after the critical velocity is reached. The stars can then be colonized and developed at leisure, and since information lag will no longer be a problem, they can be governed effectively from the center."

"Perhaps information lag won't be a problem," the Vizier said thoughtfully. "But information clog will be."

"Huh?"

"It's happened before, to other empires—and empires that were only on an Earthly scale at that. There's a limit to how much information a center can absorb and still remain effective. In the end, a ruler still has to *deal* with the facts. Keeping track of an empire of four hundred stars is a little like keeping track of a harem of four hundred concubines—a Sultan doesn't have time to get around to them all. So let the Caliphate have its closed sphere of stars. Eventually it will collapse under its own weight."

Hamid-Jones was astonished at the Vizier's dour evaluation. He'd had similar thoughts himself but had suppressed them.

"And yet you're willing to work for the greater good of the Caliphate," Aziz put in.

"I'm a realist," Rubinstein said. "The Caliphate and its Ingathering are the only game in town—for the present. One does what one can."

"What do you mean, 'for the present'?" Hamid-Jones said.

"The Sultan has had a great dream," Rubinstein said. "But every dream may be contained within a still greater dream."

"I don't understand."

Rubinstein leaned forward. "I think I know what favor you may ask from the Sultan, *ya* Abdul . . ."

He steeled himself to knock at the familiar gate. He couldn't help remembering that on his last visit he'd fled with a scarf over his face, and that on the visit before that—could it really have been all those relativistically distorted years ago?—he'd had to jump out a window with a eunuch waving a knife at him and the Rectitude police on his tail.

Then he reminded himself firmly that he had returned to Mars as a favorite of the Caliph of all Islam, that people sought *his* favor now, and that in any case he had nothing to fear from the police or other authorities of al-Sharq's and Rubinstein's newly reformed government.

He knocked decisively and the door immediately opened. Somebody must have been standing behind the peephole, watching him.

It was a new eunuch, bowing Hamid-Jones in and falling all over himself to be agreeable at the sight of the rich Centauran costume. He was a short, dumpy person with an anxious look behind the face-splitting smile. His profession was out of date, and on the new Mars he would have to be retrained for other work.

"I'm here to call on your lady," Hamid-Jones said. "Please inform her that Abdul ben Arthur Hamid-Jones is here."

"At once, *ya effendi*, this minute!" the eunuch gushed, and scurried off. He seemed to be the only servant on duty; the household had been pared down since the last time Hamid-Jones had been here.

The eunuch was back in less than a minute. "This way, *ya sidi*," he said, bowing and scraping. He led Hamid-Jones to the upstairs sitting room. Lalla was there, reclining on an over-stuffed divan, holding a veil stretched coyly across her face.

The eunuch hung around in the doorway with a toadyish expression until Lalla snapped, "Oh, for heaven's sake, Vladimir, go away!" She turned to Hamid-Jones and let the veil drop. "You were a naughty boy to come here like this without warning, *ya* Abdul," she said. "I should have made you wait downstairs a while. But my heart leapt to see you."

He advanced to the divan. Another few years had added their quota of pounds to Lalla, and the makeup was thicker. She had squeezed herself into a tight corset that pushed her breasts up over a daringly low neckline, and the skirt of her gown was artfully hiked up to show one leg almost to the knee. Her arms, bare to the elbow, clanged with gold bangles.

"Hello, *ya* Lalla," he said. "I wasn't sure I should come. But I, too, couldn't stop myself from seeing you."

She made him sit beside her on the divan. There was no curtain of tassels anymore, and he noticed that the screen had been removed from the harem door.

"You're thinking of that terrible misunderstanding with Rashid," she said. "Oh, Abdul, I can't tell you of the pain and suffering of that memory." She fluttered her eyelashes coyly. "I try to remember only our stolen moment of happiness."

"And how is Rashid?" he asked formally.

"Rashid?" she said, putting on a tragic expression. "He's dead. He was executed not long after that. He fell from favor with the Emir after his project failed to work."

"The acephalous clones?"

"They seemed to be doing well with just those little black boxes on the top of their necks, but then it was found that little heads were starting to grow there."

Hamid-Jones looked around at the sitting room. It needed new wallpaper, and the upholstery was starting to look shabby. "Then you're alone now?" he said.

She did not answer. Instead a tear trickled down through the makeup.

"There, there," he said awkwardly. "Life changes, the past must be buried." It all seemed distant and meaningless now. He was alive and Rashid was dead. He could forgive Rashid for informing on him to the police, and he resolutely told himself that Lalla had had no choice when she denounced him. It was he who had made things difficult for her by coming here as a Centauran agent.

She dabbed at the teardrop with the corner of her dangling veil. "You've become a great person, *ya* Abdul," she said brightly. "It's on everybody's lips how it was you who made possible the miracle that brought Mecca to the Sultan's doorstep. I don't understand such things myself. They say that the Sun is turning around a black hole in the sky, and that the stars are bound together in a new order of things, but when I look outside, everything seems the same as always."

"Not quite the same. The Sun still rises and sets as it used to, but these distant forces will change all our lives."

She moved closer to him on the divan. He could feel the heat of her body. "They say you're rich and famous, and that you stand at the Sultan's right shoulder," she breathed. "So whatever happened, it all came out well, didn't it? You were the only man I ever loved, *ya* Abdul."

"Lalla . . ." he began.

"Let bygones be bygones," she said. "All that matters is that you've found your way back into my life again."

Her nearness was making him perspire. He opened his mouth, closed it, opened it again. "It's true that I've carried the memory of you all these years . . ."

A man was coming out of the harem door, adjusting his clothes. The pouchy fortyish face looked familiar, and after compensating for the extra flesh, Hamid-Jones saw that it was his old co-worker Ja'far, growing comfortably into middle age.

"I knew you'd come, *ya* Abdul," Ja'far said jauntily. "I remember how you used to feel. When we heard you were on Mars, I told Lalla you wouldn't be able to stay away from her, but she didn't believe me. You're looking very well. Prosperous."

"Ja'far! You?"

"Now, calm down, *ya* Abdul."

"You couldn't wait to step into Rashid's shoes!"

Ja'far shrugged. "That's not exactly the—"

Another man popped out of the harem, buttoning his djellaba. It was Feisel, still skinny and oil-eyed, and Hamid-Jones had no trouble recognizing him despite the new seams in his face. "Hello, *ya* Abdul, it's wonderful to see how you've come up in the world," Feisel said, grinning. "It's nice to have influential friends. Are we still friends?"

Hamid-Jones tried to find his voice. Before he could speak, Ja'far chimed in.

"We've formed a syndicate, you see. To split the expenses. This is a costly place to keep up, even with most of the servants gone. It works out very well. Share and share alike. We could use another member. I know how you feel about Lalla, *ya* Abdul. Why don't you join us?"

"What?" Hamid-Jones began to sputter.

"Say, Tuesdays and Thursdays for Feisel, Mondays and

Wednesdays for me, and you could have Friday and Saturday to yourself. Or you could have your pick. We're flexible.''

Hamid-Jones turned to Lalla. "Was this your idea?"

"Ja'far's right, this is a very expensive place to keep up," she said defensively. "But *ya* Abdul, you must be very rich now. You could probably swing it by yourself."

"Now wait a minute, *ya* Lalla . . ." Ja'far said.

Hamid-Jones turned on his heel and headed for the stairs.

"Don't go, *ya* Abdul!" Lalla wailed.

"No, *ya* Abdul," Feisel called after him. "We can work something out . . ."

Hamid-Jones fled down the stairs, leaving them quarreling behind him. The eunuch stared at him, opened-mouthed, as he plunged through the front door into the clean, filtered air outside.

The orange lantern-glow of Alpha Centauri Baa' lay ahead in the sky, showing considerable disk. Beyond it, the bright yellow dot of Alpha Centauri Alif was partially eclipsed by its cooler companion.

"Halfway there," Aziz said, turning from the porthole. "It won't be long now. It's hard to believe that we crossed the former orbit of Neptune only yesterday. Have you figured out what you're going to say to the Sultan?"

Hamid-Jones looked up from the orbital diagram he was studying. "Rubinstein coached me in the right words to use. First I'm going to say that I'm formally claiming my reward. Then I'm going to say that I quake with fear that the prize may be too much to ask. Then I thank him in advance for his generosity. That way—" Hamid-Jones frowned. "—I set up a psychological obligation."

"You should tell the Sultan he's getting off lightly. You're asking for the most useless piece of real estate he owns."

"Rubinstein said that would be the worst way I could put it. The Sultan *wants* to be generous. It would be an insult to him— make it look as if he's interested in pinching piasters. No, I'm going to emphasize the gratitude of generations to come . . ."

"And the fact that it solves a problem for him as well."

"Who's the one who's telling this anyway?" Hamid-Jones said, annoyed.

"How did Rubinstein put it? 'It removes a boil from the skin of his empire.' "

Hamid-Jones threw down his pencil. "I give up! Did Rubinstein put you up to this?"

"He said you might need a little steadying. He said you tend to be a little impetuous. What's that you've got there? The orbital mechanics involved?"

"Yes. Rubinstein thought it would look better to the Sultan if I showed him that everything was already worked out. More businesslike. He put the best Martian minds in astrophysics to work on it. They did a marvelous job in so short a time. I think he got Izzat to help, too."

Aziz found that amusing. "Izzat? I'll bet that Rubinstein didn't tell him it was a favor for you."

"No. Izzat's decided to settle on Mars, you know. He's converted to the Assassins' sect. Rubinstein says that's not unusual—that when people are held captive by terrorists for long periods of time, they often identify with their captors. The Assassins seem to have gotten him off drinking, at least."

"The Assassins want a homeland, too. Have you thought—"

"No," Hamid-Jones said sharply. "Their homeland's somewhere in what used to be Syria. Rubinstein's taken up their cause. He's setting up negotiations with Damascus now."

"And removing a boil from the skin of *his* empire, eh?"

"What makes you so cynical?"

"I'm not cynical, *ya* Abdul. I'm a romantic. What are you going to say to Meryem?"

Hamid-Jones became gloomy. "Meryem? She won't want to talk to me. I've lost her, *ya* Aziz."

"Nonsense! She loves you. She's loved you since she was a little girl. Wasn't Einstein generous to lovers, to bring them together across a gulf of time? There's the hand of Allah, *ya* Abdul. He meant you to have your treasure."

"No," Hamid-Jones said. "It's no use. She never wants to see me again. But at least I can do this favor for her and her people."

CHAPTER 17

"**S**o you want Pluto?" the Sultan said.

"Yes, your Defendership," Hamid-Jones said. "That would include Charon, of course."

"And Neptune and its moons as well?"

"Yes, your Defendership. Of course if that's too much to ask . . ."

"On the contrary." The Sultan stroked his red beard thoughtfully. "But I would have thought them worthless. They have no sun—only the black hole that holds them in its clutches. They're mere frozen balls that are in the process of freezing out even those gases that still remain to them."

"We ought to pick up a sun on the way," Hamid-Jones said quickly. "It's all in the orbital diagrams . . ."

The Sultan shuffled papers. "Oho, so you want Groombridge 1618, too?"

"If your Defendership has no use for it. It's only a small yellow sun with no planets—just orbital debris in the form of asteroids and chunks of rock that formed out of the leftover gas cloud when it condensed—nothing over fifty or sixty miles in diameter. That's why nobody ever bothered to settle the system . . ."

Aziz said helpfully, "It's only a runt star—but it's a G-type sun, so it'll put the proper color light in the sky."

The Sultan peered at the printout. "Hmm, an absolute magnitude of only eight. It's not going to give you much heat."

"Well . . . we thought it might orbit us, rather than the other way around," Hamid-Jones said, "Our little black hole would be enough of an anchoring mass."

The Sultan shoved the papers back at him. "I was going to evacuate the populations of Triton, Pluto, and the rest anyway. They're hanging on so far—they never got much use out of Sol anyway—but they want to move. I've got a petition for resettlement from the Tritonian council of *ulama*."

"That's just it!" Hamid-Jones said eagerly. "All the installations would be left behind—the fusion generators, the ice mines, the ag domes and the Domed Sea, the housing. Triton could easily handle the thirty million or so *dhimmi* we envision. And besides, a good portion of the Solar System's emigrant *dhimmi*s are *already* on Triton and Pluto . . . and Nereid . . . they kept getting pushed further out over the years. In fact, the North Americans on Pluto—and they're actually a majority there—want to stay on in any case. They take a perverse pride in their hardships. So—" He finished lamely. "—that would alleviate the transport problem."

A wicked glint flashed in Aziz's eyes and vanished just as quickly. "Of course," he drawled, "there are still all the *dhimmi* in the Alpha Centauri system. Your Highness would be letting yourself in for transporting them. It would place a tremendous strain on your resources."

The Sultan recoiled as if stung. "I would not shrink from making any needed effort," he said stiffly. "At any rate, that part of the problem isn't as daunting as it might appear. The *dhimmi* population in the Triple Suns is relatively small—not mar⁻ made the jump between star systems—and they tended to settle on the less desirable low-gravity moons, so there'll be less of an energy investment in boosting them into space."

Aziz, with what seemed to Hamid-Jones to be a perverse delight, goaded the Sultan further. "Of course there's the *dhimmi* population of Earth itself. You couldn't possibly evacuate all of *them*!"

"And on Earth they'll stay," the Sultan growled. "Most of them, anyway. Earth has struggled with its burden for thousands of years, and it will go on much as always. But it was Islam that got a fresh start among the stars, and that's where our destiny will continue to lead us. Earth will remain a museum of mankind—and the place of the holy pilgrimage, which the Ingathering will now make possible for every Moslem." He recovered his composure and became charming again. "But of course I'll guarantee a spaceship berth to any Terrestrial *dhimmi* who *does* want to join this . . . this *hegira* of the infidels that Abdul here is stage-managing.''

''Your Defendership is very generous,'' Hamid-Jones stammered.

The Sultan tapped the pile of orbital diagrams and calculations that Hamid-Jones had brought along. ''It all seems to be well thought out,'' he said. ''I'll have to assume that it can work. Prince Aziz was correct—it will strain the resources of the empire for the next five to ten years. But the problem will be cleaned up by the time Tau Ceti arrives, twelve years hence.''

It seemed to be settled. At least the Sultan was talking as if he had committed himself to the scheme.

And a moment later he said the words that Hamid-Jones had been waiting for.

''All right, *ya* Abdul. You'll have your prize.'' He grinned suddenly. ''You did very well. You sound as if you've been taking lessons from that old fox, Rubinstein. Tell me, just between us, was that phrase about removing a boil from the skin of my empire his?''

There remained the nuts-and-bolts conferences with the black hole engineers of Project ''Allah's Will.'' The Sultan turned Hamid-Jones and Aziz over to the project administrator, a dour bat-eared individual named Doctor Ghazali.

''We're very busy,'' Ghazali said. ''We're still maintaining a data stream on the Tau Ceti shot, and we're just starting to crank up the Epsilon Eridani project.'' He shot out a hand. ''All right, let's see your proposal.''

Hamid-Jones handed over the sheaf of material from Rubinstein's astrophysicists. ''We don't need a very large black hole,'' he said. ''It only has to capture two planets and their moons, and later on, a small star. But if it didn't have enough mass to capture the star, it would be okay if the star captured *it*—as long as the orbit was close enough to put the planets inside the ecosphere . . .''

The administrator didn't seem to be paying attention. He was frowning at the figures and diagrams, and stabbing savagely at a pocket calculator.

''And it would only be a two-shot,'' Hamid-Jones went on hurriedly, ''not a three-shot carom. There's no need for a third black hole to speed up the caravan. It's not as if there were a *destination* to be reached in the shortest possible time. We're in no hurry. We'll be out of the Caliph's sphere soon enough."

Doctor Ghazali straightened up. "Hmm, well it all seems to be sound enough. In fact, there's a certain artistic flair to it—almost as if another Izzat Awad were involved in the simulations. We'll have to check out the math, of course."

"I'm sure you'll find it all in order, Doctor," Aziz said.

Ghazali did not appear to have noticed the interruption. "And there's one advantage to having the target bodies orbiting a megahole so closely—it speeds up their periods. They line up in a row with Groombridge every few months. So if we miss a window, we don't have to wait another ten years to try again. On the other hand, we're going to have to slice it very thin to kidnap the targets. And very, very slow. Since our"—he peeled back his lips past the gums in a grimace—"very *small* black hole will speed up inordinately as it approaches the focus of mass, we'll have to drop it into its hyperbola almost at a standstill."

"Exactly," Hamid-Jones offered. "That's what I've been saying. It only needs a two-shot."

"Well, we can spare two holemakers, if the Caliph wants to put it in the appropriation," Ghazali said.

Aziz cleared his throat. "He also said something about providing us with a small fleet of starships of our own, and a modest industrial base."

"That's entirely between you and the Caliph, my dear fellow. It's not coming out of *my* budget."

He swept up the reams of printouts and tucked them under his arm. His eyes were already wandering toward the door they'd entered by—a gentle hint.

"Er, how long do you think it will take?" Hamid-Jones said.

"These things are not done in a day, my dear fellow. Five years, if we're lucky."

"That's all right," Aziz said. "It will take at least five years to move the populations. And hit the Caliph up for a few additional amenities."

Outside, Hamid-Jones stopped Aziz with a hand on his arm and said, "What was all that about 'us' and 'we' in there? You've got *your* reward. You don't have to get involved in this project if you don't want."

"I'm glad to lend you my moral support, *ya* Abdul."

"Why, for Allah's sake?"

Aziz gave him the old raffish grin. "Maybe it's all the time I spent as your servant. It got to be a habit."

"I appreciate it, but—"

"So let me give you some advice again. Patch it up with Meryem."

"I told you, she doesn't want to talk to me."

"Then talk to Yaqub and *is-sayida* Roxane. They're still your friends, aren't they?"

"Of course."

"Yaqub can help you get things moving among the Nestorians and the Copts and the Druses, and the rest of them. There's a lot to be done. It's a full-time job. You'll need a deputy. You ought to put him on salary."

"But how? I've had my reward from the Sultan."

"Don't worry about that. I'll take care of it. I'm rich as Croesus. You should have thought of the practical details before you squandered all your credit with the Sultan. Oh well, maybe we can try for an expense account for you later."

"Thank you. I don't know what to say."

"In fact, you'll need a full staff. That bishop fellow wouldn't be bad for a starter. And some of the other mullahs in his sect." Aziz's ferret face took on a sly look. "And then, when you've become the hero and savior of the whole *nisrani* community, you can go to Meryem and patch it up with her."

"Aziz, you're impossible!"

Aziz grunted complacently. "With whole worlds to offer— complete with a sun of the infidels and an infinite future—she can't turn you down. Was ever a woman offered such a bride price?"

"I'm not going with them. It's not for someone like me. Whoever heard of a Moslem pasha with all the tribes of the Unbelievers as his flock? I'll turn the whole thing over to them, but I'll stay here. I can always go back to bioengineering."

"What do you mean, not for a Moslem?" Aziz retorted. "Don't forget that the ghettos of the Caliph's domain include the minority sects within Islam. And there are always the malcontents. And those with a taste for far horizons!"

"What species of the Faithful would they be?" Hamid-Jones cried. "Condemned to wander forever among the stars, far from

Mecca.'' All of a sudden Hamid-Jones realized that he had never made the hajj himself.

Aziz paid no attention. "What a way to see the universe!" he said. "All the comforts of home, and a planet for a spaceship. I'm tempted to go with you myself!"

CHAPTER 18

Neptune fell from the sky, a vast blue sphere that was hazy with atmosphere and striped with fluffy methane clouds. From the darkened dome of a transparent mosque jutting out of the ice of its smaller moon, a variegated crowd of people watched its slow drift toward the horizon and made appropriate sounds of awe or satisfaction; little Nereid, only a million miles away from its giant primary at this point in its eccentric orbit, offered a grandstand seat for the moving of worlds.

"We're on our way," Hamid-Jones announced, and a lusty cheer went up from the assembly of *dhimmi*. The delegation of ice miners from Pluto, a rough-hewn crew in their native plaids and twills, were the loudest.

Meryem, holding little Dmitri in her arms, turned a radiant face toward Hamid-Jones. "It's marvelous, Abdul darling," she said. "A miracle."

Hamid-Jones thought she looked very beautiful, standing there with the starlight in her hair, already big with what would be their third child. He wanted to put his arm around her, but even after living for five years among the *dhimmi*, he had not yet unbent enough to be demonstrative in public.

He compromised by picking up their oldest, Theodora. She promptly laid her head on his shoulder and commenced sucking her thumb.

"Actually it's us that're moving," Aziz said. "That's the hole reaching past Neptune's shoulder to tug at us—but it may give

us a more rounded orbit in time. But have no fear. Neptune's on
the leash, too, and Triton with it.''

Beside Aziz, Zubeideh gave a proud smile at the cleverness
of her husband. She had grown more ample in the past few
years, but Aziz thought her beautiful; she had a complexion like
cream and a small, perfect cupid's-bow of a mouth that she
painted carefully. She had adapted to her surroundings sufficiently to give up the veil on all but the most formal occasions.
Her oldest boy had opted to stay on Alpha Centauri and join the
Caliph's legal staff, but she was surrounded by the rest of her
brood. Aziz had adopted all her children, including the lawyer,
and was on the way to raising a family of his own; she had had
two more by him, the oldest, a boy of five, being given the name
Mansour bin Aziz in anticipation of the princely title he would
someday inherit.

"You said it, Aziz," boomed one of the ice miners. "Triton's
sticking closer to Neptune than a flea to a hound dog.''

Hamid-Jones raised his eyes to where Triton rested like a
small bright bubble against Neptune's bloated orb; it orbited at
a distance of only 220,000 miles—closer than Earth was to its
own moon—and looked, from this angle, as if it were floating
on Neptune's cloudtops.

It was brighter than it ought to have been, astronomically
speaking. Its thirty million new inhabitants had turned on all
the lights in celebration of this hour's event. They could afford
it. Triton was rich with the fusion power that had always had to
compensate for its distance from the Sun, and it would never
run out of fuel—not with its own methane-laced atmosphere and
with the bottomless well of hydrogen and helium that could be
mined from Neptune. Until this caravan of worlds picked up a
larger and more congenial terrestrial-style planet, Triton would
remain the jewel in the crown of the *dhimmi* confederation. It
was—or had been—the solar system's largest satellite: bigger
than Luna, bigger than Titan.

"Think of the view *they* must be having at this moment, with
Neptune stretched across their sky!" Yaqub Yordan exclaimed.
Hamid-Jones's father-in-law was grayer after the years of shep-
herding the *dhimmi* communities of four star systems to their
new promised land, arranging transport and acting as Aziz's
gadfly in getting a fleet of their own built in the Sultan's ship-

yards, but he was still a powerfully built, vigorous man who looked as if he would go on forever.

"You and Mother should be living there," Meryem scolded him. "You could be living a nice soft life in an administrative job, on a world where you can step outside without a pressure suit—just an airmask and heateralls."

"I like it better here," Yaqub said. "And so does your mother."

The Yordans had chosen a small homestead on Nereid, a domefarm with all its installations intact. The low gravity and the ample sources of water and ammonia made it possible to grow prodigious vegetables. Yaqub had taken on a partner, a retired comet miner from Charon who had proved to have a green thumb.

"Yes, Nereid's a nice place to live," Roxane said firmly. "It may not have as much to offer in the way of city attractions, but it's less crowded and we have good neighbors here."

She gave a nod that included the several hundred people standing about under the mosque's great crystal dome. They made a colorful cross-section, many of them wearing the old traditional national costumes that had lain in trunks for generations—embroidered dirndls, elaborate peasant blouses, Balkan tunics, sarongs, chesterfields, tam-o'-shanters, gray flannels, and regimental ties. There were even a few turbans and robes—mostly Druses, but including some of the Faithful.

The mosque itself was one of Nereid's landmarks, a daring architectural creation that used the jagged, icy landscape and the starry arch of heaven as its ornament. From its transparent dome and its great enclosed courtyard supported by incised crystal pillars, the worshippers had contemplated the works of Allah—the glaring faraway dot of the Sun, the clockwork progress of Triton's orange ball around the blue sphere of Neptune every six days, the swelling and dwindling of Neptune itself in their sky as Nereid left it for the farther reaches of its orbit. Moslems would always be welcome here, but an ecumenical council headed by the Episcopal archbishop planned to convert it into a church that would serve all the congregations on a rotating basis. Fortunately, the mosque was so sprawling, with so many subsidiary domes, that all the conflicts had been ironed out.

Hamid-Jones gazed fondly at his children. They would be

raised in their mother's faith—Meryem had insisted on that. But what of it? Allah was Allah, however one named Him.

As for him, he would remain a good Moslem. There were enough like him in this train of worlds to guarantee an Islamic fellowship—though one beyond the reach of the Caliphate. Zubeideh, for one, wanted to see her children raised in the True Faith. And that was as it should be.

He gazed through the crystal dome at the fierce yellow speck that was the sun. The possibility of the hajj was now denied him, but facing Mecca would not be a problem during his lifetime. The sun would be visible to the naked eye out to a distance of sixty light-years—though it would only be a sixth magnitude star then. After that, there were always telescopes.

The bishop came up beside him, still looking as fit and muscular as he had been when he was a laborer on the loading dock, though now his bare chest was covered by the queer Christian clerical garb—a black dickey with a turned-around collar.

"Well, Abdul," he said, "are you sorry to leave it?"

"No," Hamid-Jones said truthfully. "Not at all."

He smiled down at his children, and the bishop, smiling with him, tousled little Dmitri's hair.

"Do you find it ironic that you may have founded an empire of Unbelievers?"

"We're all Believers," Hamid-Jones said.

"Quite," the bishop said.

They looked out together at their little convoy of worlds. All of them could be seen prominently in Nereid's sky—enormous Neptune and an orange-size Triton on one side and the two snowballs that were Pluto and Charon on the other. There would be comets, too—thousands of them swept out of the Oort Clouds of two systems as the black hole ploughed its way through to freedom.

"It's only the beginning, you know," the bishop said. "After we pick up our first sun, there'll be others—with their planets. Will we someday become a closed sphere of stars, stagnant and crushed by its own enormous weight, as your Rubinstein predicted for the Caliphate?"

"No, never!" Aziz said in an outraged voice.

They both turned to look at him.

"We're not an enclosed cluster taking root in a volume of space that will eventually become empty, as the Caliphate is.

We're a traveling circus—an argosy of worlds setting out to explore the galaxy in the grandest fleet of all time! Oh, we'll pluck a sun here and there and take it with us. But that will only help us to stay fresh.''

He stared out across the scattered stars of the Milky Way. ''And who knows—now that we've solved the Fermi paradox and know why no extraterrestrial intelligence ever visited us, maybe, just maybe, our slow boat to forever will finally make contact. That's something the Caliphate, just sitting there, will never do.''

''Perhaps,'' the bishop suggested. ''We may need allies by then.''

''What do you mean?''

The bishop became pensive. ''The Caliphate will keep harvesting suns. And with each sun, another black hole will drop into the enormous black hole whose gravity is the glue that holds the empire together. The growing mass of all the new black holes will eventually speed up the cluster's orbit around the galactic center and send it whipping through the spiral arms. Ultimately it must catch up with our descendants on the other side of the galaxy.''

''By that time we runaways may have grown into a rival power,'' Aziz said with a wicked grin.

The bishop nodded. ''Someday two humanities will contend, as they did in centuries gone by, when rival systems clashed. Who will prevail cannot be known.'' He smiled sadly at Hamid-Jones. ''Allah knows, but does not reveal.''

''That day's a long way off,'' said Hamid-Jones.

He lifted his two children to his shoulders to show them the stars. The little train of worlds moved outward.

About the Author

Donald Moffitt was born in Boston and now lives in rural Maine with his wife, Ann, a native of Connecticut. A former public relations executive, industrial filmmaker, and ghostwriter, he has been writing fiction on and off for more than twenty years under an assortment of pen names, including his own, chiefly espionage novels and adventure stories in international settings. His first full-length science-fiction novel and the first book of any genre to be published under his own name was *The Jupiter Theft* (Del Rey, 1977). "One of the rewards of being a public relations man specializing in the technical end of large corporate accounts," he says, "was being allowed to hang around on the fringes of research being done in such widely disparate fields as computer technology, high-energy physics, the manned space program, polymer chemistry, parasitology, and virology—even, on a number of happy occasions, being pressed into service as an unpaid lab assistant." He became an enthusiastic addict of science fiction during the Golden Era, when Martians were red, Venusians green, Mercurians yellow, and "Jovian Dawn Men" always blue. He survived to see the medium become respectable and is cheered by recent signs that the fun is coming back to sf.